SWORD

—of the—

GODLESS

BY
MATTHEW C. LUCAS

MONTAG

A Montag Press Book
www.montagpress.com
Montag Press
777 Morton Street, Unit B
San Francisco CA 94129 USA

Montag Press, the burning book with the hatchet cover, the skewed word mark and the portrayal of the long-suffering fireman mascot are trademarks of Montag Press.

Printed & Digitally Originated in the United States of America
10 9 8 7 6 5 4 3 2 1

This one's for James

ADVANCE PRAISE FOR
SWORD OF THE GODLESS

A gripping fantasy about a scribe-turned-gladiator desperate to keep his humanity despite terrible betrayals... I found myself gasping out loud during pivotal moments... *Sword of the Godless* is exhilarating. Its nuanced character dynamics add to the mystique of Lucas's intricate world of revered prisoners and absent gods, and its twisty plot elements will keep readers on tenterhooks...

— *Independent Book Review*

A riveting story of strength and survival; gripping and gritty. Matthew C. Lucas weaves a tale of raw power, conniving politics, and personal redemption through the eyes of an unforgettable hero. A compelling and immersive fantasy epic of blood and valor, *Sword of the Godless* is a monument to human perseverance and the search for meaning in a godless world.

— Arkhem J. Cain,
author of *The Eighth Sacrament: A Supernatural Thriller*

ACKNOWLEDGEMENTS

As always, love and thanks go to my wife, Alexis, our boys, James and Will, and our pets, Sky and Mango. You all are the best family a guy could ever hope for. Books don't make themselves (at least, not yet); this one had an outstanding team behind it. High praise and thanks to the good folks at Montag Press, Charlie, John, Rick, and Lindsay. You all have been a pleasure to work with. Thank you, Margaret Ball, for providing helpful feedback and edits on an early draft. Thanks also to the folks at Writer Dojo for providing a friendly writing community where iron sharpens iron.

Last but not least, thank you, whoever you are, for reading this story. If you enjoyed it, I'd be honored if you'd leave a favorable review wherever you can.

PART I

THE LOWER BLUFF

CHAPTER ONE

"They're terrible," Paul Little declared. He made a disgusted noise and shook his young head with a solemnity that would have suited an old aficionado. "Look at that form. Look at the footwork. Just awful."

I wasn't entirely sure what form or footwork he found objectionable. From where we sat in the highest row of the Bajebluff Arena, on a hard, hot stone bench covered in layers of gull droppings, the two fighters below looked like nothing more than gray dots. Every so often, one dot would prod the other, move around a bit, stand perfectly still … It was hard to tell precisely who was who, or what they were doing, though it was clear enough what they were *not* doing—and that was getting around to the business of killing each other. Which, being boys who knew no better, was what we had paid good money to see.

This was my first match. But I tried to make myself sound as assured as Paul.

"I've seen better," I agreed.

It was a summer afternoon, late Harvest or maybe early Ales Month. The air was choked with grit and heat and oily cooking smoke, like every summer day that ever was in the lower quarter of Bajebluff. Paul Little and I had a row all to ourselves. Our hair was plastered with sweat. The bricks we sat on burned like oven stones through our pants. The ushers' entrance was right behind us, and stank of old, rotten food and spilled wine. But it was an afternoon with no work and nowhere to be, and I had precious few of those growing up as I did. As well, I had a friend at my elbow, and that was rare, too. No matter how paltry the day's entertainment was, no matter that Bajebluff Arena was little better than a den of dregs, no matter that I was risking the wrath of my mother simply for being here with Paul, I was inclined to enjoy myself. "Low entertainment," my mother always sniffed whenever the subject of the arena came up, a diversion suited for those who labored with their hands, not their minds. I rather liked it, though.

The stadium was an octagon of mismatched bricks that had stood in the worst neighborhood of Lower Bajebluff for longer than anyone could remember. The day's match, I learned, was "unfeatured," which meant two pence bought admission to sit in the open air and squint at no-name, low-rate criminals hacking at each other with axes. Because the fighters were at the bottommost rung of the Gladiators' Rolls, and had probably never been trained beyond learning which point of a spear was for poking, the arena's benches were as cheap as they were empty. Maybe fifty people had come to watch, and most had paid the extra pence for better seats. But Paul and I couldn't sneak down into the shaded sections because the flinty bastard who owned the place kept a battalion of ushers on the prowl to make sure no one cheated on the price of admission. The cheapest seats and the cheapest matches—but two pence was all Lower Bluff boys like us could afford. Paul heaved a sigh.

"Wish they'd get somebody from Archlé." His face brightened. "Or an Escola skirmisher. Now *that* would be worth watching. Better than this trash."

"Uh-huh."

Paul leaned back in the space between the aisles, stuffing his face with almonds he had pilfered from one of the carts outside the arena's entrance. He didn't offer me one; he never shared his food. We were the same age, but Paul stood two heads shorter and weighed at least a stone less than me. He had no parents that I knew of, no place he ever stayed for longer than a few nights. A scrawny Rogues Run orphan, one of a thousand who wandered like feral animals in this ward of the city.

We had little in common. He often grated on my nerves. But Paul was the only friend I had ever had. I might have been the same to him, it was hard to say.

Paul squinted at the action below, cupped his hands to his mouth, and shouted with a crack in his voice.

"Make a *move* at him already!"

The two specks in the arena were still circling each other. Still prodding, then shuffling off like skittish dogs. Still bearing the catcalls and boos of the lower rows who had already grown bored with the spectacle. I wondered if the gladiators heard anything down there. Paul did his best to make sure these two did.

"Come *at* him!" He made a stabbing motion with his arm. "Do it! C'mon, you gutless worm!" He buried his face in his hands and shook his head. "This is rigged. Marco's favored two-to-one. Somebody must have got to him. He's throwing the match on purpose."

"I doubt it," I said, pointing to one of the flagpoles that rimmed the top of the stadium. It bore a faded black banner, and even I, a newcomer to the arena, knew what that meant. "This fight's to the death."

Paul glanced at the piece of cloth, clenched his jaw, but said nothing. Down below, one of the fighters finally made a pass at his opponent. He stumbled, but the other jumped back at the same moment, so the fall was just that—a piece of clumsiness with no repercussion. The two froze with seeming uncertainty, scurried around a bit, and returned to their dance of poking and harmless prodding. A groan went up from the crowd.

"My man's hopeless," said Paul. He cast a long, sideways look at me. "I think I'll say a prayer for him. Care to join me, Simeon?"

I half-smiled and shook my head.

"Better not. You're the one who needs the help, since you're the one who put a mark and a half wager on him. Besides, I don't think any of the gods would listen to me."

Paul made one of the signs of the gods and tilted his chin smugly.

"Yeah, they wouldn't listen to you because you're a heathen, and they know you don't believe in any of them. Which is really strange." He pretended to shut his eyes and murmured some gibberish under his breath, and though I didn't know the first thing about prayers or invocations, I was certain whatever he was saying had never been sanctioned by any faith or creed. He finished his nonsense and looked at me fully.

"You really should take up a god or two, Sim. You'd have more friends if you did."

That, at least, was probably true. But I couldn't help how I was raised. My mother detested religion even more than the arena. She made sure I did as well.

Paul chomped on his almonds and turned his attention back to the arena floor far below. A hot wind blew over us, like an open kiln. I let the heat wash over me, inhaled the stadium smells, and relished the liberty I thought I had.

It was a pleasant, peaceful way to spend an afternoon. Yet it still held a tinge of exhilaration and danger. A fine combination. I could understand why people flocked here.

My eyelids must have drifted shut, for all of a sudden I heard a ragged cheer. Paul was tugging at my sleeve.

"We've gotta go," he said. He darted glances at the aisle that led to our section.

"Aw, did I miss it? Who won?"

Down in the ring, one of the figures was roaming the length of the arena, his axe hoisted above his head. A few of the patrons tossed coins at him.

That was when I noticed a portly, well-dressed man huffing up the steps of the nearest aisle. Ruddy-faced and urgent, he was waving for our attention.

"I think that man's looking for—"

Paul gave my shirt a hard yank.

"C'mon."

Paul was on his feet and making for the ushers' doorway.

"Hey—" I started, but he had already disappeared into the shadows.

The man in the aisle shouted up to me.

"You, there! Don't move!" Despite his girth, the man was hoisting himself up the steps, two at a time. "You're with that thief, Paul Little! I'll have a word with you—"

That was all I needed to hear. I bolted from my seat and made straight for the tunnel. As I ran, I could hear the man bellowing, "Stop, you thieves! Stop, I say! I'll call the sheriff!"

The ushers' tunnel was cramped and dimly lit with tallow candles, and the further I went, the more it reeked of rotting garbage. I tried to hold my nose as I ran, but it did no good. Fortunately, it didn't take long to catch up with Paul. I saw him up ahead striding swiftly, as if he belonged here and was not trying to beat a hasty escape. I slowed to his pace once I caught up with him.

"Who was that?" I whispered.

"My oddsmaker. I'm a little short of coins to pay my wager."

I hadn't realized Paul had made a bet with an oddsmaker. They were a secretive guild, the only ones sanctioned to take bets in Bajebluff, and they were notoriously ruthless in their trade.

"Maybe you could work something out with him?" I said. "Maybe talk to him?"

We turned a corner and the air finally freshened. An exit to the outside appeared about a hundred paces ahead. As we ran for the daylight, Paul replied over his shoulder.

"You try talking to someone with your throat cut."

"Simeon."

My mother's voice woke me.

I sat up in my pallet. Darkness, almost complete, save only a soft and vacillating glow in my bedroom doorway. I wiped the blear from my eyes, and she continued speaking in a tone that somehow sounded both weary and staccato. "I have been informed that you attended a gladiatorial match. At the arena. With Paul Little."

My stomach began to twist, like the blanket still wrapped around my legs. I blinked, and she came into focus.

Dr. Delores Severals, the tutor of Drovers Lane, holding the whalebone lantern she used for reading at night. The light guttered under her face, making shadows flicker around her chin, leaving the rest in darkness. Not that there would be much to see. A taut, expressionless gaze, flat lips, bulging dark eyes. She stooped, not bothering to hide the hunch in her shoulders. A scarecrow in silhouette. My dear mother.

"You were at the arena yesterday. Explain yourself."

Explain yourself.

A permutation of one her favorite queries—"gather your thoughts"—but it held the same inference, the same veiled contempt. I had been ignorant. I had erred.

"It was—it was just for fun." I made a plaintive gesture. "Nothing happened."

"You attended the arena against my injunction. With a boy I have forbidden you to see. Who indebted himself with a wager to the father of one of my pupils. Yes. That oddsmaker you ran from is Lyle Beedles; his daughter, Lilith, has taken arithmetic lessons from me for the past two years. Mr. Beedles recognized you." Her eyes twitched for a moment and her features, which were already drawn as tight as a drum, seemed to pull even more taut. "I was compelled to satisfy Paul's wager," she finally said. "You can imagine how … distasteful that was. So do not pretend that nothing happened. 'Something' very much happened. And now you will explain yourself."

"I …"

Any explanation would only annoy her further and prolong whatever punishment she was no doubt concocting. She knew the whole story already. So I confessed, and then I apologized, as I had a thousand times before.

It never mollified her. She let out a long, melancholy hiss of air from her nostrils.

"So," she said, "because of your actions, I am robbed of a mark and a half, and I've lost one of my students. Beedles withdrew Lilith this morning. I can't say that I blame him."

My mother rolled her neck until it creaked.

"Not that his girl held much promise," she continued. "She'll never be an oddsmaker. A merchant's clerk, perhaps, if she can ever learn how to factor. But." She clasped her hands together. "That will be another tutor's charge now. Two marks, two pence a month. Because of you and your wayward acquaintance, I've not only lost a mark and six pence from my purse, but two marks and two pence of monthly income."

She gazed at me, letting the silence unfurl in the space of my little bedroom. At last, the noise of a cart and mule rattling down the street outside broke the stillness. The driver was roaring a tavern song, slurred and off key. The cart trundled away, and the quiet returned.

"I'm sorry," I finally said, just to break the stillness.

"Indeed." She shifted her weight to lean against the other side of the doorway. "You know I've never cared for Paul Little. A base child makes a bad influence. You will never keep company with him again."

"Yes, ma'am," I nodded.

"There's more to your punishment."

And now, at last, we had come to it. My penitence; her vindication. Besides holding me inside under lock and key, and halving my meals, she would always impose a "lesson." Hauling buckets of water only to dump them in a gutter. Sweeping the dirt from one side of the street to the other. Reading books on logic to the deaf in Beggars Palace. She could be petty in her punishments. I tried to keep my voice demure, though I knew whatever she had in mind, it would be unpleasant and pointless.

"What's the lesson?"

"No lesson. A job. Since you cost me work, it seems fitting you should take some on for yourself."

"You ... want me to teach one of your students?"

"Don't be absurd."

She took a step into my room and let one of her hands rest on my writing desk. It was just a makeshift table flecked with ink stains. One of her fingers began to trace circles on its surface. As she spoke, she gazed pensively.

"Starting tomorrow, for the remainder of the summer, for however long it takes, when you have finished the day's lessons and chores, you will remain confined to your room. You will report to your desk." She tapped the tabletop. "And there you will set to work on a job I've recently contracted. You'll repay the income you have cost me." She turned to face me, and her eyes narrowed. "You will copy, in a fair hand, the entirety of the Book of Amadán."

My heart sank down to my feet.

This was beyond any torment she had ever invented. Fair hand copying was a punishment my mother often imposed. It meant writing with no mistakes, no scratches, no smudges, in a uniform, readable script. It meant hand cramps and neck aches, and it was the worst tedium, even when you were copying something interesting, like an arena handbill or a festival announcement. But what she had just told me to copy revealed a cruelty I hadn't thought even she was capable of.

The Book of Amadán was a book known only for its thickness. A thousand pages, two thousand. No one knew, because no one ever finished it. Masons nicknamed the cornerstones in buildings "Amadáns."

I swallowed my disappointment and anger, but I was a boy on the cusp of surly pre-manhood, and could not resist a retort.

"*Scripture?*" I said with exaggerated disdain. "You want me to copy scripture? I thought you said it was all superstitious nonsense."

At that, I saw the corner of my mother's lip cracking upward. For her it was what passed as a smile.

"It is," she replied. "But I've met a priest who will pay a half pence a page to copy it. And a half pence per page for a book of that heft … well, I'm willing to expose you to some superstition for that kind of a profit."

I sat in my bed, helpless, clenching my fists beneath the blanket, wanting nothing more than to punch something. Perhaps she could sense what I was thinking. Just before she left me in the darkness of my bedroom, she added,

"I'm sure it will be just as entertaining as the dregs you watched in the arena."

The days that followed were tedious. I spent the mornings with my usual lessons, my mother drilling me in arithmetic, logic, history, and alchemy. In the afternoons, while she taught her paying students the same work I had just practiced, I had to cook, and clean, and trim pens, and grind ink, and change the rushes, and fetch the water—all the chores that earned my keep, as she so often liked to remind me. When the evenings came, after supper, I worked on my punishment.

That first night, after I finished clearing the dishes, I came into my room and learned what it was to be a scribe.

Waiting for me on my desk was a lit tallow candle, a satchel of middling grade paper, an inkpot, a cane reed stylus with a fine, iron point, and the book I would have to copy.

It covered the whole of the table.

I crept close and ran my finger through the dust in its creases. I tried to lift the book. It felt like a block. I had to brace my knees and heave just to inch it over. Three stone at least, maybe four. The cover was worn, flaking around the edges, its binding reinforced with a bolted led hinge. The title, once silvered, had long since faded to a trail of faint, graying letters.

THE REVELATIONS OF AMADÁN THE PIOUS
(enscribed by Brother Odhran of North Korne Abbey)

My punishment.

Being a boy, I thought I could plow headlong into the task, muscle through, grind at the millstone, and then I'd be done. Which is to say, I approached the task like an idiot.

With a determined sigh, I creaked the heavy cover open, inked my pen, and without so much as a glance at the text, I tried to replicate, letter stroke by letter stroke, exactly what this monk from North Korne had copied centuries ago.

FOR IT CAME TO PASS *one Midwinter's night that I, Amadán, whilst tending flocks, did hear a Voice who bade me set aside the spirits of my botle and attend*
Damn.

There was no room to squeeze another "t" into "bottle." And no chance I could possibly pass off such a glaring misspelling as fair hand work. I crumpled the paper, tossed it over my shoulder, and tried again.

An hour later, I had four more ruined sheets, but had managed to get no further into the book than the initial introduction of Amadán's Voice (who turns out to be the Demigod Fifl, speaking through the form of a glowing mushroom). As I sat slumped in my chair, staring blankly and thumbing through what felt like an endless succession of pages, I felt despair pressing down upon me with all the crushing weight of the tome I was tasked with copying.

This was never going to work. Either I would have to leave my mother's house and support myself—which was alluring, mind you, but at fifteen, without any trade or connections, hardly an ideal prospect—or I would have to figure out a different approach. Because I could no more copy a thousand pages of Brother Odhran's print than become Brother Odhran himself.

While I sat listening for a long while in the silence of my room's corner, my eyes fluttering with sleep's temptation, an idea came to me. More of a realization, actually. But realizations can be the sires of good ideas. So it was with this one.

My focus was too narrow. I had been studying each individual letter, its shape and size, setting down my hand, copying the strokes, halting, lifting my hand, looking at the next letter, returning to my page, repeating the same—the process was preposterous. Like trying to paint a building with a toothpick.

What if I went line by line, and only stopped when the pen needed ink? And instead of struggling to set out the bones of each individual letter, I would hoist up their whole bodies all at once. Draw the letters in a flow, connected like a chain. The old monk could keep his stately, spired "t's" and buttressed "w's." My letters would gallop.

I gave it a try. The words came *leaping* from the dusky old book's pages onto my waiting paper. Lines, dozens of them, drifted from my head to my hand as swift as a river current. The sacred voice announcing itself, the demigod appearing in the dust, Amadán rescuing him from the mouth of one of his goats, the song of thanksgiving the two of them sang together … it all came into being once more, right there, in the corner of my bedroom.

True, my lettering looked a tad … concise. Its only ornamentation was the little trace lines strung throughout the words like thread. The text had a somewhat rambling appearance. But, then, so was Amadán's revelation.

By the time the night watchman called out midnight on Drovers, I had six pages finished, top to bottom. Each one was flawless fair script.

I must not have heard my mother opening the latch to my door. Without any greeting, she peered over my shoulder.

"Well, well," I heard her say.

It gave me a little start.

"I've never seen you so focused on your work," she remarked.

I turned in my seat, looked up at her, and nodded. She reached past me, took up my pages, shook them gently to make sure the ink was dry, and studied them. Her eyes scuttled back and forth in search of flaws. She set them down, folded her arms across her chest, and regarded me.

"You write with a curious hand."

I stretched my shoulders. I hadn't realized how stiff they were. "There's no mistakes," I said.

"No, there do not appear to be." She cast a glance at the book lying open on my table and shook her head. "So much labor. Over the rantings of a goatherder."

It was odd, but for some reason I took offense, as if she had insulted a new friend I had just made.

"He wrote—" I began, but I found that words failed me. What exactly had I been writing all night? Not a rant. Not a story, either. It was hard to describe, especially with sleep falling fast over me. "He wrote some interesting things," I finally yawned.

"Indeed?"

She was smirking, but whatever clever rebuke was on the tip of her tongue, she kept to herself. She set the ribbon bookmark in the text and closed Amadán's revelation for the night. "You've done enough for one evening. Six pages. A quarter of a mark." She turned her chin towards the doorway. "There's cold quail in the cupboard."

"I'm not hungry."

"Then time for bed."

Before I knew it, I was under the blanket on my pallet, my head rested in the crook of my arm. I fell headlong into a heavy sleep and dreamed about a rain-soaked meadow, and a hare I tried to chase down, and a man I'd never met who had a face I couldn't see. He was laughing as I ran after my game. Laughing and slapping the side of his leg over a joke I had heard but couldn't put into words.

"Oh, look at you, Simeon Severals. You're as thin as an ox tail and pale as milk."

Goodwife Rivers pursed her lips, and *tsked*, and, as if to assure herself that my skin had not indeed curdled, she pinched one of my cheeks. The grocer's wife was a solid woman, shaped like a tree stump, with tight, mouse-colored hair, strong, knobby fingers, and brown eyes that were perpetually glistening. She filled the doorway of her little grocery, her bottom pushing open the door, while a rusted tin bell gave a leaden clink over her head. The scent of flour and spices and fresh picked vegetables wafted out and greeted me like an old friend.

"Come in, come in," she half-hugged, half-shunted me into the store. Her hand clasped tight to my elbow, I followed her past the grocery's shelves and aisles and into a back bakery where an empty stool and Mrs. Rivers' famous oven awaited. It was a treat that I always relished. The Rivers never had children of their own, so Mrs. Rivers treated the kids of Rogues Run like we were her brood to feed.

"I've got a nice cheese an' onion that just came out," she said, "lots of pepper, just how you like. You'll eat every crumb of it, hear?"

"Yes, ma'am."

It felt nice being fussed over. No sooner had I settled in my seat, but Mrs. Rivers had a steaming bread pie, onion shavings falling off its top and cheese rivulets gushing from its sides.

"I've got to tend the store a bit. Say your blessing and tuck in before your food gets cold. I'll fetch something to wash it down."

The pie was scalding, but I savored every mouthful.

While I ate, I watched the fire crackling in the baking oven. My thoughts drifted back to the project I had been working on for the past three weeks. In particular, I was thinking about the last lines I had copied from the Book of Amadán—where Amadán was likening each of the gods to a different kind of looking glass, a notion I found both baffling and strangely beguiling—and it struck me that this punishment I had thought was so cruel had gradually become … enjoyable. I was almost a fifth of the way through it already. Every other sentence I had written bordered on lunacy, but Amadán was an entertaining lunatic.

Perhaps my mother had sensed my change in attitude. Perhaps she was vexed that I was enjoying the little penance she had inflicted on me. Perhaps that was why she snapped at me to take the evening off and get out of the house. Whatever her reason, I was glad for the reprieve. Though I still couldn't help dwelling on the book.

While I was reflecting on all this, Mrs. Rivers huffed back into the bakery. She had a bottle draped from her little finger and two pewter cups in her hands.

"Nothin' pairs with cheese-and-onion like small beer. You're old enough, right?"

"Yes'm."

I wasn't really. But I had always been on the larger size for my age, which made me look older than my years.

She poured us each a cup, mine filled to the brim, and as the beer washed down my throat, and the hops burst on my tongue, and the swirl in my stomach spread tingling warmth throughout my senses, I thought I could never taste anything better for the rest of my life.

"It's great," I said.

Rivers smiled indulgingly.

"Glad you like it. Now that you've got a little something in your stomach, let's hear what's become of you lately. I see every Drovers boy and girl in here at least once a week. You've been gone a month if you've been gone a day."

"I can't leave my house." I wiped my mouth with the back of my sleeve and took another pull of that glorious beer. "For all of Ales and Sunskein. Mending Month, too, most likely. This is the first evening I've been allowed out. I'm being punished."

"Your mom?"

I nodded, and her full lips drew tight. I could tell she was holding her breath. At last, she let it out.

"Well, I suppose she's minding her boy as best as she knows how." Her tone made it very plain what Goodwife Rivers thought of my mother's boy-minding. "Though I wonder what she's thinking. There's better ways to set a boy to rights without locking him in a pen. A good thump on the head. Or a strapping, pink his backside some. *That's* how a boy learns right from wrong."

"She's making me copy a book."

Rivers muttered a curse, and I think it was the only time in my life I ever heard her speak profanity. It made me smile to myself. The palm of her hand thumped the table.

"That's not right. Not right at all. I mean no disrespect to your mother. She's a—she's a very learned woman. But she's filled her head so much, she's got no room for plain, common sense. It ain't *natural* to lock up a boy and stick his nose in a book. That's not how you handle spunk. Everyone knows that. Now if *I* were your mum, I'd have your dad … oh, now," she stopped herself. In the oven's light, I could see she was blushing. "I ought not to have brought that up—about your father, I mean. May the gods hold his soul."

She tapped her forehead with her thumb twice, a sign of blessing. I dipped my head, since that was the respectful thing to do whenever someone invoked the gods.

My father drowned when I was about a year old. No one's really sure how it happened. Early one Frostlick morning down by the wharfs, a fisherman set out on his skiff and came across my father's body, bloated and gray, floating near the crab traps. And that was the end of Silas Severals, my father. I have no memory of the man. My mother rarely speaks of him except to say that their marriage had been arranged, and that I remind her of him in far too many ways. A couple of years ago I pestered some of the tavern buzzards to tell me more about old Silas. All I learned was that he had been a mason, he was regarded as clever when he wasn't in his cups (which apparently wasn't very often), and that he fought with a great number of men, some of whom were above his station.

I didn't mind at all that Goodwife Rivers had mentioned my father or that she held my mother's child rearing in low esteem. Truth was, I would have gladly traded her for my mom. Mrs. Rivers was … good. Sturdy and sweet, like her beer.

"I should be heading home," I said. I wiped my plate with a napkin and wrapped up what was left of the pie in a piece of cheesecloth she had served it with. "Thank you for the supper, Mrs. Rivers."

"But you haven't finished."

"I'm really full."

I had managed through the better part of two thirds of the pie, but I was feeling heavy, and the beer left me a little dizzy. Most of all, though, I knew it was getting late, and my mother's indulgence would only go so far. She had said as much on my way out the door.

"Be sure you put that in a cupboard," she said.

"Actually, I was going to give the rest to Paul."

Mrs. Rivers' face darkened. She tended the fire in the oven and turned to give me a meaningful look.

"I'd rather you ate it yourself."

That caught me off guard. "I don't mind sharing," I said. "And Paul could use it. He's always hungry."

She gazed at me a long while, the fire in the oven roaring behind her, and at last she patted my arm. "Do what you like with your food, Simeon. It's yours. But Paul Little's no longer welcome in our store." She shook her head sadly. "Mr. Rivers caught him pilfering the cinnamon shelf. Which ain't what hunger reaches out for. No. A hungry boy takes bread. A thief steals spices."

CHAPTER TWO

Mending Month. The rains had finally come and washed the city clean, like plunging a drunkard's head in a cistern after a night of taverning. Now that the harvest was in—and sufficiently celebrated—it was time to fix all that had been broken throughout the year. Border stones that had been knocked over in the cornfields were set aright, sagging fence posts were straightened, ax blades sharpened, livestock groomed, and laws were once again enforced, more or less.

Slowly, the neighborhood of Rogues Run settled back into the regular rhythm of the business of life. For me, this meant lessons, chores, the Book of Amadán, and, once a week, an evening to myself. The weekly outing was thanks to my progress.

I had finished half the book in what seemed a meandering, waking dream that began each dusk and ended with the street walker's cry of, "Midnight, Rogues! Midnight! Bedtime or bedlam, that's up to you, but it's midnight ..." I had stacked the finished copied pages up past my elbow. Some four hundred of them. And only seven wasted along the way (not counting my first failed attempts). At nine pages a night, I would finish before the end of Sowing Month. The Book of Amadán, copied in fair hand, in four months' time.

"You have an aptitude for copy work," my mother told me one night at bedtime.

She was right. Or I should say half-right. Anyone with a thumb and a forefinger can do fair handed copy work, as long as they concentrate. They don't even need to know how to read to copy letters. It's the concentration, keeping the focus, that's what makes scribe work a challenge. But I had no difficulty with that at all with the Book of Amadán.

I couldn't explain why. Though I knew which verse had first drawn me in. It was a question posed early on in the second chapter:

Amadán, thou art naught but these goats.
Amadán, thou art naught but a god.
Canst thou hold the twain?
In the indifferent embrace of sightless stars in their pointless promenade,
Canst thou be Goat and God,
Never less nor better than the twain?

That question has tumbled around in my head like a pebble stuck in my sandal. To this day, I have no idea what the answer is.

———————

On one of my evenings off, I happened to wander farther up Quarterman's Way than usual. As the sun began to set, a breeze wafted through the streets, and the air grew crisp. The familiar winding lane of cobblers, butcheries, pawn shops, and stall markets seemed to take on a new light. Lanterns hung in the windows, all twinkling like orange stars within the rose hue of dusk reflecting from the glass and stones. The air was pleasant and scentless despite the crowd of people; no musk or piss, no smoke or rotting fruit. Such a fine evening. My feet just carried me along.

Past the end of Quarterman's, there was a squat, rock-hewn bridge that spanned a ditch. It had an arch topped with a statue of a pudgy boy holding a lance that was too big for him, which gave the bridge its namesake, the Page. Another quarter mile east, beyond the fishmongers, I came to its companion, the Squire, with its fancy balustrades and bronze figure of a much sturdier and more handsome young gentleman carrying a sheathed sword. Now the Squire Bridge had always marked a boundary. My side, the southwest, had Rogues Run and Beggars Palace, the Bajebluff Arena, the wharves, and a handful of neighborhoods where men and women were poor, and their children ignorant, and their lives more or less overlooked by the law. It was all called Lower Bajebluff, and not because of its elevation. There were gradations in the Lower Bluff, sure; some of us lived in houses with a cellar, or had a courtyard with a fruit tree. But you could usually tell which side of the Squire a man lived just by looking at his sandals and his cloak.

It was a complete accident that I happened to venture into Upper Bajebluff that evening. I shouldn't have been there at all. If I had been paying attention instead of breathing in the nice air, and gazing at the gleaming auburn water of the river running underneath the bridge, and thinking about Amadán's latest escapade, I might have noticed some scattered disapproving looks from a well-dressed throng of people.

But since I found myself on the other side of the Squier, and since I had a pocketful of half pence coins, I thought I might splurge and buy a molasses apple at a fruit stall. As I was talking with the lady who owned the stall, and trying to point her to an apple that wasn't half rotten, I heard a noise.

"Simeon…"

I spun around, surprised to hear the sound of my name being called out, but saw only a group of porters lounging on a parked cart smoking hash. The fruit lady made a face as sour as her produce.

"Don't pay no attention to him. Little pincher. It's three and a half for the scarlet crowns, an' don't try to haggle me—this ain't Rogues Run."

"I'll think about it. Excuse me."

I left the stand, the woman's muttered curses sliding off my back, and made my way over to where I thought the voice had come from. The street was tight from the porters smoking and playing dice in a ring of pebbles and rat bones. I nudged past their game and the roadway narrowed into an alley that was lit with a single, bent lampstand. Within its glow, an armed man sat on a stool with his legs sprawled before him. A steel crescent breast plate, the badge of a Bajebluff sheriff's deputy, hung unevenly from a frayed leather cord around his neck. A truncheon lay across his lap. He lifted his chin enough to glance at my approach and scowl.

Paul Little hunched in a wooden pillory nearby.

In the flickering lamplight, I could make out a welt the size of a melon that had swollen his left eye shut. A slurry of crushed fruits and other less savory refuse surrounded him. He couldn't have picked a worse time to land in the stocks than right after the harvest.

There was also a girl. Eight or nine years old, in a sky-blue skirt and an ermine scarf, she was crouched before Paul's face, giggling, and trying to force a bean up his nose. He kept turning his head to avoid her, which only made her laugh more.

"Simeon," he said again.

"Hey," I yelled at the girl. "Clear out."

She spun around, her face as round and pale as the moon. The bean fell from her fingers. The deputy let out a warning growl. He gripped his truncheon and shifted his feet on the ground, but he didn't bother to get up from his stool. Instead, he belched.

"It's me that says who'll clear out here. As I'm in charge of this here misdemeanorant." He pulled up his belt and smirked, and I played along and looked demure and very impressed with his official sounding word, flawed as it was. "Now," the deputy continued, "if you'd like to pay for a private visit with the misde—with the prisoner, that can be arranged."

I fished around in my pocket, making sure not to jingle any of my coins, found a half pence, and brought it out to show him. His dull, hairy-lidded eyes squinted in the lantern light, studying my coin.

"You got three more of those in there?"

Two pence was a little rich, but I paid him. Another belch rumbled from within his thick neck, but at last he nodded.

"Off you go, miss." The deputy jerked his thumb to point to the street outside of the alley. The girl screwed up her face, but did as she was told, pausing only to stick her tongue out at me as she left.

"Quarter of an hour, boy," he said to me. "Then it's you who'll clear out— back to your side of the Squire."

I went over to Paul, a mound of spoiled food squelching beneath my feet, and crouched in front of his face, which looked even worse up close.

"What happened?"

He tilted his head as best he could to face me fully and then the bastard actually tried to smile. A grin marred by a set of bloody gums and a row of broken teeth. A vigorous display of impotent mockery. It is one of my favorite memories of Paul Little.

"A misunderstanding," he said, a trail of pink spittle falling from his bottom lip. "New sheriff's man, a corporal. He found a couple of pieces of ivory on me that might not have gone through the customs house. If he would've just let me—"

I cut him off. "How much longer is your sentence?"

Paul pretended to think it over. "Well, let's see. If they count the day they first locked me up—"

"They never count the first day, you know that."

"Then the day after tomorrow." His one good eye rolled up at me, as if to study my reaction. "It was only a few pebbles, Sim. I was able to dump the rest in the bay before the corporal got a hold of me. But the sheriff doesn't like it when any ivory comes through without paying his tariffs."

"Uh-huh."

I decided to leave the obvious question—how did he know to get rid of ivory that had supposedly been planted on him—unasked. It didn't matter.

I looked over at the deputy. He wasn't paying any attention, busy as he was crunching an apple and drinking from a stein. In theory, a guard was posted over the stocks to keep passersby from hurling anything harder than insults or broccoli at the prisoner. But the deputies only bothered when they were bribed. And Paul never kept any coins on him.

I turned back to Paul. An amber colored puss was oozing like tree sap from his busted eye. Two more days of this might leave him blinded. Half of Beggars Palace in the Lower Bluff was made up of poor bastards who lost their sight in the stocks. It happened all the time. I gently dabbed at the wound with the corner of my shirt.

"When did you get this?" I asked.

"Couple hours ago. From those porters." He raised his voice so that the deputy couldn't ignore him. "They should've been arrested for throwing rocks. That's against the law, too, you know."

The deputy turned his head and snorted a laugh. He took another pull from his stein. Paul lowered his voice again.

"Hey, Sim."

"What?"

"How much you have on you?"

I told him and he smiled. "That's almost enough to spring me."

It was. Small crime stocks are easy to buy your way out of. There's a robust market. The price hovers around a mark for one day. Twelve pence to buy twenty-four hours of freedom. You can't bribe off the first day. But after that, if you can slip your guard the price to cover the rest of your sentence, he'll discreetly leave your stocks unlocked and wander off to take a piss, while you "parole" yourself. It would have been an easy affair to arrange with Paul's deputy, but something in me felt resentful. The way he had asked, it was almost as if Paul expected me to empty my pockets to bond off his thievery. I frowned and stared at my foot drawing circles on the ground.

"I get it," Paul said gently, "that's a lot of money. So I'll make you a deal. Pay my parole ... and I'll take you to where I dumped the ivory. It's under a broken tile in a gutter, I know the exact place. If it's still there, we'll split it all down the middle. Twenty marks. Maybe thirty."

He was whistling for a cat, we both knew it. Whatever Paul had, he had probably stolen, and whatever he had stolen had, in turn, been stolen from him. The ivory, however much there really was, was long gone. But at least he had recognized he needed to offer me something. Even if all he had to offer was worthless. Paul gave another battered smile, and I nodded.

"Hey, sheriff's man," I called over to the deputy. "What can we do to get him on parole?"

The deputy was easy to work with. No bluster, no feigned surprise, no needless haggling: just that sly, greedy tilt of the head, like a dog that's managed to nick a flank from the butcher's stall, like what every deputy who ever wore a crescent looks like when he takes your money. He knew what the going rate was, and so he got right to the point. I paid out every one of the coins in my pocket. And as the purple dusk light melted into indigo, and the shadows in the alley grew long, and the hum of merchants winding down for the day turned into the din of revelers beginning theirs, the deputy slipped off into a bar, eleven pence richer, while I freed my only friend from bondage and walked him back to our side of the city.

———————

"This is Simeon."

My mother gestured for me to come in from the doorway of her study and greet her guests. As I stepped inside the room, an unfamiliar scent of strong coffee and freshly baked bread filled my nostrils. The drapes were pulled back, letting in the full daylight, and a fire was built up in the hearth to keep a tin and coffee pot warm. My mother's books, usually spread about pell-mell over the floor, were stacked into teetering columns and pushed into the corners to make as much room as possible.

Filling my mother's favorite calfskin chair sat an old, jowly priestess. She bore herself with the utmost dignity, though her raiment almost made her look like a carnival magician—scarlet silk vestments, purple phylactery, silver chains, and a black-and-gold mushroom miter big enough to set sail. To her left stood a girl not much older than me. She had an angular, freckled face framed by a mop of stringy mouse brown hair. The girl wore a simpler red linen robe, much cheaper than the priestess's. My first thought was how pretty the girl would be if she smiled.

The old priestess squinted, eyeing me from head to toe the way one would a foal before making the first offer to buy.

"He's rather broad," she declared in a gravelly voice. She cast a glance at my mother, took a sip of coffee from her cup, and added, "I suppose he favors his father in that respect. May Vellaunas keep his spirit warm."

With her free hand, the priestess made an absent, twirling motion, her thumb and little finger extended. She and the girl muttered something like "so be it." My mother looked at them with a bemused expression.

"He does look like his father. Simeon, I would like you to meet Her High Divinity, Gathena of the Fifth Pantheon—it is the Fifth, correct?"

Gathena gave a solemn nod. Without bothering to rise, the priestess extended her hand towards me, a slab of white flesh festooned in gold rings.

I started to grip it, but she drew it back at once, as if affronted. I turned to my mother who puckered her lips in an imitation of kissing.

"A pleasure to meet you, ma'am—er, High Divine," I said, bending at my waist and kissing the air above her fingers.

"Blessing." Gathena made another half-hearted hand wave. "This is Sister Kara, one of our postulants. We refer to postulants fraternally, as a sign of respect, until they've assumed the higher office of divine priesthood. Which, the gods willing, she will assume shortly."

I bowed at Kara, but she only glanced at me long enough to flash a tight smile, which was followed at once with a bored, disapproving frown. No one inquired if I would like any of the biscuits they were eating, or any coffee, and I knew better than to ask.

"Her High Divinity," my mother said, "is the patron of the little project you've been working on in the evenings."

"Little project, indeed," Gathena chuckled. "The Book of Amadán is a mountain—in length, mind you, not in depth. The man was a lunatic. But he's always been required reading for the seminarians. Our library's only copy of the book goes back to King Niall the Twelfth, and the mice have had their way with it. That is why I retained your service, Dr. Severals. So the seminarians will have a readable copy to slog through. Thank goodness, eh, Kara?"

"Thank goodness, indeed." Kara gave a forced laugh. Her voice, like her face, was pinched, and the pleasantry passed as quickly as it had been manufactured. Yes, she had looked pretty, for a moment.

"The postulants think we only keep Amadán around to torment them," Gathena continued. "And maybe we do. No one ever quotes it, and no priest in their right mind would ever try to preach from it. Reading Amadán is a feat. But *copying* it … well, I had to see for myself the mettle of the young scribe who has undertaken the task." She studied me once more in the same appraising manner as earlier. "I must say, he's not what I expected. I wonder what kind of work he will produce. Whether it will be worth the sum we have contracted."

My mother brushed past me. She was carrying a satchel and opened it before the priestess. She reached inside and pulled out the first three pages of my manuscript.

"I gathered from your letter that you had some concern," said my mother. "Here. You may see for yourself the quality of the boy's hand."

I worried that Gathena's thick fingers might crumple my copy work, but she plucked the pages with what looked like practiced care. Her eyes rolled in slow movements, steady, sweeping. To my delight, I noticed Kara inching closer, trying to get a view over the priestess's shoulder. Gathena went through each of the pages, her lips moving ever so slightly as she read. The fire in the hearth sputtered as the last remnants in the coffee pot boiled over. Outside, a cloud must have passed before the sun as the room slipped into shade. At last, Gathena looked up, this time with a very different expression, something between surprise and awe. Kara, too, seemed to be studying me, though what she may have been thinking was beyond guessing.

My mother broke the silence.

"He's already finished more than half."

"More than half, you say?" Gathena's eyebrows shot up. "Just since the time I hired you?"

"It's all right here." My mother patted her satchel. "You may see for yourself if you wish."

"No, no, that's not necessary. I'm sure it's just as you say, Delores. Well, young Simeon, I am impressed. Your script is flawless. Though it's in a bit of a queer hand. Sturdy, yet the letters flow. No frills or embellishments. Wherever did you learn to make letters like this?"

My mother shot me a warning glance that I understood at once. She was not to be eclipsed.

"I picked it up watching my mother," I said. "She's the one who taught me how to write."

"Did she? How wonderful."

Gathena drummed her fingertips on the chair's arm, and an enigmatic gaze settled over her features. It felt awkward standing before those placid, searching eyes, but then the old priestess clapped her hands on her knees and she seemed to brighten.

"Delores," she said, "I can smell talent when it's under my nose. You have a talented boy here. I should like to make a proposal for his services. A *new* proposal."

I looked over at my mother. Her face remained a stoic, mocking mask, though she angled her head just a trifle, as if to convey that she was listening. Listening, but not at all caring.

"We already have a contract," my mother reminded her.

"I'm proposing a novation." Gathena said. "One that could inure to everyone's benefit. I don't suppose you're a woman of faith?"

The sound of my mother's laughter, on those rare occasions that I heard it, was grating and very unpleasant, and, thankfully, always brief. Gathena seemed unbothered by my mother's laughter, though I could tell Kara was offended on her behalf. She started to speak, but the priestess held up a jeweled hand and bade Kara hold her tongue.

"I would never claim to be a woman of any faith, and though it is a terrible shortcoming of my character, I'm quite content with this world."

"I presumed as much. But you never can be sure unless you ask. May I also presume young Simeon's learning has, thus far, been confined to the secular studies? His present assignment excluded."

"You may."

"Is he bound to any tradesman?"

"Certainly not."

"Forgive me. Of course you would raise him to follow in your footsteps. He has his math, his sciences?"

"Passable geometry, poor algebra, credible grasp of philosophy." My mother shrugged. "But he does have some inclination with letters."

The priestess nodded to herself; her eyelids fluttered.

"Well-lettered children with no prospects are a rare commodity. Oh, don't pretend to look offended, Doctor. You're the widow of a drunkard. You're a friendless, over-educated tutor in the slums."

I drew a sharp breath, and Sister Kara's eyes went wide. I had never heard anyone speak to my mother so brusquely. They stared at one another, my mother grinding her jaw, the priestess exuding benevolence. Before my mother could reply, Gathena continued.

"I mean no offense. Your situation is truly unfortunate, Dr. Severals, and no fault of yours. But I took you at your word earlier. You said you were content. I wonder whether Simeon is, though."

"Get to your point, Gathena," my mother snarled.

"Very well. Our order is in need of scribes. You've no idea how much paper religion requires. And then there's the burden of the recording work we provide for the Four Duchies. All those letters, and lists, and deeds— we've a constant avalanche of pages that need to be copied, and never enough hands to tend to them." Gathena leaned forward in the chair. The legs groaned from the shift in weight. "Our seminary pays a generous stipend to anyone who recruits a lettered postulant."

"What is the stipend?"

"Two thousand marks."

My heart began to race. Thick-headed of a child as I was, even I was able to piece together what was happening. The priestess was bartering with my mother. My future was being haggled over, right here in this stuffy room that smelled of old papers, and a log fire, and burnt coffee.

I couldn't help but feel proud, though. Two thousand marks was a fantastic sum.

"We would cancel the prior contract, obviously," Gathena added. She reached towards the hearth and helped herself to a roll from the tin. "He would finish Amadán at the seminary, after he's taken his oath as a scribe. I can have the contract drawn up today, if you're interested."

Of course, no one bothered asking me what I wished, and I think I would have sputtered like an idiot if they had. The truth was, I didn't know what I hoped my mother would decide. But if I had been put to it, I suppose I wanted to stay in Rogues Run. I liked my cramped room on Drovers Lane, and roaming the streets of the Lower Bluff with Paul Little, and copying the tome of a rambling madman in a script of my own invention, so I was relieved when my mother seemed to sidestep Gathena's offer.

"That is a generous proposal, Divinity," she said. "But Simeon's almost sixteen now. He's never set foot within a temple. I would think that's too many years and too few rituals for a someone who intends to live in a seminary."

Gathena smiled and shook her head.

"Most who come to the seminary come from more, um, observant households. But not all. Kara's father, the Earl of Blithe, is known as something of a freethinker."

I tried to smile at Kara, but she stared back at me without a flicker of emotion, until, embarrassed, I had to look away. Gathena dropped her voice.

"It is a generous proposal, Dr. Severals. For Simeon and for you. All you need do is sign a bondage pledge to us."

My mother clasped her hands behind her back and dipped her head, as if in deep contemplation. While Gathena sipped the last of her coffee, my mother took a few pacing steps around in a circle. When I saw the way my mother was smiling to herself, I knew what her reply would be. She addressed her High Divinity with the thinnest veneer of respect.

"I'm so honored," she said, "that your order should offer me such generosity. But respectfully, your Divinity, I must decline your offer. Generous as it is. I have other plans for Simeon. And I suspect the boy would prove to be an odd fish in your holy kettle. He'd never unlearn all the agnosticism I've taught him. Once you've learned facts, they're quite hard to forget. But thank you, all the same."

The air in the room seemed to empty. Without anyone saying so, it was understood that the bargaining was over; there would be no deal. Gathena hoisted herself out of her chair and thanked my mother for her hospitality.

"I'll be in town, staying at the temple, for the rest of the month," said Gathena, as much to me as to my mother. "If you should change your mind…"

"I very much doubt we will," my mother replied.

There were a few abbreviated pleasantries, and the priestess and her pretty seminarian were shown the door. When they had left, my mother returned to the study, doused the fire, and started plucking books from the stacks, cradling them in her elbows, and setting them here and there in her familiar, haphazard heaps, to resume whatever project she had been pursuing. I watched in silence for a while, until my curiosity got the better of me.

"Two thousand marks is a lot of money," I said.

She was fanning through the pages of Ibid's *Prolegomenon*, trying to find her bookmark. Without looking up, she replied.

"Not really."

With a huff, she thumped the cover closed and made a face. "The trouble with Ibid is he's constantly repeating himself. I have no idea where I left off. Damn their interruption."

I was surprised—shocked—at how easily my mother had dismissed a sum of money that she couldn't hope to earn in half a decade of tutoring. Two thousand marks could hire servants, build a carriage, buy rooms on the other side of the Squire. Yet she seemed completely unconcerned. She settled back in her favorite chair, let her head fall into the comfort of a shadow and pinched the bridge of her nose, as if wearied from the ordeal of entertaining guests.

"It's just," I started. "I mean—"

"Gather your thoughts," she murmured without sparing me a glance, "then explain yourself."

"Two thousand marks is a *lot* of money." There was no better explanation for my confusion.

"Not for you it isn't." Though it was a compliment, there was no emotion, and not a hint of warmth, in her voice. "I've been showing your work around, Simeon. Once you finish Amadán, I have you hired to copy five more books, a dozen circulars, and an odd score of private contracts, memoranda, that sort of thing. At the pace you keep with that singular script of yours, you could bring in four hundred marks a year, at least."

"So that's why—?"

"Yes, that is why Gathena invited herself over. She hoped to buy four hundred a year for decades into the future in exchange for two thousand today. Assuming you live a while, it's a rather poor offer. Don't you agree?"

I hadn't realized until that moment how valuable I had become to my mother. That she would reap every pence from my work was not a point I considered. Why would I? A flushing warmth of pride filled my chest, more potent and intoxicating than Goodwife Rivers' ale.

CHAPTER THREE

"Let me get this straight …"

We were sitting outside in the relative shade of a warehouse balcony, overlooking a plaza in the roughest part of Rogues Run. Paul Little was reclining against the balcony wall, picking his teeth with a piece of chicken bone and taking his leisure, while the din and smells of the market below churned like a rushing river. It was coming on to Sowing Month, though the air still felt hot and unusually muggy. Paul twirled his drumstick like a tutor with a pointer.

"You're sitting on twenty-five marks … of copied paper?"

"Yeah," I said, staring blandly over the balcony rail.

Despite all the bustle of a market day and all the sights there were to see, I was fixated on a pigeon roosting in a stunted palm tree. The ugly gray bird kept fluttering down near a baker's table, and the baker, when he wasn't busy with a customer or sawing though a loaf or counting out change, kept having to shoo the thing away. Over and over, the pigeon repeated its sortie, and each time it was chased away, I noticed the bird had managed to creep a trifle closer to the baker's bread. Sooner or later, he was going to make a dash for it. Inwardly, I wished him luck.

"That's a lot of money," said Paul.

"I suppose."

"So what is it you do?"

There really wasn't much to explain. "Well," I said, "I set a page on one side of my desk next to a blank piece of paper. Then I just—start copying the page. When I'm finished, I go to the next one. When I'm done for the day, I set it on the windowsill to dry, and then I do it all again the next day."

He tossed the chicken bone over the rail. "And the more you write, the more they pay?"

I nodded and pulled at my shirt because the sweat was making it stick. Paul let out a whistle. The swelling had finally gone down around his left eye, though the skin was still rimmed with a deep bruise and his eyebrow seemed stuck about a thumb's width lower than its neighbor. It gave the impression he was deep in thought. For some reason, I felt uncomfortable talking about my work, so I gestured at the warehouse behind us and tried to change the subject.

"How long have you been staying here?"

He stretched his legs to their full length. "Past couple of days. Used to be a warehouse, but there was a fire. No one ever fixed it up. Took a little work to pry off the locks, but I like the view."

The building was nothing but a charred, crumbling hulk. Fallen slats from the roof let the sunlight pour through in wide, blinding bands. The floors below were carpeted with ash and broken tiles. A faint, acrid scent of smoke still clung to blackened bricks. Somehow, though, the balcony, such as it was, had been spared from the worst of the flames. A slab of mildewed flagstones propped up on a buttress and rimmed with rusted iron railings, it overlooked a dusty marketplace.

"This would be a good place to lie low for a while," I said, scanning the surroundings.

Paul fixed me with a shrewd look.

"It would. But you can't eat a nice view. A man's got to make marks, you know? When do you have to get back home?"

Over the past few days, my mother had gradually given me more free rein to roam about town, and lessened my chores and lessons. We had reached a tacit understanding. As long as I copied ten pages of Amadán a day, she didn't seem to care what else I did with my time. There were fewer dark looks, fewer snide complaints. Every now and then she would leave a half pence on my desk. It was the finest run of days in my life.

"Maybe another hour," I said.

Paul nodded. "You know," he said musingly, "I've got friends who buy all sorts of things. I'll bet they could get you a good deal for this book of yours. I don't know. Just seems to me Delores isn't being very fair with you."

I felt a flash of anger, but I kept my voice level. "She's my mother."

"Yeah, but still. You're making her a pile of coins. And what are you getting in return?" He rose to his feet and started walking back and forth in the cramped space of the balcony, and I swear he almost looked like an advocate making a closing argument. "Why should she take everything you earn? It's your work. Your skill. Alright, so she's your mother. So what? Mothers are supposed to care of their sons, not the other way 'round." Paul shook his head. "It's not right."

I shrugged, not really caring what he thought was wrong or right.

"You've got skill. I tell everybody that all the time. Simeon Severals may be mopey, his mother may be a first-grade flint, but Simeon's got skill. He gets things done. No one denies it."

I pretended to look over the balcony, hoping that Paul couldn't see the smile that was trying to break through my lips. I never knew I had a reputation. A reputation Paul was trying to burnish. The pigeon in the palm tree cooed as it eyed the table full of bread loaves.

"All you need," Paul added, "are some connections." He sat back down and tilted an eyebrow. "That's where I can help. Your mother's not the only one who's got people who'll pay for documents." He swept his hand to indicate the market. "I know lots of people in that kind of business. I could find buyers, lots of 'em, who'd pay good coin for what you can do. We'd be partners, Sim. Split everything down the middle."

It was tempting. For a moment, I actually thought about Paul's idea—me, a copy scribe, out on my own, flush with money with the business Paul's "friends" would bring us. It's a testament to Paul's honeyed tongue that I paused to consider such a stupid scheme. I did think about it, for a minute, until that pigeon finally made off with a piece of loaf from the baker's table.

"I've got to get home," I said.

You can live in the Lower Bluff your whole life, you can walk every drudging mile of every shit-filled byway every wretched day, you can take a ball of string, tie it off and unwind it to mark your route through town, but it won't matter. No matter what you do, you will end up lost in a dead-end alley every now and then.

The streets of Lower Bajebluff weren't laid out by a surveyor or a cartographer; they just kind of happened. And they're always changing. It might be a brewer who needs to expand his shop a little bit. One night, he stakes out a spot in the road by the corner of his tavern. He slips a bribe to the inspectors and the next thing you know, the next morning you find a newly built keghouse in the middle of the street and now everyone has to walk around it. A run of hovels pops up and cuts off one boulevard; a pottery kiln explodes and a new one is made. A never-ending, constantly changing labyrinth of crumbling, plaster buildings and the mud-rutted pathways snaking between them. That's the Lower Bluff. And that's why even the locals get lost from time to time.

That's why I was more annoyed than surprised when the shortcut I had been following, a narrow alley that wound behind Goodwife Rivers' grocery, led me straight into a wall of wooden crates. Hundreds of crayfish boxes, still dripping with riverweed and buzzing with flies piled up into a hill that stretched from one side of the alley to the other, from a hash shop's windowless den to the fishmonger's store. A massive, impenetrable, utterly foul bulwark. It would be days before enough of the wood was scavenged to open the alley again.

Muttering a curse, I turned around to double back when I heard the sound of a door slamming, and feet sprinting hard on the street, and a familiar voice.

"Head to the left!"

Two boys raced around a corner. The first was as tall as a mountain and laden with parcels. I didn't know him, though I recognized at once what he was carrying, just as I recognized who had yelled. Paul Little. They were making off with spices from the Rivers' grocery.

The boys came skidding to a halt. Paul's eyes went wide when he saw me. He said nothing, but stared hard, as if in disbelief, the flush in his cheeks draining away fast. I could almost read aloud the question he was asking himself: would I cover for him?

"Aw, hells," Paul's companion growled. "Alley's a dead end. What do we do?"

A breeze stirred between the buildings. An earthy scent of crushed cumin wafting from the stolen bags cut over the stench of dead fish. Paul collected himself and shot a knowing grin towards me.

"We'll just cut through the hash house, Rob. Hold our breath and make for the other door. They won't notice us."

"What about him?" Rob jerked his chin at me. "Don't like the look of him."

Paul's smile widened.

"That's my old friend, Simeon. Don't worry. He won't notice us either. Right, Sim?"

That was probably a hundred marks' worth of packaged cumin they were carrying. But all I could think about was the Goodwife, her round, kindly face, and the words she had said in the bakery:

"*A hungry boy takes bread. A thief steals spices.*"

"No," I said, my voice thin but determined.

"Simeon, what's the matter with you?" Paul hissed. He darted his head over his shoulder and nearly tottered from the stolen spices he had in his arms. The smell was pungent. "Look, if you're after a cut, I can deal you in for a couple of marks. All you've got to do is pretend you never saw us. Like what Rogues folks do."

"Those are the Goodwife's spices," I said. "You'll take them back."

"I knew I didn't like the look of him," Rob growled. He dropped his mound of parcels, stepped over them, and flexed his arms. "Don't worry. I'll make sure he forgets us."

"Wait!" Paul squealed, and tried to place himself between Rob and me. "We don't have time for this. Simeon, all you've got to do is keep your damned mouth shut—"

"No," I repeated.

Rob tossed Paul aside like a parcel and started towards me. "You're never gonna remember again."

I had been in my share of fights—you can't grow up in Rogues Run without fighting—but they were just scrapes. A few punches, wrestling around in the gutters, maybe a kick to the crotch, and thanks to my size, I had always come out more or less on top. This was going to be different. Rob was twice my weight, a smoldering volcano of intent.

Instinctively, I tried to back away. My heel caught on a broken piece of board, and I fell back into the crates. A rivulet of filthy water came cascading down over my shoulder. As I scrambled to my feet I heard Paul, exasperated, muttering at his partner.

"Make it quick."

Before I realized what was happening, Rob was on me. I was grappling, lashing, kicking, tossed about in a torrent of motion. I didn't know what I was doing, and it didn't matter. Our limbs tumbled and flailed in the dirt, into the gutter, onto the crates. It was like wrestling a bull.

For the first few moments of the fight, while I managed to keep a grip on Rob, I felt invigorated, in a way I hadn't before. The feeling didn't last long.

Rob freed one of his arms from my grip and craned it high. His fist shrouded out the sunlight. He brought it down like a smith's hammer working a piece of steel, right into the side of my head.

I collapsed in a heap. He hit me again, harder.

A tinging bell drowned out he noises of the world. Darkness rolled into the corner of my vision. It kept creeping closer, crowding out more of my sight. I was looking through a pipe, closing fast. All I could see were two hands grasping for my throat. They were hard, callused, unrelenting.

A burning pressure clenched around my neck. Rob had me pinned beneath his weight. I couldn't move. Couldn't hit. I was choking. My vision shrank to a pinprick. I heard Paul, as if from far away.

"Hurry up."

The darkness was smothering me, or maybe it was Rob. My thoughts reeled madly until an idea came churning up from the ether. I had just enough strength left to give it a try.

I tucked my chin into Rob's hold and bit the soft flesh between his thumb and forefinger. I clamped my teeth until I tasted the salty tang of blood—his or mine, I couldn't say—and then I bore down even harder.

"Ach—bastard!" he cried.

His grip loosened as he pulled his hand free.

I gulped in air, filled my lungs until they nearly burst. Now was my chance.

It wouldn't do any good to cry for help. No one in Bajebluff ever responded to that. But there was always one word you could shout that would bring folks out of their shops as surely as the sunrise over the horizon. Though my throat felt as if it had been scoured over with a whetstone, I roared as loud as I ever had.

"Thieves! Stop, *thieves*!"

I yelled until my voice was hoarse. Rob clenched a filthy palm over my mouth. I bit it again and yelled once more. As if in response, I heard the welcome clanks of shop doors being thrown open.

"Run!" Paul shouted and dropped his sacks of spice.

Other than the smoke of fire, the one thing you could count on to stir a shopkeeper in the Lower Bluff was to shout out a thief. Because the merchants couldn't count on the law, they had to count on one another. Every shopkeeper was bound to respond when that alarm was raised and do what he could.

I felt Rob's weight ease off my body. My vision returned, and I saw a small throng of cloth traders, haberdashers, fishmongers, coopers, and tinkers running down the alley towards us. Among the dozen or so in the little mob were the two grocers, Mr. and Mrs. Rivers.

Rob and Paul darted into the hash house doorway and disappeared, leaving me sprawled, soaked, and sullied in the broken crawfish crates. I tried to get up to my knees, but only managed to crawl into a mud puddle. The tastes of brine, filth, and blood filled my mouth. My throat felt like it was on fire.

Several of the merchants shouted at once:

"What's going on here?"

"What're all these boxes doing in the alley?"

"Where's the thief? Someone shouted 'thief.'"

I was still gasping, as if I had just been pulled from a lake, but I tried to respond. The words caught in my throat, stabbed it like knives, and nothing but a sputter came out.

"The—they..."

A torrent of angry noises. I think the butcher said something about fetching his cleaver. Then a woman's voice cut over the crowd.

"I can't believe it. I can't. Not Simeon. Why would he do such a thing?"

It was Goodwife Rivers. My neck clenched hard, but finally I gargled out what I wanted to say, though the effort felt like Rob's fist pounding the inside of my skull.

"Not … a thief," I rasped.

A wiry hand grasped me firmly by the elbow and brought me upright. I blinked and there was Mrs. Rivers wedged within a press of surly merchants. Her husband Mr. Rivers was holding me. I turned, my head swimming from the effort, and saw the deep lines of a shrewd and cynical face scrutinizing me closely. An unlit clay pipe dangled from his bottom lip. He scanned the ground and spoke low, as if to himself.

"They're my wares alright. But how'd the tutor's boy carry off all these packages with no sack or bag, I wonder? Must be near to two score lying 'round."

Before I could answer, Mrs. Rivers spoke again, her voice quivering.

"Why would you do such a thing, Simeon?"

She sounded so … broken. Goodwife Rivers, the sweetest lady I had ever known, the only one who ever asked how I was feeling, the finest pie cook in the Lower Bluff, was heartbroken. Tears began gushing from my eyes. I started to cry. It hurt, but I couldn't stop. Not even to explain how she had it all wrong.

Mr. Rivers let go of my arm. My legs wobbled, but I kept my balance as he spoke to the crowd:

"All of you can clear out now. I'll handle this. Thanks for answering the call. But I'll take care of this matter myself. Off with you. All of you. You as well, Goodwife."

The crowd dissipated as quickly as it had gathered. Mrs. Rivers lingered for a moment, shook her head sadly at me, and walked away. Mr. Rivers and I were alone in the alley. I wiped the tears from my cheeks.

"It wasn't me," I croaked. "It was—it was … two boys I've never seen before."

My head fell. I don't know why, but I simply couldn't bring myself to turn in Paul. So soon after a sentence in the stocks, they would have lopped off his hand. He deserved as much, but I didn't want to be the one to bring it about.

Mr. Rivers studied me for a while. At last, the grocer spat on the ground, pulled his pipe from his mouth and pointed the stem at my chest.

"You want to tell that to a judge?"

"No, sir."

He frowned, the lines around the corners of his lips spreading all the way to his cheeks.

"Me neither," he said.

Mr. Rivers narrowed his eyes and let out a long sigh, and it was as if he was sitting in judgment over me. As he stood in contemplation, the sun beat down in the alley, baking the mud and bilge from the crates into my clothes. Despite the warmth, my skin was all gooseflesh. The dirt of the roadway felt as if it was swaying; it was like trying to stay balanced on a boat pitching in the waves. At last, Mr. Rivers pronounced his verdict with the solemn conviction of a magistrate.

"Your friends—them two boys you say you've never seen before— they left you looking pretty, didn't they? You ought to keep better company, mind who you do business with." He put his pipe back in his mouth and gestured towards the scattered cumin sacks. "I'll not call the law on you. When you've got your feet under you again, stack these in my shed, the one with the lock. I'll be keeping my eye on you through the window. Got it?"

"Yes, sir."

"And Simeon?"

"Yeah?"

"It'd be best if you didn't come around the grocery for a while."

The medicine smelled like an old water trough. A putrid, pungent stench that hit me in waves. I thought I was going to retch on my bed.

My mother was sitting in my desk chair, busily mashing a paste in a clay mortar. She had the lantern as low as it could be trimmed, and the curtains in my room had been drawn and reinforced with a pair of woolen blankets. The glow sputtering behind my mother still stung my eyes every time I tried to look at her. She worked from my rickety chair, grinding, grinding, grinding, a silhouette stooped over a tiny bowl. I wished she could have worked more quietly.

After a time, she spoke, softly, though the sound of her voice drummed in my temples.

"And tell me again how it was that you ... fell in this alley?"

After I had finished picking up all of Mr. Rivers' spices, I had stumbled home. When my mother saw my condition, the first words out of her mouth had been:

"Explain yourself."

I had to tell her something. I said I tripped. Over something. I fell and hit my head in an alley behind Drovers. That was the story.

She had me strip down to my loincloth and sit on the edge of my bed while she went and fetched an old satchel I had never seen before. And now she was making medicine, which was a skill I never knew she had.

Without a word, she took my head in her hands, angled it, and carefully, methodically, parted my hair. I could feel every strand being tugged.

"You have more than one contusion here."

I felt a cool gel dabbing onto my scalp. It tingled at first, then stung, and gradually faded into a gentle, warming throb. She bound my head with a linen cloth and continued.

"I suppose it's possible that one could injure one's head in multiple places from a single fall. Although that would not explain the pronounced bruises around your neck."

My head swirled. Did that happen in the fight? It must have, but I had no idea how. At least I could reply truthfully.

"I don't remember."

"I see."

She finished bandaging my head and handed me the pestle.

"Swallow all of it."

Whatever went down my throat was like a roaring, liquid fire. I coughed and wheezed and almost lost it all through my nostrils.

"Wha—what *was* that?"

"Gin, aged molasses, kelp oil, a crushed poppy bud, and a powdered black lotus leaf," she replied. "It will keep your brain from over-swelling so that it doesn't crush itself within your skull. It will also make you sleep."

"Oh."

A strange numbness took root deep in my stomach. From there it sprouted tendrils, a kudzu plant slowly spreading throughout my body, supplanting the pain, replacing it with a blanket of blunted muteness. It was not unpleasant. I was no longer weary, simply relaxed. I also felt talkative for some reason, though my words sounded slurred.

"I never knew you were an apothecary," I mumbled.

"I'm not." She swept the mortar and pestle back into the weathered satchel and snapped it shut. "It was a course I was required to complete back when I studied in Niallex."

The thought of my mother in the capital city, poring over a classroom table, perhaps under the disapproving scowl of a master apothecary, made me smile for some reason.

"Was that where you and Dad were married?"

She had started to rise from her seat, but now she paused. For a moment she stared at me as if I had spoken in a foreign tongue. The shadows within her face grew longer.

"No," she finally muttered. "My family ran out of money to pay for the university. Then I was sent here."

So many questions, unanswered and unasked. In the warmth of the medicine, they bubbled up into my thoughts, and like a pot boiling over, out they came:

"When did you first meet him? How old was he? What did you think of him? I'll bet—I'll bet you were nervous about leaving home—"

She brought her voice down like a hammer, the weight of the words squelching the effects of the poppy and the lotus.

"Be quiet."

The sound reverberated in my head. I winced from the pain. My mother spoke more quietly:

"I do not care to discuss your late father or the arrangement of our marriage. I've made that amply clear." She leaned closer and for a moment I thought she might strike me—or bring me into her embrace—but instead she reached out, peeled back one of my eyelids, and nodded to herself. "The narcotic is taking effect."

She walked over to the window, unlocked the latch and nudged the smoky pane glass outward. A fresh breeze gusted through the narrow opening, fluttering the curtains. Sleep came blowing in.

There was one more nagging bubble, though, clinging on, keeping me awake. My eyes fluttered with heaviness, but I couldn't let it go.

"What was ... he like?"

I heard the sound of her footsteps treading into dimness and my bedroom door hinges creaking open. Before the door shut, she said,

"Like you. Go to sleep."

CHAPTER FOUR

A deep dreamless void was broken by the shrill chattering of an old tavern maid. She was in the street, not far from my window, and burning with anger. Some poor sot hadn't paid all his tab, and she was heaping fire and coals over him for trying to run out. I put my pillow over my head, but it was no use.

"—an' I'm tellin' you, Bailey," she yelled, "that was the reserve stout you drank, an' it's a full pence a mug. You drank eight, so you've shorted me four pence, you fuckin' rogue."

"Didn't taste like no reserve stout t'me," Bailey growled. "Prove it otherwise."

"How 'bout I just cut your stones from 'tween your legs. Got the knife right here to do it. How'll that be for proof?"

A long silence. There was a tingle of coins dropping onto the street outside.

"You're a flinty bitch, y'know that?"

"An' you're paid up. See you tomorrow..."

My eyes flicked open. All was dark in my bedroom. It was nighttime outside, but what night, I had no idea. A blanket twisted in knots around my body. It felt a little stiff; I must have been sweating. Gingerly I pulled myself free and felt around my head. The bandage was gone, and the swollen lumps on the side had come down a bit. It still hurt, but as a dull, pressing throb. I blinked a few times, trying to get my eyes to focus on the familiar shadows in my room.

The curtains over my bed rustled. The window had been thrust wide open.

My mouth tasted moldy and as dry as gravel. I licked the inside of my cheek with my tongue and it was like rubbing a pumice stone. I took a deep breath, let it out, and swung my legs to the ground.

A little wobble, but after a few tries, I could sit upright. Thick and groggy, that's how I felt. I sat for a while, holding my chin in my hands to clear my head. My eyes scanned the familiar shadows of my room.

Edge of the bed. Window. Rolled up rug. A heavy stick I always kept handy. The chamber pot, full (I must have gone in my sleep). My chair. The darkened lantern. The open window. My desk, clean and bare.

My heart stopped in my chest.

The Book of Amadán had been sitting out on the desktop. The pages had been weighted down with quartz stones, and a new inkpot and an uncut quill had been left waiting for me to resume my copy work when I recovered—I was on the last chapter. I remember seeing it when my mother had bandaged my head; its presence was a kind of comfort. But now it was gone.

A cold, sobering dread seized me. I knew the book and the copy had been stolen.

And I knew who stole them.

The Lower Bluff can be a dodgy place in the midnight watch. You need to "keep your hand on your purse and your head on a swivel," as the saying goes. Which is not an easy thing to do if you've just come out of a light coma and your head is still recovering from a merciless beating. But I had to get my book back, and I didn't have much time.

A dull, broken bell clanged from a watchtower. I stumbled from my house, making my way from one lamppost to the next, past the lit doorways and windows of all the hash houses, brothels, bars, and taverns that sprouted to life when the stars came out over Rogues Run. Through the winding alleys, I shuffled as fast as my weak legs could take me. The gutters were still slick with dirty puddles; it must have rained recently. The cobblestones reflected a thousand tiny marbled lights. The air reeked of mold and straw, and piss mixed with hops and hash smoke. The familiar stench of Lower Bluff revelry.

Luckily, there were relatively few revelers out. A few whores plying for clients, a stumbling longshoreman trying to find his way back to his dock, a pickpocket maybe five paces behind him, some carters and drivers making late deliveries, a lamplighter on stilts, muttering to himself. I limped past the menagerie, avoiding eye contact with anyone. Drovers Street, Vipers, Beggars Palace … I was getting close. Luckily, no one had bothered with me.

Down a run of cracked steps, through a rusted gate, I reached an empty market square surrounded on all sides by tall, silent warehouses. The square was packed with a bevy of locked-up carts, booths, tables, and empty chairs. They cast long shadows, gray beneath the alabaster moonlight. I had just found the doorway I was looking for when I noticed a man prowling around a vacant stall in a far corner. He wore a hooded cloak that covered his face.

The hood tilted up and faced me.

The hairs on my neck prickled. Quickly, but quietly, I turned away, trying not to appear as if I was hurrying, and circled back the way I had come. I would have to try the other side of the square.

When I reached the edge of the market, I hurried for the stairway. As I left the square behind, I chanced a peek over my shoulder.

The hooded man was already gone.

I picked up my pace. If I could swing around the outer walls of the market, find a lane that would lead me to the other side of the square, I could approach the doorway I was trying to reach from the opposite direction. I forced my legs, now quivering from exertion, to carry me the extra steps. I was groping my way through a byway and so focused on retracing my steps, I never heard the hidden door open. A bulky shadow slipped in front of me. I bumped headlong into its chest. It was like running into a wall. One that extended a hand to keep me from falling on my backside.

"Whoa, there, little scoundrel," the hood laughed. It was a deep, husky voice.

"S-sorry," I stammered.

The figure drew himself upright and threw back his cloak, and there stood a plain, bearded, dark-skinned man in his forties, square-jawed and broad-shouldered, his face marred by a wicked scar that seemed to cut his chin short. As he draped the cloth of his cloak over his shoulder, I noticed a short sword sheathed at his belt and a steel crescent around his neck.

A sheriff's deputy. Not the worst sort I could have run into, but a bad turn all the same.

"Little young to be out taverning, aren't you?" He bent lower to study me more closely, a faint smile playing on the edge of his mouth. I tried to smile back, but I was pretty well winded.

"You alright?" he asked.

"Yes, sir. Just—just trying to get home."

"And where is home?"

I met his eyes. They were hard, black as coals, but not unkind.

"Up ahead," I lied.

"You live here?"

"Yes, sir."

"Interesting," he nodded. "What's your name?"

"Simeon."

He waited for my surname. But if there's one thing every Rogues Run boy knows, you never say more than you have to when you're talking with the law. I left it at Simeon.

"Well, Simeon. I'm Corporal Downs. This here is my ward as of last Mending Month. We haven't met. So let's chat."

His hand gripped my shoulder and lead me to the middle of the roadway where a lone lamp post with a broken orb offered a weak, guttering, oily light. He flipped over a wooden bucket and an empty box for chairs and motioned for me to sit down. Not the most comfortable position, sitting on an upside-down pail, but a relief to finally be off my feet.

"You don't look good at all," Downs said. He slid his seat a little closer so that his knees were almost touching mine. "And you don't look like most of the folk who call this shit-sty home. So, as the new ward watch, I have to wonder what business a nicely dressed, sickly looking, well-fed, out-of-place boy might have in the middle of the night in one of the worst thief markets in Lower Bajebluff."

Instinctively, I shrank back, avoiding his gaze. Downs lowered his voice.

"A lot of smuggled wares come through here after the market closes, after the tax collector's gone." He folded his hands and he looked up at the lamp pensively. "You can make a lot of money in trade, if you can cut the tax man out. A young fellow with a few coins and a little hustle can turn a tidy profit out here. Maybe someone such as yourself?"

There was only response when a deputy insinuated you were involved in something. I recited it by rote.

"I don't know anything about that."

"Of course you don't." Downs' mouth smiled, though his eyes stayed cold and scrutinizing. "So you wouldn't mind if I searched you?"

He didn't wait for me to answer, but hoisted me to my feet and patted down my clothes, felt under my belt, jabbed his fingers through the thongs of my sandals, tapped the soles for hidden pouches—all in a swift, practiced motion. It took him less than a minute.

"Nothing," he said, that unnerving gaze never wavering.

I made a show of straightening out my clothes and lifting my head indignantly.

"I told you. I'm just trying to get home. If it's money you're after, I can pay you later when—"

"Keep your bribe, Simeon." He stretched, let out a yawn, and rubbed at the stubble around his ruined chin. Near the light post's flame, a flurry of moths floated in the air, brown wings flapping lazily. The next street over, a man was sobbing. The sheriff's deputy smiled at me.

"Sounds like I'm needed. Good night, Simeon Severals."

Before I could ask how he knew my name, Corporal Downs had pulled his hood back over his head and disappeared into the night.

The broken padlock came off easily. One tug and it clinked open. With my shoulder, I pressed against the wooden door, a soft, steady succession of nudges, so as not to make too much noise. When I had cracked it wide enough, I slipped inside into the dark building.

The warehouse was no longer empty.

Piercing the gloom at the far end of a massive high-ceilinged chamber, an orange campfire burned in a pit. The flames sent ripples of light shooting into the air. I could make out three forms huddled around the fire. One was smaller than the others. They kept their voices low, but in that expanse of space, I could still hear the muffled echoes reverberating against the unseen walls and ceiling.

I pushed the door shut behind me and crept towards the light. Slowly, very slowly, one cautious step at a time, I drew closer, crouching low to keep hidden. Thankfully, no one by the fire had posted a lookout. I was able to get within thirty paces of the fire pit. As I drew nearer, the forms came into focus and the furtive murmurs became words. The first I could make out came from a woman.

"That's a ransom. For something there's not even a market for."

She was answered with grumbled agreement.

"Malik," she continued, "has your man in the channel ever bought such ware?"

A heavy bald man looming over the glow of the fire replied with a scoff.

"Uh-uh. I never heard of anyone buyin' somethin' like this in the channel, Amma. Who'd want it?"

Amma held up her hands. In the wavering light, she looked to be in her thirties, with short hair that cut a fierce aspect around an otherwise plain face. "I'm sorry," she said, "but if we can't sell it, it's no use to us. At least," she paused meaningfully, "not at the price you're asking."

I got down on all fours onto the dusty floor, though the pain of crawling was almost unbearable. Just a little closer, so I could see who she was dealing with ...

The smallest shape, Paul Little, spoke up, spooning honey in his voice.

"I never said a hundred marks was my *final* offer. I've got a little room to negotiate, if I cut into my commission. The gentleman who's selling this has to make his marks, mind you. But we can take a few less."

"How much less would your, ehm, gentleman take?"

I could almost hear Paul smiling.

"Nice try. I'm not bidding against myself. Why don't give me your best offer, and I'll tell you if it's close to my gentleman's needs."

He was haggling. He had stolen my work, and now he was haggling over the price. Through the rolling fog in my head and the aches all over my body, a hot river began to flow. Rage of a kind I had never known washed into me, bringing new strength to my limbs and sight to my eyes.

I stood upright. Heart pounding, chest heaving, I got off the floor and marched to the fire pit, pointing at Paul.

"That's not yours to sell," I said.

The three by the fire jumped. Malik brought out a dagger.

"Who's this?" he bellowed.

"Simeon?" In the muted light, I could see Paul blanch. He started to raise a hand in greeting, thought better of it, and let it fall to his side. "Wha-what're you doing here?"

"Little bastard tried to sneak up on us ... "

Malik took a threatening step towards me, but all I could see were flames and the burlap sack by Paul's feet, a sack covering the familiar square shape of the Book of Amadán. Paul grasped at Malik's sleeve.

"No, no, he's a friend."

"Some friend," I said through clenched teeth. "That's mine. You stole my dad's book and my copy. Just like you tried to steal the Goodwife's spices!"

Amma narrowed her eyes.

"Bring him over here, Malik."

Before I knew what was happening, the scruff of my shirt was yanked backwards, and Malik had my arm locked with his. He pulled it up hard into my shoulder. I started to struggle, but then he flashed his blade before my eyes, a long, curved steel, the edge sharpened to a gleam. Malik *tsked* in my ear.

"Don't make me do it, boy."

He stood me before the fire. The flames came up high, almost to my waist.

Amma smiled at me and turned to Paul with a mocking expression. "I take it this is the ... gentleman you're representing?"

Paul shot me a warning look and replied quickly, his voice now more laden with panic than sweetness.

"Uh, yeah. This is him. His name's Simeon. So what'd you say your offer was?

"You can't sell that," I yelled. "It's mine. You broke into my bedroom and stole it."

Paul's mouth cracked open, as if he had been offended.

"I picked it up where you *left it* for me, Simeon. Like we agreed. *Remember?*"

"I thought you were my friend..."

"I am your friend." He held out his hands. "Why do you think I'm doing this? I'm getting you the best deal I can. To help you get out from under your mother, 'cause she doesn't give a shit about you—"

"*Shut up!*"

"Easy there," Malik growled in my ear and tightened his hold. I could smell the remnants of ale and onions on his breath. Smoke billowed into my face as a chair leg collapsed in the fire.

"Listen," said Paul, "this actually makes it easier. Since he's here, how about we just cut through the haggling and get to a final price. Say, forty marks?"

"I'm afraid I can't make you an offer now, Paul," Amma spoke softly, with the cutting smoothness of a stiletto. She folded her arms across her chest. "You said you were brokering these books. This young man claims they're stolen."

"Damn right they are," I spat.

"Shut up, Sim," Paul hissed from the side of his mouth. But I refused to listen, and I refused to hold my tongue.

"The book belongs to a seminary. It's on loan to my mother. The copy's mine. All the loose pages in there, that's all my writing. My work. He can't sell it. It's mine."

I jerked forward as hard and as fast as I could. If I could land one blow on Paul, one hit... But Malik was three times my size. I might as well have been a kitten trying to wriggle free of his grasp.

"Better watch out, Pauly," Malik chuckled. "Your gentleman ain't too happy with you."

"Just listen to me—" Paul started.

"No, I'm afraid this changes everything," Amma cut over him. She spoke in a serious, ominous tone, but I could feel Malik chuckling. She looked from Paul, to me, and back to Paul, with an exaggerated frown. "You see, we don't trade in stolen wares."

"That'd be a crime," said Malik.

"Indeed," Amma nodded, and I could see the grin teasing into her mouth. "This property isn't yours, Paul. It's stolen. And if it's stolen..." She left the thought dangling for Malik to pick up.

" ... it's anyone's for the takin'," he said.

I heard Paul moan next to me. Amma hoisted up the sack, and as she lifted it, part of a page poked through the opening. A fragment of my writing shone in the firelight:

"—a run with dogs. Verily—"

All of my work, and that beautiful book. Slipping away, this time before my eyes. A sob shook in my chest.

Then the warehouse exploded with a cacophony of voices. Noise, on all sides, echoing everywhere at once, a train of lights following in their wake:

"Halt there!"

"Halt!

"In the name of the Sheriff, you halt!"

"*Halt or die!*"

Torches blazed in the dark as a dozen men surged through the front door. They were outfitted in leather helms, cuir bouilli vests, and studded boots and gloves, and wielded heavy maces, the kind usually used on mobs. Each man had the same steel crescent emblem bouncing on his chest. Half the watch must have been called out.

One was dressed differently, though. In the midst of the throng, I spotted a man in a hooded cloak strolling swiftly, but with a casual grace. His hood slipped back, and there was the profile of Corporal Downs.

I had scarcely registered what was happening when Malik shoved me hard to the ground and made a run for the door. A cloud of ash and dust blinded me, but when I rubbed my eyes, I saw Malik barreling headlong towards a gap between two of the deputies.

For a man of his bulk, Malik had quick feet. Before I had blinked twice, he was twenty paces away. But the two men he aimed for must have spotted him, and closed their ranks to cut him off. At the moment the deputies braced their feet and started to swing their maces, Malik pivoted hard to his left, stutter-stepping like a dancer, and changed his angle to veer around one of the deputies.

It was a brilliant feint.

The maneuver left his opponents caught in their fighting stances, as if they were tied up under a fouled anchor. For added measure (or maybe spite), as he passed, Malik flicked his dagger hard into one of the men's legs, hardly slowing his pace as he plunged the blade in the deputy's thigh.

The deputy crumpled to the ground, clutching the handle. By the time the man let out a groan, Malik was already at the door.

Corporal Downs kept his voice level and pointed to three of his men.

"Eaves, Nightbottom, Craig, after him. Raise the rest of the watch if you need to."

The three guards peeled off from the rest and raced after Malik, their booted feet pounding in the dark. I felt the press of hands grasping me, and leather cords wrapping my wrists. I was too tired, too weak, to resist. A voice behind me spoke in a flat, officious tone.

"In the name of the Sheriff, you're under arrest."

I lifted my head and saw Paul and Amma on their knees, bound just like me. The rest of Downs' men spread out to search the warehouse. I let out a sigh. As terrible a turn as the night had taken (I hadn't even begun to wonder what my mother was going to do to me), there was one small comfort. At least the book was safe. Whatever else happened, I had kept Paul from pawning it off as his own.

I heard a crackle within the fire pit, followed by a sputter of embers and a strange, almost snake-like hiss of something burning fast.

In the heart of the fire, the burlap sack with the Book of Amadán and my nearly completed copy was curling on itself, turning to cinders. Amma must have slipped it into the fire when Malik made his run.

A small cloud of dark smoke hovered just above the sack. As the flames swept the sack into oblivion, a final fragment of one of my pages held back, stubbornly unlit amidst the inferno, but only for a moment before it, too, joined the blackened charred remains.

Who art thou? Whence come you—

Gone.

Amma caught me staring in horror at the fire. I looked at her numbly. She shrugged. It might have been an apology, or to say, "You understand, don't you? I had no choice."

"*No!*"

I broke down and wept as bitterly as any father who ever lost a child.

———————

A slender rod of dawn light pierced the bars of the cell window. A rectangle no wider than my arm with iron rebar crossed in X's allowed a crack of air and sound and light from the street outside. I was alone in a basement of sorts, a square chamber, six and a half paces by seven, surrounded on all sides by great blocks of mortared stone. A rusted iron door on the far wall was locked shut. I had a bucket, a bed of straw that seemed reasonably free of bugs, a handleless mug, a low stool, and the window. The last was a rare luxury for Sheriff Beardley's prisoners, one that I might have appreciated had I been in a consolable mood.

I sat on the floor with my back against the wall, clutching my knees, watching a pair of mice sniffing at the air. The faint noises of Beggars Palace coming to life crept through the window, a muted chorus pleading for alms.

All I could think about was my writing going up in flames.

It left me numb, and hollow, and very tired. I couldn't sleep, though.

A loud metallic clank was followed by the sound of a bar being thrown open, and the cell door slowly squealed outward.

Corporal Downs came inside. The hood was gone. He was dressed in a simple gray tunic and trousers, but he still wore his crescent. Without a word, he pulled the stool closer, dragging it across the stone, and made himself comfortable. For a long while, we simply sat in silence. The street sounds played on. The mice slipped away. Like my book.

"So," he said, clearing his throat, "let's talk about your friend, Paul Little."

It was a prompt for me to interject, to argue, to say something, anything, to get me talking—and put my neck in the stocks. I didn't make a sound. Downs nodded knowingly, and continued.

"He's a little rogue. Not your usual pick-pocketing and shop-thievery. The tax collector's convinced your friend's part of a smuggling channel. He says they've been smuggling wares through his market. Ivory, mostly. But other wares, too. And not a farthing of tax paid on any of it."

I scoffed.

"You mean they didn't pay the tax man's bribe."

Downs chuckled. "Yes, well, same difference. Anyhow, your young friend's got a mark on his back."

He shifted his weight on the stool.

"So do the two that were with him in the warehouse. Amma Grom and Malik the Mincer, and they're not little rogues. That's a hard pair. You know what I mean?"

I suppose I did, more or less.

"You, uh, ever dealt with them before?"

I looked up, bored my eyes into his, and shook my head once.

"Didn't think so. Not a nice bookish boy like you. Paul, though, I think he's had some dealings with them. I'm pretty sure of it. What do you think?"

This was getting tiresome. I rested my chin in my hands and muttered, "I don't know."

"You don't?"

"No."

A drawn-out silence.

"Well, that's a shame," he said at last. "A real shame. You see, I've got a young deputy who's going to lose a leg, thanks to Malik. And you've lost your book, thanks to Paul."

That made me wince. He must have noticed, because Downs lowered his voice, and his words came out quickly, conspiratorially.

"I can understand why you were so upset, Simeon. I would be, too. All that work, all that writing. Over six hundred pages, I hear it was. You must have poured your life into that. And here your friend steals it for his own. In a way, Paul stole a part of you. Stole your work so he could pawn it off to a couple of unlettered cutthroats."

My hands started trembling, I couldn't help it. I blinked hard to keep Downs from seeing the tears that were welling up.

"It's a crime that's worth a hand," he continued. "No, I mean it. Paul should spend the rest of his life in Beggars Palace for what he did to you. That would be justice. I'd like nothing more than to haul him into the Magistrate's Court myself."

I shot Downs an angry glance, wiped my eyes, and scowled at the floor.

"Here's the problem, though. Your book got burned. There's no evidence. And there was nothing else in that warehouse I could use in court." He tapped his finger on my knee to get me to look up at him. "But maybe you remembered seeing some ivory while you were in that warehouse. Or maybe you heard Paul talking about some ivory ... if you did, then I could haul Amma, Malik, Paul, the whole lot of them, into court. And we can start making things right. For everyone. Maybe even get you and your mother some restitution for that lost book. So let me ask you again, one more time, Simeon. Are you sure you don't know anything else about your friend Paul Little's dealings?"

It was tempting, I'll admit it. There was nothing wrong with using the law to settle a score. Lower Bluff folks did it all the time. Short of waging a blood feud or taking up knives in a duel, "swearing on" your enemies to get them taken up was probably the closest approximation to justice our lot could hope for. All you had to do was tell a story; Sheriff Beardley's men took care of the rest.

But two thoughts kept me from swearing on Paul, much as I wanted to. First, I still had this last, nagging shred of fondness for the bastard. As furious as I was, for all I would have given to have taken a hammer to Paul's skull, I felt a grain of admiration for the sheer brazenness of what he had nearly pulled off. Second, Downs was asking me to cut my own throat. I may not have been the most experienced boy in Rogues Run, but I knew testifying against someone like Amma or Malik on a false crime would eventually end with me falling down a well, or slipping off a pier, or gutted in a dark alley behind a tavern.

"Simeon?"

I looked up again.

"No. Sir."

"That's a shame."

He let out a long breath and rubbed at his scarred chin. The light from the window caught the corporal's crescent badge; the metal shone dully in the cell. Downs got up.

"So, I guess I'm stuck here," I muttered.

"For breaking the Sheriff's curfew? No. We don't jail children for sneaking out of their beds. Your mother's already paid your fine. You'll be out in an hour."

That made me start.

"I—she did? You mean she's here?"

Downs walked back to the cell door and rapped it hard three times. As the jailor on the other side unlocked the latches, Downs answered over his shoulder.

"She paid and left."

She opened my bedroom door without a knock, without any greeting.

"Pack your clothes." My mother tossed a canvass backpack onto my bed. "I'll be waiting outside."

"Al-alright."

It was around mid-morning. I had been sitting at my desk, staring at the wall for I don't know how long, my thoughts wandering back and forth between the realms of self-anger and self-pity. Before I could think of a more coherent response, before I had even fully registered what she had just said, my mother disappeared again and I heard the front door of the house creak open.

That was the first time she had spoken to me in two days.

The suddenness of my mother's appearance, and her brusque, enigmatic command, left me a little dazed. But I did as she told me. As if in a kind of dream, I gathered up my clothes and emptied my desk and started packing—though for what purpose, I had no idea. It only took a few minutes.

As I rolled up my belongings—two shirts, two pairs of paints, an oiled rain cloak, a frayed leather belt, my wool blanket—I reflected on the past couple of days.

They had been a blur.

I had emerged from the Beggars Palace Jail tired, hungry, and with a fog clouding my head. It had been a miserable trek home. The only distraction from my wretchedness was planning what I was going to tell my mother, how I would answer her questions, and how, if it came to it, I could point out, delicately of course, that some of the fault lay with her. She had, after all, been the one who opened my bedroom window.

But when I walked through the front door, before the first word came out of my mouth, she slapped me hard across my cheek and held her long, bony finger warningly before me.

"I'm finished with you."

That was all she said. She retreated to her study, slammed the door, and left me with a stinging cheek, and burning eyes, and wondering what she meant.

I cloistered myself in my bedroom, only coming out when I was sure she was in her study or teaching students. I would sneak a piece of bread, or a drink of water, or relieve myself, then, as if in penitence, return to my room and sit. I slept some, read a little, and worried a great deal about what my mother had in mind for me. I kept hoping a new book and blank pages might appear. But my desk stayed empty and bare. Two days passed like this. She went about her business, while I lingered in my room, seemingly forgotten. It had almost become a routine until this morning, when it came to an abrupt end.

I slung the bag strap over my shoulder and went outside where my mother was waiting. She looked at me for a moment then started down Drovers, leaving me to hurry after her.

She had an odd, shuffling gait, as if she had become unused to the practice of walking, but she made her way through the crowded streets as swiftly as anyone else. No greetings given or received. A silent trudge under the summer sun of Lower Bajebluff. A curtain of smoke hung in the air, carrying the stench of burning garbage. We wound our way through the fog and the gathered throng of workers and merchants, neither one of us saying a word to the other. When we reached the Page Bridge, my curiosity bested me.

"Where are we going?"

She didn't answer, didn't look over her shoulder, didn't slow her step. I hurried after her over the bridge. Soon, the flow of people we were walking with had to slow for a crowd of children, packed knee to knee in a clearing before a bright green and orange cart. It was a puppet show. The troupe was performing the *Cobbler's Magic Sole* and had gotten to the part where the cobbler's shoe suddenly comes to life. Up on the puppet stage, a leather boot with sewed on scarlet eyes and a big pair of purple lips was bouncing madly around, indignant that the cobbler had been walking upon her all this time. For his part, the cobbler was demanding that the boot shut her newly found mouth and return to her rightful place at once. The two puppets came to blows, and all the boys and girls squealed with laughter.

My mother cut straight through the performance, stepping on several of the children, ignoring their cries and the angry murmurs hurled at her back. By the time I made my way around the gathering, I had lost sight of my mother. I clambered atop a boarded-up well to get a better view over the crowds on the street. The marionette cart and the Page Bridge were behind me. Not far ahead stood the stately Squire Bridge. I scanned faces and the backs of heads, but none matched my mother. Besides the people, all I could see were storefronts, a dead orange tree, a knot of traders arguing at a grain weighing station, and an old, open-air shrine—and there she was.

I had to blink to make sure it was her.

Tucked away off the thoroughfare stood a line of marble columns on a dais. Soot-stained, and pocked with holes from untold numbers of artisans helping themselves to samples, the columns held aloft a rotting gable of timber, beneath which, on a pedestal, stood a bronze statue of a matronly figure. She held a tablet of some sort and had a disapproving glower fixed upon her patinaed face. My mother sat on a stone chair beneath her gaze.

Next to her was a table which held some papers and a lone quill. On the other side, sitting on a much more comfortable looking cushion, was Gathena, the priestess who had paid us a visit. The woman who hired me to copy the Book of Amadán.

Her Divinity was dressed down a bit from the first time we had met in the study—no silks, only fine, worsted wool; a stole instead of a phylactery; the miter replaced with an amber skull cap ornamented with onyx stones. Her cheeks had a tinge of color, as if she, too, had been hurrying here.

Cautiously, I crept into the sanctuary, feeling every bit like a burglar breaking into a home. The tile floor within was cracked and overgrown with moss, but a fading mosaic of lapis lazuli and quartz still reflected the outline of a decagram, each angle touching the base of one of the shrine's ten columns. Gathena spotted my approach, flashed a broad smile, and gestured for me to join her and my mother.

"Simeon," her voice rang with delight, "so glad you could join us. Here, come in from the sun, set your pack down."

I walked slowly, my eyes drifting from the statue, to the priestess, to my mother sitting impassively, and back, inexorably, to the statue. The goddess stood some twenty feet tall, high enough that a collection of starlings had taken up a nest in the crook of her shoulders. It was not the scale or the skill of the sculpture that kept drawing my attention. It was her face. For some reason, the visage reminded me of Goodwife Rivers, how she had looked at me when she thought I had stolen her spices.

Gathena must have noticed me studying the statue.

"Beautiful, isn't she? We are in the holy shrine of Brigid, patron goddess of commitments and undertakings. See the list she holds? With it, she tracks all our earthly oaths. The whip stuffed beneath her girdle represents her retribution if we should be faithless in their undertaking."

Her smile felt benign, though I sensed something cold and calculating churning just underneath.

"Come," she said, "stand right here. You can view the ceremony."

An airy wave of her hand pointed me to a place behind the desk. On top, I saw a loose pile of pages scrawled over with dense lettering and bright blue wax seals. My mother rolled her eyes, while Gathena closed hers. The priestess drew herself upright in her seat and lifted her arms high over her head so that her sleeves and a jangle of silver bracelets cascaded down to her elbows. She started to chant some kind of incantation. Or maybe it was an invocation. I had no idea what she was saying, or what this ceremony entailed. As I shifted uncomfortably from one foot to the other, I shot an inquiring glance at my mother. She looked right past me to address Gathena.

"Is this really necessary?"

Gathena's arms fell. Though I thought it a rude interruption, Gathena didn't seem to mind, but dipped her head as if in apology.

"I suppose it can wait until later," she acknowledged. The priestess let out a contented sigh. "What a pleasant surprise to have received your letter, Dr. Severals. And so fortuitous. My boat back to the Seminary departs tomorrow."

"Yes, fortuitous," my mother replied curtly.

"Thankfully, the temple's advocate was able to draw up a contract in short order." She indicated the papers on the table. "Do you find everything to your liking?"

My mother's mouth curled.

"No. But does it matter? You have my neck in a noose."

"Oh, I wouldn't put it like that." The priestess adjusted her vestments and repositioned her bottom to a more comfortable position in her cushion. "Not in a shrine, anyway. You are perfectly free to reject my terms."

My mother slumped in her stool.

"You know damned well I'm not."

Gathena's patient, glowing appearance didn't dim in the slightest. Behind her, beyond the shrine's boundary, life went on as ever, men and women coming and going, some laughing, some arguing, most simply meandering along in whatever current held them. In one dusty intersection, a drover whipped the shanks of a mule that had inexplicably halted. The beast refused to walk another step. Blow after blow, the poor mule flinched but never moved. I felt Gathena tapping my shoulder.

"I hope you, at least, are excited about this turn of events."

"Huh?" I blinked. "I'm sorry, ma'am. Excited about what?"

The priestess' face clouded for a moment. She turned to my mother.

"You haven't told the boy?"

"He's packed, isn't he?"

Gathena laid a hand on my shoulder.

"Simeon," she said darting a look towards my mother, "I had assumed your mother would have explained today's affair. Apparently, I was mistaken." She cleared her throat and assumed a tone that was at once formal and consoling. "In light of recent and unfortunate events that need not be recounted, there has been—how should we say?—a change of circumstances concerning your undertaking. It is quite impossible for you to fulfill your mother's contract. Just as it is impossible for your mother to return our seminary's only copy of the Book of Amadán." She paused to shake her head. "A tragic loss, for all concerned. The legal complications could have been … well, thankfully, we needn't involve the advocates since your mother has had a change of heart about my prior proposal."

My mother cut over her and, finally, spoke directly to me.

"You're going to be bound to her seminary."

I was being … bound. I don't know if I heard it, or felt it, but in my mind, there was the thunderous clamp of a great, heavy book slamming shut. Outside, the noises of the Lower Bluff droned on like a hum of cicadas; the mule began to bray.

"And in exchange," my mother said to Gathena, "I am released of *all* liability on *all* of these bonds and contracts. The loss of your paper, your materials, that ridiculous book, you'll bear every expense, expunged, without recourse."

"Yes, yes," Gathena replied. "That's all spelled out in the contract, just as your letter indicated."

My mother seemed to sink into the stone chair as she folded her arms across her chest, a kind of living statue, now murmuring to herself.

"And I receive nothing."

"You receive our thanks," Gathena practically sang. "And the Pantheon's blessing."

If only there had been another chair in the shrine. My knees were knocking. The light that filtered through the pillars seemed to fade as if a storm cloud had rolled across the sun's face. Like all boys, I had often dreamed what my future would hold, where it would lead—like all Lower Bluff boys, those dreams never ventured past the Lower Bluff's wharves, the arena, and the Squire Bridge. Now I would be shunted off to a foreign place where the people would speak a foreign language—the language of religion—that I had been raised to loathe.

I had been sold to an enemy.

Though the enemy seemed surprisingly nurturing. Gathena peered at me like a kind and wizened owl helping a chick that had fallen out of its nest.

"Don't be afraid, Simeon," she said. "I think you'll come to like the seminary. Once you've become settled in our ways. You'll be able to put your talents to a higher purpose. Here, take up your pack. There's a carriage on the other side of the Squire that will take us to my boat, and thence to your new home." She turned to my mother and strained a smile. "It's time, Delores. Do you—do you wish to say farewell to your son?"

Without a word, my mother leaned over the table and grasped the quill and scratched her name across the bottom of the page.

"Mom?"

But she was already up from the chair and walking away in that familiar, jarring shuffle. She had turned around without a word and left me. Before she had reached the edge of the shrine and disappeared back into the press of Lower Bajebluff, I thought I heard her mutter.

"He's his father's son."

PART II

THE SEMINARY

CHAPTER FIVE

For a boy who had never set foot beyond the quays of the Lower Bluff, the Most Holy Seminary of the Fifth Pantheon of Deities seemed like some kind of a mystical citadel, a far-away palace shrouded in mystery.

In truth, all that shrouded the seminary was swampland. Miles of it.

Far from any town or city, straddling a loose border between the Four Duchies, the seminary had stood for nearly two centuries as a tiny bastion of civilization dropped alongside the bank of the Hillswash River's wide, flowing brown waters, an oval-shaped compound set on a plateau of weeds. Standing atop one of the basilica's towers, one would see only undulating marsh, mangroves, scrub, reeds, and a scattering of fetid, mosquito-infested lakes. A pathless realm of wilderness. Those who bothered to call it anything called it the Glades. Mereborough, a river town of perhaps five hundred souls a mile south of the seminary, was the only other habitation in the Glades.

And yet, the seminary was a place to behold. Like a gemstone that had fallen from a merchant's pocket on the road to the market, it was something shining, and beautiful, and out of place.

Hidden behind stone walls overgrown with strands of duckfoot, past a lone portcullis gate wrought to resemble the ivy so closely that from afar, you wondered where nature's leaves ended and the iron works began, a collection of six crimson brick buildings rose from among granite boulevards, orange groves, gated vegetable gardens, fountains, and a bounty of art works. From the moment I passed beneath the gate, everywhere I turned, there was another masterpiece—a mosaic of scripture, a frieze of the gods hunting a stag, a sculpture of a woman in deep contemplation, a leering gargoyle, a shrine with a bubbling stream of water and festooned with bronze pelicans—all of these heaped together and on top of each other, so that not a finger span was wasted. Even the brickwork had been laid with a dizzying, beguiling geometry.

It was a riot of beauty. Beauty beyond my wildest imaginings. And yet, somehow, it was also perfectly ordered. Gathena was right, I thought to myself. I was going to like living here.

On my first day, her High Divinity breezed me about the grounds, pointing out statuary that was particularly to her liking, pausing to chat with a visiting Wizerian monk, and talking in her easy manner about the seminary's great history, its proud service to the Four Duchies of the Kingdom, and my good fortune of being bound to its service. As tired and road-worn as I felt after our long journey, I couldn't disagree. I tried to take it all in, to hold onto every detail, but in the end, my first day at the seminary became a marvelous blur.

One memory, though, stands vividly.

As Gathena led me toward the dormitory, as we crept up the short run of worn steps, the doors creaked open, and three girls in seminarian robes came barreling outside. They had been giggling about some private joke, but when they noticed Gathena, all three came to a halt, bowed their heads, and greeted her reverently.

"It's good to finally be home, sisters," she said. "I've a new scribe here. His name's Simeon. He will be taking his oaths tomorrow morning. We're just getting him settled now."

Two of the girls gave me a polite, if somewhat stiff, welcome, while the third simply pretended not to notice the ragged street boy Gathena had in tow. She was the prettiest of the trio, her brown hair shining with glints of orange in the dusk light. She gave me the same haughty glare I remembered from my mother's study.

"Kara," said Gathena, "you recall meeting Simeon when you accompanied me to Bajebluff?"

She made a wicked arch of her eyebrow. It was followed by a perplexed expression.

"I can't say that I do," she replied. "That was such a busy trip, High Divinity. And I was only with you in Bajebluff for a couple of days."

"Ah, that's right, I had forgotten," the priestess said, nodding. "You were passing through on your way to visit your father. And how is His Grace?"

"Very well, thank you. He sends his warmest regards."

From afar, a bell rang. The other seminarians milling about the seminary began to congregate towards the refectory. The three girls before Gathena stayed more or less still, though they clearly wished to take their leave and join their companions. The high priestess waved her hand over them in dismissal.

"I won't keep you from your suppers. Off you go."

The girls wished Gathena a very good evening and ran down the stairs, their peals of laughter echoing against the beautiful brick walls that surrounded us.

Dawn came with a rap on my door. The muffled voice of a young man called from the other side.

"Simon?"

I shot up out of bed with a start, bleary and confused by the strange surroundings. I was in a darkened dormitory room, not much larger than my old bedroom, and much the same in the way of furniture—a desk and lantern, a bed with an old mattress, a chair, a crate to hold my few possessions, and a rug—though it was laid out differently. My eyes blinked at the shaft of sunlight that came through a lone, arrow-slit window.

"Simon," the voice repeated and the knock came louder.

"It's Simeon," I said, getting up. Dressed only in a long shirt, I threw up the latch, and opened the door.

A boy on the cusp of manhood slouched in the doorway. He had a wide, friendly mouth, ears that stuck out from the side of his head, and knobby jointed limbs as thin as cattails. A curly mop of sandy hair sprouted from his head like a mushroom. He wore a simple dark blue robe with a red sash tied around his waist. A similar set of clothes was tucked under one of his arms.

"Hey," he greeted me with a half-smile. "I'm Alec. My room's at the end of the hall." He gestured to some point over his shoulder. "I'm supposed to take you for your oaths."

"Hi, Alec."

"Here." He handed me the clothes. "You have to put this on."

He turned around as I changed. When I had finished dressing, he helped me tie the sash correctly, took a step back, and frowned. The sash looked short, my sleeves barely covered my elbows, the end of the robe fell well above my shins. I had to keep my arms close to my side for fear I might rip the shoulder seam.

"They're a little tight," I said.

"You're a little big," he replied. "We'll head over to the commissary later. Get you a bigger set of robes. Come on."

Alec took a bone lantern hanging from a ring on the door jamb and led me down the narrow hall of dormitory rooms, to the stairwell, and down the flight of worn, marbled steps that took us from the boys' floor to the girls', and at last to a side doorway of the building. Outside, the seminary grounds were still draped in a hazy gray light. Wisps of fog clung about the ornamental shrubs and a nearby copse of fruit trees. The last cricket was winding down its night's song. It already felt warm, though a weak breeze strove to keep the air mild.

"Over there," Alec pointed as we walked, "is the refectory. That's where we eat. There's the observatory. Meeting hall. Scriptorium. That's the theater. Don't get your hopes up, though. They only put on tragedies or religious plays, and the actors are always bad."

I followed the bobbing light of Alec's lantern past an avenue of bronze statues and around the back of the refectory. Along the way, I spotted shadowy shapes of priests and postulants along the granite roadways. They moved in groups of twos, threes, and fours. A few snatches of murmured conversation, the sound of wooden shoes on stone, but mostly they were silent.

"Where are we going?" I asked Alec.

"The basilica."

There was no need for him to tell me which building was the basilica. Situated in the center of the seminary, a great temple trimmed with marble and stained glass stood as tall and proud as a king's throne. A silver dome crowned the basilica's roof, topped with a spear-shaped spire that pierced the gray sky like a needle. Anchored to the corners of the basilica, four round, slender minarets rose higher still, overlooking the holy grounds below.

It seemed to be drawing everyone, Alec and I included, towards its doors.

I was about to ask Alec about my oaths, when the air was suddenly rent by a blaring noise from high above. A slew of gongs sounded from the two minarets closest to us, sending a flock of crows that must have been resting on the parapets off into the sky, cawing irritably. An answer to the gongs came from the opposite two towers, a high, piercing note of ram's horns. Five times, the call and response—heavy gongs followed by shrieking horns—reverberated.

No one seemed to pay it any notice.

"Hurry up, Simeon," Alec tugged at my arm.

I followed him to the front portico of the basilica where we melded into the larger throng that was slowly making its way into the entrance of the basilica, the part Alec called the narthex. I kept glancing around, as discreetly as I could, partly to take in some of the faces of the people that were congregating, but mostly in the hope I might spot Kara again. I didn't see her, but I did behold a bewildering collection of outfits. All around me there was silk and fine wool, and gold and silver trim, and rustling waves of tassels. The priests and seminarians were dressed as fine as nobles.

Alec jerked his neck around and held a finger up to his lips, and then, for the first time in my life, I entered a holy place.

My first steps into the basilica were like taking flight into star-dusted heavens. Soaring, vaulted ceilings had been painted indigo with swirls of gray and pinpricks of white to resemble a clouded night sky. Somehow the clouds seemed to be floating, the stars twinkling. Below, hundreds of burning candles glowed with real light from scores of brass candelabras. The melting scarlet cylinders illuminated a gallery of paintings that spanned the narthex walls. I had never seen illustrations like these. They were all on canvas in gilded, golden frames, but they weren't the crude drawings you would see in wharf taverns or outside the arena. These were like mirrors of real people, with sallow cheeks, and haughty smiles, and hooked and bulbous noses, and hair so perfectly drawn, you could almost count the strands reflecting in the painted sunshine.

There were alabaster water basins set in a line along the front. As soon as we came inside, Alec went to the closest one, dipped his fingertips and proceeded to touch his forehead, breast, and stomach in a single, hurried motion. It looked a little foolish, like a children's exercise, but when I saw everyone else copying the ritual at the other fonts, I tried to look natural in my imitation of them, as if I had been blessing my mind, heart, and body in sacristies all my life. I could have happily wandered up and down the narthex gazing at the portraiture, but Alec yanked me by my arm to hurry to our seats.

We passed beneath a span of carved mahogany that rose almost to the height of the basilica's ceiling, and then we came into the main temple. I couldn't take in all the sensations. Statues of mighty men and women were poised upon pedestals, as if they were about to descend upon the mortal world, while the breaking dawn poured through stained glass windows, each as tall as a tower. The light flowed like cataracts of colored light—amber, ruby, emerald, sapphire, garnet, and amethyst—as if an ancient glazier had somehow caught and corralled the rainbow itself. Rows upon rows of censers sent clouds of beeswax, cinnamon, and incense into the air.

When that first sense of awe had finally settled, and all the sparkling arcs of light and incense and statues began to fade into a kind of backdrop, I felt a very different, more pointed sensation. Anger, I think. Or resentment. That my mother had so casually dismissed such wonder as this and deprived me of knowing it sooner.

The crowd gathered in the pews. I counted some eighty seminarians filing in, many still groggy from sleep, shuffling to find their places. The prospect of reciting lines under the gaze of so many strangers made my stomach knot. Where was I supposed to stand? What was I supposed to say? Were there more head-to-chest-to-gut dances I was expected to know? I tugged at the ends of my new robes, trying to pull them down to look more like everyone else's. Unaware of my mounting anxiety, Alec stood up on his tiptoes, searching for something along one of the far walls. I leaned over to whisper in his ear.

"So should I—should I go up to that, that altar-thing up there?"

He turned and looked at me as if I were an idiot.

"Why in the gods' names would you do that—oh!" He brought his hand to his mouth to stifle a laugh. "They're not here for you. This is just morning paidir. First prayers of the day. We do this every dawn for a quarter of an hour. Then again at noon before the midday meal. Don't worry. Just kneel when everybody kneels, and chant when everybody chants." He held up his finger to emphasize a point. "But you can't skip it. You don't get anything to eat unless you go to paidir first. We scribes sit over here."

We made our way over to a plain, wooden pew, far removed from the rest of the congregation. Eight blue-robed, red-sashed men and women moved over to make room for Alec and I. Before Alec could introduce me, a gong sounded, followed by a single, soft note from a brass horn. All the hushed conversation in the sanctuary came to an end.

Thanks to Alec murmuring in my ear, I got through my first of many paidirs without embarrassing myself. An older priestess led the ritual, while Gathena sat contentedly on what looked like a throne adjacent to the altar. The old priestess chanted something. We chanted back. She knelt, so did we. I suppose if she had stood on her head, everyone would have followed, but thankfully, that wasn't part of the ritual. Near the end, she dropped her formal intonation for a minute to make announcements. Brother Maynard had fully recovered from his apoplexy and appreciated our prayers; Divine Gathena had returned from her business in the Archlé Duchy (which was met with a smattering of applause that her High Divinity acknowledged with a bow); mulberries were in season so breakfast would include jam (which was welcomed with cheers); everyone should continue minding the building work around the baths. There was no welcome for me or mention of my presence, which left me slightly disappointed. Then the priestess held up her hands, gave us all a blessing, and eighty-odd clergy touched their foreheads, chests, and stomachs and replied in unison, "Be it so."

With the paidir over, the congregation began to dissipate. Alec motioned for me to follow him. The flow of clerics was heading back toward the narthex, but we moved toward the opposite corner of the basilica. As we drew near the wall, I saw that what seemed to be a solid face of veined marble had a pillar that concealed an inset brass grate. It served as the entrance to a tunnel that sloped down into the floor.

Alec approached the grating, helped himself to a taper burning on a nearby stand, grasped the gate's handle, and yanked it hard so that it slid open with a loud rattle. Before he went inside, he paused.

"Are you ready?" Alec gave me a searching look. "You can still turn back, you know."

"I ..."

I had no idea what I was supposed to be readying myself for. And why was he looking at me that way? It almost seemed like Alec was playing a game, but that couldn't be. I didn't know much about oaths, but from what I had read, they were considered solemn occasions. "Yeah," I said, "I mean, I guess I'm as ready as I can be."

"There's no guessing about oaths, Simeon." He angled his taper, using the flame to point to my chest. "You're going to be calling the gods to come down from the heavens—to here." He stomped his foot to emphasize his point. "The holiest patch of ground in Four Duchies. There's a real chance one of them could show up. Oh, yeah. Don't look at me like that. It's happened. Believe me. And if a god should appear for your oath, you'd damn well better be ready. Or else ... " With his fingers, he made an exploding motion just above the taper. "They'll take your soul. Burn your body to cinders. And I'll have to clean up what's left. Understand?"

"I'm ready," I said, this time with a little more conviction.

"Alright ... "

He descended the steps and entered the tunnel. The space was tight. We could only walk single-file, and I had to hunch beneath the low arched ceiling. Gradually, the corridor widened as we wound underneath the floor of the basilica. In the wavering glow of Alec's light, I could make out dusty, iron-bound wooden doors along the walls. We hadn't traveled very far before he came to a halt in front of one of them.

He turned to me, and I thought I detected a smirk reflecting in the gloom.

"This is the Sacred Chamber of Oaths," he declared solemnly. "Are you ready to stand before the gods and make your pledge?"

This was it, then. I was going to present myself and make a promise—to invisible gods. I could almost hear my mother sneering.

"Gods are nothing but figments for fools."

It's a hard thing for a young man to turn his back on his mother's teachings. But I was so ensorcelled from the splendor of the basilica (and, truth be told, stinging from how my mother had left me at the shrine), I made up my mind about the path I was going to follow. There, in that murky passage underground, I decided if I was going to be bound to the gods, I would do it freely and fully. Without reservation or equivocation. I'd *make* myself believe, and unlearn what I had been taught all my life.

"Well," Alec patted me on the shoulder. "Are you ready?".

"I'm ready."

Alec pushed on the door. It swung open easily. "Go on," he said, and stepped aside to make way for me. "An oath-taker must make his pledge alone." His smirk had grown into a silly looking grin. "But if you do so with a false heart, a god will appear and strike you dead. Seriously, this is your last chance."

"I said I'm ready."

I felt his hand clap me on the shoulder. He craned his head as if trying to hide his face.

"Good luck, Simeon."

The door clanked shut behind me, and I was alone inside a room not much larger than my mother's study. A pleasant light from burning brass lamps cast a warm yellow glow over the room. The ceiling, walls, and floor were rough-hewn stone, but the space was finely furnished with a thick woven rug, tapestries, and a long scarlet curtain drawn across the far wall. Bookcases held a small collection of leather-bound tomes. An ebony altar and a pedestal stood in the center. Atop the pedestal stood a familiar bronze bust of a dour, heavyset, middle-aged woman I had met not long ago. The Goddess Brigid. But she was not alone, for each of the walls were dotted with sconces that held a collection of different idols—amalgams of men, women, and animals—staring down from their perches. In front of the altar was a velvet kneeler. Otherwise, the room was empty.

"Hello?"

No answer. I fidgeted with my new robes and scanned the chamber again. Unsure of what I should do, I crept closer to the altar and saw that it bore a tarnished silver plate with the husks of dried flowers upon it. I leaned over, sniffed at the withered plants, and waited. The lamp flames guttered. The chamber grew so quiet I could hear the flames hissing.

A voice shattered the solitude, a bass resonating with such power I could feel the floor vibrate.

"Who art thou?"

I fell down backwards, right on the tail bone, but quickly scrambled to my feet, my head swiveling to find the source of the sound. I rubbed my bottom, and the voice rang out again.

"I am Ogma, lord of magic, master of words, keeper of secrets. I know all, and yet I know thee not. Who art thou?"

My jaw hung open. The noise was deafening. It seemed to rattle in my chest alongside my racing heart. It was a man's voice, one that echoed and emanated from a deep iron well, but I noticed it held a certain nasal affect. All the a's sounded flat, so that "magic" and "master" came off almost like "mayejik" and "mayester."

Whoever this god was, he came from Lower Bajebluff.

Another thought occurred to me, an old memory. I had heard that kind of down-a-well echo before—at a puppet show. I suppose I should have answered with my name, but I was still puzzling about the accent and the sound effect. Ogma apparently grew angry at my hesitation.

There was a loud crash of a cymbal and the curtain on the far wall flung open. It revealed an archway from which silver smoke now billowed, rolling like a dam break across the chamber's stone floor. Emerging from the fog of the arch, a silhouette appeared. Shorter than me, its arms extended, and backlit with a quivering azure light, the figure approached slowly, as if floating on a cloud. He wore long, ragged robes and a bronze mask depicting the visage of a laughing, leering maniac. The mask went all the way down to his chest.

And at that moment I recognized every one of the phenomena for what they were. These were stage props. I stood firm as the figure approached. He kept his arms wide, step by step, sapphire light wobbling in a halo behind his head, until the mask's hollow pointed eyes were inches from mine.

"Well?" he boomed.

I shook my head, smirking.

"I've seen better."

The mask came off. In its place, a short, wiry man with squinting eyes, and bony cheeks, and a nose wrinkled as a rotting apple, glared at me. He looked to be in his forties.

"It was the heavenly light that gave it away, right?"

"Yeah." I nodded. "I can see the glass." I pointed to a wine bottle suspended from the capstone of the archway. It was filled with a blue liquid. The lantern hanging behind it cast a cerulean hue.

"Dammit," the man swore. Then he shouted over his shoulder. "Alec, he's already smoked it out. I told you the heavenly light was overdoing it."

From behind the folds of the curtain, Alec reappeared, his idiot's grin replaced with consternation.

"Gathena told you, didn't she?"

"Not a word," I said. Turning to the costumed man I asked if all new scribes had a "god" appear for their oaths.

"Nah." He leaned against the altar, propping his feet on the kneeler. "Not any more. Gathena frowns on oath hazing; says its juvenile. She only lets the scribes do it. The last one we hazed was little Alec here." The man fell into chuckling. "He pissed his robes."

"I did not," Alec snapped. Seeing me laughing, he added. "At least I didn't fall flat on my ass."

"That voice was scary," I said. "How'd you manage that?"

The man hoisted the mask up to his mouth and spoke into a hidden slit and his voice boomed deep and metallic once more.

"Behold the magic of Ogma—a lead echo chamber."

He let the mask drop to the floor with a clang. "Shit, but that's heavy. Name's Marcus," He flashed a smile of crooked teeth. "I'm the Master Scribe here."

Alec pretended to whisper from the side of his mouth. "Which puts him just below archbishop of chamber pots."

"I'll tell Gathena to put you in penance." Marcus gave Alec a punch on the arm.

The three of us settled around the altar, leaning our elbows on the edges as if we were at a tavern bar. Marcus turned to me.

"So you're from Lower Bajebluff from what I hear."

"So are you." I tapped my ear. "From what I hear."

Marcus nodded and seemed to puff out his meager chest.

"Born and raised on Chandlers Row. Don't see any reason to try and hide it."

"I'm from Drovers."

"Know it well. Used to get our wicks from the Rivers' grocery."

The reminder of Mrs. Rivers gave me a brief pang. "How long have you been here?" I asked.

Marcus scratched at his head pensively. "Took my vows in Sunskein of the seventeenth, no eighteenth, year of Niall the Nineteenth, so that'd make it…" He counted on his fingers. "Right around twenty-six years. Hard keeping track of time. No reason to. I haven't set foot past the Hillswash since I came."

"Really?"

"Sure. The food's good. So are the rooms, once you've been here a while. We scribes, we may not be all high and mighty as the priests and seminarians, but we've got it good. The work's not bad, either. Beats scalding your hands off making candles."

"Though Marcus'll load you up with so much copy work, you'll wish you could burn off a hand," Alec said.

Marcus made a face at him and turned back to me. "I hear you're a fast writer. You'll be working in edicts with me and Alec. At first, it'll feel a little overwhelming, but you'll get used to it. In a few months, you'll be saying you're the luckiest Rogues Run boy ever to get out of Bajebluff."

For some reason, I had no trouble believing him. Alec and Marcus seemed like a pair I could get on well with. I found myself smiling. Friendship had always been a scarce commodity for me. In less than an hour, my store had more than doubled.

"You hungry?" Alec asked me.

"Yeah, kind of."

"Alright, alright." Marcus got up and stretched his arms. "Time for me to do my Master Scribe duties."

I caught Alec rolling his eyes. Marcus gestured for me to kneel before the altar.

As I took my place, I cast a quick glance around the little stone chamber. The candle and lantern light, the carpet, the books that probably hadn't been cracked open in decades, the ridiculous theatre props, the smell of earth and burning wax, the presence of two new friends—all of it suffused me with a warm, welcoming glow. I cleared my head, letting that feeling wash over me in what, I imagined, was how one prepared oneself for holiness. I closed my eyes and heard Marcus's voice, his real voice.

"Let's make you a scribe," he said, "then we'll get you some clothes that fit you—gods, but you're beefy for a scribe—and then we'll get breakfast." Marcus reached over to put me into position. "Place one palm on your forehead and the other on your heart. No, like this. There. Now repeat after me …"

I recited Marcus's words, the call-and-response of our voices—one, a bored sounding middle-aged man's; mine, thick with youth's earnest solemnity—seeping into the walls, soaking in the stones, one more oath for them to bear witness to:

I, Simeon Severals, before Belanos, Brigid, and all the deities of the Most Holy Fifth Pantheon, hereby swear this oath upon the air of my breath, the water of my blood, the earth of my flesh, and the fire of my soul.

I will faithfully serve the Pantheon and its Priesthood as a scribe. I will obey their just commands. I will attend to the rites, rituals, and holy obligations thereof. I will devote myself to the duties my superiors shall assign me from time to time. And I will ever proclaim, by my thoughts, words, and deeds, the divine truth of our Pantheon.

I will not profane the sacred. I will not be slothful or gluttonous. I will not steal or bear false witness. I will not kill or covet. I will not lie with a brother or sister in holy orders. I will not bring shame or dishonor upon the Pantheon or its Priesthood.

So help me, gods and goddesses, keep me steadfast, and may my mortal life be forfeit and my immortal soul partitioned if I am ever faithless in this oath.

CHAPTER SIX

On my second day, I learned my place in the seminary. After morning paidir, breakfast, and an hour for leisure—it was time for labor. At least, for the scribes. For the seminary, I soon discovered, was every bit as sorted and divided into castes as Bajebluff. As in Bajebluff, I was nearer the bottom.

The seminary's postulants, the "brother" and "sister" seminarians, were, by and large, the younger children of the wealthy and the nobility. An earl with one too many daughters to match, or a baronet with a son inclined more to arts and letters than swords and shields, or an alderman whose tryst in a tavern left behind a child that resembled him a little too closely, they could all find a discreet convenient dumping ground in the seminary. For the price of a thousand marks, their excess offspring could be "fed, read, and spread" throughout the countless shrines and temples of the kingdom's four duchies. Five years in the seminary followed by a sinecure and a comfortable livelihood was a far better prospect than the hope of a sibling's charity. Probably nine in ten of the seminarians had a parent in someone's court. They took classes in the morning. Their afternoons were spent in leisure along the river, or music in the nearby town of Mereborough, or a boat trip to one of the Duchies.

For scribes, the afternoons and evenings were devoted to work. Not unloading barges on the river dock, or skinning potatoes in the kitchen, or harvesting turnips in the gardens (there were servants who lived outside the seminary for those kind of tasks), but money-making work. The kind that filled the bellies of the two hundred odd souls who called the seminary home. The kind that made it a place of fabulous wealth. Marcus explained my work—and my place—on my first visit to our workplace.

The scriptorium of the seminary had a special name. They called it the Holy Vault of Records. It was a vast hall as wide and long as an arena, with beveled skylights that lit the whole of the room as brightly as an open-air stadium. Every crack and corner of space was filled as tight as a tinderbox with parchments and papers, all bundled, rolled, stacked, collated, and bound throughout a seemingly endless array of wooden cases that stood as tall as trees. Some cases had shelves, while others held drawers, while a few were honeycombed with diamond-shaped apertures. All of them, though, were stuffed to overflowing with paper. A stepladder graced the side of each case to reach their upper shelves.

There were desks positioned beneath the skylights where scribes hunched at work. Writing, stamping, sealing, more writing. Like a hive of red-and-blue-clad bees—but instead of honey, they made documents. Reams of them.

"Every piece of paper that's worth holding onto," Marcus said with a grand wave of his arm, "is filed and recorded here. We break them down by duchy. Thuadeigh's in the dark oak shelves; Sheer is mahogany; Dheas is the pine cases (they take up the most room); and our own Archlé is the honey oaks. You'll get lost at first. Everybody does. But once you get the lay of the land, it'll start to make sense."

I scanned the Vault in dumb awe. I had never seen—never imagined—so much paper congregated into one building. It was like trying to peer through a rainstorm while keeping your eyes on the individual drops.

"Come over here," said Marcus. "I'll show you what you'll be doing."

He walked me over to the nearest desk where a woman around Marcus's age was busily scratching a scribe's pen across a mostly blank broadsheet, copying a page of gothic writing weighted down on the desk with a sandstone. Her hand moved deftly, letter by letter, reproducing the fanciful script in a perfect imitation.

"This is Sister Emma," said Marcus. "Em, Simeon here just took his oath and is learning the trade."

"Welcome to the Vault," she greeted me, without pausing her work.

"Hi." I peered over her shoulder to read the document she was copying. The word "Nuptial" had been deeply bolded, probably written over four or five times for extra emphasis.

"Every few days," Mel explained, "barges ferry in from the Hillswash. They come from all four Duchies, and they'll all be loaded with three things. Food and wine. Money. Documents."

"What do we give them in return?"

Emma let out a sardonic laugh. "We give them a good leeching."

Marcus gave her a slightly disapproving look. "What Sister Emma means," he said, "is that we don't exactly trade for our goods. I mean, we're not merchants. Our seminary provides the Duchies' temples with priests—"

"—also parasites," she smiled, still not looking up.

"Emma," Marcus chided. "Let the boy settle in before you make him a cynic." He folded his hands and continued his explanation. "Besides providing new priests, we also serve as the scribes for the Duchies." He indicated Emma's desk. I saw that besides the paper, there was plenty of ink, spare pens, a sand jar, fresh rags, and a special drawer underneath the table. "The Duchies send us all their official records," he said. "We file them for safekeeping, and whenever someone needs an official copy, we make it. For a small fee. Deeds, contracts, records, court judgments, censuses, statutes. We take them all. What are you working on now, Em?"

She tapped her pen into a meaningful comma and finally looked up.

"The Marquis of Dunwoody's latest marriage contract."

"You're joking."

"I'm not." She shook her head. "Six thousand marks, two ranches, and a vineyard is what it's costing him."

Marcus chuckled. "How many marriages is that now?"

"Four." Emma held up four ink-stained fingers then hesitantly extended her thumb. "Five, if you count that orgy in Connol as a wedding ceremony. The court still hasn't decided."

"By Brigid," Marcus murmured, "his grace should find a new hobby."

"Hold on," I said. The enormity of what was in this Vault was slowly sinking in. "So every city, every court in the Four Duchies ... they send their papers ... *here*? To a swamp? Why? Why not just keep their own documents, like in a basement, or a courthouse, or something?"

Marcus gave me a long, searching look, and even Emma held off from her gothic reproduction of a marquis' marriage contract to arch an eyebrow at me.

"Because," said Marcus, "we keep our word. We have to. Or the seminary wouldn't survive."

I cocked my head, puzzled at what he had just told me.

"Think about it this way. Suppose you had a house in the Upper Bluff, but someone files a lawsuit in the Magistrate's Court saying they own it, not you. Now suppose the person suing you is a Beardley."

Malcolm Beardley had been the Sheriff of Bajebluff for as long as I could remember, as was his father before him, and his uncle before him. They say the Beardleys of Bajebluff had been keeping order and taking bribes since the city walls were first built.

"I suppose I'd lose that case," I said quietly.

"Of course you would," Marcus agreed, "if you had to rely on one of Beardley's clerks to find the official deed and not burn it, or scratch through it, or just replace it with a rank forgery. You'd be a fool to hope for an honest record." Marcus thumbed through the stack of blank pages on top of Emma's desk. "No one trusts people in power to play fair with records. But that's a problem because the only way people can do business with each other is with trust. That's our service, Simeon. We trade in trust. Your deed's safe here in the Vault. No one's going to alter it or throw it in the river. And if a court needs a copy—a trusted and true copy—we can make it."

"Your scribes," I said with a tone of growing respect, "they must have to work in here every night."

"Not a chance," Emma scoffed.

Marcus shook his head and pointed to the skylight windows in the ceiling.

"Only when the daylight's good, when we can see our work. After the leisure hour until dusk, those are our working hours."

"What, no midnight candles?" I joked.

Emma *tsked*, while Marcus shot me a grave look.

"No," he said softly. "No flames in here. Not so much as a flicker should ever pass through that doorway. Ever. If these records caught fire … but then … " His somber expression softened. "From what I hear, you know what happens when old papers catch fire."

I felt my face flushing hard. Alec laughed and cupped his hand on my shoulder.

"Not to worry. Nobody'll ever miss *that* brick of a book. Bel's balls, you should have heard the cheer that went up in the basilica when Gathena announced the Book of Amadán 'had been tragically burgled.' Ho, ho."

"I'll make sure not to bring a lamp in here," I said, trying to change the subject.

"See that you don't. And don't touch any records, unless you've got an assignment that requires you to. Browsers always end up leaving smudges."

Emma had finished her copy of the contract. I watched as she pinched a bit of sand from the glass jar and spread it to dry the ink. She blew it off, then reached beneath her desk, opened the drawer, and produced an iron ring about the size of her palm. It looked like a thick, heavy coin. Carefully, she flipped it open on a hinge, dabbed the inside with ink, and pressed it hard onto a patch of blank corner in her document. When she lifted it, there was a round, cunningly drawn picture on the page. The profile of the Goddess Brigid, surrounded by a ring of stars encircled with a tiny splay of words.

Seal of the Fifth Pantheon. Fidelity is Blessed. Forgery is Cursed.

"These seals," Emma said to me, "never leave the Vault. Whenever we finish a copy we stamp, sign, and date it. Return the original to its shelf. Drop off the copy—once the ink's dry—in your work bin. Then move on to the next one."

"That stamped and signed copy," Marcus continued, "is worth a fee of three marks, two pence. Storing the original is a mark and five."

I whistled to myself. I couldn't help it. All these records, all these documents from the Four Duchies. All these fees.

"Niallex?" I asked.

"The capital has its own section," Marcus made a sweeping gesture towards his left. "Those ten cases over in the northeast corner."

"Which still isn't enough room," said Emma.

"Gathena says she's hiring carpenters to build us more space."

"Uh-huh. I'll believe it when I see it." Emma rolled her eyes.

A thought occurred to me.

"What about Bajebluff?"

"Oh, sure," Marcus smiled, pointing to a forlorn looking set of cases against a far wall. "Bottom three shelves there."

"Provincial towns don't need much space," Emma added with a wicked grin.

"Says the hick from Dubhlington," replied Mel, his Bajebluff accent coming through thicker than ever. "Can you even call that sty a village?"

"Hey, we may be small, but we have culture. We built a library to teach our people letters. You Bluffers built an arena."

"I'd take the arena," Marcus joked with me.

But I wasn't really paying attention any more. All I could think about was that dusty wall of the Vault, shrouded and tucked away, far from the warm illumination of the skylights. The records of Bajebluff, dutifully, faithfully recorded. I gazed and wondered what documents I might find buried in the shelves of those three cases, what stories they could tell, what secrets I could learn.

The days rolled by at the Seminary of the Fifth Pantheon, each one melding into the next, drifting steadily like the brown, silted waters of the Hillswash River. A hot, dank summer became a warm, humid autumn. Sowing Month turned into Long Eaves. The rhythm of gongs and ram horns, morning and evening paidirs, good and plentiful meals (better than I had ever known), and work.

For the most part, I liked my new routine.

Each morning, after paidir and a meal of eggs, grits, and palm hearts, I would spend my hour of leisure time sitting in the back row of a classroom cellar, or an amphitheater, or sometimes by the riverbank, to learn about the gods, their deeds, their works, their foibles. As a scribe, I was permitted to attend the seminarians' lectures (though I was the only one who ever did). They were ... beguiling. A cacophony of stories I had only ever heard allusions to, all of them so baffling, and strange, and yet satisfying. Studying divinity was like mastering, at long last, a foreign language that had been spoken freely around me all my life.

I learned every god and goddess of the pantheon, their names, their origins, their lineages and progeny. I found out that Belanos sired the entirety of the Fifth Pantheon (even though he was also somehow begotten of his daughter, Brigid). And that his twelve-legged mule Padraig pulled the sun across the sky every day, past the fences of the worlds and into the moors of the dead, who would catch the poor beast and feast upon its flesh until Aengus, the goddess of rebirth, would chase them off and pluck out a scrap of the animal's heart, breathe new life into it, and birth a new mule for a new day. I learned that the mad goddess Bog was the source of all confusion and was responsible for the admixture of water and earth that made marshes. I heard that kindly Lugh was blind, and yet the source of all light. In the stars, looking through refracting glass lenses, I discovered that those points of shimmering lights were also huntresses and hounds, dragons and daemons, sickles and centaurs, each with its own story, its own myth, its own wisdom. Slowly, like a new swimmer mastering his strokes, from floating to flailing to moving forward, I learned to believe in things I could not see.

After lunch, I was in the Vault, working, until the sun crept behind the skylights and it became too dim to write. My assignments were edicts.

"You're going to bless these," Marcus explained the first time he dumped a sizeable pile of papers on my desk to copy, "with officialness."

"Do I have to take another oath?"

"No, no, this is serious." He plucked the top paper from the stack and showed it to me. "This here's an edict. It's how official people officially talk to the rest of us and tell us, officially, what to do."

I scanned the paper he had laid down.

"*An Edict of the High Alderman of Lake Tinny-by-the-Dale Concerning the Revised Registry of Weights and Scales.*"

"Everyone in charge," Marcus continued, "from king to constable, has to use edicts to make their rules. But here's the problem. They can't just write up an edict, tuck it away somewhere, and hope everyone will find out and then follow it. They need official copies. Ones they can post in different places with our seal telling everyone it's real. Then, folks who can read will tell their neighbors what their edicts say."

"So I make a copy of this?"

Mel grinned at me somewhat wolfishly. "No, you make *four* copies of this. See the little notation in the bottom corner? That's from our receiving clerk. It says the alderman's paid for four copies."

I looked at all the edicts, the blank pages I would have to fill, and my shoulders slouched.

"I don't know if I can finish all these in one day, Marcus. But I'll try."

Marcus stared at me for a moment, then he barked out a laugh. The scribe's face made a mocking expression as he mimicked my voice: "I don't know, but I'll try ... hoo, but that's good! I like your pluck. This is your work for the month. You've got thirty days to finish it all, which is manageable for a new scribe if you stay on task and don't fool around too much. But, listen, if you can knock all this out in a day, may the gods keep your knuckles. Gathena'll make you a saint ..."

That first stack of edicts ended up taking a little over nineteen days. Marcus was impressed, so much so that he asked to watch me as I copied a relatively short edict that had arrived that morning (commanding the commoners in the earldom of Saibhir to stop pinning daisies to their dresses).

"That's the damnedest way of making words I've ever seen," Marcus said as I finished the first half. "I mean, it reads fine, and you're fast at it, no question. But it sure is bizarre. Here, let me have a try." He helped himself to my pen, dipped it in the ink pot, and set his hand to my method of flowing the closest parts of neighboring letters into one another. I watched as he furrowed his forehead, and scrunched his eyes tight, and with painstakingly slow motion, etched a few words in my writing style: "*It displeases Her Ladyship to see flora wasted...*"

"Ah, forget it." He dropped the pen back on the desk, shaking his head. "So what do you think of edicts?"

I'm sure Marcus was expecting I'd say they were dull as browning leaves, or something banal, like "alright, I guess." And in truth, copying edicts was boring and a little tedious. But only on the surface. Kind of like the Book of Amadán, in a way.

"You learn a lot," I said, "about what's happening in the world."

Marcus's eyebrows lifted.

"That you do." He looked at me pensively for a moment and nodded. "You're going to do fine here, Simeon. Take the rest of the day for yourself. We'll get you some more work tomorrow ... "

Gathena propped her elbows on the podium and shifted her girth so far forward I feared she would topple over the wooden prop that held her notes. She lifted up on her tiptoes. It made her look a little silly. But holding a ridiculous position was one of her innumerable ploys to keep her students' attention.

"I'll say it again," Gathena intoned from atop her perch. She bobbed her head every so often for emphasis. "Our *greatest* task as called and ordained priests is to *squelch* sectarian strife. Which requires us to glean the *intersections* between seemingly disparate faiths. Which are *abundant*."

It was mid-morning, and her High Divinity had deigned to give a rare lecture. Some twenty seminarians had gathered in a meeting hall of the dormitory to learn how we could find symmetry among all the wildly divergent faiths of our kingdom. How one could preach, fervently and without conveying a hint of doubt, that the world was a disk resting upon the fulcrum of a tortoise shell, while at the same time acknowledging that it could just as easily be a rind left over from when the tree of the universe was cut down, or the entrails of a dragon, or a stillborn song. How one can profess a pantheon of gods while breaking bread with a monotheist.

As usual, I was the only scribe from the Vault. I sat in the farthest corner of the room, a barricade of empty chairs between the rest of the students and me.

"So we seek intersection," Gathena said, easing back into a more ordinary stance behind her podium, "throughout the sects of the kingdom. That is to say," she drew out a lengthy pause, "we strive for fusion ... not friction."

She drummed her fingertips on the ridge of the podium, a prompt for us to be dutifully impressed with a conclusion that was both succinct and alliterative. Several of the seminarians nodded along like weathervanes. My attention had been wandering, because Kara, who sat near the middle a few rows down, had raised her hand. I leaned forward in my seat as Gathena recognized her.

"Yes, Sister Kara?"

"What do we do if we have a zealot in our congregation?"

"Ah." Gathena exhaled and looked slightly panged. "The zealot. The marginally learned who has found a cause—a god, a downtrodden people, a language, a leader. Sister Kara poses an apt question. Because at some point in your ministries, you will be confronted with a zealot. They can be … trying. Trying, I say, because a zealot is one who can't change his mind and will never change the subject."

There was a smattering of polite laughter.

"Find me the priest who has never lost an afternoon of her life indulging the wide-eyed, open-mouthed rantings of a zealot after temple, and I'll show you a contented cleric. Alas, we who have perceived cosmology in its infinite capacity must bear with those who stare at dirty floors with blinders on their eyes. It is a vexing duty, truly, but one every one of us is sworn to discharge."

She seemed to have finished. Kara cocked her head, her hair bouncing slightly on her shoulders, and spoke again.

"High Divinity, with all due respect, I know I'll have to deal with a zealot sooner or later. My question is, how do I do it?"

The room fell quiet. I could feel my pulse quickening, not because a student had pressed the head priestess of the seminary in a public lecture, but because the sound of Kara's voice, so clear and firm, rang in my heart like a gong. I'm sure I was grinning, though I did my best to hide it. Gathena stood impassively, though her drooping gray eyes twinkled with a mirthful light.

"Sister," she said softly, "I just answered it."

A soft murmur rippled among the students, confused as to whether her High Divinity was being humorous, or obtuse, or both. Kara started to stammer something more, but Gathena held up her hands and spread them apart.

"You squelch the zealot by giving him half of what he desires. You listen, which gives him his audience. But you do not contend, which deprives him of its reward. When you speak to the zealot, keep your talk three levels above his zealotry. If he's stuck on the dire sins of the township, you lament how the world is a sinful place. If it's the mistreatment of lepers, you blather something about the sorry state of medicine. If he's fixated on poverty and malnourishment, you fixate about justice and equity." Gathena made a clapping motion with her outstretched hands so that they deliberately missed. "Stay above his meanderings, and he'll quickly tire of the discourse. Just like I did with you, Sister. But if all else fails," she finished with a wink, "tell him 'I shall give your point my close and prayerful consideration.' That always dampens their ardor."

It certainly seemed to dampen Kara's spirit. She shrank a few inches, slumping into her chair. I could see the back of her neck turning pink. It bothered me that Gathena had made something of a jape out of Kara's question, when all she wanted was an honest answer to what sounded like an honest inquiry. More than that, though, Gathena's words cut into the root of something that had been germinating inside of me these past few weeks.

In my time in seminary, I had slowly come to embrace faith.

Kneeling to statues still felt a little awkward, and the words of my newly learned prayers sounded strange in my ears, but all in all I found the whole of religion to be something both profound and beautiful. Like the statues and stained-glass windows that surrounded me. True faith, I thought, ought to be faced fully, not side-stepped in a dance of words. Gathena's condescension toward sincere faith was as bad as my mother's ridicule. Worse, in a way. At least my mother engaged it head on as an enemy.

As if of its own volition, my hand rose in the air.

"High Divinity?" I asked.

She seemed startled that I had addressed her. A score of heads swiveled around to gape at the Vault scribe who had spoken. I could hear the girl sitting next to Kara mutter loud enough for all to hear, "What's he even doing here?" Gathena, though, tried to sound cordial.

"You have a question, Simeon?"

I imagined this was what it would feel like in the pit of an arena. Where strangers stared at your whole person, scrutinizing your mettle, before you grappled with an opponent. Gathena was looking at me with a guarded curiosity, while Kara stared as if one of the kitchen hounds had just piped up to address the head cook. In the sunlight coming through the window, Kara's eyes were more hazel than brown.

"Um … " My throat felt like it had a clamp around it. "I was wondering—you know, just thinking—about, um, Sister Kara's point." At the sound of her name, Kara's eyes blazed with a venomous light, but I pressed on. "What if, uh, what if the zealot … you know, is actually right?"

The seminarians in the class shook their heads and whispered loudly to one another, and judging from the derisive glares they shot back at me, considered me an idiot who should never have opened his mouth. But my ideas were beginning to coalesce into something cohesive; as my mother would have said, I had gathered my thoughts. I raised my voice over the growing murmur.

"What I mean is, it's like all these saints and seers whose scriptures we read, they were all zealots once. When they were alive, everyone made fun of them. Ran them out of the temples. Beat them. Put them to death. Then, years later, someone would go back and, you know, actually read what they had written and suddenly they weren't a crazy zealot anymore, they were prophets. I guess what I'm asking is … how can you know if a zealot isn't the next Gealtach, or Mearbhall, or-or—"

"—or Amadán?" Gathena's eyes flickered with a bemused gleam.

The classroom fell silent. All the ambient conversations came to a halt when the head priestess spoke.

It still stung to be reminded of the book I had copied and lost, but I nodded in agreement. "Yeah," I said.

Gathena narrowed her eyes, and steepled her fingers, and seemed so intent on whatever was passing through her thoughts, I wondered if perhaps she forgot she was in a lecture hall before a crowd of students. Kara and the rest of the seminarians had turned their attention back to the podium. But Gathena paid them no mind, breathing slowly, staring at a point somewhere over my shoulder. At last, her High Divinity stirred and for once, I thought, her words were sincere, and not a performance. She said simply,

"You can't."

Gathena smiled, it seemed, a little sadly. When she spoke again, it was as if I was the only one in the room. "You really can't. Your Amadán, for example, was deemed a heretic in his day. Somewhere in that millstone of a tome he had written something, something along the line of, 'the one god's … one god is one for …' now how did it go?"

I recited the passage instantly from memory:

"The One God is the God of One."

"That's the verse." Gathena let out a long breath through her nostrils. "They threw him into an oven for that little tripe. Oh, yes. Wouldn't give it a thought today, but back then … that was heresy. It threatened what everyone knew to be true about the pantheons." She sighed again. "Zealots—whether they're right or wrong—always make trouble. They pit their will against their betters, against all righteous authority, against the gods themselves. They make their own right and wrong." She bore her gray eyes hard into mine. "That's why we do not engage with them, Simeon, why we shun them. And why, if necessary, we kill them."

After the lecture, I lingered for a while outside the dormitory feeling sullen and a little lonely. I had a few more minutes before the mid-morning gongs would call me to work in the Vault. A sheet of low, steely clouds covered the sky, filtering a harsh, colorless light over the seminary grounds. The jasmine and orange blossoms had long since fallen, leaving the air scentless.

I went on an aimless walk, more or less in the direction of the refectory, though I took a roundabout path since I had no desire to be around anyone. With shuffling steps, I stared down at my feet, my frayed sandal-straps treading the carefully laid cobblestones. I made for the one place within the walled seminary where I never felt beneath my station, and where the students seldom bothered coming. Past a terrace and a portico, tucked behind one of the basilica's buttresses, was a small avenue of statues, my favorite group of artifacts.

Two rows of a dozen figures standing upon unadorned plinths barely taller than the shrubbery, so you can look each figure in the eye and take their measure. Carved from humble sandstone rather than marble. Plain-faced women with their hair tied in buns; pot-bellied men, some stooped from age; people with hooked noses and knobby knees and balding scalps, who held staves instead of scepters, and wore caps instead of crowns. A collection devoted to demigods, not deities. But they were carved with the same pride and valor as the Almighty Father God Belanos himself (may he forgive me, if that's blasphemy). It was a place I often came to be alone.

I looked up, and there was Kara.

She stood underneath the shadow of Buisteir, the one-handed lord of butchers, leaning her shoulder against the handle of the demigod's stone cleaver. The last blossoms of a lavender azalea bush hung like ornaments behind her. She seemed to be waiting for someone. I froze in mid-step, neither coming closer (as I wanted) nor retreating (as I probably should have). It was the nearest I had been to Kara since arriving at the seminary. In the leaden half-light, poised in the quiet of the statuary garden, with her hair stirring in a breeze around her bare shoulders, I could almost picture her standing on a pedestal of her own.

She saw me. And the moment our eyes met, I thought I read in her face the expression of a dockyard cat about to pounce. But then her eyebrow tilted and she cracked the barest hint of a coy smile, and that first impression, along with all my thoughts, went careening off with the breeze. Her lips parted, and she spoke to me.

"Who do you think you are?"

It was not at all what I expected her to say. She had her hands crossed across her chest, and her head angled slightly, and I wondered … well, I couldn't really say what I wondered because my mind went blank from the shock of speaking with her.

"Wha-what do you mean?"

"I mean," she said, slinking out from under Buisteir's shadow, "why were you at a lecture for seminarians? You didn't belong there. You're just a scribe. A scroll-scratcher."

I tried to appear unconcerned and shrugged my shoulders.

"Lectures are open to anybody."

"Not for you, they aren't." She shook her head, never letting go of my gaze, and took another step towards me. "How old are you?"

"Sixteen."

"Youngster," Kara chided. "Listen. I don't need a gutter-born boy to speak up for me in a class where he doesn't belong."

My cheeks went warm. The heat quickly spread to the back of my neck. My fingers curled into fists. But Kara didn't seem to notice, or to care.

"I've seen you staring at me," she whispered.

"I don't—I don't stare at you."

"Yes you do. All the time. It's really rude."

She took three more steps. Kara was near enough that I could smell the lilac of her perfume. My mouth went dry, but I made myself sound incensed.

"I haven't been staring at you … Sister."

The coy smile widened, crinkling the edge of her lips. She slitted her eyes and lowered her voice.

"Don't lie to me, Simeon. You took an oath not to bear false witness." Kara leaned forward to peer into my face. Her eyes ran down the length of my body. "You're built like a farmhand. All big and brown."

My chest inflated. She was looking at me, studying my body, and a wild, maddening part of me hoped she liked what she saw. Nearby, a pair of squirrels scuttled up one of the statues, their little claws clicking against the stone in a chase that ended as suddenly as it began. I couldn't tell whether they caught each other; I was fixated on the beige flecks in Kara's eyes and her thin, mocking lips. As if sensing my thoughts, she drew back, turned as if to leave, but paused long enough to crane her head over her shoulder.

"You know I'm an earl's daughter." She said it threateningly, the way a man armed with a dagger would warn a would-be pickpocket.

"I know."

I bit down on my tongue for letting that slip. Kara's forehead lifted, as if in triumph. She faced me fully and drew out her words at length, like the cut of a carving knife.

"Then you know you should stop staring at me."

"I … I don't… "

A clatter rang down from the basilica's minarets. The mid-morning gongs. Noises of people scurrying towards the great hall intruded into the solace of the cloistered avenue. With a flick of her hair, Kara slipped away to join them, her last words gilded with laughter, fading in the clamor of brass sounding from high above and the thrum of my heartbeat pounding from within.

"Back to work, Simeon… "

CHAPTER SEVEN

A lec trudged ahead along the marsh bank. Each footstep seemed to be an effort for the boy's spindly legs, a struggle marked by the squelch of loam, soaked sand, and what looked like centuries of fallen, rotting leaves. I had to help him pull his feet out of the muck more times than I could count.

Dawn had just broken. A few rivulets of sunlight leaked through the canopy of oaks that surrounded us, but otherwise the Glades lay shrouded in a shadowy haze. Great, gnarled eaves draped with flowing capes of moss twined overhead. A few woodpeckers tapped at palmettos for breakfast, a lone mockingbird twittered through her run of tunes, but otherwise, there was only the sound of our bare feet sloshing through the mud and the clatter from the gear I was lugging—a wicker basket, serrated knife, hooks, rope, and two gig spears. For his part, Alec carried a walking stick. I didn't mind, though. The load wasn't that heavy, and Alec was acting as our guide.

A sweat-plastered, out-of-breath guide, at the moment. His head swept the landscape slowly, as if he was searching for something. The Hillswash was still to our right. Alec ran his forearm across his brow and turned towards the river.

We wound our way to the river's edge, picking through tangled branches of mangroves until the waters were licking at our toes. The water felt surprisingly cool. Here and there, strands of river grass drifted by in the current as water beetles scurried between the clumps of vegetation, casting tiny arrow-shaped ripples in their wake. Alec came to a halt and gestured with his staff.

"We're here," he announced with a huff of triumph.

Up ahead in the river, just past a stand of cypress trees, a jetty of lime-stone boulders jutted out in a perpendicular line from the riverbank. The rocks looked worn and slick, with weeds that sprouted like hairs from their crevasses, and green mold that covered every bit of their surface. A couple of frayed ropes still knotted around rusted bolts hung limply, their ends twirling in the river's current. It was a somewhat jarring sight to see stones out here in the heart of the Glades. Judging from the angry murmur of the river pushing around the jetty, it seemed the river shared that opinion.

"It was going to be a bridge," Alec explained. "Long time ago, they cut a road through here and started hauling in stones to cross the Hillswash. Some big project that was supposed to give everyone work to do. Then, this townie from Mereborough pointed out how no one in his right mind would *walk* through the Glades when you can just paddle a canoe, so they stopped the whole thing. Didn't take long for the swamp to take back the road. But the rocks are still here." He crept around the cypress roots to pat one of the jetty stones. "A bridge to nowhere. But it makes a great fishing spot."

"It's all the same river," I remarked with a shrug. "Why should the fish like this patch of water better than any other?"

The question seemed to stump Alec, but only for a moment. He waved his hand curtly.

"What does a Bluff boy know about fishing?"

We had become fast friends over the weeks, Alec and I, so that now, in that timeless tradition of young men, our every conversation had to carry a taunt or an insult.

Alec clambered out onto the rocks on his feet and hands, like a crab, and headed for a long, low, flat boulder that jutted out from the pile. I followed his example, though it was a bit of a trick with all the gear I had to carry. The stones felt smooth to the touch, and very cool. I joined Alec on the boulder and looked about. We stood just above the surface of the Hillswash, facing upriver. A wide vista of featureless brown water framed with overhanging jungle.

"So you ever fished before?" he asked.

"Couple of times. But only with a net. Which you don't have."

He pursed his lips and snorted. "Can't use a net on a river. That's why we brought gigs. Here, hand me one and I'll show you what to do."

I set down the gear behind me and picked out one of the spears. It had a long, thin shaft of oiled wood, and balanced easily in my palm, between a rusted eye bolt on one of its ends and a barbed spearhead on its other. Alec tied a length of coarse string through the bolt's hole.

While he worked on untangling the line, I studied the water. It was brackish, a beer-colored slurry that licked the jetty's limestones with a soft, steady ripple. At first, I could make out nothing in the river, but slowly, as my eyes unfocused, I could see shapes here and there, shadows moving just beneath the surface of the water, appearing then fading, like ghosts.

While I studied their movement, Alec shared his store of fishing lore.

"Don't waste your time on any of the gray ones," he said, gesturing at the spectral shades. "That's all spiny lips. Slimy, bottom-feeders, got poison spikes on their cheeks. There's a million of them, and they're terrible eating. Look for fish with color. The colorful ones are the only ones worth eating … that's what we're—"

Alec flicked his arm and launched his spear. I was hardly one to judge, but I could tell it was a poor throw. The gig veered before it struck the river's surface so that the gig splashed and sunk harmlessly to the river bed.

"Dammit."

Alec was already rewinding the line, hand over hand, looping it back over his shoulder so that he could make another toss.

"It takes a few tries," he muttered.

About a dozen, apparently, I watched Alec hurl the gig over and over, calling out curses and murmuring prayers between shots, and never striking anything other than the water or the river grass. Since there was only room for one of us at the ledge's outer tip and that was where all the fish seemed to be, I soon grew bored. The sun crept further into the sky, warming the air.

"Hey, Alec," I asked, trying to sound insouciant, "what do you think of Sister Kara?"

"I don't." He threw again, and missed a flash of orange gill by the thinnest of inches. "Dammit all to Bel's bloody *balls!*" He started rewinding the gig's string, then stopped and fixed me with a scrutinizing gaze: "Why? Don't tell me you've an eye for Kara Blithe?"

"No. 'Course not."

"Good. Because *that* will get you gigged, my friend." He finished looping the line, adjusted his belt, and returned to his fishing. "No bedding with seminarians."

"I know, I know. The oath—"

"No one gives a fart about the oath. There's always priests and seminarians pairing off. Scribes'll bed one another every now and then, too. It's not a problem so long as you stay on your rung. You're a scribe. That means you can never lay with a seminarian. There'd be trouble if that ever got out. And if you ever put a baby in one of them … " He let out a long, low whistle. "Listen, if you don't like the look of any of the scribes—and I can't blame you if you don't—there's a dozen Mereborough girls for us if you're ever feeling—you know—like you need some company." He made a jerking motion with his hand. "Marcus sneaks over there five, six times a month. Emma, too. She has a lady friend who tells fortunes. That's where we're allowed to fish, if you catch my meaning."

"Yeah," I replied with a snort, "I get it. And I don't fancy Kara. I was just … curious where she came from, why she's in seminary. That's all—"

At that moment, Alec heaved the gig and finally struck something. "Ha!"

The line went taut. Alec wrestled with the string, yelping as the running rope burned his palms. His arms started to flail, so I came over, grasped a fistful of his shirt with one hand to keep him from falling into the river, and gripped the last length of line with the other. I could feel the fish thrashing.

"Must be a big one!" Alec exclaimed. "Help me bring it in."

I leaned my weight back on my heels and dragged the line in until one of the shadows came close enough to the surface that it gave a great splash. It was like hauling up an anchor. Alec gave a few tugs, more for show I suspected, but as the splashing grew louder and the fish drew closer to the ledge, his face fell. He let out a crestfallen curse.

"Belanos' balls. It's just a spiny lips. Gods, they're everywhere."

So it was. I brought the wriggling gray mass out of the water by its tail. Alec's gig had skewered it clean through, but it was still thrashing, still flaring its two long spikes from its cheeks. The fish's silver mouth gasped for air it couldn't breathe. I watched it flop helplessly on the surface of the stone. Without a word, Alec grabbed a loose piece of stone and smashed its head in.

He jerked his gig free from the fish, taking care to avoid its spines, and nudged the carcass with his foot. It plunked into the river, and no sooner had it begun to sink, a flurry of spiny lip fish was swarming about it, tearing their erstwhile companion into shreds. Eating their own. I watched Alec crinkle his nose. He handed off his gig for me to have my turn.

"Remember," he said, "aim for color. Those are worth the throw. The ones that stand out are the ones we want to kill."

———————

Wolven, the final month of the year, brought to the seminary what passed for winter weather. The few maples that dotted the boundary between the walls and the Glades cast off their meager offering of autumn leaves. The squirrels vanished from the grounds. There was no snow, not even a hoarfrost, but in the mornings, if you blew out your air in a hot, hard breath, and you peered really hard, you might make out a puff of silver fog in the sunlight.

It was the time of year at the seminary when barley loaves made way for pumpkin bread, and potatoes were replaced with buttered corn, and the ale—well, ale never stopped flowing in the seminary. Day after day, the river boats brought an endless succession of harvest feasts from the Duchies, so that within a fortnight I must have put on another stone of weight and had to trade my robes again for the largest set the commissary had. Oh, how I would stuff my face in the refectory! Three helpings every meal, then I'd sit on my arse all day in the Vault to copy edicts. I should have had a belly like an elephant's, but Belanos be praised, somehow all that wonderful food packed on as muscle. What a blissful season of my life.

I was in the refectory one day, clearing my plates and utensils to tote them back to the kitchen. My scribe companions had already left for work at the Vault; most of the seminarians were gone, too. . I strode briskly, balancing my plates in my arms, when I noticed three girls at one of the tables huddled in conversation. One of them was Kara.

It's a hard trick trying to walk by a pretty girl while pretending you're not carrying a pile of dirty dishes, while also pretending you don't care that you are. I utterly failed in every regard. As I drew close, Kara stopped one of her friends midsentence, spun around in her seat, and smiled at me.

I stopped so hard, I nearly dropped my plates. My heart thrummed hard in my throat.

"Simeon!" She greeted me so warmly, I thought she might ask me to join her. She lifted her plate, a pewter dish with a few wilted leaves of salad and a crust of pumpkin bread, and a cherry tomato. I couldn't fathom why she was raising her dish like that. I didn't care. Kara's voice dripped sweet, like amber honey.

"Simeon?"

"Hi."

Her brow knitted, as if something bothered her, though her smile never dimmed.

"Well?"

"Well … what?"

She dangled the plate before me.

"Aren't you going to take it?"

The girls tittered. My face turned hot. A volley of urges welled up and raged against each other, like the little red fruit bouncing across Kara's plate: whether to take the dish with a stiff formality, or pretend I didn't hear her and walk away, or dump the thing over her head. I settled on a question, asked with pretended innocence.

"And why would I do that?"

Now it was Kara's turn to flounder. But she quickly recovered herself.

"Because you're poor," she said. "You're here for service; it's all you're good for. Really, you should consider it a privilege to clean after your betters…"

Without a word, I set my own plates in front of a startled Kara.

"You're right. It is a privilege."

There was a collective gasp from the table, followed by a hush. An old washerwoman wiping down the far benches paused in her work, though she pretended not to be eavesdropping. Kara's cheeks turned as red as that little tomato.

Before she could collect herself and unleash the inevitable tirade, I fled the refectory, satisfied that I had held my own and despondent that I had been forced to.

I must have copied ten thousand edicts. Word of my flowing script had spread fast so that in the humble circle of the Vault, I became something of a celebrity for the singular talent I had mastered. By the time another scribe had rounded out a paragraph, I had finished a page. For ordinary grist, writings where the customer didn't require much formality or ornamentation, I could produce twice what the swiftest scribes had ever managed. My flowing script even had a name now. The scribes had taken to calling it "severaling." A few of the younger Vault scribes were even trying their hand to mimic it.

But it had its limits. It was only good for bulk work, never anything of importance. The subject matter of what I was copying—lists, tallies, petty ordinances, legal notices—had quickly grown tiresome.

It was a pleasant surprise when one afternoon, Marcus interrupted me in the middle of copying a voter roll, propped his leg on my table with a knowing grin, and dropped a small satchel in my lap.

"Thought you might like this," he said, "so I set it aside for you. Finally got a bit of work from home."

I looked at the satchel. It was tattered and thin and couldn't have held more than a couple dozen documents.

"We don't get much from Bajebluff," Marcus continued. "You want it?"

"Yeah," I nodded eagerly. "Thanks, Marc."

Marcus shrugged his shoulders. "There's nothing juicy. I already looked. There's a plague running its course, but that's nothing new. Some smugglers got sideways with Sheriff Beardley."

"I'll get right on it," I said.

"No rush." He swung his leg back down. "Like I said, it's pretty bland stuff. But I figured you could use some news from home—since, well…"

It was an unspoken understanding between Marcus and me never to mention the painful fact that, although I had sent her five letters, my mother had not written to me once.

"Have fun," he said with a wave, and left to check the other scribes' work.

The sun through the skylight gave the dusty satchel on my desk a soft glow. I pushed the voter roll aside, smearing a line of wet ink in my hurry. It didn't matter. I finally had some news from home. I hadn't realized how badly I longed for news.

With the eagerness of a child opening an unexpected gift, I threw aside the satchel's cover and began thumbing through its contents: a list of updated tariffs, a certificate for a new crematorium at the arena (I guess it was cheaper to burn dead gladiators than to bury them), an edict that directed all plague-infected houses to bear a warning symbol, and a small stack of forms, about twenty in all, each a replica of the other except for a blank line near the top filled in with names, ages, places of residence, and crimes. Death warrants from the Sheriff. The second to last caught my notice:

Amma Grom, aged 30-35, Lower Bajebluff, smuggling

The thief in the warehouse. The one who burned my book to hide her crime. Maybe Paul Little testified against her, or maybe that corporal planted a piece of ivory on her, or maybe a jailor bludgeoned her until she confessed. However they managed it, they were able to convict her. But, then, the Sheriff always wins his prosecutions. It was odd, but I found myself feeling sorry for Amma.

I peeled back the page and read the last warrant.

Paul Little, aged 15-20, Lower Bajebluff, repeated larceny

My eyes went over the line again and again, refusing to believe the words before me.

Paul was dead. His crooked smile, his gangly limbs, his cocksure capers— gone forever. Cut down on a headman's block.

A soft patter of rain began to fall on the window overhead. I stared at the page in my hands, unable to move, unable to think. The emptiness left me numb. I finally shook my head and came back to my senses. As a storm brewed outside, I settled in my chair, folded the warrant, spread out the satchel's papers, and attended to my duty as a scribe of the Fifth Pantheon.

CHAPTER EIGHT

The Day of Padraig's Reprieve falls in the last week of Wolven Month. It's the day when nighttime runs its longest and the daylight dwindles to its shortest span. According to the Gospel of Feirmeoir, on this one day of the year, poor Padraig, the perpetually eaten mule, gets a holiday as his master, Belanos, the god of the sun, pulls his own freight across the sky. No one knows why the haughty father of the gods deigns to relieve his beast of its toil and misery for the shortest day of the year. Feirmeoir doesn't say. I suppose the story's meant to show that even the most imperious arse has to show a piece of kindness once in a while.

There is no real theology surrounding the Day of Padraig's Reprieve. It isn't even mentioned in the Pantheon's Calendar of Holy Days. No special rites or prayers mark its observance. But the seminary venerated the day like a high festival.

Paddy's, as it's called, was a rare day off, when everyone—from the high priest, to the scribes, to the groundskeepers and cooks—got to do as they liked. For most, that entailed a copious amount of drinking at a carnival.

There was a small field about an acre wide between the edge of the Glades and the seminary's eastern wall. Overnight it had been transformed into an outdoor festival. Booths, tents, stalls, and tables were set up and festooned with bright orange flags and ribbons. The town folk of Mereborough sold slow-cooked meats, honeyed cakes, roasted nuts, mulled ales, and spiced wines. The aromas in the air were intoxicating.

Within those carnival grounds, student and scribes could gamble at card games like Castes, or sing songs, or get into fistfights, or find true love for a few hours; anything they wanted, really. There were contests everywhere:

ring-the-barrel, clash of canoes, footraces, wrestling, and the seminarians' favorite, gator-tail, a roving challenge to knock over whatever drink someone was holding by whipping their hand with a rolled-up orange terry cloth. I never fully understood the rules, but it was a fun game to play.

The carnival was a familiar kind of diversion. Despite being in the middle of a remote swamp, the atmosphere reminded me of an Ales Month festival in the Lower Bluff. Only with better company and much better drink.

A brisk evening fell over the bank of the Hillswash River, and the Paddy's festival, well underway since before dawn, showed no sign of abating. The sun cast a jasper sheen across the face of the water while the shadows of the palmettoes and oaks of the Glades crept deeper into the haze of noise and cooking smoke. Torches pinned to wicker stakes flared like fireflies in the field. Judging from the shouts and peals of laughter, the revelers seemed determined to see the party through the end of Paddy's Reprieve, all the way to midnight.

As for me, I was into my fourth or fifth ale and feeling a fine tingle in my cheeks. I'd left my red and blue postulant robes on my bed and replaced them with a more comfortable shirt and pants. Alec suggested I "blend in" on Paddy's, and that turned out to be wise counsel. There were scores of young, rough looking men from Mereborough milling about, and few of them seemed to hold esteem for the seminary's attire.

But I fell in right among them, wandering with no other direction than my pleasant inebriation, taking in the sights. There was a fire eater, who nearly ignited the hair of one of our seminarians. Over to my left, a toothless, half-blind derelict tried to put on a magic show. A pair of children straddling a fence post thumped one another with meal sacks, each hoping to knock the other off. Just ahead, one of the town's butchers had his cleaver in hand to guard a shallow pit where a hog lay roasting over embers, the grease hissing as it fell against the coals. I glanced over my shoulder and caught sight of a woman walking around on stilts. Another woman was pulling her down from the planked legs, laughing uproariously, her dark hair flowing unkempt. Somehow they ended up embracing, and everyone around them cheered. My fellow scribe, Emma, had found her lover.

I heard a loud crack, and a painful sting lashed my wrist. My cup of ale tumbled, spilling down my chest. I spun around and saw Alec brandishing a wrapped-up terry cloth, grinning like a madman.

"Gator got you!" he crowed.

"You son of a whore." I rubbed the back of my hand and gave Alec a thump on his shoulder.

"Ow." He winced. "You've got to buy me *two* drinks now. One for the drop, the other for the punch."

"Fine. But I'm only into you for ales, since that's what I was drinking. Right?"

"Yeah, yeah," he said. "I should've gone after Marcus over there." Alec pointed with his chin, past a small throng of people, towards a booth where the master scribe, now dressed like a merchant, was busy sucking oysters off a tittering young woman's bare stomach. He was trying to reach down her blouse with one hand while balancing a wine glass with the other, and succeeding at neither.

"He's got a Niallex port," Alec said wistfully.

"You'll get a Mereborough cask. C'mon."

We made our way to the nearest keg stall where I settled my gator-tail loss with Alec. Then we tried our luck at a few of the games on offer. A crooked three-card shuffler took a mark off Alec, but paid it back the next hand when Alec pointed out, quite loudly, how he was palming the show card. I earned five pence when I threw a dart ten yards and made it stick in a dead frog's corpse, but lost my winnings when I went for double or nothing. A run of half-pence wagers on a brightly painted wheel of fortune ended with neither of us worse nor better off. We had a fun time with all of it, though. If you break even at a carnival, you've come out ahead.

In a moment of drunken graciousness, Alec bought the next round. As we emptied the mugs, we rested our backs against one of the many drained casks piled about. I gazed at a flickering torch, watching its orange flame curl about itself as it sent shimmers of heat into the night air. The noise of the fair washed over us. My legs felt like I was on a barge at sea.

"Just one more after this," I said to Alec. "Then it's bed. Did you hear me?"

Alec's eyes were fluttering shut. I took another sip, and when I turned to him again, he was curled in a ball, passed out in the grass.

I was debating whether I should nudge him awake with my foot or leave him be, when I felt a warm breath on the back of my neck. A scent of wine and perfume wafted up.

"Hello, Simeon."

I craned my head, but my vision lagged a bit behind it, so it took a moment for my eyes to focus—on Kara.

"Hi," I said.

She wore a woven winter dress of deep orange. Her hair was braided and tied up with a black silk band. The torch seemed to play with her eyes. She was smiling.

"So I've made a wager," she said, and all I could see were her lips, pink and glistening in the torch light, forming pretty words. The world spun underneath me. All I could manage was,

"Oh?"

"Uh-huh."

I felt her hand on my shoulder, her fingers drumming thoughtfully. I had the sense she was playing a kind of game, like so many others in this field tonight. A game I couldn't refuse. My words came out thick.

"What kind of wager?"

Her eyebrows tilted and her smile widened.

"Everyone's always talking about how big and strong you look, and— Simeon, are you blushing?"

I must have been, for my face was burning hotter than the torch I had been staring at. But I shook my head and mumbled that I wasn't. Kara drew her words out like honeyed mead.

"Well, someone—don't ask me who—made a bet. Would you like to hear it?"

"Yeah."

She leaned closer. Her hair brushed against my cheek.

"They bet ten marks you couldn't carry a person to the top of a minaret."

I felt a grin plying at the corners of my mouth. I sniffed out a laugh. The stairwells in the minarets were steep and narrow, and probably a lengthy flight to climb, but the musicians who traipsed up them every day to sound the gongs and horns for paidir were no athletes.

"I guess I could manage it," I said, "but who would I have to carry?"

Her face beamed, even as she dipped her head demurely, and I could sense that not only was I playing the game Kara had in mind, but I must have been playing it well. For I was following her lead. She leaned into me, slid my hand around her waist, and answered softly.

"Me."

A cold full moon had crested above the seminary walls. It cast the stone avenues and statues in a marble glow, where shadow and light mixed together, so that the familiar grounds seemed ethereal, spectral, and exhilarating. A wind blew between the buildings, scuttling the piles of raked leaves near the gardens. The sound of our sandals scampering over the stone walkways broke the stillness.

Kara's hand clasped mine, as it had since we snuck through the gate. Wherever she pulled, I followed. Her laugh, the strands of her hair flowing like wisps of ivory in the moonlight, her coy glances had me plodding along as faithfully as old Paddy ever had. Her triumph—oh, yes, I could see that in her eyes, too— burned as bright as a star. She wasn't trying to conceal it. And I didn't care.

The basilica doors would be locked and barred, but there was a servants' entrance in the back, where the chandlers and cleaners could come and go between services. It was a plain and narrow wooden door in the wall, with no awning and no rails or steps to lead into it. A humble accommodation suited for menial workers. Discreet, too. I couldn't count how many times Alec and I had used this entrance to sneak into paidir when we were late from fishing.

Kara leaned against the basilica wall, tilted her head, and let the moon wash over her. I was staring at her, I know I was. She fixed me with an arch look.

"It's locked. But you'd have a key to get in, wouldn't you?"

A playful barb, but a barb nonetheless. Meant to remind me of my place. I, a lowly scribe, would surely consort with the sextons and sweepers by sharing their keys. Yet in my inebriations—of ales, of exhilaration sneaking into the seminary, of Kara's closeness—I couldn't feel the sting of it at all.

"Don't need a key," I said with a swell of pride that I knew something she didn't.

Her brow knitted. It was true, though. There were so many doors scattered throughout the seminary, the servants didn't want to bother lugging around heavy keys. So the locksmiths had built special latches into all the servants' entrances.

I clasped the heavy, iron door ring, but instead of pulling at it, I gave it a three-quarter turn to the left, then back to the right, and left again, until a latch clicked.

"My, my," was all she said.

I shouldered the door in, and Kara and I entered the darkened temple.

It was breathtaking.

The candelabras and chandeliers were all extinguished, and yet the whole sanctuary blazed with pearlescent light pouring through the glass windows. All the familiar statues, the pews, the altar, the alcoves, were aglow with a sparkling whiteness, bright as hoarfrost. A sense of awe fell over me. It was like gazing at a constellation of stars fallen to the earth.

Out of habit, I knelt, made the holy sign, and shut my eyes, but my prayer was cut short by Kara's mocking laughter. It echoed softly in the emptiness.

"Aren't you the devout little scribe. Wait." She paused and gave me a chary look. "You're not a zealot or something, are you?"

"No, of course not. Just seemed—I don't know—like we should be respectful."

She stared at me a long moment and nodded. "Alright. Let's do this properly." I felt her sliding next to me, kneeling, her hip brushing mine, and any thought of the gods tumbled out of my head. Kara hastily touched her forehead, chest, and stomach and held a hand up. She lifted her voice in what, at first, sounded like an impressive benediction.

"Oh, great Belanos, father of the gods and wellspring of the bold, we beseech your divine favor. Give this servant, Simeon, strong legs and arms and a sturdy back. So that he can make his penance. For drinking too much tonight, and for barging in on the classes of his betters, and for staring at one of your priests with very impure thoughts…" She started giggling. "And not taking her plate to the kitchen, like he should have—"

"—Be it so," I finished and started to rise, but Kara only laughed and pulled me gently by the arm to rejoin her on her knees. A smirk still lingered on her lips as she whispered the rest of her prayer.

"And if he can complete this penance and win me my wager … may he be richly rewarded."

Her lips pressed into mine, her hand grasped the back of my head. It was rank blasphemy what we were doing. I had acquired enough of my new faith to feel a pang of guilt, which somehow only made it all the more intoxicating. I don't know how long we knelt there, kissing in the sanctuary, but I could have stayed there forever. At last, she pulled back, smiled, and purred at me.

"So are you ready?"

"Yeah." I nodded eagerly and repeated with more conviction. "Yeah."

"Then let's get to the minaret."

She was up, gliding, a specter floating through alternating bands of light and shadow in an empty, moonlit basilica. There, then gone, then there again. I raced after her.

Past the altar, through a doorway that led into the vestry, and down a narrow hallway, we came at last to a cyclopean wall that held a stairwell. The steps spiraled upwards into darkness. Kara paused, glanced up the stairs, and extended her arms out from her sides. She had an expectant expression. Not really thinking, I leaned forward to kiss her again, but she laughed, and turned her face away.

"Not until you win my wager. Now. Carry me…"

A year and a half of rich food and sheltered desk work would have left most men soft, out of shape. But thank all the gods, I was still in the prime of my youth. It was as easy to hoist Kara into my arms and carry her up the circular run of steps, as it was to lug fishing tackle out to the river with Alec. Cradled in my arms, nestling her head against my shoulder, whispering in my ear for me to hurry, the girl felt as weightless as a feather.

I have no other memory of climbing to the top of the minaret tower. I must have managed it quickly. One moment, I was pumping my legs in the dark like a bull in heat; the next, I was thrusting open a hatch into the platform at the top of the minaret. A bead of sweat and a thumping heartbeat were the only signs I had exerted myself at all.

I blinked and drew in a chest full of night air and beheld the vista from atop the tower. Truthfully, it was much cruder on the inside than it appeared from the ground. A cramped, dusty enclosure, perhaps ten feet in diameter, shaped in a perfect circle, the tower's edge was marked by a low brick wall, topped by bronze columns that held a conical spire above our heads. A heavy bronze gong hung from wires caught a glint of light. Otherwise, it was just an empty stone platform.

But the view was breathtaking.

The whole of the seminary, alight from the full moon, was laid out like a map beneath us. Beyond the seminary's walls, there was the carnival field, twinkling with orange embers from scores of torches, and beyond that, the twining brush and mangroves of the Glades, gray all the way to the horizon. I don't know how long I had been standing at the edge of the minaret wall when I felt Kara slide her hand over mine. She turned me around to face her.

Kara had already slipped out of her clothes. Her pale skin prickled from the cold. I reached for her, but she held me back one last time, intent on finishing this game she had in her mind. Her eyes gleamed with victory.

"You won my bet," she said approvingly.

I grinned. "So how much did I win you?"

"Oh, the bet was with myself." Her eyebrows tilted. "I couldn't make you carry my plate to a kitchen … but I bet I *could* make you carry me up to the top of a minaret. You did it. And I won. Well done, servant."

I didn't know what to say. My tongue fumbled over itself, lost in the whirl of feelings beating in my chest, in my groin.

"And now," Kara continued, "you're going to serve me some more … "

And at last we embraced. We were on the floor, the fruition of all I had hoped for washing my senses away. Kara straddled herself on top of me the whole time, she the beautiful spire, me the meager pillar, and I didn't mind in the least. This was all a game to her, played to assuage her noble ego, but I didn't care about that either. Despite my inexperience, I like to think I served her well that night.

It was a tryst, nothing more. That was made very clear before dawn had broken.

We were lying together, uncomfortably, on the cold stone floor of the minaret, and sleep was still the farthest thing from my mind, when Kara suddenly winced and pulled away from me. She propped herself up on an elbow, and in the moonlight, fixed me with a stern, almost priestly expression.

"It's time for me to go."

"Oh … alright."

Her eyes hardened for a moment, a wrinkle marring her forehead. She started getting dressed.

"This was just for Paddy's, understand? You have your place, Simeon. I have mine. So don't try to talk to me again. I'll be leaving soon, anyway." Her face fell into something almost like an apology. "It was nice, though."

She slipped down the stairwell, her feet hardly making a sound, while I lay naked in a dusty, empty tower, a little dazed, feeling the breeze for the first time.

That was the end of our affair, such as it was.

From then on, whenever our paths in the seminary crossed, Kara gave me no more regard than the furnishings, an object that had been utilized once when it had been wanted, but now could be ignored.

It stung a little, at first. Once I tried to catch up with her, on her way between classes, after paidir, in the refectory. Just to talk to her, in private. Kara's friends were nowhere around, and I thought if we could share a few more moments together, if I could touch her hair, or hold her hand.

"Kara? Kara? Wait, I just want to—"

She rounded on me, eyes ablaze.

"How dare you speak to me? Impertinent whelp! Get back to the Vault where you belong. Go copy some handbills, or whatever it is you scribes are supposed to do …"

I learned a lesson that day, an important one. If a woman doesn't wish to be bothered, she ought not to be bothered.

Kara cut into me hard and cruel, buried her barbed quills deep. She yelled at me and heaped scorn over my head until I stormed off, flushed and on the verge of tears.

So be it, I thought angrily. If I was relegated to nothingness, so was she. If I was a forgotten bench, she would be a forgotten statue. A piece of artwork in the background, like all the others in this miserable seminary.

Springtime.

It came one day out of the darkness of the Glades, sudden and unannounced, hot and in full bloom, with the frenzy of a rampaging army. Pink and yellow blooms broke through the mangroves, like scouts peeking through the trees in enemy terrain. They were followed by the oaks. All at once, as if some divine order had been given, the trees spewed pollen. In clumps as cumbersome as burlap sacks, great mounding heaps of yellow-green strings cascaded down from the limbs and eaves in a steady, relentless volley. It was like being trapped within a storm, one that lasted for days. Every flagstone, statue, roof tile, and step inside the seminary was draped with the stuff. It fell into the food we ate, clung to the air we breathed. The fog swept in, swallowed us all, and left us sweltering.

And sickly. Every year when the pollen arrived, a score of seminarians would end up in the infirmary. You could hear their hacking coughs and groans and sneezes all through the night.

When I went a span of days without seeing Kara around the seminary, I thought little of it. I figured she was probably bed-ridden with all the other asthmatics. Hopefully, lying under a coarse blanket and wracked with fever, if the gods could hear my vengeful prayer. As for me, I had friends, and fishing, and, once this damned pollen cleared out, a comfortable life ahead of me (or so I told myself to salve my pride).

One hot afternoon, I was making my way back to the Vault, shuffling along a path that had been swept through the fallen pollen. I was alone, still brooding, and not paying much attention to anything besides my feet, when I happened to walk within a broad shadow.

I looked up, and there was Gathena. She was flanked by a half dozen helmed men in ringmail armor. Each one had a sword strapped to his belt. Gathena's cheeks sagged from a frown.

"Simeon." Gathena said my name without warmth.

"High Divinity?" I gaped at the men-at-arms. "What—what's happening?"

Her mouth pulled tight. The men surrounded me, but before I could react, Gathena laid her hand on my shoulder and said in a firm voice:

"This man took a holy oath. He's sworn to the gods themselves."

One of the men replied in a grave, respectful, tone.

"Alright, Divinity. We'll treat him proper." The others grunted their agreement, as they closed a circle around me.

"What's happening?" I repeated.

"If any harm should fall upon him," Gathena warned, casting a dark glare at each of the men, "the one responsible will be guilty of clericide, and—Simeon!"

I may have softened in my months in the seminary, I may have grown a little numb from ale, and leisure, and easy work, but the instinct of a Lower Bluff boy doesn't die easily. I reacted the way you had to when a posse of the sheriff's deputies came for you. I tried to run.

Hands, bodies, shouts rained down on top of me.

"Hold 'im!"

"Lil' bastard!'

"Easy there, boy. Strong 'un, isn't he?"

Gathena's high-pitched squeal cut over the men-at-arms.

"This is holy ground! *Holy ground!* Damnation, Simeon, stop fighting them, stop—"

I felt the press of men bearing down on me. But in a crack of daylight in the torrent of limbs, and leather, and curses, I spotted an escape. I sprung headfirst for my last chance at freedom. It was a good leap, strong, determined. If these had been Bajebluff deputies, it might have been enough. But these men were as strong and determined as I. An arm grappled me around my throat. The air cut short, I thrashed as madly as a speared fish.

"Stop!" Gathena squealed. "Stop, I say!"

Through the noise of the scrum and Gathena's protests, I heard the sound of a steel blade drawn from its sheath. There was a brief flash of light. A pounding, stinging blow to the side of my forehead. Then I knew no more.

PART III

THE ESCOLA

CHAPTER NINE

There's not a commoner in the Four Duchies who, at some time or other in the course of their dreary childhood, doesn't dream of one day coming into Niallex, the capital city. For me, it was as a knight. I would have a banner, something with a dragon in gold and garnet, and wear gleaming silver plate armor, a helm topped with an ostrich plume, and a flowing yellow cape. Of course, I'd be wielding a sword (I went through a series of names for it—Reaper, Scourge, Sunstrike, that sort of thing), for I was a conquering hero, coming home from war to a stately, grateful king. A great, coal black charger would carry me high through the city's streets thronged with cheering crowds.

Some of that dream came true.

I was coming into Niallex, and I was riding on the back of a black dappled steed. A pony, actually. Not armed, but under guard. I was led bound and gagged through one of the city's innumerable back gates. The only witnesses to my triumphal entry were a legless beggar, a cat, and a cluster of children carrying water buckets to the outer parapets of the wall. Only the cat paid any attention to me.

My guards walked alongside the clopping mount I was tied to, their ring-mail clinking dully against leather vests, their helms lusterless from dusty roadways. We had traveled together ten days. Ten aching, saddle-sore days of hunger and thirst and cramps.

The men who had arrested me kept mostly to themselves, and by the end of our journey, they still seemed unsure whether to treat me like any other prisoner, or if they should afford me the respect of an ordained priest. The strange compromise we had reached was still awkward after half a fortnight.

They were rough, but not overly so, and the few times they spoke to me, it was always in a tone between a man-at-arms' command and a polite request: "Time to take a piss … your Divinity, if you have a need to." "Here, drink this … or it can wait 'til later." As I said, they didn't talk to me overmuch, and in the sour, self-pitying mood that had gripped me, that was perhaps a small blessing. Though it would have been a greater blessing if one of them would have dropped a hint as to why they had taken me prisoner. All they would say, though, was that I was wanted in Niallex.

So to Niallex I came.

They say the city was spewed from a volcano, one that vomited buildings instead of lava. If you squint your eyes from afar, Niallex does look like a little like a mountain rising from within a rolling plain. But instead of rock, its slopes are packed with teetering structures piled on top of one another, almost like a pyramid. At the top, there's the palace. I'm sure it would have been a lovely place to see.

But I never came within a mile of the palace gates.

Instead, we wound through one of the outer wards, a run of cramped streets packed with somber, featureless buildings, and peopled with somber, expressionless men and women who walked about with their noses in the air. The streets were tight, littered with carriages in various stages of delivery, but otherwise fairly clean. Every few feet we would pass a sign post that, to a one, was plastered over with handbills that fluttered in the breeze. I knew without being told that we had come into a neighborhood of petty, minor officials.

We reached a low wall with an iron gateway. Another guard wearing the same garb as the men who brought me let us through. Once inside, I beheld what would become my jail. It was a sandy courtyard some two hundred feet square with stables, a well, a guardhouse, and in the center, a round tower dotted with arrow slits no wider than two or three fingers.

I spent thirty-four days in a locked room in that tower. The cell was small, but not uncomfortable, with one off-center arrow slit window for light and air, a straw bed, a chair, and a dented chamber pot. Two meals were served in the courtyard each day, always black bread and some kind of thin soup, followed by vinegary wine that was barely palatable. Each meal was followed by an hour of exercise in the courtyard with a dozen other prisoners who kept to themselves even more than my guards.

No one would tell me what I had done, or why I was here. Though I asked a thousand times in a thousand different ways, my every request was answered with either an indifferent shrug or a palm—an open palm held upright at my chest, the universal signal for a bribe. But as I had no money to give, my jailers had no information to share.

I passed a month of days feeling sorry for myself. I woke up angry. At noon, I would fool myself to believe I could accept whatever fate the gods had ordained. By nighttime, I cried like a child. More than I should have, really, since all things considered I was being treated fairly decently compared to my fellow prisoners. I prayed a great deal more than I did when I was in seminary. Prayed, pleaded, begged, bantered, cajoled, cursed—the gods got quite an earful from their servant.

On the thirty-fourth day, they answered my prayer.

While I was ranging around the courtyard on my morning exercise, I heard the wall gate creak open and shut, and in scuttled a figure dressed in red and blue. The gate guard pointed me out for him, though there was no need to since the man was already striding fast straight towards me.

It was Marcus.

He looked tired, road-worn, his hair a mop of frizzled wisps. His nose and cheeks were sunburnt as red as his robe. But the gods of the Pantheon be praised, it was Marcus, my old friend and mentor. My eyes watered with joy, I spread my arms to embrace him.

He only glared at me, licked his dry lips, and without so much as a greeting, spoke in a thick Bajebluff accent.

"You really are an idiot."

We sat in my cell, me on the bed with my knees brought up to my chest, Marcus on the wobbling chair. Thankfully, the jailor had removed my chamber pot. A long thin blade of sunlight cutting through the window marked a boundary between us.

Marcus took a long drink from a wine pitcher. His face screwed up, and I thought he would it spit it out, but he managed to swallow it down.

"Bel's balls." He stuck out a purpled tongue and wagged it to shake off the taste. "They'll kill you off before your trial if you drink this stuff."

I gave a start. "What trial?"

"What do you mean, what trial?"

For a painfully long, scrutinizing moment, we gaped at one another, neither comprehending the other. At last, Marcus cursed and then ran his fingers through his hair, spiking the strands. His voice dropped low. "You do know why you're here, don't you?"

"No."

"Hell and balls, boy! How can you not know?"

I hit the side of the wall with my fist and let my temper loose. "Because no one's told me a damned thing! I've begged, *begged* everyone I can to tell me—something, anything, why I'm here, what's happening. All the guards ever do is stick out their palms for a bribe."

Marcus threw his in the air. "So pay them. It's just like back home. You've got to pay your toll."

"I *can't* pay them! They knocked me on the head before I could get my things, my money."

"Ah," Marcus nodded, "and whose fault would that be? Who had the brilliant notion of making a run for it from a troop of regulars? Or were you thinking those were just sheriff's deputies that came all the way out to the Glades to come fetch you?"

My head felt like a millstone. I cupped my face in my hands and replied between my fingers.

"I—I didn't think."

"Damn sure you didn't. They'd have taken you back to your room to get your things if you hadn't turned the situation into a scrum. You're lucky they didn't do you worse than a thump on the head."

I felt my shoulder being jostled. When I looked up, Marcus's sweat-smeared brow and tired, bloodshot eyes filled my vision.

"You're a Bluff boy," he said with a tinge of pride, "you've got some book learning. Use your head. What do you think's happening here?"

"I ..."

My mind went whirling down the same rabbit holes I had been chasing for the past month. Every possibility I could imagine still led into the same dead end. For some reason, though, with Marcus sitting before me, his red and blue robes turned beige from the road, a new possibility, one I hadn't considered before, dawned on me. And with it, a cold dread squeezed my insides, as if to confirm its truth. It came out as a whisper.

"Kara?"

Marcus sighed through his nose and nodded. He leaned closer so that his features were almost blinding in the bar of sunlight as he hissed at me.

"You laid with a seminarian, a noble seminarian, less than a month before her ordination as a priest."

Indignant now, I rose from the bed and paced the small length of the cell.

"But-but it was just that one time. We were in a minaret—Paddy's—she *dared* me to carry her—"

"Sit down, you fool boy. Now."

I came to a halt from the force of his words. Slowly, I slid back onto my bed while Marcus, his thirst overcoming his revulsion, forced down another swallow of my jail cell wine. He licked his lips for a bit, as if considering the best way to instruct a particularly dim novice. At last his face settled, and he said more calmly.

"Why do you suppose, Simeon, that scribes have to swear they won't lie with a seminarian?"

I had never thought about it before.

"So we'll ... so we'll focus on our work?"

Marcus arched a dubious eyebrow, as if to say, I couldn't possibly believe that was the reason. I didn't. I gave a more honest answer.

"So we'll keep to our caste. Not tangle up nobles with commoners."

Marcus nodded again.

"That's one reason. We've got the Duchies' finest afterthoughts in our care at the seminary. We're paid hefty sums to polish them up and turn them into something respectable. So when the Earl of Blithe tells his dinner guests how his eldest daughter just married the fourth son of Duke Thus-and-Such, and his second daughter is betrothed to Sir What's-he-Called's youngest, when he gets to his last girl, Kara, he doesn't have to admit he ran out of money for a decent dowry. He can say, 'And we're so proud of our youngest, Kara, who heeded the gods' calling and pursued holy orders and was just installed as second vicar in a temple in Dheas.' And all his guests can nod along and say how lovely that is."

Marcus managed another drink, this one with a little less effort. "Kills your taste after a time," he observed and followed it with another swallow. He wiped his mouth with his sleeve and continued. "It's all a lie, of course, but it's the useful sort. As long as the image of it can be maintained. But it's kind of hard to keep up the charade if 'the gods' calling' means rolling around in the stables with the children of pig-keepers, or wharfmen, or—"

"—or tutors," I finished for him. "Yeah, I understand." I chewed on my bottom lip a while, for something still bothered me. "That doesn't explain this, though." I waved at the walls of my cell. "No one saw us. I never told anyone. And Kara …" The memory of her spurning me still made my cheeks burn. "Kara wants nothing to do with me."

Marcus heaved another sigh and took another drink, this one finishing the pitcher. He shook his head with a melancholy look.

"This," he said, indicating my cell, "is because of the other reason we have you take that oath."

I stared at him as cold anxiety crawled up my spine. The master scribe spoke slowly, his words thick with cheap wine and sympathy.

"Kara Blithe is with child. Your child." He paused, shook his head, and added, "And now you have to answer for it."

On the whole, the Niallex Court of Chancery was an unremarkable place. Situated less than a mile from my tower jail, the courthouse was a long, rectangular room with a magistrate's bench at one end, a gallery of pews at the other, and a half-circle of desks in between. The windows had been greased over so that no one could see in or out, and only an oily light from the sun could shine through. A bronze bust of a kindly, bald man, one of the countless Niall kings who nominally ruled over their Kingdom of Four Duchies, looked down benignly from above the judicial bench.

As my guards opened the courthouse door and motioned for me to enter, a middle-aged woman paused her hushed deliberations with an older, bored-looking woman seated at a bench. The former was an advocate, I could tell right away. She stopped her shuffling of papers long enough to gaze at me with cold, vacant, apprizing eyes. Like a vulture that's spotted a dying calf. The magistrate looked at me in much the same manner. Thank the gods I had Marcus with me.

"May it please the court," the master scribe announced.

"It doesn't," the judge snarled. She was old, and gnarled as an oak tree, and just as stiff, and when she spoke, her voice grated like sharp thorns over skin. I saw only her upper half, but it was covered in dark purple, the color of the law, and a flowing headdress, all of which announced that Her Honor was the judge and this was her domain. "Tell your guards to close the damn door," the judge added, "it's hot as a hell today."

Only two jailors had accompanied Marcus and me, and in the heat, they had left most of their arms in the barracks, carrying only truncheons and short swords. But the heavy manacles they left on my wrists and ankles were all they really needed to ensure I wasn't going to try and run off.

The guards shut and locked the door, found a bench in the shadows, and made themselves inconspicuous, as the advocate dipped her chin ever so slightly at Marcus.

"Well met, Divinity," she greeted him. She was a tall, spry woman, dressed in the same hue as the judge. Beneath her arm, she held a curled parchment of considerable heft, a document she bore like a sheathed weapon. The woman regarded me coldly. "And you must be Severals."

Marcus acknowledged her with the slightest nod and, casting off his Bajebluff accent, replied in a formal voice I had never heard before.

"Well met, Counselor Nelphia. You may call me Marcus. Though I do not have the privilege of priesthood, I am charged by the Seminary of the Most Holy Fifth Pantheon of Gods with representing our oath-bound scribe, Simeon."

Not knowing if I should wave or offer to shake hands or bow, I simply stood, watching this strange parley unfold. Nelphia gestured for us to join her at her table, her eyes darting between Marcus and me as we approached. The parchment crinkled threateningly in her clutch.

"You'll forgive me for asking," she said in a tone of pained politeness, "but given the unfortunate circumstances of this meeting, I had rather expected the intervention of her High Divinity Gathena. Or at least an ordained priest. Though I've no doubt you command her High Divinity's trust and authority, her absence is, um ..."

"No more unusual than the absence of your client." Marcus made a point of staring at her. It seemed like they were grappling with one another somehow, like players striving for a good first position in a contest, I could sense it. Neither would budge. "Her High Divinity has authorized me to speak and negotiate on behalf of the seminary and our clergy and scribes. Including the scribe your client has taken by force of arms."

"Yes, well." Nelphia tapped the document she held and waved her hand absently. "His Grace is very busy with his official duties. That is why I carry his authorization. And why Judge Lankley has graciously agreed to provide her able assistance—"

Judge Lankley cut over her.

"The Earl wants this problem taken care of quietly. As do I."

Nelphia dropped her voice, as if she were about to share a deep confidence. "Can we speak candidly?"

Marcus shot me an expression that said he would be doing all of the "candid talking" before he nodded to the advocate.

"Kara is starting to show," Nelphia said. "The whispers are becoming murmurs. In a few more days, it will become tavern talk."

I felt my stomach clenching. I started to open my mouth, but Marcus set his hand gently on my shoulder to keep me from talking. "Surely his Grace has a chateau or a manor. Someplace in the backwoods where she could wait out the pregnancy."

Nelphia shook her head. "Kara had accepted a call to the High Temple in Cultacai. The installation ceremony had been scheduled. Announcements were plastered all across the duchy. His Grace was quite proud ..."

"I see," Marcus frowned.

Judge Lankley spoke, her words hitting like a cudgel.

"If it weren't for the boy being oath-bound to the gods, he would have already been tried and trussed. He behaved like an animal. Rutting a poor, innocent girl, and at the top of a tower, of all places!" Nelphia nodded along in eager agreement as the judge's voice rose into a righteous, indignant timbre. "The Earl would be well within his rights to have him gelded and hanged for unlawful congress with his daughter. I've handed down a hundred such sentences, and for infractions far less severe." Judge Lankley's eyes narrowed into two razor slits, sharp enough to do the emasculation themselves. They cleaved right through me. "You ever seen that before, boy? They cut you in the public square and make a necklace of your stick and pebbles. Your naughty bits dangle from your neck while you dangle from a rope. That's what'll happen. All His Grace has to do is ask me for justice."

The blood drained from my face, from my feet and fingertips, pooling into my groin, where it tingled with mounting alarm. Sweat beaded my forehead. I found myself twisting my knees together, as if to ward off the pruning blade the headsmen used to make examples of men who dared to bed their betters. Men like me, apparently. I started to stammer.

"S-sorry—I—I—"

"His Grace *won't* ask you," Marcus addressed the judge in a respectful, but firm tone, "because if he does, his scandal will be out in the open. For all to see. Which is why we are here today, isn't it?"

"His Grace would prefer not to ask for justice," Nelphia corrected him, "if he can keep this affair out of the open, and restore some measure of his honor."

Marcus drew himself up, lifted his chin, and folded a bit of his blue robe in his hand, assuming the mien of a wise, old counselor. "Then let us cut to the heart of the matter. This proceeding," he waved his hand around the courtroom, "has been convened with neither a petition nor a plaintiff because its purpose is to take care of this problem—as discreetly as possible."

A long, slow nod from Nephalia was followed by an imperious sniff from Judge Lankley. Marcus continued.

"We accept that our oath-bound scribe's conduct fell beneath what we expect at the seminary." He cast a severe sidelong glance at me. "He accepts his responsibility for his actions, and for the child he has made. Doesn't he?"

Everyone in the courtroom, the judge, the advocate, the priest, the guards, awaited my response. I swallowed dryness and finally managed to speak.

"Yes." I dropped my head to show how deeply ashamed I was supposed to be. "I bedded Kara. I'm the—I'm the father of her child."

So peculiar to speak that word aloud. Father. A medley of images came to my mind, of countless children I had seen in Bajebluff: girls tailing after their dads on the way to market, boys sweeping shop floors beneath a scrutinizing gaze, children getting whipped, toddlers squealing with laughter. My own father was nowhere to be found in my ruminations. Would Kara's baby, my child, feel the same absence that I did? My reflections were interrupted when Nelphia addressed the judge.

"Will the Court accept Severals' admission in confidence?"

The judge waved her hand impatiently. "Yeah, I'll adjudge him the father and seal the paper. Get on with the haggling already."

Marcus nodded.

"The Seminary is willing to return His Grace's sponsorship."

"That is an insult of an offer." Nelphia's teeth clenched. "Your Honor, we might as well schedule the trial—"

"It is only the first offer." Marcus held his palms up defensively. "What does His Grace envision?"

"To start, ten thousand marks. And a fortieth of the Seminary's recording fees in perpetuity."

Marcus scoffed. "He's an earl, not the king!'

"True. But as an earl, he is entitled to remuneration. A noble's remuneration."

"To be sure. And we will give him such meager compensation as we can. But we are oath-bound not to share our fees ... perhaps His Grace can accept a delayed payment, over a term of years?"

"Depending on the number of years. Perhaps. With sufficient security, of course."

"Depending on what you would define as sufficient security …"

The two of them, Marcus and Nelphia, went on in something between bargaining and bantering for a long time. Proposals, counter-proposals, pretended indignation, followed quickly by some levity, turning then to yet more proposals. Judge Lankley made no pretense of being interested, but made herself a lunch, right there on the bench, of what looked like sliced bread and anchovies and a small bottle that, judging from the apple glow in her cheeks, held a drink stronger than my jail wine. I too found myself bored with the drone of negotiating, and a little hungry. I stretched my legs from my chair, rubbed at my manacles, and gripped my stomach while the back-and-forth between the master scribe and the advocate ran its course. At some point, they began poring over the advocate's document, scribbling notations here and there, striking through pages, adding text in the margins. A mounting anxiety began to take hold of me. It occurred to me that when they bothered to look over at me, Marcus and Nelphia regarded me with much the same expression—I was a problem they were resolving. With that realization, it also dawned on me that Marcus, my brother scribe, might not have been sent here for my sake.

I had not long to dwell on this, though, for at last they came to an agreement over money, and signed part of a page, each one looking equally satisfied with themselves.

"But now we must turn to the question of what is to be done with Simeon's person," said Nelphia, after she blew dry her signature. "His Grace is willing to forego the customary punishment, but he must have some measure of justice."

"What does he have in mind?"

"Imprisonment, I should think."

"A scribe in a common prison? That would bring disgrace upon the Seminary."

"No worse than the one brought upon the earl's household."

"His Grace's disgrace," Marcus showed a wry smile, "will pass soon enough. A few months of awkward questions, a brief 'holiday' while his daughter gives birth, that's all. We could always shunt the boy into the kitchens."

It seemed they were bartering again. This time not over money, but over me.

"Yes, and the Seminary will keep making money off his scribe-work and have him clean your dishes," said Nelphia, wagging her finger at Marcus. "Nice try, Master Scribe. You can have him, but only if His Grace receives the fees he earns."

I felt a flutter of hope.

"That sounds fair," I said. "I'm a fast copier. My work'll make His Grace a fortune, over time."

I could see Nelphia's eyebrows tilt, and the look on her face, like a merchant about to fleece a customer, told me her client would be thrilled to reap my scribe fees. But Marcus set his jaw and hardened his face. Without sparing a glance at me, he returned to the advocate.

"I told you, the Seminary cannot share its fees. Ever. It's absolutely forbidden." He scratched his chin and thought to himself for a moment. The noise from the street outside hummed softly in the courtroom, masking the soft snoring of Judge Lankley, now napping, from her perch on the bench.

"The army?" he countered.

"No," Nelphia shook her head. "The army is too honorable. Some soldiers are venerated as highly as priests."

"But not quite as highly as advocates." Nelphia let out a little titter, which sent a chill down my spine. "I've got it." Marcus leaned close to her, as if he were drawing the advocate into one of our sacred mysteries. She inclined her head to receive it. His words, cloaked in that pretentious Niallex accent he still affected, landed with harsh, brutal thuds in my ears. "The arena," he said.

"The arena," Nelphia repeated. Then, with a waspish grin, she nodded. "The arena," the advocate pronounced the words like a death sentence, "would be acceptable."

The guards stirred from the shadows and hoisted me to my feet, while the advocate gently woke the judge to inform her that a settlement had been reached. A few pen scratches from Her Honor, and it was finished. Judge and advocate retired to Her Honor's chambers, leaving me with Marcus and the men who held my chains, men who would soon be taking me away.

Marcus was busying himself rolling and re-rolling one of the large parchment sheets, a copy he would take home—his home, mine no longer. No doubt he'd show it to Gathena who would heave a melancholy sigh and say something sagacious-sounding about the good of the Seminary, before she had the paper filed away in a special shelf reserved for the Seminary's private affairs. Marcus would get on with his life, the routine of paidirs, and scribe work, and meals. His wench in Mereborough would soon blot out my memory. He might already be forgetting me. I watched Marcus as he set his chair back in place under a table, snapped some twine around the rolled document, and scrupulously avoided looking at me. When there was no more paper to move about, he jerked his chin at one of my guards, and I was pushed back towards the door.

The empty courtroom passed by, a blur of blandness. Marcus didn't bother to walk with me. I jerked free from one of the hands that held me, but only so that I could say one last thing to Marcus. I'd be damned if I was going to be forgotten that quickly.

"You're a bastard," I said.

He stood there before the desk, his stare still fixed on that precious paper, the one that officially sold me into an early and brutal death. The one he had signed.

"Bastard," I said again, and the word echoed against the colorless, plaster walls.

At last he looked at me, without so much as a hint that he would lose a moment's sleep over the choice he had just made. One of the guards started to step between us, but at a curt shake of Marcus's head the guard withdrew. When Marcus spoke, his voice was pure Lower Bluff again, harsh and gritty as a scab.

"I told you," he said quietly, "when you first came to us. We've got one thing we sell."

"Yeah," I snarled, "trust. But you didn't keep it with me."

"We *sell* trust," he replied, a bushy eyebrow raised high, "to paying customers." Marcus drew closer to me, close enough to poke me in the chest with his finger and glare up into my eyes. "You're the one who bedded a noble. You're the one who broke his oath. So don't get all high over me, boy. I did what I had to, to fix the trust you broke."

I wanted to strike him with my fist, smash my manacles into his eyes—and yet I felt so drained, so bereft of will, all I could do was stand there, and breathe, and hate him. There is a kind of impotence that comes over a man when he feels powerless over life's indifference; I hadn't yet learned how to conquer it.

"Sorry," he muttered.

I was pulled away again, tears falling freely down my cheeks, blurring my sight, but before the guards had shunted me out of the door, I heard Marcus say,

"The gods be with you, Simeon. Good luck in the Rolls."

CHAPTER TEN

I n the late afternoon of an autumn day, an armored wagon trundled across the cobblestones, carrying a score of rag-clad pickpockets, rapists, lunatics, burglars, drunkards, and a disgraced and miserable scribe. I was chained alongside them all, knee to knee, shoulder to shoulder, stripped of my robes and my position so that nothing distinguished me from this wagon-load of Niallex's refuse.

A team of oxen pulled us along at the whip of a shrill-voiced teamster, while we prisoners shifted in what little space there was, chained within a cage like penned cattle. A few people in the streets paused to watch or to hurl curses and refuse in our direction, but there was little interest in prisoners being sent away. A troop of archers strode alongside the wagon, arrows nocked in their bowstrings, lest any of us threaten trouble. None of us did.

We went to the outskirts of the city through a sequence of keeps, over a bridge, and out into the countryside. It was a cramped, uncomfortable ride. Quiet, though. We were all sullen, for every one of us knew well (except, perhaps, one wild-eyed man who kept talking aloud to his thumb as if it were his dearest friend) that this ride was taking us to our deaths.

As I squinted between the bars of the cage, I watched the undulating plains and dreary villages of Niallex's borders transform into foothills ripe with grain, orchards, blossoming berry bushes, and grape vines. My eyes drank the beauty of the land greedily, like a man who finds himself at the last water well before he journeys into the desert. My dark thoughts turned to Padraig, that pathetic celestial mule, who, if the stories were true, had finished his labor today, and was now being rent apart for his troubles. It was a grim musing that held me bound for the rest of a brief journey.

They called the compound the Escola. An academy where, from time immemorial, men had come to learn the craft, which was what they called killing other men for sport. There were other gladiator schools scattered across the Kingdom of the Four Duchies, but the Escola was the only one ever spoken of with a shudder and a whisper. It was a place that made masters (or monsters, depending on your view of the arena). The gladiators who came forth from its hallowed gates, those who had survived its ordeals, did little to dispel its reputation. It was rumored to be a house of horrors.

From the outside, though, it looked more like a large, off-the-road inn. A nice one, actually.

Set atop a steep rise jutting from the darkened fields and foothills of the country, a two-storied rectangle of barrel-tiled buildings loomed over us. White plaster walls glistened in the moonlight. Lanterns twinkled from windows, almost inviting. If it weren't for the iron portcullis barring the gateway, I would have expected to hear a strain of tavern singing.

We unloaded from the wagon and trudged up a run of cracked stairs in the hillside, our manacles clanking in time with the tired thud of boots, yawns, and the half-hearted grunts of our guards, who seemed eager to deliver their charges so they could find a proper inn for their own comfort. I lingered towards the rear, keeping to myself, but I could still make out the gate opening at our arrival and the backlit shadows of a dozen broad-shouldered, pot-bellied men outfitted with helms, clubs, and short spears. One of the new wardens took the lead chain and led us inside.

Save for a few plain obelisks, there was no statuary, no gardens, no busts or statues, no embellishment whatsoever in the Escola. Just a long open expanse, divided into sections and surrounded with plain, featureless buildings. It was stark, not a stone wasted for adornment.

We were brought into a courtyard illuminated with hanging braziers. The long stone expanse held a dozen rings of low walls. Miniature arenas. In the center stood a towering obelisk. And that was where we were led.

Our line marched slowly, all of us taking in our new surroundings. It struck me how each of my fellow prisoners tried to hold themselves—some thrust out their chests or spat on the ground in defiance, others gaped like travelers on a holiday. Most kept their eyes on their feet. As for me? A little of each, I suppose.

As we walked the span of the courtyard, one of the wardens intoned a practiced speech.

"Prisoners, you are now in the custody of the Escola of Niallex. I am Silas Tate, the watch sergeant. Here are the rules. You will keep your mouth shut. You will do what you are told. You will not try to escape. That's it. Pretty simple. Follow those rules, and all will be well. Break any of those rules ... " He pointed vaguely towards the obelisk that now loomed over us. We could see in the moonlight that its spire was pure white alabaster, its base was festooned with iron rings and darkened with the stains of gore from countless floggings. After a suitable pause, Tate concluded. "Break the rules, and you'll be broken."

One of the prisoners' voices cut through the stillness. It was the thumb-talker. He had lapsed into an argument with his delusion. I suppose he couldn't help himself.

"We'll pick the blueberries *later*, Duggan. Later, after they leave. There'll be plenty left, yes. I hear ye, I hear ye, but be patient, Duggan dear—"

Tate gestured at the closest guard, who untied a club from his belt and with a practiced flick, brought it down upon Duggan's skull. He struck the man skillfully—hard enough to do his work, but not so hard as to kill his charge. The madman and his talking thumb crumpled to the earth, quieted, but not dead. Without a word, every one of us drew a step away from him, while one of Tate's wardens undid his chains and dragged him off.

"To repeat," Tate said as if nothing out of the ordinary had occurred, "your mouth stays shut. You don't try and run. You do as you're told. Those are the rules. Now you're going to line up by that table over there. On the other side of the Block. That's this big fellow here." He patted the face of the obelisk as if it were an old friend. "Break the rules and you'll get to know the Block. Over here, now. Queue up! Doctor Broward's waiting. He's going to have a look at you and assign you to your Roll."

On the other side of the Block, shrouded within shadow, a small table had been set up. A lantern burned low, showing an urn, a ream of papers, a few medical tools, and a heavy-lidded woman in a faded physician's cloak who looked like she would much prefer to be in bed. The doctor gripped a quill pen between her knuckles and, as we approached, gave it a lazy flick, her only acknowledgement.

At that cue, Tate grabbed a pair of shears from the table and went down the line and cut off our clothes. It only took a few minutes, and there we stood, a score of naked, chained men—and one woman—in a midnight courtyard. The woman was tall and muscular, the color and build of an oak, and she kept her hair cropped close to her scalp. She hadn't uttered a sound for the whole ride, which I suppose is why I hadn't noticed her before. It should have been awkward. Yet she stood defiant beneath the glow of the lanterns right alongside the men, her broad shoulders squared.

A chill breeze blew across the length of the courtyard. In my mood, I hardly felt it. Silence hung as thick as the night sky; the thumb-man's example had squelched any idle chatter.

When we were ready for our examination, Doctor Broward scraped her chair back and rose with a grunt. Starting at the front of the line, she worked through our group in a steady routine: she pulled back our eyelids, then pinched our chests, arms, legs, stomachs, and groins while she sniffed the entirety of our bodies, then felt inside our mouths and counted our teeth. Only after that did she speak, checking our names against a list she carried, and asking each of us the same three questions:

"Have you had any pox or plague since last Raven Month?"

"Have you been purged for worms in the past twelve months?"

"Have you ever laid with an animal of any kind?"

Sometimes a guard would bleat like a goat when the last question was asked, but we all knew without being told, and no matter how bald a lie it might have been, that every one of those questions had to be answered with a firm "no." The Escola had no place for the diseased.

The old physician would spend a moment or two quietly considering the slab of flesh before her, mumbling under her breath or squinting in the wavering lantern light, before she told Tate what our Roll would be.

The Rolls, I came to learn, was a play on words. They were lists, but also assignments. The kind of craft we would learn here—and one day perform— was our Roll. There were only three in the Escola—Warrior, Skirmisher, and Grappler—and it quickly became obvious how they were assigned. Only the strongest and sturdiest became Warriors; the wiry, those with thin but working limbs or who were in relatively decent health were made Skirmishers (that was most of our group); and a squat cutpurse who had once been a tumbler with a carnival became the lone Grappler.

One by one, the doctor did her assessments and decided our fates. The two chained ahead of me were quickly deemed skirmishers, and Dr. Broward came at last to me.

"Severals, Simeon," she read. Her fingertips probed my body. They felt cold and bony, but filled with studied purpose. Her nose, I noticed, protruded at an angle, and when she sniffed me over it sounded like she had a head cold. I answered her three queries about my poxes, worms, and bestiality, and she settled her eyes on my chest.

I found myself squaring my shoulders, and flexing my muscles. Miserable as I felt, dejected, self-pitying, tired, hungry, but when a woman's gaze fell on me—even one who was practically a crone—my natural reaction was to flex. Broward must have spotted what I was doing, for a slight smirk spread across her thin lips.

"Yeah, there's a frame under the flab, I see it." She made some more mouth noises as she pondered what to do with me. I realized she was chewing on a set of wooden teeth. She muttered to herself. "Still kind of young. Hard to tell with youngsters, which way the body'll grow. Maybe you've topped out, eh?"

I kept quiet as she rubbed her chin. Suddenly, Broward turned her head and called for Tate.

"Sergeant," she said to him, "this one's a bit of an in-betweener. Can we have a quick aptitude test?"

Tate eyed me briefly. He shrugged, and then, with astonishing swiftness, pulled his blade free from its sheath.

I heard the metal hiss, saw the sergeant's tired face twist into a grimace, felt the ground tremble beneath my toes as he lunged. The world seemed to freeze in motion—the tip of Tate's sword poised a finger's width from my throat, the blade gleaming orange in the torchlight, Dr. Broward watching with her arms crossed across her chest, and without knowing what was happening, I drew back, spread my legs as far as my manacles would allow, and brought my hands up. They had formed into fists.

I panted hard, my heart thumping madly, my sorrow and despair replaced with … something else. Tate re-sheathed his sword.

"More warrior than skirmisher, I'd say."

The old doctor nodded.

"So he is."

Three of us were to become warriors. The first, a mountain of a man who looked as if he had been born of a she-bear and a giant, went by the name of Posey. Next to him was the lone woman in our wagon. She spoke with a strange accent and muttered something about being a sailor, though I suspected her work was probably more in the line of piracy. Her name, which she only pronounced once, was impossibly long, so it became simply Kik. Posey the giant. Kik the pirate. And I, the scribe, was the third.

The three warriors in training stood inside one of the rings of the Escola courtyard, as the first rays of sunlight broke over the rooftop. We each wore white, the color of novice gladiators—loose white pants tied with a cord, short-sleeved white tunics with low necks, and light sandals with thongs that strapped around the ankles. A pair of wardens sat idly on the wall nearby, their spears balanced across their laps. The ground felt hard. The air held the promise of a hot day to come. In the distance, I could hear a mockingbird twittering a mindless tune. Posey seemed determined to outdo him.

He had not stopped talking since he introduced himself. His tale was meandering, incoherent, and held more lies than truth. Posey claimed he had been imprisoned in two different duchies, served a stint in a border legion, was expelled (for reasons he kept changing), returned to the legion, was captured (under circumstances that seemed rather questionable), until he escaped and came into Dheas Duchy.

"And if you can believe it," he said with dramatic indignation, "there was a warrant out on me. Some flinty bastard claimed I swindled him on a lead mine that didn't pan out. Now I never took so much as a farthing from the gentleman—'least not for that particular mine—but he had his judgment on me, which never should have been entered seeing as I was off fighting for our Good King when he got it. But there's no arguing with a judgment once it's got a seminary stamp. So I got taken up. Magistrate wouldn't listen to a word I said. Told me my extensive record," he paused to breathe, purse his lips, and roll his eyes, "*required* him to send me to the Rolls. As if it pained him to do it. Injustice was what it was. If only I could've afforded a good advocate—"

A shadow fell over Posey that brought his ramble to an abrupt halt.

"If there were better advocates," the shadow said, "I'd never get a novice."

In my short lifetime, I had heard many voices. Some were grating, some gravelly, two or three I'd call pleasant. Most were unmemorable. Only one ever struck me with fear.

The voice of the man who had spoken had no accent, no inflection, no feeling, no bottom.

The three of us turned to face the figure who had entered the ring.

He looked wholly unremarkable. A man in his mid-thirties with a wrestler's build, he stood only a little taller than I. A leather vest and wrist guards covered a suit of black clothes. His face was broad, almost simple looking, with heavy eyebrows and a set of pale, melancholy lips wreathed with a bushy blonde moustache that hung to his chin. He might have been any man you would bump past in a market.

A wide pair of eyes fixed on each of us in turn, eyes of no particular color.

"Welcome, novice warriors," the man continued. "I am Frederick. I will be training you. Let's see what we have here …"

While we stood at attention, Frederick slid quietly between us, sidestepping, turning delicately, his movement fluid and never ceasing. His face was indecipherable, though I soon realized he was assessing us, much as Dr. Broward had the night before last. When he had finished, he put his fists on his hips, made his moustache bristle, and declared, "You look rested and fed. Good. We can begin at once."

From the corner of my eye, I saw Posey raise his hand, and without waiting for Frederick to acknowledge him, he began to speak as if he were addressing an innkeeper whose service was not to his liking.

"Look here, Frederick, I think there's been a mistake. By which I mean, I don't belong here. No offense, mind you, I'm sure it was an honest mistake, but, see, I'm a corporal in His Majesty's Sixteenth Legion, and that gives me the right to—"

Before Posey could finish telling us what his rights were, Frederick pivoted on his back heel and spun his leg around. It was swift and graceful; his movement was like a dancer. And when he landed his foot in Posey's throat, it brought the conversation to an abrupt ending.

Posey doubled over on the ground, clutching his neck and gasping for air. Kik and I drew back. Still fighting for breath, Posey managed to get to his knees.

"Bas-tard," Posey wheezed.

The novice charged the trainer, heedless and headfirst. Frederick made a lazy movement backwards and angled to his right. Posey stumbled to grasp at him, but caught only empty air, while Frederick dipped swiftly to his left. As Posey lurched by him, Frederick struck with his forearm, a quick slash to the precise point of Posey's neck he had kicked before.

The sun broke full across the expanse of the ring. Beneath its glare, Posey writhed in the dirt, his furry beard now caked gray with dust, his eyes rolling, his long shadow contorting into strange shapes. Over on the wall, the guards laughed. Frederick crouched next to Posey, a pitiless smile on his face.

"You do not speak unless I tell you to," he said softly. "It will go much better for you if you remember that."

Frederick rose to his full height, adjusted his vest, and continued, his voice cutting over Posey's gasps, while Kik and I stared straight ahead, trying our best to pretend that the man splayed on the ground wasn't on the verge of suffocating.

"So as the soldiers would say," Frederick continued, "I have some sugar and some shit to give you. The shit must come first. Here it is." He paused to let out a sigh which, I gathered, was meant to seem empathetic. "All three of you are going to die in an arena. It will be a brutal, painful death. No one will mourn you. In fact, an audience will cheer as your life bleeds out for their entertainment. Cuts and gashes. Blood and bile. Agony. And then ..." He snapped his fingers. "You'll be dead."

The sun felt warm on my cheeks, and a muggy heat was already rippling up from the ground. I looked down at my feet. Somehow they seemed miles away. I remembered the match I watched with Paul in the Bajebluff Arena. A pair of men whose names I never knew were made to kill one another for no reason other than we had paid some pocket money for them to do it. What had I felt at the time? I couldn't remember. I looked up as Frederick brushed a bit of dust from his sleeve.

"Your term on the Rolls is twenty years," he continued, "some eighty fights, give or take. Only one in a thousand lasts the whole of their term." He shook his head once, emphatically. "You won't be that one. Banish that hope now. Accept your fate. Harden your will. It's all you'll have."

He made a long, slow sweep with his eyes. In the light of the full morning, I could see now they weren't colorless, but multi-colored—concentric rims of gray, blue, hazel, and brown. Frederick clasped his hands behind his back.

"For generations, the Escola has furnished the greatest gladiators in the kingdom. Colm Black, Maddox the Maniac, Ella the Left-handed, the Orc. Legends. Each one passed through these gates. Each one was made here." He thumped the earth with his heel. "Right here. The Escola sends out less than a half dozen new warriors each season. But they fetch the greatest prices. You three will be worth a fortune. Once you've learned the craft."

Frederick took a step closer to us, his hands still behind his back, his chin jutting upward so he could look down upon us, in what was almost a perfect imitation of the pose my mother used to assume when she taught lessons. Posey had finally gotten back to his feet, wobbling and rubbing his swollen throat, bearing a pained and angry grimace. Frederick cast a brief glance at him and continued.

"In the coming months, I will train you in your craft. I will break you. I will reform you. Then I will break you again. Again, and again, and again. Until you are empty of everything you are—except your will. That alone, you keep. For that is what we are training here."

He paused, turned to me, and flashed a smile that reminded me of an alligator I once spied sunning itself on the banks of the Hillswash. "Those you who hold to gods," he said, still smirking, "should say your farewells. Pray, if you wish. But understand, they can't help you here. They can't change your fate. You will be trained. You will go and fight. You will die. That's the shit of it." Frederick shrugged again. "If there are any questions before we begin," he looked at Posey, "*now* you may ask them."

To his credit, Posey was not cowed. With one hand still clasped around his neck, he raised the other, but this time he waited for Frederick to nod at him.

"Yeah," Posey wheezed, "you said there was shit *and* sugar. What's the sugar?"

The alligator grin widened, showing all of Frederick's teeth. For the first time, he seemed genuinely pleased. "Right you are, Posey. I nearly forgot. So the shit is you'll die soon enough in an arena. The sugar is … it won't be in this one." He let the silence draw for a moment until he chuckled and added, "Though you'll soon wish it were."

CHAPTER ELEVEN

Frederick was true to his every word. In the weeks that followed, I came to hold my life in contempt.

Our regimen began each day at dawn when Posey, Kik, and I were pulled from our cells and forced to sprint ten times up and down the stairs of our wing. Whoever finished last took a scourge to the back. Every warden carried a scourge, a short leather cord tipped with something like a beaver's tail. It wouldn't break the skin, but the slap always brought tears to my eyes.

Then we ran around the perimeter of the Escola courtyard, never fewer than fifty laps. The jog ended at the mess hall, the one place where we could mix with the other Rolls, for a hurried breakfast. These mealtimes were the only thing that kept me from hanging myself, especially in those first days. As warriors, Kik, Posey, and I were given heaping bowls of hot sausages, potatoes, onions, grits, bacon, granola, and, always, half of a lemon that we either sucked dry or took a scourge (it was Frederick's order and it had something to do with scurvy, I later found out). The skirmishers were given a loaf of bread and an egg, while the grapplers, who had to keep a lighter weight, got vegetables and a flank of meat.

Sometimes we would talk, Posey, Kik, and I. Kik always spoke tersely when she spoke at all, but from what I could piece together, she had been involved in a rebellion. Who she was fighting against, or why, she couldn't really explain, at least not in the Duchies' common tongue. It seemed the magistrate spared her the noose only because she was a woman who could fight; and a woman who could fight in an arena could potentially fetch a lot of coin.

Posey talked incessantly. But he was one of those rare people who could hold an entire conversation with himself and yet, somehow, those around him didn't mind. I don't know if a tenth of what he said was truthful, but it was always entertaining. I also met a few of the skirmishers, who were, by and large, a decent lot of serial criminals and low-rate brigands.

As for me, I shared only that I was from Bajebluff, and that there had been a misunderstanding about a stolen book that had been worth a lot of money. My time in the Seminary, I kept to myself. The last thing I wanted was to seem like I wore a higher caste's cloak—and the gods knew, most folk held anyone connected to the priesthood like a higher caste. Fortunately, it was a time-honored tradition among prisoners to accept each other's misfortunes as unvarnished, unassailable, misunderstood truths. I kept my half-true tale simple, and no one questioned it: I was a petty thief who got caught with a rare book and thrown into the Rolls by a bastard of a judge who had it in for me.

After breakfast each day, we spent the mornings in drills. Sometimes we would work with the skirmishers, but most days, it was just the three warriors, Frederick, and a couple of wardens. Gathered in the center ring, Frederick would show us the morning's maneuver, and we would imitate him. Repeat and repeat and repeat, until every muscle moved and every joint angled exactly where Frederick wanted it. Stances. Strikes. Parries. Counterstrikes. Endlessly grinding, pitilessly grueling repetition. We worked with wooden short swords—our "little pricks," as Frederick called them—and wore heavy pads to get used to the weight of the armor we would one day bear in the arena. The pads were woolen and sweltering hot. The pricks were made of solid oak and weighted down with lead so that by the end of the morning you could scarcely lift your hand. But you never dared complain in the ring. And the gods help you if you staggered or fainted (as I did more than once). Frederick once boasted he could "scourge a man back from the dead," and I came to learn that he probably could.

After we were done with the day's maneuver, we lunched, and then we sparred. Since they were close in fighting skill, Kik would usually be paired with Posey, leaving me with Frederick. Which meant I received a daily beating. I would try to use the maneuvers we learned, but I never landed a blow. Frederick would dodge, or feint, or parry with a bored, lackadaisical flick of his practice sword. He seldom spoke—not for correction, nor for taunt-ing—he simply fought me, and won. Time and again. The only words he would say, after drubbing me, were:

"What did you do wrong?"

At first, I floundered, or guessed, or sputtered like a whipped child, and was answered with a scourge. But pain can be a most effective pedagogy. After a few weeks of welts, I finally began to pay attention to what I was doing when we sparred. One day, after I skidded headlong across the ground trying to slash at Frederick's throat and the dust had settled, I saw Frederick's dim shape crouching next to me.

"What did you do wrong there?"

This time I knew the answer.

"Too much weight," I grunted, rubbing at the sting of sweat and blood in my eyes. "I led with too much weight. Didn't keep any back."

A slow, knowing smile broke across Frederick's face. "You really wanted to kill me, didn't you?"

I looked up at him. "Yeah."

"Good." He hoisted me back to my feet. "Your weight is down here." With his sword's tip, he poked my lower chest, my stomach and each of my legs. "And your weight is your power. Never spend all your power, Simeon. No matter how tempting the target. Keep a little back, for balance, for defense. The only time we put our entire weight into a blow is when our foe has yielded to receive his death. Only then do we give our entire body to the strike, and that is to make a quick and honorable kill. Do you understand?"

I nodded.

"Then try again …"

After that bout in the ring, Frederick paired with me every day, and every day he beat me like an ox. I despised him. But slowly, as I began to learn the craft, and the soft, pliant flesh of study came to be replaced with taut strength, with each passing day, Frederick began to show more interest in my progress. He scourged the three of us equally, he trained us all, but I was the only one he deigned to teach.

The morning came on bright, and cloudless, and biting. The courtyard's surrounding walls cast long, gray shapes against the sand that sparkled pink as poor old Padraig pulled the sun over the cusp of the gatehouse. At its top, fluttering in the stiff breeze, a white flag on a pole proclaimed another day of training, and a reminder that no one should die.

Before I had woken fully, before I had the first biscuit of breakfast, I was shuttled out of my cell and into the courtyard, where I was outfitted in full padded armor, helm, shield, and, as always, my "prick." By now, I had handled that damned wooden training sword so much it actually felt like a part of my body.

Today there would be a mock match.

I stood before the low brick wall in one end of the ring, while Posey faced me from the far side, a bored expression on his bearded face. My stomach grumbled, but I did my best to observe the formalities that would be expected in a gladiators' match. Between the two of us, the wind stirred the sand into little cyclones. Frederick, draped in his usual black garb, paced back and forth through the gritty breeze.

"A good arena," Frederick raised his voice so that it carried across the length of the training ring, "will match you against an opponent of an even weight. There shouldn't be more than a stone of difference between you. It keeps the fight fair, and interesting. There's no sport in watching a twenty stone giant rip apart a ten stone scarecrow." He regarded each of us in turn. "But that doesn't mean you won't find yourself in the ring with someone who doesn't look much like you. There are less reputable venues in the backwoods of the Duchies and they'll do anything to anyone if they think there's a chance to make an extra mark on a side wager. In my time on the Rolls, I fought in some truly bizarre pairings."

He paused and stroked his moustache pensively. The bristles sparkled amber in the breaking dawn's light.

"This morning we will fight a mismatch. It's the bear of the Sixteenth Legion versus the Bajebluff book-thief."

I ground my teeth, but did my best not to show my annoyance at the sobriquet my trainer had bestowed. It was bad enough to be made to fight a man twice my size before breakfast; worse still to be made fun of for it.

"At my signal, you'll begin the fight in the fashion as I've taught you. I'll halt you when I think appropriate. Listen to my instructions. Use what you have learned." Frederick strode across the ground and through the ring's gate, which he locked behind him. "And use all the weapons you have. They can even out any pairing."

From the corner of my eye, I could see Tate and two of the other guards leaning against the wall, whispering and exchanging coins. Distantly, I wondered what odds Tate had given against me. Three to one? Four? I repositioned my left arm in the shield strap, shook loose my sword arm, checked my helm. My stomach began to churn. This was the first time I had fought in anything like a match, and not simply a practice skirmish.

Straddling an archstone at the top of the wall, Frederick stood looking down on us. A passing breeze stirred one of his black sleeves as he held up a hand.

"Warriors, salute!"

Posey and I, as one, approached one another and held our wooden training swords before us upside down, then slowly turned our blades to point to the sky as we came together. I had practiced this little ceremony countless times, but it always looked stilted. When we reached our marks, Posey winked at me, whether to be friendly or to intimidate me more than I already felt, I couldn't tell. My voice sounded thin and scared when we chanted the gladiators' salute together:

"We have one death to die.
One chance
by death to be remembered."

A wind rustled across the ring, whistling softly through the ear holes of my helm. The top of the rising sun cleared the Escola's entrance. I tried to keep my gaze steady, but Padraig's load was blazing right behind Posey's massive head. My sight filled with floating purple clouds. I had to turn away. Frederick called out from his watching perch.

"Begin."

I had no sooner brought my shield to the ready when I heard a wild, half-strangled scream. The ground shook beneath my feet.

Thank Belanos, my feet moved before my brain realized what was happening. My left leg swept back, the ball of my foot finding purchase under the loose sand, and I sprang aside, just as Posey barreled past, his arms outstretched, wooden sword dangling from his hand. The noise of his cry echoed in my ears, but my vision was still plagued with an orb from where the sun had blinded me. I drew back to put more room between us.

Posey turned to face me, and I could make out that he was in a regular fighting stance. I heard him chuckling. Frederick, however, was anything but amused.

"Terrible!" he yelled down at us. "Posey, you couldn't possibly think a gang rush would work against an Escola gladiator. We trained for that nonsense in your second week." Then to me, he added, "And had your opponent followed his dodge with a back-strike—as he was taught—you'd have one less kidney."

I felt my cheeks flush. It wasn't that my sword arm hadn't primed for that very move, but I couldn't see the target. The damned sun was in my eyes. I pushed my helm back a little from my forehead and blinked, and finally regained the better part of my vision.

"Fight on," Frederick barked.

Once again, Posey came at me fast and hard. Only this time he raised his sword over his head and struck. No feint, no fake of the head, just an overwhelming rush of force. Easy to meet, but the shock of the blow was like an avalanche that reverberated over my shield, down the length of my arm, all the way into my chest. It left my fingers numb. I couldn't return the blow, but had to draw back once again.

Frederick's voice pierced the sound of my heartbeat thumping in my head, and how I wished the mustached bastard would come down here so I could strike the knowing smile I was sure was plastered on his face.

"Now you've felt it," he said, like a parent explaining a hot oven to a child who's just burnt his fingers. "Hurts, doesn't it?"

I grumbled under my breath, but I was busy sidestepping another blow from Posey. This time, though, he made a feint. At the last moment, Posey turned the arc of his sword so that instead of my head, he went for my side. I got my shield down to defend it just in time, but once more the blow left my arm pulsating with pain. But he had come close enough within my reach, and his move had forced him to drop his shoulders, so I could finally give him something of my own. I brought my practice sword around, swung hard, and heard the satisfying crash against Posey's shield. It felt like striking a hammer against a mountainside.

We traded a few more blows, pulled back, and engaged in a kind of dance we had long practiced, each trying to outflank the other. After a little while of that, I made it look as if I was about to change direction, then charged and stabbed with all the force I could muster. My sword deflected off his shield and skimmed the padding on his shoulder.

Posey drew back, shook his head, and laughed.

"I felt a draft. Did you feel that?"

"Simeon!" Frederick roared. "You can't trade blow for blow with a man who's twice your size. You'll never win that way. Do something else."

I had had enough. If I got scourged for insolence, so be it.

"Like what?" I shouted up to him.

He didn't come down and beat me, but answered in a flat voice. "Use your other weapons."

I clenched my jaw and went at Posey as hard as I could. He stood fast for the assault, neither moving nor really trying to deflect my blows, for the ones that got past his defenses seemed to have no effect on him. I heard a loud clang in my helm, felt the world warble, and heard what I thought was a gong banging between my ears.

He had buffeted the side of my head, but once more, my feet knew what to do, and I was able to regather my wits and senses.

"Ready to yield?" Posey sneered through his beard. He was panting hard, but I was in much worse shape. I couldn't get enough air into my lungs, and yet the more I breathed, the more I feared they would burst. "No shame in it," he continued. "Frederick won't scourge you. C'mon, I'm hungry."

"Eat this!"

I charged again, hacking wildly. We grunted, we cursed. I snuck a hit on Posey that did nothing. He landed a blow that left me dazed. Sometimes the guards would cheer, or groan, or curse. Twice I snuck the tip of my sword over Posey's shield, but each time it skidded harmlessly off the pads on his breast. After the second hit, Posey let out a roar, lunged at me, and knocked me to the ground. I landed on my face, cold, chalky dust filling my mouth, and rolled as fast as I could.

Posey's boot slammed into the dirt, not a thumb's width from my nose. I rolled again, barely missing his sword flailing the ring's dust, and sprang back to my feet.

"Enough!"

We both turned as Frederick dropped the six feet of the wall's height, landed nimbly on his feet, and walked purposely towards me, his brow crinkled, a disgusted expression fixed on his face.

"Give me that," he hissed, and plucked the wooden training sword from my grip. He didn't bother taking my shield before he turned into a fighting stance and faced off with Posey.

"Come at me," he commanded.

Posey cocked his helmed head, as if unsure he had heard the trainer rightly. Frederick was no heavier than I, and a bit shorter, and, other than the practice sword he now held, completely unarmed. A firm thwack with the flat of the blade on the side of Posey's head brought him around.

"I said, come at me!"

With a grunt, Posey surged towards Frederick. Step by step, never breaking his stance, like an ox pulling a plow. It was a slow, steady onslaught of weight and force, one where Posey kept his shield in Frederick's face as he brought his sword down in swift, methodical chops.

"Good," Frederick huffed as he dodged another blow. "Keep pressing. You've got every advantage. Wear me down with your weight. Very good." He was retreating, though it almost didn't seem like it. Frederick's backward steps were quick and at an angle so that he made a long, sweeping spiral. Within a few moments, he had traded sides of the arena with Posey.

And then I noticed what he had done. Frederick had maneuvered Posey so that it was he who was now facing the sun. Posey's sword faltered. His eyelids became slits. He tried to turn Frederick's flank, but now Frederick went on the offensive.

A swift hack at Posey's exposed shin, and the big bear let out a howl.

Frederick hopped aside well before Posey swung his sword in a wild sweep. Another strike, this time to the knee, and Posey's legs wobbled. They went back and forth, Frederick prodding for space, Posey on guard, but it didn't last long. Three more blows, all to Posey's legs, and down went the giant. He crumpled to the dirt with a soft thud, a cloud of dust wafting up over him. Angry welts were already swelling through the hair on his legs.

Frederick regarded him for a moment, turned, and tossed my practice sword back to me. They had fought hard, and yet the trainer was not winded at all. He fixed me with a sardonic look.

"However did I manage that, Simeon?"

"You—you used the sun, didn't you?"

He smiled. "They say it's quite bright. Hard to look at for very long. But you found that out for yourself at the start of the match." Frederick clasped his hands behind his back and began to pace in the center of the ring. "That was a weapon, Simeon. But you didn't use it. Why?"

I was still panting, still recovering from my skirmish. My head felt heavy. I had no answer for him.

"Listen to me." Frederick turned on his heel and stared hard at me, while Posey sat on his rear, rubbing at his legs.

"Anything can be a weapon," he said. "Anything. Your arms and armor, of course. But also the sun," he gestured towards the gatehouse, "the wind, the walls that surround you, the dirt at your feet … "

Suddenly, Frederick flicked his toe into the ground and kicked up a cloud of dust right into my face. I coughed and sputtered and had to rub at my eyes. The next sight I had was Frederick, now a hand's span away from me. His round, colorless eyes glinted, the only spark of life in that plain, expressionless face. He spoke very low, so that only I could hear him. "Your eyes, your fingers, your legs, your blood, your *mind*. Oh, yes. That especially. Whatever can be put to use. Whatever extends your will … is a weapon."

The sun broke fully behind the trainer. There was a distant murmur, the skirmishers coming out from breakfast for the day's training. Frederick's eyes never wavered. His fingers came towards me, long and spindly and pale. He lifted my chin so that I couldn't avoid his gaze.

I thought I caught a glimpse of fondness. It was brief, fleeting.

"You have many weapons, Simeon."

Four of us sat huddled around the table in my cell: Kik, Posey, Sergeant Tate, and me. We were playing cards for farthings, old tin coins that were almost worthless these days (ever since King Niall VIII minted a billion of them to pay off his army). Thirty-five farthings trade for about a pence, if you can find a banker or a merchant willing to take them. There aren't many. It was the closest thing there was to worthless money in the Kingdom of the Four Duchies. But here in the Escola, they still served as currency. You could always worm a few from a cook, or a jailor, or a nurse if you didn't mind doing a little grunt work. The tin pieces could then be traded back later for an extra portion of honey cake, or a dram of gin, that kind of thing. You could also steal any farthings that weren't being looked after close enough, which was no doubt how Posey had accumulated the sack he brought into my cell.

By now a kind of companionship had evolved between the three warriors-in-training. From Posey's endless chatter, I could recite every detail—real and imagined—in the wild, winding course of the man's life. If you paid too close attention, he contradicted himself, sometimes profoundly, but Posey's voice was always a source of amusement, if not accurate history. He brought the brusque joviality of an army barracks wherever he went.

Kik was more reticent. She came from an island off the northern coast that was peopled with a seafaring tribe who shared neither the language, nor the customs, nor the faith of any of the Duchies. What she called a rebellion, the Kingdom deemed piracy, which was how she had ended up on the Rolls. Most of the time, Kik held her thoughts to herself, but every once in a while, she would erupt with a belly laugh so deep and powerful it shook the room like an earthquake.

It was the beginning of Frost Lick Month, and in this part of the Kingdom, that meant a succession of cold, sunless, gray days, interspersed with deluges of rainstorms. A nasty one had been blowing over the Escola since the night before, leaving the courtyard flooded with a hand's breadth of water. Too dangerous for maneuvers, much less any skirmishing, which meant we warriors enjoyed a rare day off. After some light exercise indoors, they opened our cell doors and let us visit for a few hours, under guard of course. Sergeant Tate, never one for subtle graces, suggested a card game, and since he happened to be closest to my cell when the idea came to him, promptly volunteered me to host it.

I'll confess the fare I had to offer was paltry. Like everyone else, I had managed to stash away a small amount of food when no one was paying attention in the kitchen. Some black bread and raisins, a half a round of cheese, a flagon of porter (pilfering that had been a feat). All of it was technically contraband, so of course Sergeant Tate helped himself to the greater part of my spoils. But I didn't mind. For a short span of that afternoon, when I didn't think overlong on it, I almost felt like I was in an apartment, playing a game of Castes among friends.

Through the closed shutter of the barred window in my cell, the din of the downpour droned outside. A trickle of water seeped between the slats, scurried down the stones, and hissed in a small fire I had built up in a brazier. One of Tate's guards had brought in a lantern, and between the two flames, my jail cell almost looked cheery.

Sergeant Tate took a long pull from the flagon and spread the deck of cards flat across the table in a line. He flipped them over in a wave, then back again, a skill he showed off whenever he could. The cards were old, bent, and faded. I suspected they were marked, since the largest pile of farthings, by far, had accumulated at his part of the table.

"Alright, boys," Tate said cheerily and dipped his head to Kik. "And lady. Next game. Let's have your toll."

We each tossed a farthing into the middle of the table, and eight cards slid across to the tables' corners.

"Y'know," Posey mused aloud, peering at his cards with a disapproving scowl, "in the army we played Blind Fives for gin. More a game of chance, mind you. Though if you're good with numbers you can pad the odds a bit. I'm 'bout ready for a switch—"

"We're playing Castes," Tate cut over him. "Fives is for children and cretins—and soldiers, I guess." He sniffed. "Castes is a gentleman's game."

"Well then how'd you get so good at it?"

Kik barked with laughter, which was followed by Tate drubbing the side of Posey's head. I tried to hide my smile. Posey was going to be cheated out of every last farthing he had stolen. I looked down at the hand I had been dealt.

Beggars and Farmers mostly, and none of them in any sequence. But three had pictures showing clusters of men working mills, binding books, and stoking forges, which gave me hope. I had drawn a trio of Journeymen, the seven, eight, and nine. We put in our first bets, traded in for new cards, and it was all I could do to keep my face steady. Of the five I took, one depicted six masons chiseling away at a cornerstone, turning my trio of Journeymen into a quartet. One was a useless Farmer. But the last three were a good draw in their own right. Each card depicted a triangle of three different pictures: gleaming, golden crowns on one, stooped and sullied peasants on the other, proud and cocksure noblemen in between. The three of Beggars, three of Nobles, and three of Crowns.

I cast a furtive glance around the table. Kik's face remained as impassive as ever. Posey was smirking and rubbing the stubble around his chin, and by now I had played enough hands with him to know the cards he was holding were garbage. Tate narrowed his eyes. Though he pretended to be studying his hand, his eyes were peering over the top of his cards so that he could study mine. After a time, the sergeant called for the final bet.

Posey drew a loud breath in through his nose, let it out as a satisfied grunt, and pushed the last twenty farthings he had into the middle of the table.

"All in," he announced. With a meaningful glare at Tate, he added. "Let's see if this, uh, gentleman's got a pair of stones on him!"

Kik cocked her head thoughtfully. Her dark eyes roved the pot, and I thought she might fold. But with a slow, fluid motion, she flicked a matching number of coins to join Posey's.

"I got the stones," she smiled.

"Me, too." I pushed my coins into the pot.

We waited for Tate. He made a show of indecisiveness that would have been worthy of a bad theatre troupe. Finally, he shook his head mournfully, laid down his cards without showing them, and slid them to the bottom of the deck.

"I'm out," he announced.

"What?" Posey's head spun. "You haven't folded all game. What're you about?"

The sergeant leaned back and laced his fingers behind his head. "Somebody's pulled a good hand. I can tell."

"Yeah?"

"Oh, yeah. Gotta know how to read your table, Posey."

"Or their cards," I muttered under my breath.

I don't know if he heard me, but the corner of Tate's mouth curled a fraction of an inch. He crossed his arms over his chest and said,

"Let's see what you have, warriors."

Kik flipped her cards over with a firm, confident flourish.

"Two pair," she said, rolling the r's with her accent. "Twos of the Nobles and the Beggars, Eights of the Journeyfellows and the cursed Crowns."

Posey blurted a triumphant noise and slapped his cards over Kik's. In his enthusiasm, he almost knocked the table over.

"Gotcha beat, sailor girl! Look here …"

For once, Posey hadn't bluffed. He had a quartet of Beggars, nine to twelve, and a pair of ones, Farmer and Crown. "How d'you like that? Set you all up this whole game, didn't I? Ha!"

His hairy arms stretched across the table for the farthings. Tate was shaking his head even before I had shown my cards.

"Hold on," I said.

Posey paused, his fingers dug into the coins, his face still glowing with expectation. I drew the moment out longer than I needed to.

"You can't beat a run and a pair," Posey challenged.

"I can," I replied, and, flipping my cards over, one by one, added, "and I did."

Posey's bottom lip quivered. His mouth gaped dumbly at my winning hand. From the other end of the table, Tate was clapping sarcastically. Even Kik nodded with approval.

"You little prick," Posey snarled. "You lucky little prick." He flopped back in his chair and waved for me to take the pot. "How'd you pull a quartet and a three of a kind?"

I shrugged innocently. "Like you said. I'm just a lucky little prick."

The sergeant took a swig from the flagon, wiped the dribble from his chin, and leaned over the table edge with a knowing wink.

"Or maybe blessed," he slurred.

Something in the way Tate was smirking at me made my cheeks and ears warm. It suddenly occurred to me that while my mates in the Escola would only know what I had told them about why I ended up on the Rolls, my guards would have the records. Apparently, Sergeant Tate had read mine at some point.

"You do know," he said with a hiccup, "you poor sinners have been playing against a priest. Isn't that right, Divinity?"

Now my face was burning, as hot as the fire in the brazier.

Kik's head tilted once more, while Posey blinked incomprehensively. "What the hell're you talking about, Sarge?" Posey asked.

Tate's eyes glowed with drunken mischief. "Young Simeon here— excuse me, Divine Simeon—came to the Escola ... from a seminary."

"Oh, c'mon!" Posey scoffed.

"He ... he's a man of god?" Kik's eyebrows lifted.

My face fell, and my hands felt numb. I couldn't even gather up my winnings. When I finally lifted my eyes, I saw Kik first. She had an intent, inscrutable expression, as if she was no longer sure what to make of me. Posey looked much the same. I felt the sergeant clapping me on the shoulder hard.

"Yes, indeed," he chuckled. "Simeon's a holy. Here, I'll tell you his story—"

"No," I said, my voice thick. "I'll tell it. It's my story to tell. I'm not a holy. But I was in a seminary ..."

My three companions settled in their chairs and passed around the remnants of my ale, as I recounted how a tutor's son ended up taking a scribe's oath in the Seminary of the Fifth Pantheon, how he spent more than a year of long and lazy days copying records for other people's profits, how the first girl he ever bedded ended up with a baby, and how that girl's father, an earl, had him shunted off to the Rolls. I left nothing out. It must have been a spell-binding tale, for not even Posey interrupted, except once to guffaw and make a crude gesture when I got to the part about my dalliance with Kara in the tower.

All the while, I felt a strange relief wash over me, a lightness, as if a weight I hadn't known I was carrying had been lifted from my shoulders. By the time I finished, the storm outside had stopped, and the flames in the lantern and brazier were starting to gutter. No one spoke a word for an uncomfortably long time, though Sergeant Tate's head bobbed slightly and, I couldn't help but think, approvingly. It was Posey who finally broke the silence.

"Holy *hells*!" His enormous hands thumped together like a peal of thunder. "That's the funniest damned thing I ever heard! Ho-ho, *shit*! My man blasphemed the gods *and* breeded with a noble's bitch? In a seminary? Ho-ho! You're a spawn!"

Tate patted me on the shoulder again, and when our eyes met, he gave me a wink.

"Story like that was bound to come out sooner or later. Don't worry, Divinity. We'll still flog you."

"You'll be cursed if you do," Posey snorted. "You hit a priest, and your prick'll fall off. Everyone knows that."

I held up my hands, smiling with relief.

"Your manhood is safe. Like I said, I was just a scribe." Seeing Kik's incomprehension, I added, "Even though I took an oath, I wasn't going to become a priest. No one would ever call me 'Divinity.'"

Posey waved his hand as if such a trifling detail could detract from a story he was, no doubt, already embellishing beyond all recognition. While Posey blathered on laughing, Tate began to sweep up his deck of cards. Only Kik seemed troubled. She tapped the table for my attention and asked, with an almost child-like sincerity:

"You—you took oath to gods? You serve them?"

"Yeah," I nodded. "For a while. For all the good it did me."

We gathered in the shadow of the gatehouse, the morning yet to break behind us. Every student, every guard, every cook and cleaner had been brought outside in a throng that was kept more or less together by Tate and a line of spearmen. Puffs of fog trailed into the air from our breath. As we clapped our arms and stamped our feet against the biting wind, our guards stared sullenly at us from within their bundled cloaks.

Duggan, the lunatic who talked to his thumb, was chained to the towering white obelisk in the center of the courtyard. He had been stripped to his waist, but his neck, arms, hands, legs, feet, even his stomach were bound tight. His head sunk as low as the manacle beneath his chin would allow. I think he may have been weeping.

Kik, Posey, and I were together, and though we had been put with the rest of the Escola, the other students naturally afforded the warriors a pace or two of separation. None of us knew precisely why we had been roused from our cells and made to stand in the freezing dawn without our breakfast. That didn't stop Posey from opining.

"It's going to be a flogging," he announced. "Saw my share of these in the army. Poor crazy bastard."

I had no reason to dispute Posey's prediction, but Kik was shaking her head.

"Nobody get flogged with face front. This … be bad."

One of Duggan's fellow skirmishers, a tall, stringy man with a round head that reminded me of a scarecrow's, chimed in.

"Whatever he gets won't be any less than he deserves."

The skirmisher next to him asked, "Why, what's he done now?"

"Nothing," the scarecrow replied. "That's been the problem with him all along. Just lolls around talkin' to that damned thumb of his."

That was answered with a round of murmuring, mostly in agreement. It seemed to be common table knowledge among the skirmishers that Duggan was hopeless as a gladiator. I didn't hear a single man speak up for him. Posey raised his voice to nearly a bellow.

"Whatever he did, I *still* say it'll be a flogging. I once had a captain, a right flinty demon, who'd have the whip man work your frontside all around your prick so that every time you'd—"

Tate cut him off with a shout.

"Shut it! Here comes the Trainer."

From a doorway on the far side of the courtyard, Frederick's form emerged. He was followed by another, I couldn't tell who it was. Tate addressed us all in a dark, warning tone.

"Listen close. Every one of you better keep your eyes on this. No matter what happens, you *watch* it. And don't make a sound. If I hear so much as a fart, the man that passed it will find himself up there next to Duggan. So help me, he will."

Frederick crossed the length of the courtyard without so much as acknowledging the gathering he had convened. In his wake, struggling to keep up, was Dr. Broward, carrying a medicine satchel. When Frederick came to the obelisk he paused to whisper something in Duggan's ear. I heard Duggan respond, "He c-can't," before he fell into a fit of sobbing.

Frederick drew back as if to study him. But only for a moment. He turned to face us and addressed the entire crowd in his firm, toneless voice.

"Our student, Duggan, attempted to escape the boundaries of the Escola last night."

There were a few startled gasps, for though it was a subject that we often fantasized about, no one had actually tried to break out of the fortified school. Every door and window was barred, and it seemed like every ten paces you took, you ran into another guard.

"That is an unpardonable offense. It is worse than refusing to fight. What it reveals is a lack of will. It shows that Duggan doesn't have the heart to serve his sentence on the Rolls."

Frederick paused to sweep his gaze slowly over the crowd. He was apprising us, one at a time, as if weighing each man upon scales of his own devising. Judging from his expression, found us little better than Duggan. I shifted on my feet uncomfortably, but kept my face forward.

"Look closely, gladiators," he continued, "pay heed. Any man who attempts to escape from his lawful confinement on the Rolls, any man who ever declines to fight, any man who doesn't have the heart to be a gladiator … forfeits his heart."

Frederick concluded his terse announcement. Duggan hadn't moved. His shoulders trembled slightly, but otherwise he was perfectly still. Frederick nodded at Dr. Broward.

The doctor passed her hand over the length of her face. She looked pale and unsteady as she fumbled through her satchel. Posey whispered from the side of his mouth.

"She's drunk."

For once, Posey was right. Dr. Broward was mumbling to herself, and hiccupping, and warbling on her feet. She was so far in her cups, I wondered what medicine she could possibly practice. At last, she brought out a shining metal scalpel and, without bothering to clean it, staggered over to the obelisk.

Still Duggan wouldn't lift his head. Dr. Broward pried at Duggan's eyes, scarcely bothering to examine them, and felt around his neck, and put her ear to his chest. She gave him a kindly pat on the shoulder in what almost seemed like a gesture of apology—or farewell. Duggan stirred, and I heard him rasp,

"M-mind y'don't hurt my dear thumb."

"I won't touch it," she answered quietly.

The doctor plunged the scalpel into Duggan's abdomen.

A horrible scream tore the quiet and echoed across the walls. Duggan's body exploded with contortions. He writhed, his veins pulsated, his muscles constricted. I saw his jaw open wide, he seemed to be biting at the air. But the chains held him in place. He could not twist a finger's span away from Dr. Broward's relentless blade. With every cut, the doctor rasped, "I'm sorry," until a wide, straight gash had been opened in Duggan's left side. A river of red flowed from the wound, puddling at his feet. The fall of his blood sounded like rain drizzling down a rooftop. Duggan kept twitching, kept screaming.

"Finished yet?" Frederick asked.

Dr. Broward scowled at him. Despite her inebriation, the doctor kept a steady, practiced hand. She cut the final length of incision, withdrew her scalpel and spoke some final words to Duggan, but he was surely too pain-wracked to understand them. With a last, dark glance at Frederick, the doctor stormed away, her satchel clattering on her shoulder.

Frederick looked at us once more to make sure we were still watching. He approached Duggan, and without pausing, thrust his hand deep into Duggan's chest.

"Dear gods," Posey breathed. Kik shook her head. No one else made a sound.

When Frederick pulled his forearm free, he was holding a quivering pink mass of flesh. Duggan's heart squirted blood through the trainer's gore-drenched fingers. He paced the length of the guards' perimeter to show the awful thing to us. Casual, as if he were passing a piece of food off to a table-mate. Not a man among us dared avert his eyes. Kik made the sign of the gods. I felt as if I was viewing the whole terrible spectacle from the highest row of an arena.

"Remember," Frederick said, and I thought he was only speaking to me, "if this is the death you want to die, then by all means. Run. Try to escape. Tell your minders you won't fight. You'll remember this sight—when it's your heart pulled from your chest."

CHAPTER TWELVE

The days drifted by, unmarked and uncounted, within the cloister of the Escola. A steady, relentless stream of fighting, and drilling, and eating, and more fighting. The skirmishers worked through various weaponry—javelins, tridents, nets, the glade (a short, stocky spear with a ridiculously curved and ornate head)—while our exercises only ever used the gladiator sword, for that tool was "the culmination of the craft," as Frederick liked to say. For a time, the men could talk of nothing but Duggan's execution. I always found an excuse to leave whenever the talk turned to him. It was a foul thing to have been forced to witness.

Not long after that awful morning, Frederick brought weights into our training regimen. Though at first the work left my limbs burning with fire, the strength I soon gained from hoisting casks over my head and pulling sleds loaded with quarry rocks and curling cauldrons was beyond anything I could have imagined. Twice, they had to exchange my padded armor to accommodate my broadened chest and arms. Frederick complained of the expense, but he didn't beat me for it. Even Posey began to look at me with new respect.

We trained, day after day, week after week. Constant learning, constant repetition, yet the work never became monotonous, for Frederick was constantly changing it, if only slightly, and always to make it harder.

The seasons passed. Freezing rain turned to fat flakes of snow that piled up in the corners and gray slush that covered the grounds, which the kitchen staff were made to sweep so that the rest of us could keep on with our training. Then one day it warmed again, and the sparrows returned, tiny harbingers of spring, to flit through the windows and nest in the rafters. In the cracks of the walls, weeds with slender pink flowers began to poke through. The girls in the kitchen wore less clothing, and blushed a little longer when we leered at them.

But nothing else really changed about the Escola. In its bones, it was as it had been since the night I first arrived. Rock walls, beige ground, a patch of sky overhead, and an endless routine. The tedium only broke when I would collapse in my bed each night and plummet into sleep so deep, it seemed a foretaste of death. Some days I would have welcomed the end.

I also stopped praying. New habits can be the hardest to break, but this one proved easy to leave aside again. The truth was, I had nothing to say to the gods. And since it seemed they had nothing to say to me, I decided I had better stop bothering them.

One day, without announcement or fanfare, I mastered the craft. Or the craft had mastered me. Either way, I was told, without so much as a congratulations or a handshake, that my training was coming to an end.

Late one night, I was sitting on the edge of my bed, watching the last of my lantern's light oil sputter. On a lark, I decided to spend a small portion of my sleep time for writing. I had wrangled some scraped paper and cheap ink from one of the cooks and was trying to remember Amadán, that ponderous and beguiling tome, trying to work out bits and pieces of verses as they came to me. It was like snatching after minnows, but every so often I would recall a line, and it pleased me for some reason to practice "severaling," my old trick of flowing script, to record the mad old prophet's heresies. My door opened with a creak, and there was Tate, slouched in my doorway, a bone lantern lighting his unshaven face. He looked tired and put upon.

"Simeon. Frederick told me to tell you to put out that damned light and get to sleep. You're fighting a match tomorrow. In Niallex."

The Arena of Niallex was a wonder.

The sights and sounds of the city left me dizzied. An endless run of stone, and markets, and spectacles, and people—so many people—of all different tongues, and dresses, and features. I rode in a dog cart (which, in the daytime, was all that could fit through the packed avenues in the heart of the city). Though it was a humble conveyance, when Tate bellowed, "Make way for a gladiator!" the throngs begrudgingly parted for our cart.

We came to a high wall of ancient bricks that marked a kind of boundary between the commerce outside and what lay within. We followed the road along the wall until we reached a keep, its great doors left open and its portcullis drawn high. Lines of people passed through freely, or gathered around stalls to haggle and barter, but not a guard or watchman bothered to challenge our approach.

"This was here before the city," Tate explained. He had to raise his voice to be heard over the curtain of noise that seemed to hang over every piece of space in Niallex. "It was originally a trading fort. But they made it out of sandstone, so it was easy to sack. When Niall the Eighth built out the first wards of the city, he left the walls standing, but scraped all the buildings inside and turned it into an arena. Which turned out to be a good bet—"

"That ain't how it happened," one of the guards in the cart. "First off, it was Niall the Fifth who built the wards. And second, everyone knows the arena used to be an asylum. That's why the walls were so shoddy."

"Shut it, Brockman. Why would anyone go to the trouble of building a keep just to hold lunatics inside?"

"Depends on the lunatics," Brockman said, with a wink to me.

I had never seen so much white veined marble. It was as if a mountain of alabaster had been brought into Niallex and carved up by artisans. The arena itself was set near the front of the grounds, a soaring, shimmering bowl with an undulating rim, almost like the lip of a clam's shell, which gleamed as bright as a pearl in the sunlight. A great white banner fluttered from a spire that jutted into the sky from one of its ends. Beneath its shadow, countless inns, and betting houses, and baths, and walled villas spread from one end of the sandstone walls to the other. Not a spot of trash or graffiti could be seen. Incense and spices swirled in the air to cover the smells of the city.

It was the villas, in particular, that held my attention. As we passed by, I noticed some were simple cottages, while others looked like mansions, with fountains, and hanging gardens, and statuary. All of them, though, whether humble or grand, had high, thick walls with locked iron gates and a pair of guards barring the entrances. When we came upon an especially rich one, I asked Tate about it.

"That would be Colm's quarters," he replied. The other guards nodded knowingly, as if out of respect. "Pretty nice, eh? I hear he's got a wine cellar down there that the Lord Mayor borrows from." Tate elbowed me in the ribs. "You win forty matches without so much as a hangnail, and you'll have a place like that, too."

My mouth dropped. For the first time in my life, I saw what a common-born man could have, and I'll confess, it whetted my appetite for this new trade of mine. As if sensing my aspirations, Tate added,

"Don't get ahead of yourself, Divinity. It's a rough room with beer and bread until you start making some money. And today's just a training heat. No one's dying, so it won't count for much. But who knows? Colm started off as you are."

With that thought to buoy my spirits the rest of my journey, we came into the arena. I wish I could describe the grandeur within, but I only caught a few snatches of the sights before I was shuttled down into a warren of tunnels. But what I saw took my breath away. It was like being cast into a sparkling sea of white granite. Arches, corridors, plazas and pillars, even the bins for garbage, were all crafted from the finest stone in the Duchies. It almost made the seminary seem a paltry place. We went down a run of steps to a portico where a massive slate board had been hung upon a wall. This was the oddsmakers' board, and around it buzzed a hive of sharp-looking men and women, chalking the names and wagers of the day's matches. The air was satiated with the smell of spiced wine and roasting meats. It was intoxicating.

But no sooner had I swiveled my head to take it all in, than I found myself in darkness. Tate and his men led me into a queue of porters, and armorers, and cleaners, and together we shuffled down another stairwell, this one like a corkscrew that seemed to have no ending until, at last, it opened into an arched stone tunnel that was as wide as a main street. The vaulted ceiling was held aloft by pillars every dozen paces, followed, more often than not, by a junction with another equally massive tunnel. Near the roof, there were slits for air and slivers of daylight.

We walked for some length until, at last, I was brought to a holding cell. A plate of bread and olives and a jug of small beer waited on a table. Tate found the sergeant of the ward, a retired soldier with a bad leg and a scar that ran down the length of his neck. The man was named Anders. The two seemed to know each other well enough. After they traded their news and their grumblings about work, Tate got around to telling Anders who I was, and signed a form to officially transfer my custody to the Niallex Arena.

Before he left, though, Tate motioned for me to come to the bars that separated my cell from the corridor. Through the space between, he extended a few fingers of his hand for mine.

"The gods be with you, Divinity," he joked. I rolled my eyes, but then he grew serious and dropped his voice to a hushed murmur. "Listen. Even though it's a skirmish, you're fighting for a prize. Make no mistake about it."

I stared at his shadowed face and wondered what he meant. He leaned close so that his cheek touched the bars.

"You've been favored to win, Simeon. So win. If you don't… Frederick will be disappointed. Good luck."

I nodded and gripped a couple of his fingers. Tate took his leave, and Anders and two of his assistants came into the cell to outfit me for the match.

The shield was round and much the same size as what I had trained with. Anders called it a "platter," I suppose because of its size—bigger than a target shield, but still much smaller than a proper cavalryman's shield. There would be no armor; in fact, not even a shirt. Beneath Anders' watchful gaze, I had to change into a white loin cloth and a slitted skirt.

"The crowd loves to see your beautiful chests," Anders explained with a leer that left me wondering who it was that enjoyed it most. "Here."

He handed me a metal blade. My face must have shown my surprise.

"Usually, you don't get your weapon 'til you're in the arena," he said. "But this here's just a trainer. It's got no point, no edge. Feel it."

So it was. I doubt it could cut the loaf on my table. But it seemed to float in my grip. I slashed it through the air in the space of my cell.

"Little lighter than the prick you're used to playing with, isn't it?"

"Yeah." I practiced a twirling parry and was amazed at how fast I could maneuver the blade. "How come we don't use these in the Escola?"

"Well, look how you're making it dance," the jailor answered, as if it were perfectly obvious.

It made sense. After months of swinging a weighted down hunk of oak tree in sword drills, an actual sword, made of lighter steel, felt as easy as lifting air. As my match was only a training skirmish with hardly any crowd in the stands, there would be no priests to perform rites or blessings, so I was left to prepare myself however I liked.

"So, uh," Anders dabbed at the sweat on his forehead and licked his lips before continuing. "You want to get on your knees and pray? Heard you was some kind of a priest once. I could sure use a blessing. What kind of priest ends up on the Rolls, I wonder, hmm?"

I drew a step closer, holding his eyes with a hard gaze and replied in a dead voice.

"The kind who cursed the gods. And forever carries their curse."

It had the effect I hoped. If there was one trait all soldiers shared, it was a primal fear of omens. Anders' face blanched.

"I-I'll just, ehm, leave you to it, then," he stammered, and scuttled away.

I nibbled a few bites of bread, ate one olive, and left the beer in its jug. "Only eat enough so that you don't fight on an empty stomach," Frederick had once explained. "And liquid courage," he said, "will make you brave, and dead. Let your foe drink himself into a bold stupor. An Escola warrior keeps his senses as sharp as his sword."

I didn't have to wait long before I was brought out of my cell and into the arena.

Walking up the steps and into the ring, I felt oddly at ease. When we passed beneath the portcullis, I touched my blade to a capstone where the gladiators' salute had been inscribed, the letters faded from countless touches of weapons and outstretched fingers. I felt small once I stepped into the arena. It seemed to stretch all the way to the horizon, a smooth floor of packed sand hemmed in with walls twenty feet high. There were only a few hundred in the audience, and they clapped politely as a woman's voice boomed through a trumpet to announce the training heat. She mispronounced my name, which annoyed me more than it should have, and when she said I had come from the Escola for my first training match in an arena, a bawdy group of men in the front row took up to chanting,

"Virgin! Virgin! Virgin!"

I don't remember the name of the man I fought. He was of my age and height, lighter skinned, much lighter in weight. Tate told me after the match that the poor bastard had only been trained for a few weeks in some hell-hole of a jail, and that he had been promised his freedom—outright freedom from the Rolls—if he could best an Escola warrior.

He fought boldly for the chance. But the match was brief. He came at me with wild, sweeping blows that would have worked better in a field of wheat than a field of battle. I let him take a couple of passes, parried the one strike that came somewhat near my shield, and then brought a swift sideways cut into his kidney. I heard the wind leave him. He nearly crumpled over. A moment later, I added two more purple bruises to his torso. From the way he was trying to hold himself upright, one of the blows looked as if it might have broken a rib.

I remember his face, a boy's face, smeared in dust and streaming with tears. I wanted to tell him I was sorry. But he howled and made a desperate charge. I cleared the blow easily and brought the handle of my sword down onto the top of his head.

There was no need to ask him to yield. He lay sprawled in the dust, unconscious.

I had won.

My heart was thrumming like a tambourine, not from any exertion but from the exultation. I had defeated a man. Brought him down through my will. The feeling in my chest was better than wine, better than love.

I looked up into the crowd, saw only blurred faces and wisps of censer smoke, and was rewarded with sustained, respectful applause. A few whistles. The men who had shouted "virgin" were now raising goblets in mock toasts. I drank in their praise, loving every moment.

Some who were sitting in the front rows reached over the edge. I saw a few metallic glints fall like rain. They were tossing coins. Gratitude for the victorious gladiator who had entertained his audience with a spectacle. I hurried over and started to scoop up the coins, and the applause turned into laughter. I couldn't make out what anyone was saying, but it was obvious it was at my expense. Out of one of the shadowed gates, Sergeant Tate came over, shaking his head and looking a little embarrassed.

"Don't stoop, Simeon. They'll send out some foundlings to gather up your gratitude. Just make sure you tip the child that brings it." He paused and eyed me with favor, and despite my apparent breach of etiquette, my chest was still swelling.

"That was good," he said with a nod. As he led me back through the shadowed gladiators' entrance, he added, "You're almost ready."

I returned to the Escola before dawn the next day. My fellow novices commemorated my triumph with the kind of bawdy, foul-mouthed backslapping that passes for congratulations among fighting men. The kitchen cooks served me a bowl of my favorite gravy with a plate of biscuits still warm from the oven. Friendly handshakes and congratulations greeted me at every corner. The Escola almost seemed a pleasant place.

But it was a short-lived joy. As I was licking creamy sauce off my fingers, Frederick walked up to me, as dour and stoic as ever. He knocked the biscuits away, pronounced my performance "a bland mediocrity with an atrocious defense," and proceeded to put me through the most pitiless day of shield work I had endured in all my training. When I returned to my cell that night, my left arm felt as heavy as a bar of iron.

But Tate, Kik, and Posey were waiting for me, ready to celebrate with another card game. Once again, we played Castes long into the night, and once again Tate relieved us of our ill-gotten farthings (most of my gladiators' gratitude was gone after the first five or six hands). But the sergeant made up for it, in his flinty way of accounting favors, by treating us to two bottles of aged Niallex port. It went down sweet and strong, and almost made up for the ache in my arm and the loss of my coins.

By the time the watch changed, I was well into inebriety, laughing like an idiot, swearing oaths of eternal friendship and fidelity, losing my money and not giving a damn. It seemed the gods didn't give a damn either. But, then, their blessings are always fleeting. Like wine. A delight that drains away all too quickly, and leaves you emptied, and tired, and saddened, with only the faintest memory of what they were.

That card game would be our last time together.

And those were the last people I counted as friends in my life.

———————

I was brought down from my cell early the next morning, still stiff and bleary from drinking the night before. My mouth felt like it had been scoured with a wire brush, and my temples thumped angrily. The gray gloom of half-light that hung over the Escola courtyard matched my mood.

The sound of our footsteps, Tate's and mine, crunching over the gravel on the way to the training ring, was the only noise that broke the silence. I rubbed at the stubble on my cheeks, dreading the morning, when I noticed something that brought me to a halt. We were near the gatehouse, and great iron portcullis had been left wide open. A prisoners' wagon, like the one that had brought me to the Escola, waited in the opening. A team of mules had already been hitched, some luggage was tied down in the back, and the driver was working to release the brake. A lone figure sat crouched inside the cage.

Tate drew a few steps back and pretended to slowly retie his sandals. I gaped at the wagon for a moment, until I finally caught the sergeant's hint and made my way over to the gate.

The person inside the wagon was wearing a traveling cloak, but I could see the manacles on the wrists. She threw back her hood at the sound of my approach, jerked her head toward me, and smiled.

"Kik?"

The smile on Kik's face broadened. "Simeon, my friend."

A glow warmed in her dark eyes. And something else. She almost looked … relieved.

"What's happening?" I asked.

"Is my time to go." She shrugged, as if she were as indifferent to her fate as she was to the weather. "Posey leave little while ago. Someplace east, I think. He will fight well, wherever he go. As to me, I go to Dheas Duchy. Big city. Funny sounding name. Agent waits for me there. Says a woman make much money in their arenas. We'll see."

I shook my head dumbly, trying to piece together what was happening.

"I—I'm sorry," was all I could say.

But Kik only hunched her shoulders. "Is my fate, no? I sign good contract with agent. I hope. Maybe see ocean again. I will hope." Another shrug. She twirled her finger, making the chain of her manacles jingle, and looked upwards. "The gods are on the move. What can I do but follow?"

The weight of the moment settled on me. The odds of us ever seeing one another again were about as likely as the odds of us surviving twenty years on the Rolls. This would be my only farewell. I wanted to make it meaningful. I choked down tears.

"I hope you fight well, Kik."

"Yes. Yes." She nodded. "That good. I like your hope. But, ehm … I like better your blessing."

That took me off guard.

"You want me to bless you?"

"I do."

My first reaction was the one I had been taught in the seminary.

"Only a priest can bestow a blessing, Kik. I was only a scribe for hire. It—it wouldn't be proper." The excuse sounded paltry and Kik's expression said as much. "Besides," I continued, "every arena will bring in priests before your match. They'll give you any kind of blessing you want."

Kik leaned back against the bars of her cage and gazed thoughtfully at the looming gateway. The haze was finally beginning to clear. In some distant barnyard beyond the horizon, a rooster crowed. Kik broke her silence with a sudden, scoffing vehemence.

"Blessing from a stranger?" She shook her head with disgust. "Is useless as a fart. Only one who *knows* you can give you blessing. Whether priest or scriber, however you say, is no matter. You took oath to the gods, Simeon. What you speak below will be heard above. You know me. Will you—will you not call the gods for me?"

I wanted to tell her no. Truth was, as I stood there on the cold gravel and thought about it, I was no longer sure what I believed about the gods, whether they were or were not, whether they deigned to care about our affairs, whether they heard us. To presume to invoke them and to proclaim their intentions would feel … false. But when I looked into Kik's face, the guileless hope, I saw, for a moment, what true faith looked like.

It would have been a sin to douse something so beautiful. A few words would cost me nothing. And as for the theology of who could bestow blessings and who couldn't, well, it occurred to me how far beyond Gathena's admonition I now was. I, Simeon, was completely free to bless whoever I damned well deemed worthy, for whatever it was worth. Kik was an easy choice.

"Bow your head."

Kik shuffled close to the cage bars and did as I bade her. I touched my forehead, chest, and stomach, and squeezed my hand through the bars to touch the top of her head. I quickly cobbled together a few pieces of the paidir I remembered, garnished with some poetic verse of my own making, and pronounced the words with all the solemnity of the highest holy day in the basilica.

"Kik, beloved of the gods. The blessing of Our Father Belanos, and all the gods and goddesses of the Holy Fifth Pantheon, and the one god of Amadán, be upon you and remain with you always. May your arm never fail and your heart never falter. May your name never be forgotten."

Looking satisfied, she rose and stood as best she could in the cage, made a sign of the gods with her forefinger, and thanked me. The wagon's driver was ready. With a snap of the reins, the mules trudged forward, and Kik's wagon rumbled through the gate. I watched her leave, wondering if my blessing would do her any good.

Loneliness.

That old, familiar companion had come again. Alone I woke up in my cell house; alone I went to bed. The time between was an intolerable chore. Drills, and sword work, and meals that tasted like nothing, and boredom. I was not alone, as such. The Escola was as packed as ever—with guards, novices old and new, kitchen cooks, medics—but my two companions, those who had first learned the craft with me, who had lived in the cells next to me, who drank and ate and fought and laughed with me, my mates, they were gone.

Once, I asked Frederick why Posey and Kik had gotten contracts while I had not. He looked at me with his inscrutable face, and stroked his moustache.

"They were ready. You're not."

I was left to ponder what that meant for two more months. In that time, Frederick continued to work with me, though it was more sporadic, and often he had nothing to say. After a new batch of novices arrived, I hardly saw him anymore. He and Tate were busy in the ring, molding the next coterie of the Escola's finest. My training had become a kind of sustained exercise, a series of practices that took the better part of the morning, beginning with footwork and ending with weights. It grew into a ritual of sorts, one I would carry on faithfully for the rest of my days.

And then one evening, my time came. I was finishing a mock fight with a newly arrived skirmisher named Aric. He was a wisp of a boy, an eager, energetic swindler from Dheas. He reminded me a great deal of Paul Little. Aric was sure he could convince Frederick to change his entered Roll to a warrior. While I was showing Aric how to better balance his weight when advancing, Frederick snuck up behind me.

"You're almost ready," he said, as if resuming an earlier conversation. It always startled me how he could vanish and appear as quiet as a mist, though I tried not to show it.

"Thanks." I toweled off the sweat from my face with a rag.

"Aric," Frederick said to the skirmisher. "You've been working hard. Tell the cook to serve you an extra portion of beef."

Aric's face lit with pride. "Thank you, sir!"

A bell rung, the signal for supper in the dining hall.

"Off you go," Frederick said, smiling.

When Aric had left, his gaze hardened.

"Tonight you will come back here, Simeon." He let out a long, contemplative breath. "After tonight … you'll be ready."

I nodded, though I had no idea what he could mean. Frederick's mouth formed a half-smile, bereft of feeling. As he turned to walk away, he offered the only hint about what awaited me.

"Yours should be a light meal this evening, Simeon. And don't drink anything harder than water."

The walls of the Escola's center ring were topped with torches that blazed in the darkness. Tendrils of smoke and shimmering waves of heat fluttered in the air above, while on the ground below, the shadows on the ground danced teasingly. A score of guardsmen dressed in mail and formal cloaks, spears and shields at the ready, stood at attention.

One of them held a standard, a pole that bore a black flag.

Beneath the banner was Frederick, hands clasped behind his back. His eyes flickered in the torchlight.

"Simeon," he said.

Coldness crept down the length of my spine when he called my name. I knew before he said another word what I was to do. The silent understanding passed between us in the span of a moment when he indicated with his eyes for me to go into the ring. A strange, detached sensation came over me as I crept down the five familiar steps to enter the ring. Sergeant Tate opened the gate, a somber expression on his face. One of his assistants was waiting for me on the other side.

"Just get it over with quick," Tate whispered as I passed through.

The guard inside handed me a platter-sized shield made of bronze and a sword. A real sword. The blade was polished steel, sharpened to a lethal sheen. It felt as light and natural as a finger on my hand.

Some twenty paces away, roaming around in a nervous circle, was Aric. All of fifteen years perhaps, no doubt proud of the reddish stubble he passed for a beard, the skirmisher who would be a warrior. Like me, he was armed with a sword and shield.

I looked over my shoulder and cast a glance at Frederick, one that I hoped would convey my anger. Once again, the trainer seemed to read my thoughts. Without any ceremony, without any greeting, Frederick held up his hand and spoke in that cold, heartless voice I loathed.

"Every novice who passes through these gates is entered on the Roll he is deemed most fitted to. But Dr. Broward is not infallible. Occasionally we make adjustments. Aric of the Duchy of Dheas believes he should be on the warriors' roll." Frederick shrugged. "We shall see. If he can best a warrior in the ring, I'll admit we made a mistake."

I started to object. "This is a mismatch. It's not fair. He-he doesn't have—"

"He doesn't have a choice anymore," Frederick's voice boomed. He was hunched forward, leaning over the wall's ledge like a vulture eyeing its prey. "Neither do you. The match will be to the death. Whoever wins ... " His head pivoted slowly so that he was facing me fully, speaking as if I were the only one in the ring. "Whoever wins will live, as a warrior."

I had to turn away to hide my disgust. Aric could scarcely be called a man. He hadn't trained nearly long enough to cover his boney frame with any muscle. I had every advantage—in weight, reach, strength, speed, and training. Killing this boy in the guise of a gladiator's match would be worse than wrong—it would be obscene.

That was not my only qualm, though.

Through the slits of the gate, Tate called out to us.

"Gladiators, salute. Then join in combat." His face pulled into a grimace, as he added, "The gods be with you."

Aric hesitated. I could see the sword quivering in his grip.

"Frederick—" I started.

"You were told to salute," he replied flatly. "You were told to fight. As you both know, gladiators who haven't the heart to fight ... forfeit their hearts. That would be a pity."

The threat brought Aric out of whatever terrified reverie he had been stuck in. I heard a clank against his shield. He held up his sword before him, and it swayed like a reed in the wind. May the gods take pity on the boy, but his voice cracked with a sob as he recited the salute. I mumbled along with him.

"We have one death to die. One chance by death to be remembered."

That night, it would be Aric's chance. I am ashamed to say his only battle was not at all memorable.

I remember the wavering torchlight, and how the dust on the ground sparkled. I remember my breath misting in the air. I remember Frederick yelling at me, but I couldn't hear his words. And Aric finally mustering the courage to commit to a real attack … and then there was a deep, red gash in his spindly thigh. My sword blade dripping. Aric was in a heap, clutching at his wound, crying like the child he was.

That was the end of the match, such as it was. At least, that is all I care to remember of the fight. But what happened after he fell has been seared into me for all time.

I kicked Aric's sword to the other side of the ring and stood over him. The cut in his leg was deep. It must have hit an artery for all the blood that was flowing. A dark, crimson rivulet gushing in a steady rhythm. The ground beneath him quickly puddled. Aric whimpered.

"Mum …"

I wanted to say something, to do something, anything—to comfort him. I didn't want him to end like this.

"Up," I hissed at him. "Get up. You have to fight."

His face twisted with pain, and settled into an expression of betrayal, as if I had broken some kind of unspoken trust.

"Look," he blubbered, pointing at his leg. "Look what you did …"

Frederick's voice came cold and impassive:

"You were right, Aric. We had you on the wrong Roll. You'd have made a poor skirmisher. Give him a swift death, Simeon."

Aric flailed his arms, kicking up the dust and smearing himself with grime. He was trying to elbow himself away from me, slink into a corner, like a wounded animal searching for shelter.

It was all in vain. There is nowhere to hide in an arena. They're always built round and open, so the spectacle can always be seen. Not really knowing what I was doing, I paced near Aric, saying useless nothings, whispers, prayers, hoping I could do him some good.

I heard a soft thud behind me, and when I turned around I saw Frederick approaching me. His steps were swift, like running water. He had a dagger in his hand. "Why are you prolonging this boy's death?"

"He—he doesn't deserve this. There's still time. If Dr. Broward—"

"Black flag," he replied, pointing to the banner. "He must die. And you will hasten it. Now."

I looked over at Aric. He was gasping, fighting for every breath. I shook my head.

In an instant, Frederick's blade was pressed to my throat. The metal felt warm for some reason. The smell of lilac and wine on Frederick's breath filled my nostrils and made me shiver. He whispered in my ear.

"You will give this boy a swift death, with all your weight—or I'll kill you."

Tears rimmed my eyes. I hated that Frederick could see me cry, almost as much as I hated him.

"Why?" I pleaded. "Killing him—there-there's no *point* to it."

The dagger blade trailed closer to my artery, but Frederick answered, his words rapid and pitiless.

"There's no point to *any* of this. Fighting, dying, living, fucking, eating, it's all pointless. It all comes to nothing. We're here, and then we're not. What remains in between—is your will."

Aric had stopped trying to move. His face had become as pale as the sand beneath his head. His mouth was moving, speaking unintelligible words only he could understand.

"Time to choose," Frederick said softly. "Your will to kill that boy. Or your will to die."

The tears wouldn't stop now. "But-but *why?*"

"Because it is my will." He moved to my side to speak into my other ear. "I can't send you out a virgin, Simeon. That is why I've held you back. Posey and Kik had killed plenty of men before the Rolls. This is your final lesson."

I let out a low moan. My head thumped like a hammer. I could hardly see for all the tears. My sword hung in my grip, as heavy as an anchor. Its grip felt … vile.

But in the end, I did as I was told. I gave Aric all my weight and thrust the point of my sword through the base of his neck, as I had been taught.

With all my will, I killed a man. The first but not the last.

PART IV

THE ARENA

CHAPTER THIRTEEN

My first match was at the Cove a small, wooden stadium about a mile outside of Niallex in a place called Ballast Bay, a brackish gulf of dredged-up islands and oyster beds rimmed with sage brush. Too shallow to be any use as a port, and too unsightly to have any allure for pleasure seekers, Ballast Bay was peopled with fishermen, the kind who walked with a stoop and a squint and cursed the city mongers who bought their catch. Besides a brothel that would probably leave you poxed if you so much as touched its door handle, the Cove served as the hub of Ballast Bay's entertainment.

The fight was unusual in how it was arranged. A local oysterman no one much liked had been caught stealing from a crab trap in the middle of the day. Ordinarily, he would have paid a fine, lost his boat, and gotten a beating, but the bastard stood twenty hands tall and weighed nearly twenty stone, and apparently had a terrible temper. A fight on the wharf turned into a bloody scrum. In the end, the oysterman had been chased into the Cove, roaring how he'd kill any man who dared try to lay a hand on him again.

This gave the arena's oddsmaker an idea. She decided to turn the oysterman's challenge into an impromptu match. The oysterman would be called out on his word, the crab trap's owner served a measure of justice, the town would have a little sport, and the oddsmaker would make a few marks.

Since the Escola happened to have a newly trained warrior on hand, it was short work to find her man an opponent. Frederick signed a contract that very afternoon—not an official match, according to the verbiage, but an "exposition"—and off I went to Ballast Bay.

I spent the night in an inn that reeked of rotting seaweed, and though there was nowhere to run, the door to my room was barred and guarded.

The place was a sty. They served a decent chowder, though. The fight was scheduled late the next morning, when the tide was out and all the bay's denizens could watch. The arena grounds were small, soggy, as if the whole place had been built on top of a bog (which it probably was). Horseflies buzzed everywhere. But the dozen rows of benches were packed. And over the hum of excitement, there was the jingle of coins changing hands.

The man's name was Peter. A native of Ballast Bay, but the picture of him—slouching, heavy-boned, round-bellied, skin tanned to umber, a sneer for the world, a fist at the ready—reminded me of countless dregs I had crossed paths with in Lower Bajebluff. He looked like he had just come out of a hard week's drinking and wanted nothing more than to hit someone for his pains. I felt a flutter in my stomach. Not from fear, though.

I knew I would kill this man.

There were no shields, no armor. Just a pair of swords tossed down to us. The blades were notched, their gleam dull from whetstones, but mine was well balanced and had a workable edge. Watching the oysterman swipe his weapon in practice strokes, pausing every few swishes to leer at me, it was clear he had only ever handled cleavers and fillet knives. The oddsmaker made her announcement, a lusty shout went up, and we went to it.

In truth, I could have just gutted the bastard the first time we came together. Peter held his sword over his head like a bouquet of flowers. But instead, I worked him the way Frederick had taught me that day I faced Posey in the training ring. After his first clumsy lunge, I went to his left flank, brought myself close into him, and struck him at his roots.

Three hacks to his knees, a stab into his upper thigh, and down Peter went like a felled tree. He turned himself over, craned his neck and looked at me. The insolence was gone. His face paled with confusion, then darkened as my shadow fell over him. His eyes went round, he opened his mouth to speak, but my blade cut his breath short. And that was how my first real match ended.

The stands of Ballast Bay's arena shook from all the cheering. Not a tear was shed for that oysterman. But as elated as they were with the killing, they were flinty with their gratitude. Eight half-pence coins, that was it. That was all that was thrown down. Even for backwater poor-mouth fishing folk, it was awfully flinty. Still, I raised my sword and saluted, and they shouted all the harder.

No sooner was the match finished, but I was packed up, manacled, and carted back to my cell at the Escola. A strange sojourn, finished as quickly and spontaneously as it had begun. As it happened, though, that first foray, an unsanctioned (and probably unlawful) gladiatorial "exposition," set the course for the rest of my career.

The next day, Frederick interrupted my morning drills to call me into one of the Escola gatehouse's inner chambers. It was a private, windowless room I had never been in before. It could have passed for a scriptorium if it had better light. A scuffed table was surrounded by chairs and held a pair of wooden candelabras. The dozen lit candles cast a soft glow over the space. A glass carafe of coffee steamed on top of a tray nearby. Otherwise, the room was bare.

Frederick sat at the head of the table. Next to him was the oddsmaker from Ballast Bay, the woman who had arranged yesterday's impromptu fight with the oysterman.

She was middle-aged, and of middling weight, and wore an unremarkable dress of light blue linen, but I could tell she had taken some pains to look presentable. Her peppery hair had been neatly combed into a silk net, and the earrings that dangled almost to her shoulders were good amethysts. Frederick introduced her as Olga Reeves.

"And this," Frederick indicated the man who sat across from Olga, "is Caspar Cartier."

My first impression of Caspar was of an unctuous money changer, the kind who would smile and clap you on the shoulder and ask after your wife and children while he sold you silver-plated dross and took your life savings. Caspar rose from his chair, flashed a set of enormous, pearly teeth, and extended his hand. Every finger wore a ring. I tried to look pleasant and made myself comfortable at the table's remaining chair.

"There he is," Caspar greeted me as if we were old friends. Every word he spoke was like a merchant extolling his finest wares. "Simeon Severals. Just finished his training, and already a master and a marvel of his craft. But

I would expect nothing less from the Escola." He turned to Frederick and clapped his hands. "Well done, sir!"

To my surprise, Frederick inclined his head. Caspar, it seemed, was one who was allowed some liberty with effusiveness.

"You're a credit to this hallowed school and her devoted trainer," Caspar said to me. He paused and his mouth bent downward in a very good mimicry of a disappointed frown. "So how, I was just asking Frederick before you came in, *how* could a warrior of the great Escola have made his debut—forgive me, Olga—in Ballast Bay, of all places?" He paused and tittered into his hand. "Pray, don't take offense. The town has its charms, I'm sure, but it's not often we see our finest diamonds paraded in an oyster pond!"

"It wasn't a debut," Frederick corrected him. "It was only an exposition."

"A fair point," Caspar said, nodding eagerly, "and a good point."

Olga spoke up, and though she answered Caspar, I noticed she was eyeing me.

"So long as it leads to profit, doesn't matter what you call it."

"Indeed," said Caspar.

Frederick cleared his throat for my attention.

"Caspar is an agent, Simeon. A good one, actually."

I nearly gasped, for in all the time I had known the trainer, I don't believe I had ever heard a compliment pass Frederick's lips.

"He was in the stands yesterday," Frederick continued. "A fateful happenstance. Caspar was able to see you perform."

"Such a happenstance!" Caspar sang.

Happenstance, indeed. The glances shared between Frederick and Caspar all but proclaimed they had an understanding. Olga too, judging by the comfortable smirk she was wearing.

"A happenstance that wouldn't have happened," said Olga, "were it not for the Cove."

"For which the Cove will receive the customary gratitude," Caspar replied. A flitter of annoyance clouded his joviality, but only for a moment. He served himself a cup of coffee from the carafe and indulged a long sip.

"Ordinarily, we agents must labor on nothing more than a roster report—name, age, weight, height, and convictions—maybe a rumor from a friendly guard, but little else. Standing on its own, your report would certainly paint a …. colorful story, Simeon. The gods know, we don't see many seminarians come through the Rolls. On paper, one might question your suitability. A bit on the lighter side, a bit young, and as I say, one would naturally wonder how a scribe would fight. But Frederick happened to mention your exposition, and so I was able to see for myself, take the full measure of the man." He leaned across the table towards me, twiddling his jeweled fingers together greedily. "What a man I saw! Here we have strength forged with skill and buttressed with stamina. But there is more." He held up a finger for emphasis and nearly tipped his coffee over. "Here," he said, his voice lowering dramatically, "we also have intelligence. And that, young man, is a rare amalgamation in this world."

From the folds of his tunic he produced a folded document and spread it before me.

"I should be honored to represent you, Simeon Severals. Here is a contract. I daresay you can read it better than I, but it's all the standard terms."

I drew the papers close and my eyes wandered over the script, a decent if somewhat crimped hand. In my days in the Vault, I had pored over and copied countless contracts, but never before had I really considered one. The verbiage was as I expected: larded with legal jargon, obscure, needlessly grandiose. The gist of it, from what I could gather trying to read hastily while three people stared at me, was that Caspar would arrange my matches, negotiate the fees for my appearances, promote my interests, and keep most of the money.

"This seems," I said a bit hesitantly, "kind of one-sided."

Caspar seemed to take no offense. To the contrary, he bowed his head in acknowledgement.

"So it is. As I said, though, the terms are all standard. This is how our trade works." He held up his wrists together as if he were bound. "I can hardly change the world."

"But—but why do I need an agent at all, then? Why not just—I don't know, represent myself. Make my own deals with arenas."

Even as I said it, it sounded preposterous. Olga chuckled to herself, while Caspar gave me a hard, level look.

"A gladiator acting as his own agent? You'll have a corpse for a client. Only the dregs represent themselves, Simeon. No warrior from the Escola has ever gone unrepresented."

Frederick spoke up and, as ever, drove straight to the point of the matter.

"You're under a sentence, Simeon. No one has to pay you to fight. And so they won't. They'll simply use you, day after day, like a mule, until you drop." His forehead crinkled as he regarded the contract before me. "That gives you leverage. An agent—the right agent—can mean the difference between dying as a pauper or living years in luxury. Your choice of an agent is important."

"The most important choice you will make," Caspar added with grave solemnity.

Frederick held me with his strangely colored eyes, and I could almost sense a trace of some kind of emotion lying buried behind them. I would have called it wistful if I thought the man was capable of such a feeling.

"Choose wisely," he said softly. "I didn't. Much to my regret."

Olga slipped a pen into my hand. I was being worked over, like a bumpkin farmer trying to deal with a sharp city merchant. It vexed me; but, then, what did I know? I knew how to read and write. Now I knew how to battle and kill. But when it came to the dealings of the world, the bartering of understandings, the trading of opportunities, I was, as ever, a naïf.

Frederick, who I hated but respected, had vouched for this man. So I bound myself to him.

Much to my regret.

———

"You need a name."

I felt a scowl cover my face. "I have a name."

Caspar leaned back in his chair, studied the ceiling, and took a deep draught of wine. We were in the infirmary room under the arena in Telos, a rising town five or so days' ride north of Niallex. I sat upright on a stretcher, covered in a film of sweat and grime and blood from the match. Most of the blood was my opponent's, but a well-timed thrust under the lip of my shield had left a nice gash in my side. It wasn't deep, but it stung badly.

A withered old woman who called herself a medico had stuffed the wound with a salve I watched her concoct in a mortar and pestle. I wished I hadn't seen it. Brine, a dram of gin, a lump of curdled milk, and a bundle of mushrooms made a wretched looking paste that put off a smell like a dead halibut. "Balm," she called it. Supposedly a disinfectant. Between the reek and the burn, I would have preferred infection.

While she worked on me, Caspar tapped his front teeth thoughtfully with a finger, as unmindful of my nakedness and injuries as the woman slathering foulness into my open wounds.

"I've got it," he said, brightening. "The Holy Warrior. A nice melding of your past and present, don't you think?"

"No good." I clenched my teeth. The medico had finally finished with the balm and was starting to sew up the skin. "Makes me sound like a zealot. Which I'm not."

The agent considered. "Hadn't thought of that. You're right. No one likes a zealot. Too virtuous." He took another drink. "The Sage of Swords? The Wizened Warrior? Uch, no, those are both terrible."

She pulled the thread taut, leaned her balding head over my groin, and bit the end of the string off.

"How long?" Caspar asked.

"A month," she said without looking up.

Caspar pursed his mouth, but shrugged.

"Ah, well, that gives us time to come up with something."

I tried to lie down, felt a sharp stab ripping in my side, and immediately sat back up.

"It'll bite for the next three days. Try not to move too much. You can drink a little wine to blunt the edge. No exercises for the next ten days. No women either. I'll not answer for those stitches if you try swinging a sword—or your prick—before ten days has run. After that, you can work back into your routine, so long as you do it slow."

She packed up her satchel, Caspar paid her two marks, and the medico hobbled out of the room for her next patient. When she had gone, I tried to find a comfortable position. But the stretcher I sat on was coarse canvas, and the wall behind me a rough-hewn stone that scraped my bare skin. I slouched, holding myself upright on my elbow and tried to make conversation so that I could take my mind off the pain.

"Why can't I just be Simeon Severals? It's my name."

Caspar snorted. "Because a warrior must have a moniker. Something that is both intimate and unattainable. Something they can all cheer—or jeer, it doesn't really matter—so long as it's something they can remember. That's the only way you'll gain a following."

It seemed silly to me, but I could tell Caspar was very much in earnest. He set his cup down and tossed me a linen cloth to wipe myself off.

"No one would travel across the Four Duchies to cheer on a bow-legged, bucktoothed miner with a missing nose named Jakob Felix. But 'the Orc' ... ah, now that's a name folk pay their purses to see. So they do. And so you must have a nickname. A good one."

I supposed there would be no rest until we came to a conclusion of the matter. I let out a sigh, but could come up with nothing better than what Caspar had already suggested. I told him as much.

"Your background is so unique, Simeon. It would be a shame not to make money from it. I don't know much of theology or pantheons. Was there a particular god or goddess you held closely in your seminary days? Perhaps we could weave their name into yours somehow ..."

"No. Not really. Truth is ... I'm not sure what I believed. Or believe. Growing up, we never kept any gods. And what I learned at the seminary ... well, it didn't make much sense. I liked the stories, but—to tell you the truth, I don't really have a god of my own. Sorry."

Perhaps it was light-headedness that made me sound so vacuous, or the slicing pain in my side. But Caspar's face lit with delight at my answer.

"That's perfect," he said. The palms of his hands pressed together, as if he were squeezing oil from an olive. He leaned towards me. "I've a *perfect* arena name for you. Dark, yet beguiling. Stoic, yet deviant. The kind of name that will make the women *tsk* with disapproval, as they whisper to themselves: 'What poor, tortured soul would call himself that? Would a night of my love heal his brokenness?' Oh, it's absolutely perfect! Listen closely. Because when you're all healed, your next match will be in Niallex. If we play this well your new moniker will be the talk of the city!"

My return to the Niallex Arena entailed a good deal more pomp than the training match a year before. Mine was a featured match. Not the top-billed (or the second, third, or fourth), but it was listed as a part of the show. My appearance would earn a mention from the announcer, a line on the hand-bills, and a space on the oddsmakers' chalk board.

It also put me in the ceremony.

I remembered watching the opening rites the one time I went to a match at the Bajebluff Arena. Everyone rose to their feet in silence, while one of the local clergy made a benediction, and we all mouthed along the first verse of "So Long as Niall Sits the Throne," and then the fun began. It seemed trite to me, but I suspected for many of the souls in the Bajebluff stands, it was what passed for religious observance.

The opening rites in the Niallex Arena were of another realm, perhaps another world, from the one I had experienced.

In a sun-dappled tunnel, we gladiators waited, queued into two lines. The featured warriors were nearer the front, followed by a pair of grapplers, the skirmishers, and last, a troupe of acrobats, jesters, and jugglers—it was like taking part in a parade. Our entrance corridor spanned three hundred paces and was wide enough to run a trio of chariots abreast, and still we were packed in, shoulder to shoulder. The tunnel was dank and hot as a fever. The only person who could move about somewhat freely was a bald man dressed all in silks, and carrying something that looked like an imitation of a scepter. He was called a verger, and his only function appeared to be fretting. Skirting in and out of the crowd, he hissed directions, and frumped outfits, and tisked, and shooed, and herded the motley lot of us into a semblance of order.

Set apart from the unruly mob, a score of clerics held a cordoned off plot of floor next to the portcullis that opened into the arena grounds. It was the best lit and ventilated space in the tunnel, and yet the priests and priestesses seemed to grouse the most. I scanned the group until I found a set of red and blue robes. The Fifth Pantheon's delegate was a long-faced priestess with moping eyes and disheveled hair, and she kept yawning as if the bloodshed she was about to bless was a bother. My fingernails dug into my palms as I marked where she was among the clergy.

Out in the arena, a deep booming voice rose over the hum of the crowd. It echoed into our entrance tunnel, and instantly everyone grew quiet.

"Nobles, yeomanry, and commoners, give heed! Forth come the brave and the dead. Forth comes the spectacle!"

All at once, horns, drums, fiddles, bagpipes, and a deafening cheer hit us like a crashing wave. Up went the metal bars of the portcullis. The sun poured in freely. Perched on the edge of the open archway, the verger stood on his tiptoes, his face locked in a grimace, his voice lost in the noise, flapping his arms madly for us to march.

Movement. Slow and ambling, but we trickled out of the tunnel and into the blinding maelstrom of the Niallex Arena. As I passed into the stadium, I drew a deep breath through my nostrils and smelled a thousand scents— incense, and fried meats, and bodies in need of a bath, and spiced wine, and dust. I blinked and scanned the crowd, not caring how it must have looked, awed at the mass of the people gathered.

I never thought so many could be brought together into one place. Above our procession, tens of thousands of faces melded into a nameless, featureless blur. A torrent of indecipherable cries rained down on us. We circled the perimeter of the arena twice, the verger at the lead, directing us with a brisk, assured formality that would have befit a high holy day in the basilica. I had to give him credit. In less than an hour, the verger had brought a mob of priests, ex-criminals, and entertainers together, and led us through a credible procession. On the third lap around, all the performers were made to veer back into the tunnel so that only the fighters and the priests were left on the arena grounds.

The verger motioned for us to come into the center of the ring, where he sorted us, clergy and fighters, into two lines facing one another. When he was satisfied with our appearance, he made a flourishing turn to face the announcer's pedestal high in the stands. With his clothes flapping about him, and a slather of sweat trickling from his temples, he bowed his head and took his leave.

For a while we simply stood there. At length, though, the announcer brought the crowd to silence. The sound of his voice in the speaking trumpet made my heart flutter. Not because of the forthcoming fight, but the prelude of its ceremony.

"Nobles, yeomanry, and commoners, pray give due reverence as your fighters receive their blessings from the gods."

As the crowd settled, the gladiator at the farthest end of our line approached the line of clergy. He crossed the space, knelt before the Declanian priest, received the blessing, then rose and returned to his place. Down the line, one by one, each gladiator sought a benediction from one of the assembled clerics. All the while, I eyed the Fifth Pantheon's priestess. Slouching and sour-looking, she scarcely bothered to raise her hands the one time a skirmisher sought her deities' protection. In the middle of her benediction, she broke into another yawn.

The man next to me went for his blessing. And then it was my turn.

I took a deep breath, and walked straight for the red-and-blue robed priestess, taking my place before her. She cast the briefest glance at me, licked her lips, and twirled a finger for me to hurry up and kneel already.

Instead, I glared at her, hard. It took a moment for her to notice, but when she saw a gladiator standing over her, fixing her with his war face, she brought her hand to her chest and gave a start.

I drew the moment out, just as Caspar had instructed me. Not a sound could be heard in the arena. I stood there tall and defiant, bathed in the noon sun, a man before the gods. Their representative shrank before me.

And then I spat.

Right at her feet. A long wet train of spittle landed in the dust, almost grazing her sandaled toes.

One can hear a great many things in the stands of a stadium. In Niallex that day, there was a long minute of stunned silence. It broke with a collective gasp, as if the air had been sucked out of the arena, and then it came. Just as Caspar warned.

Confused murmurs quickly coalesced into a furious chorus. Boos and hisses poured down. Shouts, and jeers, and hocked spit flew from every direction. Guards had to keep some in the front rows from spilling onto the grounds; apparently, they meant to do me harm in the name of their affronted gods, which I found more than a bit ironic under the circumstances. The hound-faced priestess stood and gaped. By the time I had turned my back on her and rejoined the line of gladiators, I could almost taste the derision and hatred.

I soaked in their scorn and kept my face an expressionless mask. I stood my ground, not flinching, not shrinking, while the rage of the clamor grew.

It wasn't nearly as hard as I had feared. In fact, the longer it went on, the more I felt a new strength beginning to course in my blood.

The man standing next to me, a grappler, muttered from the side of his mouth.

"What'd you do that for?"

I didn't reply, didn't spare him a glance, but glared straight ahead into the maw of the angry mob. It took a while, a few bashed heads in the lower levels and the announcer pleading for order, but at last the stands settled down, though their anger still hung heavy in the air. The rest of the line received their blessings with no further theatrics, and we were sent to our cells to await our turns.

My match was unremarkable.

It was the fifth of the day's featured fights. I faced a warrior from Southport. He was a credible opponent, equal in strength and speed, but, unfortunately for him, he had been given far too short a shrift in his training. Early on, he tried to buffet me with his shield. When I grappled his shield arm with mine and locked our elbows tight, it was obvious he had never practiced for this scenario.

I had.

I threw myself close, dropping my sword low, and the moment I had him in position, I slid the point through the space between his armpit and shoulder. The blade went right through his lung. He fell from my grasp, wheezing, blood frothing from his mouth. Without wasting a moment, I gave him an honorable ending. I put the whole of my weight into the final thrust in his neck.

Another spell of quiet fell over the crowd, as if they were unsure now what to make of me. Then, begrudgingly, a few scattered claps came, followed by some whistles. I lifted my sword in salute while the man from Southport leaked the last of his life's fluids at my feet. A polite applause was soon followed with a smattering of coins, my gladiator's gratitude. My heretical prelude had apparently been forgiven. Prowess covers many sins, it seems.

As they gave me applause, they gave me a new name. Caspar had been working discretely for the past few days to help its spread—whispering to the oddsmakers and writers and aficionados who always shaped the public's perception of the arena—so the moniker wasn't exactly spontaneous. But from that day, I wore it into every match I entered. At first, as an embellishment wedged between my given names, but in time, it wiped away Simeon Severals entirely. Word of the priest who had spurned the gods to become an Escola warrior spread fast.

And thus I became "the Godless."

CHAPTER FOURTEEN

Five years of gold, glory, and gore. I took my share of the latter two. Caspar helped himself to the gold.

We went on tour: me, Caspar, a teamster, a cook, a physician, and a troop of guards. It was like a merchant's caravan, and I was the ware. We stopped in cities and hamlets, port towns and crossroad villages. Wherever there was an arena and an oddsmaker, there we went, and there I fought. Some of the victories were hard-won; twice I feared I had made a fatal misstep. But most of my wins were swift and never much in doubt.

When a match was finished and Caspar's accounts paid off, we set off for the next appearance. I rode in a comfortable carriage and wore vellum-lined manacles and sometimes played Castes with my guards. Usually, I let them win, for I made more in gladiator's gratitude than they earned for their watch.

I ate well enough. I trained every morning of every day—sword work, conditioning, weights, footwork. About once a month or so, I had a match. And for five years, I repeated that petty little contrivance of spitting at the feet of whichever poor cleric happened to preside over the match's opening ceremony. It became a kind of standard of mine. The crowds who, at first, denounced my heresy, slowly began to accept—and then applaud—my irreligious idiosyncrasy. In this way, what began as an anti-ritual turned into an actual ritual. Only the gods and I could appreciate the irony.

Some evenings, when there weren't any inns or stables nearby, we camped by the roadside and I gazed out on all the strange lands of the Four Duchies. If I had had the talent, I would have put charcoal to paper to capture the wonders that I saw.

How the proud heights of the Alahambrian Mountain jut like an angry fist into the belly of the leaden skies above, as if in defiance of their ascendency. How the Theken Fields stretch from one horizon to another, aglitter with amber heather and wild barley, until a snowstorm rolls in, blotting out the colors of the world, and the rolling plains shed their earthen colors to wear a mantle of frost, sparkling like a curtain of fallen stars. And the towering waves that crash upon the ashen beaches of Pau Methelmapau. How they glisten like liquid jade, turgid and wild, and the wave caps rise to weave frothy crowns of diamonds, only to cast them down in their fury. The panorama of date palms I saw outside of Southport, miles of tall, swaying palm fronds sighing in the wind. Their seed pods, each as long and heavy as a man, burst open with heaps of scentless, colorless flowers strung together in strands. The swarm of honey bees that flitted through the abundance, and in their bustle, made the flower petals fall like a soft rain that captured sparkles of sunlight.

Those memories, those scenes of nature … I treasured them. For there were other images etched into my mind in those days—a montage of corpses, limbs hacked and hewn, faces wracked in pain, eyes forever fixed in sightless, accusatory stares …

Better to think about the pretty trees.

By the time we returned to Niallex, I had saved enough of my gladiator's gratitude to lease one of the smaller villas I once admired. It was a pleasant place with an open feel to its rooms (despite the barred windows and doors), and a cellar lined with empty shelves. Instead of wine, though, I bought books. Histories mostly, biographies of long-dead generals, some books penned by self-proclaimed aficionados of "the gladiatorial sciences" (which were, to a one, either vapid or wildly wrong), and, though I called it a passing fancy, religious tomes. The more esoteric, the better. As for the recent spate of fantasy tales scratched out on pulp paper, I never wasted a pence on any of those.

I also had a few trysts, now that I could afford them and my name was being spoken in the lower quarters of the city. They were satisfying, I suppose, in a way. A pleasurable release, a diversion, another means to keep the horror of my work at bay. But meaningless. Sometimes, as I lay awake in bed,

I would dwell on that night in the tower with Kara, and shake my head in disappointment at the sleeping woman next to me.

One morning, as I showed a tittering red-head to my villa's door, the guard outside unlocked it before I had even knocked. He pretended to look the other way as the girl slipped out, and told me that Caspar wanted to have breakfast with me. Before I could splash any water on my face, there was my agent, with a trio of servants in tow, bearing covered platters. A fourth was not far behind balancing a glass jug of black coffee that must have just come off a fire judging by the steam.

"Simeon," he sang, "I hope you don't mind the intrusion, but I wanted to catch you before your morning exercises." His dark eyes sparkled knowingly. "I hope I didn't interrupt anything?"

"I was just about to look for something to eat," I replied.

"Look no further! I've brought my feast to your table."

Caspar clapped his hands, and his servants hurried about to set my table with silver plates and utensils, white linen napkins, the jug of coffee, a separate carafe of orange juice spiked with white wine for Caspar, and a bounty of food that could have served a dozen fighters. Hot biscuits flecked with seeds, salted ham, kebobs of lamb and peppers, a rainbow of cheeses, honeyed apple slices, and a beef soup that smelled wonderful. Since I still had my training regimen before me, I only took a biscuit, a bowl of soup, and a mug of coffee. Caspar indulged himself.

He passed a few trivialities, and as I watched him eat, it occurred to me how much fatter he had grown, and how much finer the cut of his clothes appeared since that day we first met in the Escola. Oh, he had a few other gladiators under contract—some skirmishers, a handful of warriors—but he was making his fortune off my successes, and my scars.

As he finished his second plate, Caspar finally got around to the business that had brought him here.

"It occurs to me," he said, stifling a belch into his napkin, "that it is past time we choose a permanent residence for you. Stake out a home base, if you will."

This caught me by surprise. For five years, I had been taken around and told where to go, where to stay, what I must do. The idea of choosing where I might live seemed utterly foreign.

"I just assumed I'd stay here," I said, looking around. "It's a nice little place. There's a good book shop—"

Caspar shook his head vehemently. "Niallex is too crowded with talent. You'll never get out from under the shadows of Colm or the Orc. And if you stay here, sooner or later you'll have to face them. That would be a shame." He quickly added with a reassuring smile, "By which I mean, a shame for them. Their agents will be *furious* when my prize warrior slaughters off their biggest earners. No, we need to find another arena—the Godless' arena. Where the locals will rally around you and call you their own, and aspiring fighters will have to come to you, and we can reap the first fruits from all the fees they'll have to pay for the privilege. That's the way to fortune, Simeon."

I had never imagined where I might go if I were offered the choice. Never given it a thought. But when Caspar put the question to me, I didn't hesitate in my answer.

"Bajebluff," I said. I felt a tinge of excitement at the prospect, though I couldn't really say why. "The Bajebluff Arena," I repeated.

Caspar's finger rubbed the flesh of his bottom lip. His brow knitted. His face grew clouded, as if he had swallowed something unexpectedly sour.

"Bajebluff ..." he said, more to himself. "But has anything good ever come out of Archlé?" As if in answer, he shook his head. Then, slowly, a shrewd grin broke across his face and eventually settled into a satisfied expression. He took a few sips of his breakfast wine, and that seemed to settle the matter for him. "Your hometown, is it not?"

"Yes."

He finished his glass and refilled it. "It's different," he finally declared. "But, then, that is your motif."

The bird once flown can never come home.

It's an old piece of tripe everyone's heard (Goodwife Rivers must have sighed it once a day), but it's a truth, and a hard truth at that.

When our caravan rolled through the outer gates of Bajebluff, my first thought was how small everything had become. The streets felt cramped, the grain silos that once seemed to tower over the city looked meager, and the Squire Bridge, with its balustrades and bronze statue, would have passed for a livestock bridge in Niallex. The roads were as mired with muck as they ever were; that at least had not changed. Nor had the scents of familiar spices. The smell brought memories of sitting in Goodwife Rivers' kitchen, and pilfering the merchants' carts with Paul Little, and evenings spent roaming the market squares without a care.

I persuaded my guards to take a detour into Rogues Run. Few of the faces were familiar. As the covered carriage trundled down the street, they turned and stared, but I paid them no mind.

The old house was still there.

I gazed at the door for a long while, saying nothing, thinking only of the memory of its feel—how the knob stuck unless you gave it a good tug, and the lower hinge creaked whenever it rained ... For some reason, I couldn't bring my thoughts any further than the doorway. I had all but forgotten my bedroom. My mother once had a study. I had spent countless afternoons within, but if I were pressed, I couldn't have said anything more about it.

For that matter, as I thought on it more, I had forgotten my mother's face. A vague, shadowed image, like a ship in a fog-shrouded harbor, was all that remained. She was ... thin. And disappointed. That was all I had left of her.

"You, uh, wanna knock or something?" The teamster had turned around from his driver's perch on the wagon and was eyeing me warily.

I did. But I didn't.

"Oh, look there," one of the guards piped up. "This was a plague house. That bad one that came through a few years ago. See, you can still make out the red death's head picture over the transom. They tried to cover it with white-wash, but it's still there. Bet you whoever lives there now was able to buy the place for pence."

So the plague had taken Delores.

I watched the front of the house for a while in silence, my thoughts hollow, like my heart. The local folk milled by, the wagon's horses champed impatiently. At last, I told the teamster to take me to my new home in this old neighborhood of mine, my newly built villa in the arena.

———————

The Arena Square was still a derelict place. The old Dirk & Dirge tavern billowed its usual oily black smoke from its chimneys, while a mob of thieves, cutthroats, and whores spewed from its doors. The stalls and stores were much the same, though their merchants might have changed. The same shoddy wares and spoiled groceries piled high, concealing the same smuggled contraband that would be sold with a wink and a slippery palm. The flagstones were still overrun with refuse. The place still reeked. Nothing had changed at all.

Except for the arena itself. The crumbling, soot-stained octagonal stadium now boasted a new annex. Three stories in height, made of gleaming white granite with adornments and graceful arches, there was no attempt to blend the new construction into the old. Like an ivory handle fastened onto a shit pot. Caspar had insisted on building this vainglorious project and, true to his tastes, had made it the most ostentatious construction ever built in the Lower Bluff.

But the annex became my new home. At its northeastern end, a spired gatehouse led into a courtyard, which featured a run of small townhomes opposite a grand villa. The villa was mine. It boasted its own private courtyard with a grove of orange trees and a small fountain. The home was spacious, but also a gladiator's residence, which meant every window had strong iron bars. The restraints were also artisan, so that what imprisoned me looked fine and graceful. The window bars were painted and scrolling, the locks gleamed with bronze sculptures, and my front door could have served a basilica's sacristy. The rooms of my new home had high ceilings and arrow slits in every wall to invite cross-breezes. With a dozen rooms, a cellar and kitchen, and even a covered exercise ring for days when the weather was bad, this new opulence was far beyond my wildest imaginings.

The only feature I cared about, though, and the only room I was given complete leave to design to my liking, was the study. I chose cedar paneling for the walls and ceiling, and a thick burgundy carpet for the floor, with book-shelves built into every wall. A wide oaken hearth offered plenty of heat, and yet another shelf to hold books. Caspar tried to play the part of an indulgent father, declaring that his warrior should have "the finest tomes in Bajebluff," but thankfully, he left it to me to select my own catalogue. That was decent of him, since the entirety of the annex project—as well as the manse Caspar built for himself in the Upper Bluff—had been financed from the money I had earned.

The extravagance wasn't entirely wasted, though. The townhomes across from my villa were for visiting gladiators, and much finer than the cells beneath the arena. For the privilege of facing me in a featured match, roaming warriors and their retinue would be treated to their own plush accommodations, an excellent cook, a personal servant, whatever escorts and private entertainment they fancied (some of which were unutterably bizarre), and the acclaim of walking through the annex's private entrance into the arena grounds.

Where they would die.

Those who came to Bajebluff to challenge me were slaughtered. Every one of them. I say this as neither boast, nor unburdening of uneasy conscience. It was simply that the Godless had become very good at his craft. And he felt nothing when he killed these aspiring fighters, nothing at all. Some began to call my talent great.

But not so great that there wasn't always a line of hopefuls who thought they could best me.

For the opportunity, their agents had to pay a handsome fee to Caspar; but then the agents would more than recover their investment (and the loss of their fighter) from their share of the oddsmakers' bookings. In this way, the men and women of business always stood to gain. The amount of money I brought into lower Bajebluff was like a river. Folk from far-flung towns and cities found their way here to tour the "rustic" Archlé city, behold the Escola warrior who resided in its modest arena, feast and fornicate far from their native metropolises—and make wagers. Wild, spectacular bets. And every inn and pub was filled with paying customers. For every mark that changed hands, there was Caspar's palm ready to catch a piece of it.

I'll grant Caspar this one accolade: the man could wring silver from sand. He was soon counted as one of the wealthiest men in Bajebluff, almost as rich as a Beardley. I did well, too. The first year of fighting in Bajebluff, I cleared more money in gladiator's gratitude than I had the previous six. Enough that I could afford trainers who knew their art, an occasional tavern woman who knew hers, and a library of good books, which I read whenever I had the leisure.

One afternoon, I think it was in Wolven Month because I had a fire built up in the hearth, I was sitting in my study. With one hand, I was knuckling out the last knots in my thighs from the morning's exercises, while with the other I held open a book. As I remember, it purported to be a discourse on the Prophet Cormac's Forty-Second Revelation, though it was little more than a polemic on libertine theology pasted over scripture. My eyes had moved over the same sentence for the fifth time when I heard a knock at the front door.

A set of keys jangled on the other side, the outer locks turned, and one of the doormen, Elliot, poked his head inside.

"Beg your pardon, Godless."

Inwardly, I cringed.

"Simeon," I corrected him.

"Right, sorry. There's someone here to see you."

I set the book aside and got out of my chair with a grunt. I had only just gotten comfortable, and my legs still ached from the last round of lunges I had finished this morning.

"Who is it?" I snapped from the study.

Elliot slid inside and quietly shut the door behind him. He was young, not particularly clever, and, at the moment, clearly befuddled.

"It's a lady."

I blinked at him.

"At first, I told her to come back around dinner time," he continued. "Y'know. Figuring she was that kind of company." He palmed the back of his neck nervously. "But then she pulls back her cloak, and, uhm ... "

"What?"

Even from the study I could see his face screwing up tight in consternation. He hissed across the room, as if he were divulging some hidden secret.

"She's a holy."

I shook my head. "What?"

"Priest's garb, head to toe. Twirled me upside down to see it, that's for certain. Didn't know what to make of it. And then she looks down her nose and says, 'I would speak with the master of this house.' And the way she spoke all grave and serious, I knew she wasn't no forgery. It's a real priestess out there that wants to see you."

"Maybe—" I found myself faltering. "Maybe she has the wrong house?"

"That what I thought. So I asked her. And she nearly took my head off, and told me if I didn't want to be working off a curse, to tell Simeon Severals that she wants a word with him."

I leaned against the doorway to the study and ran my fingers through my hair to gather my thoughts. The doorman, mistaking my silence as a direction for him to further explain himself, kept talking, his nervousness gradually mounting.

"Knowing how you are … with folks of that particular persuasion—holies, I mean—well, I wasn't sure what to do. I s'ppose I could tell her you're busy, if I had to. But lying to a holy, well, that's—"

"No, no," I said, waving off his reticence. "Show her into the study."

"Yes, sir." Elliot nodded with obvious relief and hurried back out. I seldom had company who warranted the work of cleaning up. I brought a pile of loose sheaves of paper into a neater stack and cleared off a chair and was halfway finished folding up a blanket when Elliot appeared in the study's doorway and cleared his throat in a pretense of formality.

I looked up and felt my breath knocked out of my chest. The blanket fell from my hands. Standing just within the shadow of the hallway, her head rising no higher than the doorman's shoulder, a woman faced me, an impassive, inscrutable expression fixed on her face. Elliot announced my guest, though I knew her already.

"The Divine Kara Blithe."

She took tea with a wedge of lemon. Her fingers, draped around the curve of the glass handle, were as I remembered them when they had been clasped with mine. Long, lithe, but blunt at the tips. She had always had comely hands.

Kara propped herself on the very edge of the chair, her back as straight and stiff as a spear shaft. The auburn-tinted hair that had once bounced about her shoulders had been cropped close, almost up to her jawline. Her robes, the red and blue of the Fifth Pantheon, hung loosely from her frame, and though her tailor had been careful with his stitching, I noticed several patches had been sewn into the hems. She neither smiled nor frowned, but sipped from her glass politely. Chin tilted up, eyes fixed upon the space between us, legs crossed primly, she still bore herself as the daughter of an earl.

But that was all that remained of her station. A leathered tan was seared into her skin, and faint crinkles cracked her forehead and the corners of her lips. Her eyes had lost some of the luster of their former imperiousness. They looked … tired.

I had already greeted her (pleasantly, if not enthusiastically), offered her a seat and refreshments, said a few banalities, and now a silence had settled, and I found myself striving for suitable words—which is to say, any that were not curses.

Once, I had hated this woman who ruined my life, almost as much as I loathed the trainer who had destroyed my faith. So many nights, curled on the mattress of my cell in the Escola, I cursed Kara and dreamed of what I would say if I ever saw her again. And now, here she was, sitting in my study, drinking tea.

Instead of cursing her, I tried to smile.

"Sure you don't want a biscuit?"

"No, thank you."

She shifted in her seat and for the first time, appeared uncomfortable. The log crackled in the hearth and sent up a cloud of embers. She drew her cloak tight around her shoulders. Kara set her glass aside on a table, and when she spoke, it was in a soft, flat voice.

"I used to hate you," she said.

There was no accusation, no feeling in her words. Yet my hands clenched into fists. Anger flushed in my cheeks. Before I could reply, she added.

"I'm sure you felt the same about me. Perhaps you still do. I hope not. I stopped hating you a long time ago, Simeon."

As quickly as it had come on, the rage dissipated. Its ebbing left me hollowed. I let out a series of breaths and watched the flames in the hearth dance in the air, meaningless flares of light, there and then gone. I could think of nothing to say, except the question I should have asked when she first passed into my home.

"Why did you come here?"

Her head bobbed. She brushed back the bangs of her hair from her eyes.

"Because the gods willed it."

From anyone else, I would have rolled my eyes and laughed. For so many, the presumption of what "the gods willed" always carried a convenient alignment to what they already wanted. A discursion to distract you as they pilfered your pockets. For others, it was a balm for life's tragedies. 'Your wife and brother burned to death while asleep in each other's arms? Ah, well, the gods must have willed the fire.' Sometimes it was meant as a shoulder shrug, an acknowledgement that the world moves as it moves and nothing much can be done about it.

But I could sense Kara meant it in none of the usual ways. The way she declaimed the will of the gods—she truly believed it to be so.

Nonetheless, I cast a sardonic look at her and asked,

"So what is it that the gods want, Divinity?"

She stiffened.

"I mean, whatever their purpose," I said, trying to soften my cynicism, "it was … good of you to heed their calling. And it's good to see you're well. It's been a long time."

I was staring at her. The years had given her lines, made her features taut, but she was unchanged in the essentials. The same facile plainness was still there, the kind that fell away the longer you studied it. The angular jaws, the narrow nose, the limp hair, the eyes that seemingly never blinked. No one would have carved a bust of Kara Blithe, but she was pretty. Time had not changed that.

"It's been a long time," she agreed. She took a deep breath, as one would before plunging into a hard chore, and finally launched into what she had come to say.

"I'm sorry to trouble you; I only have a couple of matters I need to address, and then I'll leave and never bother you again, I promise."

"Alright. Let's hear it."

"I'm the vicar of the Temple of Morrigan," she announced it with no more pride than if she were telling me the weather. "You wouldn't have heard of the temple. It's a small parish just on the other side of the Squire. Yeomen and tradesmen, mostly. They're good people. Honest, hard-working."

"I know the kind."

"Then you know how the gods give their lives meaning. How they hold their faith—and their clergy—in sincere regard. You can understand how proud my parishioners were when the Sheriff announced our temple had been chosen to perform the rites for your upcoming match. As the vicar, it falls to me to discharge this service. I will provide the blessings for the gladiators next week."

My eyes rounded in surprise. Kara continued.

"That's why I've come here." She hesitated a moment and took another sip, and for the first time, would not meet my eyes. "From what I've heard about … about what you do before your fights, how you participate in these blessings, how you call yourself Godless … " She paused again and her hand started to make the sign of the gods, but she caught herself. "I'm here to ask you to respect my gods, Simeon. Regardless of how you feel about their representative. If my parishioners saw—"

"I won't spit at you," I said. "If that's what you're worried about."

"Thank you." She bowed her head, and then raised it, as if she had been relieved of a heavy weight. Her eyes lifted and she began to speak more tenderly. "I … I can understand why you lost your faith, Simeon. I'm sorry for that. I truly am."

Her pity was genuine. For some reason, though, I found it galling.

"You don't know a damned thing about what I believe."

The words came out harsh, more so than I intended. She retreated a fraction of an inch, her breath catching for a moment.

"I suppose I don't," she said.

From outside, the muffled noises of the villa percolated into the study—workmen breaking from their labor for lunch, complaining about the mortar they had to work with, a baker's helper singing a bawdy limerick as he kneaded dough, a pigeon cooing. We each gazed at the burning log in the hearth, saying nothing as we shared its warmth. At last, I broke the quiet.

"You said there were a couple of matters. What else do you want?"

Kara pinched the bridge of her nose. When she faced me, she had pulled her lips in tight; the bottom one quivered. The faintest trace of moisture clung to one of her bottom eyelashes.

"I want nothing," her voice trembled. "But our daughter would like to meet you."

CHAPTER FIFTEEN

"And then," I called out, heaving in a lung-full of air, "I do the same drill, but with my body a quarter turn to the left."

I angled myself slightly, so that the side of my shoulder now faced my sparring partner, the door guard Elliot. Like me, he was filmed with sweat, bare-chested and stripped down to a slitted skirt that covered a loin cloth. It was snowing heavily outside, so we practiced in the villa's indoor training ring, using weighted, oaken training swords, working through one of my many sword work exercises. The one was called the pentacle, a drill I only bothered with occasionally as it was used in a fighting style I seldom employed. But as it involved big, flashing movements, quick lunges, and sudden contortions, I thought the girl might appreciate it.

But she only sat, cross-legged, at the far edge of the ring, her chin resting in her hand, a book still open in her lap, a pen and ink pot at her side.

"How many more of these do you have to do?" she asked. It wasn't quite whining, but she was obviously bored.

I turned to Elliot who was doubled over and panting. Though all he had to do was rain down blows for me to parry and counter-strike, the man was completely winded.

"I suppose we can take a break," I said.

"Thank you, Godless," he gasped, and nearly collapsed into the compacted clay of the training ground.

I walked across the length of the ring, picking up my shirt and a mug of water along the way, until I reached the girl. She looked up to regard me. A pair of brown eyes filled with challenge. My daughter.

She was a nine-year-old replica of Kara, but with darker skin, and hair that fell in ringlets, and (I, alone, shoulder the blame for this) a frame like a marble block. The girl was dressed in worsted, undyed wool, with a scarf that was much too long for her wrapped around her neck, and a pair of leather shoes that had a hole in one of the toes. She arrived early in the morning, introduced herself, and announced—demanded, actually—that she would visit me. My suggestion for her to return this afternoon, after my exercises, was unacceptable, because she had a calligraphy lesson. So we retreated to the villa's training ring, and I tried my best to work through my regimen while she lobbed questions at me like sling stones.

The day's practice was ruined, but it was the best morning I had had in years.

The girl's name was Sarabella. Her mother alone, she said, could call her Belle. I was to refer to her as Sarabella, and she would call me by my given name. By the time I finished my warm-up stretches, I had learned that Sarabella had read over a hundred books, could do algebra, excelled at rhetoric, and had memorized all the major and minor holy days of the Fifth Pantheon. She aspired to become a seminarian of the Fifth Pantheon, just like her mother, whom she would assuredly surpass in accomplishments. Bajebluff, she proclaimed, was beneath her talents. I told her I couldn't agree more.

I took a deep draught of water and pulled my shirt on. She was peering at me closely, as if unsure how to measure what stood before her.

"You do the same drills every morning?"

"Mostly."

"Why?"

I sat down next to her, close, but not too close. "Why do you suppose your mother says the same prayers in temple all the time? It's the only way you get good at anything."

She started to open her mouth, and I could tell the girl had a wicked retort nocked like an arrow on a long bow. But she held it. Instead, her eyes narrowed.

"That is a specious argument, Simeon," she declared.

I had to turn my face to hide my laughter. "Is it?"

"Fighting and praying are totally different things. You might as well liken prayer to farming, or brick-laying, or forging horseshoes. No. One single prayer can invoke the gods, change the world—if the person who says it has a pure heart." She eyed me in such a way that made clear her opinion about my heart's purity. "But you wouldn't know much about that, I suppose."

Gods, but she was a little viper! Yet I was enraptured. I replied with exaggerated indignation.

"Why do you say that? I happen to think I'm a decent enough man."

Her face screwed up with disgust.

"You call yourself Godless. You kill men for money. You're practically a criminal." She paused for a bit, chewed at a fingertip thoughtfully, and lowered her voice. "And my mother told me how you ended up on the Rolls."

"Ah."

Out in the ring, Elliot had finally recovered enough to get back on his feet. He looked over and saw Sarabella and me talking to one another, and apparently took it for an opportunity to conclude the exercises early. The guard began picking up the training weights and lugging them back to their racks, while I stretched my shoulders to loosen some of the knots.

"What did she tell you?"

"That you were a scribe, and that you were young and impetuous, and broke your oath with her. She also said you were clever."

It was absurd, but a flutter of pride rippled in my heart. I decided to change the subject and pointed at her book.

"Is that for your handwriting work later?"

She clutched at the cloth binding, as if I had threatened it, but nodded. "Yes. Master Caiaphas will give me three pages of scripture this afternoon. I have to copy them all, in fair hand, before the sun sets. His other students can only manage two. Three is quite difficult." She sniffed. "He says if I ever deigned to lower myself to the station, I could be a gifted scribe."

"Indeed?" I cocked an eyebrow at her. "Let's see it, then."

"What?"

"Let's see this gift of yours. You watched me at my work. Let's see you at yours. Show me how you write."

Her almond eyes slitted again, and her bottom lip pouted. As I suspected, it was not in her nature to back down from a challenge.

"Here," I said, waving for Elliot. "Let's fetch something from my library and you can show me how well you copy it. Elliot! Run into my study and get the book that's on the top of the credenza. The one with the vellum cover."

From the corner of my eye, I caught Sarabella's mouth dropping open. When he returned, I opened the book to where the marker was, laid it in the space between us, and pulled off the top of her inkpot. At first, she seemed hesitant to touch my book; an understandable hesitation since the paper, binding, cover, script work, and silk ribbon were as fine as any blessed tome in a temple.

"Whenever you're ready." I folded my arms across my chest.

Reluctantly, she smoothed down the opened page and squinted at it. After a long moment, she looked up at me defiantly, threw open her writing book, and plunged her little stylus into the inkpot as hard as any sword thrust.

Her hand was meticulous, perfectly angled, every serif and turn a perfect right angle. But watching her write was like watching maple sap flow from a tree. A quarter of an hour later, and all she had copied was:

> *"Brother Odhran's trial for disseminating the heresy of Amadán was highly irregular in numerous respects, beginning with the indictment, which failed to identify, much less describe, a single law,—"*

"No, no, no," I said plucking the pen from her hand.

"Hey!"

"You'll never finish three pages at that rate, not unless they're handbills. Here. Watch."

Now I hadn't put pen to paper in days; and that was only to jot a few notes and figures. But once the letters started flowing, once I dove back into my "severaling," it was as if I was back in the scriptorium, copying my day's allotted work, while the world ran its course around me. In the span of a couple of minutes, I had tripled Sarabella's output.

"—canon, injunction, or holy writ he had allegedly violated. Nor did Divine Thomas a' Cairn, the Chief Inquisitor and the author of Odhran's indictment, cite a single passage in the Book of Amadán at any point in the proceedings. The latter irregularity would span the entirety of the trial. Indeed, Odhran's prosecutors never described what the heresy was—other than to say it had 'caused great injury.' This has led many (including this author) to conclude that Brother Odhran was tried, convicted, and executed for transcribing a book none of his prosecutors had ever actually read."

"What is that?" Sarabella demanded.

I lowered the stylus and felt as if I had come out of a dream. I looked over at her. Her young face was filled with affront, but also curiosity.

"It's fair hand copying."

"No it isn't. No one writes like that."

"I do." I handed Sarabella's copy book back to her. "It's called severaling, and it's how I did all my scribe work. There's over a year's worth of sealed documents in the Seminary in that hand."

She leaned over the page in her book, her curled hair shrouding her face, studying what I had written more closely. At last, she turned her head and the distaste had fallen away from her expression. For the first time, she touched me. Her hand clasped my shoulder. A trifling gesture, meant only to keep me from getting up. Yet the feel of her palm sent a warm current coursing through my body.

Fittingly, she accompanied it with a command.

"Show me how you do that."

The day came when Kara performed the gladiators' blessing in the arena. It was a gray Wolven afternoon, damp, the cold gnawing at the bones, the kind of day most preferred to spend with indoor diversions. The season was drawing to a close, and the stands were less than half filled. Before the match began, Kara came out into the middle of the arena. She wore a heavy robe of crimson, fringed with glistening azure tassels that seemed to flutter like grass in a windy field. She held a chain with a censer of burning incense. The smoke floated behind her in long silvery tendrils.

My opponent approached her. He was into his fifteenth year on the Rolls, a decent but aging warrior, now past his prime. His left leg had a limp, either from arthritis or the chill in the air, or perhaps both, and his hands faltered, but he managed to make a sign of the gods, and Kara murmured a blessing and swung the censer toward him, bathing the old warrior in sweet smoke.

Then it was my turn. Kara's eyes met mine. She carried herself tall and proud, neither questioning nor afraid. I drew myself up to my full height. The crowd grew still, awaiting my usual act of practiced heresy before a holy, waiting for me to sneer and then spit at the feet of the gods' representative.

But this time, this one time, I stood still and simply regarded the priestess. Kara held my gaze. The moment drew out. And I kept my defiance of the gods to myself that day, just as I had promised.

After the match, I expected Caspar would scold me for breaking the routine, but to my surprise he was giddy with delight. So much so, he had come down from his private box, bundled from head to toe in ermine, to meet me in the private corridor that led back to my villa.

"Brilliant!" he exclaimed, clapping his gloved hands. "Absolutely brilliant! Completely unexpected, totally unexplained. And on a day of low attendance—*that'll* teach them to miss a match when it's a little chilly, ha!"

"I suppose it will," I replied, and dipped my hands into a wash bowl to clean away the gore on my fingers. I wanted nothing more than to have a hot bath and slip under a blanket.

"Oh, they'll be talking about this all winter! 'Why didn't Godless profane the ceremony like he always does?' 'Was it because of his opponent?' 'Or the priestess?' 'Is he finding his faith again?' What a perfect way to end the season. Showmanship at its finest."

"Glad you approved."

"I do." His unctuous smile faltered ever so slightly. "And I don't entirely blame you for keeping your little ruse a secret from me. I might have been tempted to fan some flames ahead of time, and that would have spoiled the surprise." Caspar held up a cautionary finger. "But should you have any further ideas of this sort in the future, pray share them with your agent first. There are ways to turn these little controversies into profits, you know."

———————

The season finished. My seventh on the Rolls. One of the last things Frederick imparted to me before I left the Escola was to always take advantage of the winter and heal myself—however I could. Most gladiators would drink themselves into oblivion, or sally forth into the taverns and rut like stags; every now and then, one would take his own life, or someone else's. My restorations had always been of a milder sort. A journey to the seaside, a pilgrimage to a library, a philosopher's lecture in Niallex, that sort of thing. Always under heavy guard, of course.

This winter was different, though. Not long after that final match, Sarabella began to visit my villa, with stylus, ink, and a calligrapher's book in hand. She would come in the afternoon every three or four days or so, and I would give her writing lessons. As snow piled up in the streets of lower Bajebluff, Sarabella sat in my study and learned the flowing script of severaling.

I had never met a child as clever as my daughter.

Whenever she came, I made sure there was a plate of warmed biscuits, or honeyed scones, or bacon-wrapped apple slices waiting for her, and she would eat every crumb without ever a word of thanks. Then we would practice clusters of letters—first, I would show her how to form and link a pair, and then, like in the Escola, I would give her exercises. It was a challenge. She was, in a sense, unlearning what had been deemed the right and only way to make letters. For her, it came reluctantly. Every lesson she found something to complain about, whether it was an imagined pain, or ink that was diluted, or frosted windows that didn't let in enough light. Sometimes she would break down in tears. I learned I had little knack for teaching—she told me as much.

But she kept at it, and in a few weeks' time, Sarabella was looping her letters together, curving their ends to meet in the spaces. "Making the lines swim, like a river," as I explained it, a metaphor she declaimed was hopelessly muddled. Regardless, she was well on her way to mastering my method of writing, copying fair hand in twice the speed she had when she first came to me.

Every once in a while, when her duties allowed, Kara would accompany her. Not often. But enough for me to learn a little of what befell her. While Sarabella practiced her lines, Kara and I would visit over a pot of tea.

She had changed. There was still an imperious air about her, the nose always angled upward, the sense that she found her surroundings mildly displeasing. But the years of her vocation had cut away much of her worldly arrogance. And kept her terribly busy. I never knew a vicar had so many duties—praying the daily rituals in the temple, balancing its finances, visiting the sick, officiating the weddings, praying over the newly born, blessing the soon-to-be departed, comforting the bereaved. The Divine Kara had become a dedicated minister to the working poor of Bajebluff. The gods know Bajebluff's poor needed ministering to.

One afternoon when Kara came to fetch Sarabella, I met her at the door and saw that she had brought a parcel with her. It was wrapped in terry cloth, and I could tell it was heavy from the way she balanced it on her hip.

"What's this?" I asked, taking it from her.

"A present. For all your work with Sarabella."

I glanced towards the study where Sarabella pored over a book she had almost finished copying. "You didn't have to buy me anything. Truth is, I've enjoyed this."

Kara smiled. "I can tell. So has she. She talks about you all the time."

"Really?"

At that, Kara laughed. "Oh, yes. But don't ask me what she says—we girls keep our secrets. Aren't you going to open it?"

I looked down at the wrapped package tucked under my elbow. It had to weigh half a stone. I threw back the ends of the cloth and saw it was an old book. The cover was bare and weathered brown at the corners, and the binding was a bit stiff, but it was in good condition. I cracked it open, turned past an opening page with a crude drawing of a flock of sheep and a shepherd who seemed to be distracted by a ray of sunlight, and read aloud:

"For it came to pass one Midwinter's night that I, Amadán, whilst tending flocks ..."

The Book of Amadán. I snapped the cover shut and stared at Kara in wonder.

"Do you like it?" she asked hesitantly.

"I can't believe it. Is it a complete copy?"

She shrugged. "As best I can tell. I thumbed through some of the pages. I think you're the only one who's ever read that whole book, Simeon."

I felt as if I had just been handed a treasure. An open gateway back into my childhood. I had to swallow my emotions. My voice stuck for a moment.

"But ... how can you afford something like this?"

It was perhaps not the politest observation to have made, but Kara took no offense.

"Actually, it didn't cost me anything. A few days ago, we started building a new transept for the temple—ever since your last match, we've had a lot of newcomers coming around, so we need more room. It's a small addition, nothing grand, but we're very proud of it. Anyhow, while they were digging the foundation, they came across an old chest. Not much was in it. Some parish records, a few boxes of incense that had lost their scent, a bag of farthings, and that book. As soon as I realized what it was, I thought of you." She turned her face away for a moment, and I thought I saw the slightest hint of blush rising in her cheeks. "I remember you used to quote it. Which everyone thought was ... well, strange, for a scribe. But now I realize the book must have spoken to you." She faced me fully. "Whatever you may think of them, the gods meant for you to have this."

I didn't know what to say. I set the book aside, as gently as if I were laying an infant in a crib.

"Thank you," I finally managed. Over in the study, Sarabella murmured a string of curses—probably because her "L" ended up as a "P" again. My throat was clenched, so I cleared it and tried to change the subject.

"She'll make a fine seminarian," I said, nodding at Sarabella with approval. "And if she's like her mother, an excellent priest."

I felt Kara lay her hand on my arm. For a moment we were in the Seminary again, in a hidden courtyard, her hair dappled in sunlight, and she and I were the only people in the world. But beneath her smile, I could sense there was something aching.

"That's kind of you to say," she said softly. "The priesthood is her dream … my dream for her, as well, truth be told. But I doubt those prayers will be answered."

"Why?"

She took a deep breath and let her hand fall. "My father's last act of kindness to me was to find a parish that would hire an unwed mother as a vicar. The Beardleys owed him a favor, apparently. I'm grateful he did as much. For many reasons. But that was the end of our relationship. He's not spoken to me since. He's never acknowledged Sarabella. Never will. I couldn't possibly ask him to fund her sponsorship. And even with these newcomers, my stipend will never be enough to afford what the Seminary requires."

I pretended to study Sarabella at her writing, but I was working calculations in my head. This annex, my books, and all the trifling extravagances I had acquired had depleted most of my coins. Now I regretted every pence I had spent. If I lived frugally and laid aside all of my gladiators' gratitude next season, and the season after, and the one after that, I might save enough to cover most of Sarabella's costs. But that would be three years from now, and Sarabella might be too old for the Seminary to take her (assuming they would look past her parentage and accept a reduced payment), and, of course, I might lose a match. Gladiators seldom planned far in the future.

"She's gotten good at fair hand copying," I suggested. "Maybe Gathena would take her on as a scribe. Find her a place in the Vault …" My voice trailed off.

Kara's face hardened. "You of all people know how scribes are used. Is that really what you would wish for her?"

"No."

"She'll be a clerk," Kara pronounced it like a court sentence. "Maybe a notary. She'll learn to be grateful for her place. Like I have."

A piece of scripture came to me, one I had read many years ago.

"*In Time, verily, oh proud mountain, ye shall bow to the sea.*"

She shot me a quizzical look. "Amadán?"

"Mm-hmm."

It was only half the verse, though. What I kept to myself, and ruminated upon in the innermost chambers of my heart, was the second part. An echo of the prophet's great unanswered question—can you be a god and a beast at the same time? A query I still hadn't resolved for myself. But for Sarabella, I was coming around to a conclusion. Or a conviction. Like embers stirred from cold, dormant ashes, it began to spark and shed light.

In Time, verily, oh proud mountain,
ye shall bow to the sea.
Or stand firm, for all time,
and make Time bow to thee.

CHAPTER SIXTEEN

"What in the gods' names are all these for?"

Caspar jerked his thumb at a bookcase teeming with my more recent purchases. He had invited himself over, unannounced, and shown himself into my study, where he helped himself to a goblet of chilled wine from a decanter I had been saving for later.

"The books?" I asked.

"Yes."

"They're for reading."

His moistened lips pursed with disapproval.

"What a dreadful hobby." He took a gulp from his goblet, settled into my nicest chair, and gestured for me to have a seat on a nearby stool. We had business to discuss, apparently.

My agent, however, simply sat in silence, drinking, letting the dust motes float about him. He studied me closely for a long moment, and then asked:

"Do you know who Colm Black is?"

The question was so inane, it caught me off guard. Colm was one of the brightest stars of the arena. A warrior ranked either second or third in all the Kingdom, depending on whom you asked. He had been the resident champion of Niallex for more than a decade and had over sixty victories to his credit. He was almost certain to finish his twenty-year term on the Rolls, and that, too, was a spectacular feat.

"We've never been formally introduced," I replied, brushing my finger-nails on my tunic.

Caspar stared at me blankly, then burst out laughing.

"That droll wit. So rare for a gladiator." He wagged a finger at me. "You always surprise me, Simeon."

I dipped my head. "I try."

I could have added that Caspar's uninvited intrusion into my study to ask me about one of the most famous gladiators in the Realm was something of a surprise as well. Surprising and disconcerting. But I kept a note of levity in my voice.

"To answer your question, Caspar, yes. Although my nose might be more buried in books than you like, I've heard of Colm Black. And his sixty-three victories. Including the one last Sunskein Month when he decapitated Jakob "the Orc" Felix in a rounding maneuver. Why do you ask?"

The agent leaned forward and steepled his fingertips together. Two bands of sunlight streaming through the bars on my window cast his face in a jagged light.

"He's coming to Bajebluff."

"Strange place for him to take a holiday."

Caspar didn't blink.

"He's coming to fight you."

"Ah."

I pretended to study an open book that happened to be lying nearby. A tract on metaphysics. It had been a tedious read, but that wasn't why the words refused to come into focus. I set the book back down, along with the pretense I was unconcerned. My palms had left damp marks on the calfskin cover. Caspar apparently sensed my apprehension. He sat back in the chair, sipped his wine, and nodded.

"You have every right and reason to be concerned. Colm is one of the best. In speed and technique, he has no equal."

Hearing that from my own agent stung me hard. I clenched my jaw.

"Now, now, Godless. Don't look so stricken. An agent must always be honest with his fighters. Here." He walked over to the decanter, refilled his goblet, and poured me one, as well. I was in no mood to drink now, but I obliged him all the same. "I was as surprised as you to learn this news. The official announcement won't come out until next month, but the arrangements have already been made. Colm is to go on a grand tour of the Duchies' farthest corners to seek out new and worthy foes. He's coming to the slums, gracing our humble backwaters with his fame and prowess. He will face the finest warriors outside of Niallex. You—" he extended a ringed finger to point at my chest, "—are to be the opening match of his tour. That was Colm's personal request."

I'll confess I felt a tiny flutter of pride that Colm Black knew who I was, and that he thought me fit to open this grand tour of his. Only for a moment, though. I could almost hear my mother's voice scolding me as a fool for not recognizing that the honor of Colm's acknowledgement meant my imminent death. I shook my head to gather the swirl of thoughts tumbling around.

"He's touring? I've never heard of a settled gladiator going out again on tour. Why?"

"Business."

I cocked my head. "How is leaving *Niallex* good business? It doesn't make any sense."

Caspar drew a deep breath and let it out slowly. "It makes perfect sense. Colm never loses in Niallex. Never falters. His matches are almost never close. Year in and year out. The same. Agents stopped sending their best to match him years ago. Can't blame them for that. Why waste their talent? The problem is all these lopsided matches have dwindled attendance. The Niallexers aren't watching his fights anymore. It's like going to a play you've seen a hundred times. They're getting bored."

"Can't blame them for that," I said.

"Indeed. But boredom is like poison to an arena. First it settles, then it spreads, then it kills the whole enterprise."

I made the sign of the gods. It was in jest, but Caspar joined me with the fervor of an acolyte at prayer.

"So," I said, growing more serious, "I have to die to liven up Colm's draw. I'll be sacrificed on the altar of entertainment. How comforting."

Caspar's soft fingers slipped around my wrist. He clasped it, tenderly. I looked up into his eyes, and they radiated concern and care. Of some sort—whether for my welfare or his investment or a measure of both, I couldn't tell. I doubt even Caspar could say.

"Simeon, listen to me." He lowered his voice as if he were letting me in on a conspiracy. "I try not to burden you with all the tawdry financial details I must negotiate on your behalf. But I'll tell you this: a local champion's agent is perfectly free to reject any outsider's bid for a fight—even when that outsider's Colm Black. Why, then, do you think, after all I've invested in you, that I practically leapt at the chance to sign this contract?"

"You … you think I can win?"

A slow, knowing nod.

"You are the finest gladiator I've ever worked with. Not because of your strength or your speed or your skill, though you're certainly credible enough in all those regards. No. You are great because you are *resourceful*. Your fights are seldom pretty, but you always manage to find a way to best your opponents, even those who are your betters. In your own rough-spun, make-it-work way … you're an artist. Don't laugh. I mean that."

"Writers are artists. I'm just a Lower Bluff boy who learned to swing a sword."

Caspar scoffed. "Oh, please. Spare me the false modesty. You're very good at what you do. And you know it."

I was good. And I knew it. It was nice to hear it from him, though. Especially under the circumstances. A passing cloud shrouded the daylight in the study. The agent fixed me with another hard look and spoke so softly I had to strain to hear him.

"You're very good, Simeon. But Colm is great. So put away the books. Tell this daughter of yours who's been coming around lately, she'll have to leave you be for the next month. Train like you're back in the Escola." He tilted his chin with a proud, almost fatherly bearing. "I'm betting all I have on you to win."

Word of Colm's coming spread like wildfire. Before the first handbills had been printed, before any official announcement, whispers raced through the city, from one side of the Squire Bridge to the other, that Niallex's champion would face Bajebluff's in a month's time. I half-suspected Caspar had fanned some of these rumors, though he professed his innocence with the most solemn oaths.

Colm Black was coming to fight the Godless.

You could hear the talk in every tavern, outside every alley, throughout every market. Even among those who never set foot in the arena, there was no other topic of conversation. The whole city thrummed with excitement.

Which proved to be an annoyance. Every time I went outside, a crowd would somehow appear. A gang of men and women eager to catch some word, some hint, about the upcoming match that hadn't been talked over and chewed on already. They plied me with their nattering.

"What do you think, Godless?"

"Can you take him?"

"Of course he can take him!"

"I don't know. This is Colm, after all ... "

"He could be the one."

What a nuisance.

Worse, though, was the vacillation. It was so palpable, I could feel it. My adoring public, the throngs who had cheered my triumphs and showered me with coins and gorged themselves on the blood I spilled for them, they'd become ... torn. Unsure of who they should back. Because, gods forbid, any of these fools should be known to have gotten behind a loser. Around the streets, I started seeing black and white bunting—Colm's colors—fluttering outside homes and over shop doors. More and more, I would catch sideways glances or hear someone clicking their tongue. Even my guards wouldn't look me in the eye.

Fickle bastards.

When the oddsmakers posted five-to-two odds against me, that cut to the quick. But it also set something ablaze. My annoyance turned into anger; and the anger became a new fuel for my fire. I stopped going out. I posted the numbers 5 and 2 in every room of my villa. They became a constant reminder. Every time I happened to see those two numbers, they would strike a chord of fear and rage in my chest that would spur me on and keep me true to my new training regimen.

I spent every hour of daylight in training. Stretches, drills, weights, sparring, more drills. Again and again. Day in and day out. It was a self-imposed exile, a return to my days at the Escola, where I assumed the role of the piti-less trainer over myself.

Sarabella raised a mighty fuss when I had a guard tell her there could be no more lessons with me until the match was over. I could hear that shrill voice of hers cutting the poor fool to pieces all the way in the courtyard. It made me laugh.

I felt bad for having set her aside like this. Just when we were getting to know each other. But, then, that's what fathers have done with their off-spring for time out of mind. If, somehow, I survived this bout with Colm, I'd make it up to her. I'd have her over every day, I'd indulge her with whatever she wished. She deserved it.

Sarabella. That clever, clever girl. My daughter who was already master-ing my skill in writing.

Sarabella became the last piece of kindling I heaped on the flame inside of me. Fear. Anger. And Sarabella.

A conflagration that burned through thirty-one days like a fistful of matches.

The first day of Sowing Month was the day of the match. It dawned gray and wet. A rare autumn rainstorm had blown in overnight, settled itself over Baje-bluff, and, by mid-afternoon, showed no sign that it would be on its way any time soon.

Any other match would have been canceled for the weather. Not this one, though. Taranis himself could not have brewed enough rain in his heav-enly casks to keep this match from happening.

When I emerged from my preparation room and went into the gladi-ators' entrance, garbed in the agreed upon armor—a long mail shirt with short sleeves, leather wrist and ankle guards, standard round shield—I was engulfed in the roar of a packed arena. Chants and cat-calls and whistles of thousands upon thousands echoed against the narrow stone walls of the tun-nel. The portcullis that barred the way into the arena was dripping with mois-ture and veiled what little light there was.

When my eyes adjusted to the dimness, I saw him standing before the gate, a powerful silhouette framed against the iron bars. He was outfitted as I was. A sculpted, perfectly apportioned figure, flawless, with not a thumb's weight of flesh that wasn't muscle. Two long, powerful arms stretched wide as the man came up to me and brought me into a warm embrace.

"Simeon! What an honor to finally meet you."

Never before had a gladiator greeted me thus. It was deeply disarming. I stepped back and offered my opponent a respectful bow.

"Colm Black. The honor is mine, sir."

"No formalities." His face, a dusky and handsome one, was wreathed in a smile. Two bright, probing eyes looked me over, top to bottom, and then one of them winked. "If you call me sir, I'll have to call you Divinity."

I tried my best not to grimace; he meant it kindly.

"I suppose that's fair," I said.

He studied me again with no pretense at all about what he was doing. "You are just as impressive in person as the reports I've heard. A proud product of the Escola. I'm glad to finally face you."

Another bow. "As am I."

His smile fell a fraction of an inch.

"It's a shame you weren't able to accept my invitation to dine at the Sheriff's."

"I—"

"—need not apologize or explain." He clasped me on the shoulder as if I were an old friend who had arrived rather late to his invitation but was welcomed all the more for the absence. "My agent told me you had doubled your training regimen and that you would take no wine. I completely understand."

Tripled would have been more accurate, though I had snuck a glass of wine in here and there. "Just so," I replied. "Still, I'm very sorry to have missed your hospitality."

Neither one of us could, in good conscience, pass off the usual pleasantry of, "perhaps another time." This would be our one and only conversation before one of us killed the other; it would have been rank hypocrisy to pretend otherwise. Outside, a rumble of thunder was met with more chants and even louder cheers. The crowd sounded like they were ready to pull the arena down to rubble.

Colm raised his voice to be heard.

"But they told me Bajebluff was like a desert." He gestured towards the gate and the rivulets of water seeping into the tunnel.

"It usually is. This time of the season. Once every four or five years we'll get a downpour like this in Sowing. The streets all flood. Whole city swims in shit. Everything shuts down." I smiled at him. "Only Colm Black could bring all the Bluffers out on a day like this."

"Oh, I have a feeling Simeon Severals has much more to do with this crowd than I. But thank you, all the same. You know, I like you, Simeon. You and I will have an excellent fight."

He meant everything he said. Completely and sincerely. It was as impossible for Colm to conceal his genuine delight as it was for me to comprehend. I didn't have long to dwell on this, though, when the sound of trumpets cut through the din outside. There was a loud groaning noise as the portcullis clanked open. A mad and wild cheer went up.

Colm grasped me on the shoulder once more, smiled, and said, "Good luck, my friend."

I struggled for the right response; in the end, all I could say was, "Thank you."

The two of us marched out, side by side, into the soaked grounds of the arena. The storm was still falling, light but unrelenting, and had done nothing to dampen the crowd's fervor. I had never seen the stands so packed or whipped into so much tumult. They were all on their feet, stamping, howling, shaking their fists in the rain. A teeming, undulating mass. How many bodies had they piled into the stands for this match? Tens of thousands? How many marks had Caspar fleeced?

The crowd's roar, the blare of trumpets, the thump and *tat-a-tat* of drums, the swirl of a million noises, it made my ears ring. Beneath the stench of all the bodies, I smelled mildew and damp, muddy earth, the arena's rain-soaked grounds. The sand had turned into clumps of muck, in some places, puddles. At one end, something close to a pond was forming. The rain fell on, almost straight down, so that by my tenth step I was wet all over; by the twentieth, I was soaked.

Without meaning to, without even realizing it, I fell into step behind Colm.

He kept a steady stride, his arms loose and swinging, and only once did he lift a hand in greeting to a section that was holding up a black and white banner as wide and heavy as a sail. It read simply, "Colm Has Come." So he had. At his wave, a low, ominous call echoed all around the arena. At first I thought they were boos, but then I realized, no, they were chanting a name. In a steady cadence, their voices a drum:

"Colm. Colm. Colm ... "

We came to a canopy that had been hastily set up in the middle of the grounds. Servants held poles in place that draped a length of red and blue colored canvas overhead. Under that meager shelter, four guards flanked a young, nervous-looking priest. His red and blue robes, heavy with wetness, swallowed a scarecrow's frame. Though I did not know this priest, I recognized his amulet, and the colors of his vestments. A divine of the Fifth Pantheon.

Ah, what irony. Or, perhaps, a portent? I'm sure this good cleric trembling like a bowl full of water could divine the difference.

Colm and I came to a halt before the pavilion and drew a few steps apart. The horns sounded again, a trilling run of notes that signaled the match's ceremony was about to commence. The crowd begrudgingly quieted enough for a speaker's trumpet to be heard from the nobles' box up front:

"Nobles, yeomanry, and commoners, give heed. I said, give heed! Thank you ... Today, you shall bear witness to the fight of the ages. Today, you shall see the greatest match in the history of the Four Duchies. Today, two legends shall fight to the death for your entertainment. Give heed, for the Battle of Bajebluff is today!"

A wild, rabid cheer came crashing down from the stands and washed over me like a tidal wave. It was almost more than I could endure. I stole a sideways glance at Colm. He seemed perfectly content, smiling to himself as he re-tied the laces to a wrist guard. When there was finally a lull in the noise, the speaker continued:

"Forth have come the brave and the dead. They need only the blessing of the gods before the battle can begin. Let us stand in silence as the gladiators receive their benediction."

The priest under the canopy took a cautious step forward. Water beaded down from his robes. He could barely lift his head to face us. Part of me almost felt sorry for the boy. Colm looked over at me expectantly, but with a curt nod, I indicated he should have the honor of the first blessing. Such as it was.

As the rain splattered down, Colm approached the canopy and bowed his head. The crowd went completely silent for the first time. The cleric raised a trembling hand over Colm's head and clutched his amulet with the other and stammered a prayer:

"Um. Hear us, you most high gods and goddesses of the—of the Most Holy Fifth Pantheon. We, um, are gathered here to, to ask for your favor and blessings on these two warriors." He swallowed hard and his eyes roved about, searching, it seemed, for the words to the rest of the prayer. His mouth opened and shut several times, but if there were any more words to his benediction, they weren't budging. Murmurs rippled through the crowd. With a sigh, I put an end to his awkwardness.

"Be it so," I said loudly.

"Be it so," the priest echoed and hastily touched his forehead, chest, and stomach.

Colm shook his head, chuckling to himself, and made a sign of the gods. He took a position about twenty paces away from me and stretched his arms one final time while I presented myself to the holy. I decided to cut my usual godless ritual short, just so the poor fool wouldn't faint. I strode quickly by the priest and pretended to spit at his feet, but he jumped as if I had hurled a javelin to skewer his legs. His reaction was met with uproarious laughter from several thousand in the crowd. Many thousands more jeered the sacrilege. In this way, I could tell who in the stands were my supporters, and who were with Colm.

Five to two. That was about the proportion, I estimated.

The priest and the servants holding the canopy folded up the cloth and scurried away. I walked a few feet away and faced my opponent. He smiled at me. I rolled my head to crack my neck.

The guards broke off into pairs; two went over to Colm, and two to me.

My men patted me all over, searching for any hidden weapons, bits of armor, poison phials. When they finished, one of them unwrapped an oil cloth bundle he had brought and handed me a blade a little longer than the oaken pricks we used for training and about half a hand wider. I tested the edges and the point, gave the pommel a few tugs to make sure it held fast, held it at arm's length. Sturdy, steady in its balance, sharp as a razor.

"It'll do," I grunted, and the men withdrew.

Across from me, Colm was giving his blade a few lazy swings. The arena's speaker called for attention a final time.

"Gladiators, give your salute."

Colm and I turned in unison to face the royal box that bore the king's crest. With the rain streaming down our faces and our swords held high, we said:

> *"We have one death to die.*
> *One chance*
> *by death to be remembered."*

I remembered a deafening shout and the chime of a gong. And then the world outside of the space between Colm and I faded into shadows.

He struck first, like a serpent.

A brisk stab with his sword's point aimed at my neck. Without thinking, I jerked my head aside instead of parrying or blocking with my shield, for I knew the downward sweep he would follow up with would be instantaneous. It came, faster than the thought had formed in my head. Thank the gods, my sword hand knew what to do and angled out reflexively in defense. The flat of my blade blocked the edge of his with a loud clang not two inches away from my kidney.

My shield was free, so I made it a weapon. With my shoulder, I thrust as hard as I could into Colm, but he was already leaping back so that what should have been a blow that knocked the wind from his lungs scarcely brushed him and landed no harder than the friendly clasp he had given me in the tunnel.

All this happened in the time I had blinked twice.

Another attack. This time, he tested my legs, but my shield was back at the ready. A couple of glancing slices left a fingernail shaped notch on the edge, but nothing more. We lunged, he and I, back and forth, working through a score of attacks, blocks, counters we had mastered in the Escola. When a lull finally came, I swung my sword in a wide arc to put some distance between us.

We were both breathing hard, but neither was winded. The rain pattered down on us. Our boots were caked with mud. Colm bore a wide grin.

"Flawless." He shook his head with wonder. "That was perfect."

"Thanks." I wiped a leather wrist guard across my eyes to clear away the moisture. He did the same.

"Ready?" he asked.

I drew a deep breath and let it out. "Yeah ... "

I came at Colm hard, but he was gone before I could put any weight into a blow. A loping side-step and half-turn put him on my sword's flank. I had to abandon the attack before I could begin. My front foot went back into a defensive crouch just in time to withstand an onslaught of blows. Then he was moving again, twisting, coiling round and back in concentric circles, fast and graceful. He was trying to flank me.

At each of his turns, I would have to change my position or the angle I faced him or my stance. Never had I seen footwork like Colm's. He struck, and moved, like a viper.

Our blades rang. His sword hacked into my shield. I countered with a back-strike that cleaved empty air and a jab with the bottom of my sword's handle that came nowhere near Colm's jaw. His sword's tip snuck past my shield arm and scraped my mail. I retreated, my boots nearly coming out from under me. A chorus of boos came down with the rain, but I scarcely heard it.

He came at me, again and again. Constant motion, never the same way twice. Like quicksilver. My lungs were gulping air.

I couldn't put him on defense. Nothing would land. He never revealed an opening, and I dared not try to make one. He was too quick, too slippery. One lunge too far, one off-balance step, one over-extended blow, and Colm would have his sword in and out of me before I knew what I'd done wrong.

He feinted to my left, but I was too slow, or too tired, to catch his diversion. I didn't see the blow. Cold steel bit hot. A gash to my shield arm, just behind the elbow.

The gasp of thousands was followed by the whoop of thousands more. I swung my sword upwards with all my might, a blow from crotch to crown. The blade whisked through the air with a noise like a buzzing hornet, but it touched nothing. Colm had drawn back a couple of feet.

That damned smile. How I wanted to slice those lips off his face, burn them, stuff them down his throat.

"You," he panted, "are the finest warrior I've ever faced."

I stole a glance at my arm. There was a shallow red gash about the length of a feather midway between my shoulder and elbow. He'd gotten me just beneath the mail's sleeve. The blood trickled underneath the leather guards on my wrist, warm and slick. I watched pink droplets, my blood mixed with the rain, drip from my fingers clutched tight into a fist behind my shield. Colm brought his shield up at the ready. I lifted mine, though it felt heavier now.

"They undersold you, Simeon."

"What?"

"They undersold you. On the odds." Colm shook his head. "Five to two was an insult. You're better than that. Here. Show them."

With a laugh, he barreled straight for me. No circling, no sidesteps, no false strikes. A bold, undisguised charge right into my front. It was the last thing I expected.

I threw nearly all my weight into a sword thrust, stretched my legs and my arm as far as I could.

Had it only been a little more to the left, I'd have skewered him. I would have run my sword clean through his armpit. Instead, I felt a jolt in my hand and heard a loud thump as my blade dented the side of his shield. The noise was followed by another sharp cut and a fresh wave of pain. He had sliced low, under my defending arm, and ripped another gash above my left knee.

A low grunt of pain slipped out of me. It belched forth like a guttural wave, one I could no more keep at bay than change the tide. Only the two of us would hear it over all the bedlam in the stands. Still, I wished I could have held onto that show of weakness and kept it locked away.

But Colm said nothing. He halted his attack and dipped his head in respect.

"Brilliant counter. Almost killed me."

I suspected he would have paid me much the same compliment had my blade hit true. I checked my leg. A deep wound, bloodier than the first, though, strangely, it hurt less. It would be my undoing. He had thoroughly marked my shield side. I was losing blood and stamina, the cuts were burning, the muscles underneath spasming. The inevitable had drawn close enough for me to see it plainly. Colm would resume his swirling footwork, flank me on my wounded side, which, slowed from hurt, would yield an easy target. Then the killing blow. It would come, as surely as this rain would keep me wet.

At that moment, I had a revelation. A moment of profound lucidity, so bright and clear, it cut through all pain, all thought. Three insights blossomed into certitude in the span of a single breath.

I knew this man could not be beaten. Colm had been made for this manner of fighting. Forged and formed for this one, awful purpose. And he reveled in it, the way the hawk takes joy in her flight, or the lion proclaims his lordship when he roars.

I knew also that I had been a fool for not realizing this sooner. I'd forgotten the lesson with Posey. In that practice arena of the Escola years ago, when Frederick had me face a man nearly twice my weight and size. A bigger—or better—warrior cannot be bested if you fight him in his element.

And last, I knew I had a weapon yet to use. It had been waiting for me this whole time, since before the match began.

Over there. No more than twenty paces. That patch of ground near the northern end of the arena. Though we had ranged wide across the arena throughout the fight, we had kept clear of that one area. It was near a wall, and it was flooded.

The water stretched as wide as a small lake and was deep enough to cast a blurry reflection of the audience above.

Colm took a few, prodding jabs to set up his next attack, but instead of engaging him, I took a long step to my right. My hurt leg throbbed from the motion, but I kept going, a slow sideways gait, my shield tucked up to my chin, my sword raised to parry. I was putting distance between us, a trail of blood marking my passage.

To the crowd, it looked like a retreat, and they let me know how they felt about that. Jeers. Curses. Scorn. So much vitriol, I could bathe in it, gulp it down.

Colm cocked his head. He studied my movement from afar and saw where I was heading and looked utterly confused. Good.

I made it to the edge of the pond, and I kept going. Freezing water enveloped my feet. Each step sent up a splash of mud and debris. But I didn't stop. Not until I'd reached the deepest point where the water lapped up over my shins. That was where I halted and came back into a fighting stance.

Colm still hadn't moved. He was staring at me as if I'd lost my mind. Perhaps I had.

"Come!" I waved my sword for him to join me.

He mouthed the word "come," as if questioning whether he'd heard me right. His gaze swept over the pond I was standing in, and then comprehension dawned on him. A loud belly laugh burst out of the warrior.

"Clever. Very clever. How's the water?"

"Come and find out."

Colm chuckled. My toes were going numb, whether from the cold or the loss of blood, it didn't matter. It was all I could do to keep from shaking.

"Come at me!" I yelled.

Colm held for a moment before he nodded once, as if making up his mind. He knew what my gambit was. Knew it and respected it. He pointed his sword at me in salute.

"This will be remembered," he said.

Colm trudged out into that ankle-deep pond. Into icy water covering slick, soaked ground that would mire those thrice-blessed feet of his, weigh them down like anchors, and turn every sideways shift into a coinflip he'd fall over headlong. Of course, those same risks held for me, too. But out here in the water, I had evened the odds. And Colm was walking straight into them.

We crossed swords again. This time on a straight line. No more of his serpentine circles or sudden feints to exploit an opening on my wounded side. It was straight blade and shield work. Metal rang on metal. Shield clashed on shield. Fast, arcing sword swings, countered with lunges, thwarted with buffets, shoulder blows, elbow strikes. Water churned around us like a falling cataract.

We were evenly matched once more. The spectators loved it; their roar was deafening. For the span of a minute.

With a sudden flick, Colm thrust his shield into mine, levering his weight so that my left side was pinned. Our blades glistened with rain. And then Colm's was stained with more of my blood. He had brought his sword across our bodies and snuck the point into my shoulder so quickly and smoothly, it would have been a credit to a surgeon.

My arm went cold. I could still clench the hand, flex the elbow somewhat, but the weight of the shield felt like a millstone. Colm started hacking away at it, just as pleased as a woodcutter who could hear the creaking timber of an oak about to fall.

In the Escola, we had trained for wounds such as this. For when a leg's been crippled, or hand severed, or what have you. That part of the body must be retired, protected from further injury, while the unhurt portion must become your new center of fighting. Doing so yields angles for your foe, but it preserves your ability to mount whatever defense the rest of your body can muster.

The water at our shins was black and dappled with raindrops. So cold, and deep.

Instead of withdrawing, I leaned my left side into Colm's. There was a flash of uncertainty in Colm's smile. With a painful groan, I grappled my shield arm over his, linked the two, and held his wrist hard in my grasp.

Then I dropped my sword. And with my free hand, I grabbed his sword arm's wrist.

It wasn't any kind of warrior's defense; it wasn't even a grappler's move. It was how a lower Bluff boy would wrestle in an alley. Colm struggled to pull away, but I held him fast. He shook, but I didn't let go.

"What're you ...?"

Before he could finish, I came into him in an embrace. I clasped him as if we were lovers, and then I threw all my weight backwards. We hurtled down into the water, Colm and I. At the last moment, I twisted hard, so that I was on top of him.

His blade was in my side. Down my right torso, he had gotten the point through the arm hole of my mail, pierced the meat, and thrust it deep between a rib. Even in a wild, gutter brawl, Colm Black remained a swordsman.

The pain was more than anything I had ever imagined. Torrents of searing, blinding pain. So much pain, I was nearly driven mad. I couldn't breathe. The light of the world faded at the edges. All I could see was the side of Colm's face pressed against mine, and the water.

"*You have many weapons.*"

Frederick had trained me well.

I have my weight. I have this water. I have my opponent.

With the last scrap of my dwindling consciousness, I focused on those weapons in my grasp. I curled my legs around Colm's and hugged him as tight as I could with my arms. I forced my weight down, pressed it on top of his thrashing body. On his back, half-submerged in the pond, he couldn't gain any leverage. Colm had to crane his head at a hard angle to keep breathing.

My right hand wriggled behind Colm's neck; my fingers, pale and soggy and flecked with mud, probed to find purchase on the side of his head. A fingernail clamped onto his eye socket. The rest of my hand wormed its way around until I had his head in my grasp.

I pulled it down.

His face slipped beneath the surface of the water. The smile vanished, at last. I was so close, if I tilted my chin down I could have kissed him. But instead, I watched. I never closed my eyes. I gave my opponent all my weight and all the strength I had left in my dying body. I bled and grunted and grappled to keep my leverage over Colm, to keep his head under the pond. He bellowed under the water, an awful, muted roar followed by an eruption of bubbles. He thrashed about madly, but I had him pinned. Stuck on his back with his limbs braced in mine, with the weight of my body and all this armor pressing down, Colm couldn't escape. And I refused to let go. He kicked and heaved and convulsed. I could barely draw a breath for the blade that pierced my chest. And still I kept his head under the water. My life's blood flowed out like a stream, and still I held him down.

We were no longer men; we were animals, flailing in our death throes.

So much blood. It fell like rain into the pond, into Colm. Who had stopped moving.

My sight began to fade. I was plummeting down a deep, dark well. A yawning maw that blotted out my senses. From afar, I could see the surface of the water going still and my tiny hand clamped fast around Colm's head and a last, lone bubble of air floating up from his nostril.

There was nothing after that.

CHAPTER SEVENTEEN

The Dirk & Dirge Inn had always held a dark reputation, even among the denizens of Lower Bajebluff. Not because it was a brothel, and smuggler's cove, and unsanctioned gambling house; it was all those things, but so were a dozen other buildings within a short walk of the Dirk's covered porch. Not because it catered to the lower classes who tended to brawl a bit more frequently and a great deal more loudly than Upper Bajebluff's more refined citizenry. One was no more or less likely to wind up with a broken nose, or a knocked out tooth, or a blade in the back if he dined at the Dirk than if he went for drinks down the road at the Copper Bowl, the Four Green Ducks, or the Kobold. The Dirk & Dirge Inn welcomed all, as long as they had coins.

What made the Dirk singular was that it was reputed to be a place of high intrigue. Where schemes were free to ferment and graft was freely pollinated.

Caspar and I made our way past a table of patrons who had been playing cards. They stopped their betting long enough to gape at me and fall to whispering, which, half a year after my match with Colm, was still the most common reaction whenever I ventured outdoors. I followed Caspar past a well-worn bar and down a hall that ended in a door. Without bothering to knock, the agent went inside and I followed.

An elderly man rose stiffly and beamed.

"The Risen Godless!"

"Cedric Fallowfield," Caspar greeted him with a warm handshake. "May I introduce you to my champion, Simeon Severals."

"Oh-ho," Cedric chuckled. "Colm's Killer needs no introducing. An honor, sir."

"Pleasure to meet you," I replied somewhat icily.

I'd acquired two more sobriquets since my match with Colm Black: the Risen Godless and Colm's Killer. The latter was seldom meant kindly, and never spoken to my face. Caspar's eyes darted at me. He made a discrete motion with his hand, as if to say no insult was intended.

"Outside the arena," said Caspar, "he prefers to be called Simeon."

"Then that's what I'll call him. Pray, have a seat."

We settled ourselves around a circular table. It was shadowy inside the room, and quiet, for there were no windows, and the chamber door was unusually thick. As were the walls. A wooden chandelier hung from the ceiling with all the candles lit. Bowls of dates, olives, and raisins, a platter of cheeses, and a chilled wine flavored with blueberries had been set out. Caspar settled his bulk comfortably and consumed enough food for the both of us, while I picked at the raisins.

Cedric, I learned, was one of the tavern's proprietors, though from his dress, he could have been mistaken for a patron. His hair was slicked and combed to cover a balding pate, and his shoulders hunched beneath a patched shirt that was much too big for his frame. His eyes were globular, almost on the verge of bursting from his sallow face. He portrayed himself as a simple, friendly tavern keeper, but there was shrewdness underneath his humble bearing. Though he smiled constantly, it never seemed to quite reach those moon-round eyes.

Cedric shut and barred the door behind him. He pulled a chair close to Caspar and I, and served himself a glass of wine.

"Sorry we have to use a backroom," he said, "but there's this fellow who's been coming around lately and making himself a nuisance.

"A friend of the Sheriff's?" asked my agent.

"Yes." Cedric took a deep drink and his eyelids settled, momentarily turning his eyes from full to gibbous moons. "A newly made sergeant. Says he's going to sweep up the square. Clear out the criminals." He pinched the bridge of his nose. "Which means he'll cost me twice the usual."

Caspar tsked in sympathy. "It's the unexpected expenses that always prove the costliest."

"Isn't that the truth?" He drank some more and as he set his cup down, Cedric's eyes drifted down to my hands, which he studied for a moment.

"I see they've already removed your manacles for the visit. Good. We're all friends here."

"Simeon is a man of honor," Caspar tutted. "We lock his villa and keep a guard with him for propriety's sake, but he is committed to serving his time on the Rolls."

Ordinarily, I would have indulged Caspar's puffery, but the idea that anyone would freely serve a twenty-year sentence on the Rolls was absurd.

"He's also committed to not having his heart forcibly removed from his chest," I popped a handful of raisins in my mouth. "It's a remarkably unpleasant way to die. I've seen it done."

The glass in Cedric's hand quivered and his face blanched, but Caspar laughed it off.

"As you can see," said Caspar, "my client is also a man of candor." He shot me a chiding look. "Sometimes overly so. The truth is, when a gladiator reaches a certain level of fame, such as Simeon has, now that he's bested the best gladiator in the Kingdom, he can be afforded a little more liberty of movement. His fame binds him, you see. If Simeon Severals were to ever take leave of all his senses and desert his obligation, there would be a hue and cry raised across the Four Duchies. He'd be recognized in an instant, caught within moments, and, ehm, as he mentioned, punished quite swiftly." Caspar waved his hand as if this line of conversation were some malodorous scent. "But here, we've digressed before we've even begun. Let's attend to business."

"Yes. To business." The proprietor leaned in close to study me, his eyes roving up and down my body. "So how goes the recovery?"

Caspar had his answer at the ready with the words I'd heard repeated so many times I could recite them myself.

"The doctors couldn't be more pleased. He's training at full strength and speed. Nothing short of a miracle. Indeed, not four days ago, Simeon had his first foray back into the arena and, though I'm somewhat partial, I'd say he acquitted himself quite well." He gave a respectful dip of his chin towards me and winked. "As I knew he would."

My agent would have made a fine bard. Like all good tales, the one he'd just told Cedric was built upon a truthful foundation. My recovery had been a miracle. Her Divinity Kara Blithe, who had chanted a funerary paidir for my soul, proclaimed it so.

I had died.

My heart had stopped beating, or so I was told. Bled out in that filthy pool alongside Colm's drowned corpse. But Caspar's physicians or Kara's prayers or some strange god's twisted sense of humor brought me back. I awoke that night in my bed, stitched and glistening with salves and wrapped in a mile of linens. That much of Caspar's story was true.

As for the rest … when I first came to, my every breath was like a hot dagger stabbing in my side. Colm's blade had barely missed my heart, but not my lung. Those days after the match were wracked in unfathomable pain. The tiniest movement brought waves of agony. Sometimes I fainted. Most times I wished I'd died. It was a month before I could sit up, and another month before I could take my first cautious steps around my bed chamber. The recovery since then had been slow, and far from complete.

Yes, I'm able to train now. To a point. I can work through most of my exercises, but the motions are labored, slower, and they wear on me. I have to take rest often. The old forms are all still there, the muscles in my limbs still know what they must do, but their range of motion has lessened.

And, yes, a few days ago, I'd won a contest in the arena. The stadium was nearly full (unusual for a white-flagged match where no one would die). I defeated a deserter whose only training had been whatever the Dheas Duchy regulars drill into their conscripts before shipping them off to war. I suppose my performance was "well enough" for an opponent of that mettle; but for Caspar to suggest it was anything beyond rank mediocrity strained all credulity.

The truth was, my body was still healing. It would get better, in time. But I'd never be as good as I was when I faced Colm. Caspar knew that perfectly well, though he wouldn't utter a word to the contrary, not even to me.

"Well, I'm glad to see you all mended, Godless," said Cedric in a way that indicated he was finally ready to broach whatever it was he wanted to talk about. "Now, um, has your agent mentioned my business proposition?"

Caspar picked at some fruit but kept his face perfectly impassive.

"Actually, he hasn't," I replied.

"He hasn't," Caspar leveled the tavern keeper with a placid gaze, "because this is *your* venture. I am merely here to facilitate this meeting and advise my client."

Cedric licked his lips and nodded.

Though it was only the three of us, and the door was shut and barred, his voice dropped to a conspiratorial pitch.

"I'm acquainted with a few oddsmakers, up-and-comers, who specialize in—how should I put it?"

"Exotic?" Caspar offered.

"That's the word. They offer *exotic* wagers for arena matches."

I couldn't imagine how a bet on who will kill who could be any more exotic than it already was.

"What do they do?" I asked. "Give longer odds than what's written on the boards?"

"No, no, no." Both men shook their heads firmly, as if I had uttered some kind of blasphemy.

"That would be most improper," said Caspar. "Posted odds are as sacrosanct as holy scripture."

"Yeah, and the oddsmakers' guild don't take kindly to anyone who tries to undercut them," Cedric added with a slashing motion to his throat. "No. What I mean is, these oddsmakers who are friends of mine, they offer different *kinds* of wagers on the fights. Winners and losers are what most folk put their money on, but that's not all there is to a fight."

My agent leaned closer to me, resting his elbow on the table edge.

"You know there are recorders at every featured match."

I'd heard of the trade, in passing, but had never really paid it much attention "Sure," I replied. "They keep track of the matches, how many fights we've had, who won, that sort of thing."

"They follow much more than that," Caspar said archly.

Now it was Cedric who was bending over the table, as if to gain my confidence. I began to suspect the two of them may have arranged some of this conversation beforehand.

"Everything that happens in a fight," the tavern keeper said, "everything, they write it all down, put it in their books, and hand it off to arithmeticians— who turn it into gold." His eyes gleamed with greed as naked as a burlesque.

He held out a spidery hand and began to count off his fingers. "Who strikes first, what kind of blow, how many hits, how many stumbles, how the man dies—they watch it and write it. Every bit of it. And once a fighter's gotten a few matches under his belt, they can give odds on just about anything that will happen up until the final blow."

"Wait." I shook my head. "Are you saying there are people who actually place bets on whether I have to stab my opponent four or five times to kill him?"

"You'd be shocked," Caspar replied sagely, "at how robust that market is."

"Robust, that's the word," Cedric agreed. "Your last match with Colm was a fine example of how it can work. When that terrified stripling of a priest declared you had gone to the Gods, and then you choked up a lungful of blood and muddy water…"

"What are you talking about, a fine example? They *rioted* when the odd-smakers closed the books on that fight and said there were no winning bets."

Caspar had tried to keep the news from me while I recovered, but my guards couldn't stop wagging their tongues about the news. Fighting in the streets, fires burning outside the arena, statutes being smashed. The whole city went in an uproar. The sheriff had to call out the garrison to restore order. Since both gladiators had died on the field, the oddsmakers declared neither Colm nor I had won the match. I had killed Colm, sure—but, as he'd done the same to me, we had both lost, according to how they read their rules.

Which had a measure of logic, I suppose. It also, coincidentally and quite conveniently, meant the oddsmakers would keep all the wagers that had been made on our match. Millions of marks flowed in like a tide; not a farthing would go out. Everyone lost except the oddsmakers. Oh, there were some actions at law wending their way through the courts, but the oddsmakers had the finest advocates in the kingdom at their beck and call. They'd come out ahead, as always.

The two men seated next to me shared a knowing look and smirked.

"Apparently," Caspar chuckled, "there was one winner."

"Some drover from Westfield," said Cedric, "rolled into town for the match, drank himself into a stupor, and placed the one and only wager …

that you both would lose. Five pence got him eight-six marks. Wildest gamble I've ever heard of, but it paid off. For him."

"Well," I said, leaning back in my chair. "Good to know someone profited off that fight. The gods know I didn't. Thank you for enlightening me. But I'm sure you didn't set up this meeting just to tell me about some drover's lucky bet."

"Oh-ho," Cedric laughed. "He *is* clever, isn't he."

"I told you," Caspar grinned. "Simeon, Master Fallowfield's business proposition concerns these exotic oddsmaker friends of his. And you."

I raised my eyebrow, showing neither eagerness nor unwillingness to entertain what I already knew would be their proposal. Caspar parried with his own nonchalant gesture, cutting off a generous piece of cheese, enjoying a few bites, licking his fingers clean.

"If a certain warrior," he mused aloud, "of particular talents knew ahead of time what the given odds were on certain features of his match that were in his control to alter—say, whether his first strike comes from his sword or his shield, or how he will render a finishing blow—then one who was in that warrior's confidence could, in theory ..."

I couldn't help but smile at the brazenness of the graft.

"Make a wager against the odds," I said, "and earn a nice sum of money."

Caspar's face beamed. He looked every bit like a proud teacher whose favorite pupil had just solved a difficult problem. "You have it exactly. And of course, we would share a portion of those sums with you."

"We'd insist on it!" Cedric exclaimed.

The table went quiet as the two waited for my response. I rose from my seat. With a pensive expression, I paced about my chair, gradually looking more and more worried. Mid-step I stopped, feigning as if something unpleasant had just occurred to me.

"But surely this is unlawful."

"Gray area, I'm told," Cedric answered at once.

"Now, now, Cedric," Caspar clicked his tongue. "If you wish to bring my client into this venture, he deserves your unvarnished honesty. Simeon, it is indeed against the laws of every Duchy to purposely conspire with gladiators for the purpose of underselling the guild-sanctioned odds of any wager. That is what an advocate would tell you."

"What would be the penalty?" I asked.

"It is almost as severe as the penalty for trying to escape the Rolls. Anyone convicted would have their limbs hacked off with dull saws—apparently, that's supposed to be apropos for one who has 'shaved' the odds. Needless to say, if you were to agree to work with Cedric, we would engage in the utmost care and secrecy in how we managed the affair."

"Keep the wagers on the smaller side and spread them out," Cedric agreed. "Three or four hundred marks on each bet, no more than that. And make sure to lose a few. Never speak a word about it, except to tell you what to do in your fight."

"Every precaution would be taken," Caspar added.

"Yeah. Our arms and legs would be on the block next to yours."

Caspar cleared his throat disapprovingly. "Simeon, if you wish to think on this, by all means, we've plenty of time before the next season starts. Focus on your recovery. In the meantime, I'll answer any questions you may have. I should only add that, though there is a small risk, it is eminently manageable. The potential profits, though … my friend, they are beyond your imagining. Thousands, nay, *tens* of thousands of marks, potentially."

If there were no other concern in my life, if these confidence men had approached me months ago at the beginning of last season, I would have politely, but firmly, told them they had misjudged me. That my wants and needs were simple and more than amply met with the coins of gratitude I received from my matches. I would have returned to my villa, knowing I had probably disappointed my agent and not really caring because I had already made the man as rich as an earl. I wouldn't have given it another thought.

But all I could think of was Sarabella. She had visited me once while I was still bedridden. She had seemed impatient, as one would expect that from a child paying a call on a convalescent, but she had asked after my health before she demanded that I resume tutoring her again. With enough money, I could buy Sarabella a priesthood. I imagined her face, radiating with joy, once she learned she would go to Seminary, not as a scribe, but as a sponsored student.

I pictured her mother, reluctant to accept my generosity, but crying with joy as I insisted it was for Sarabella. Sarabella could have her dream and become a cleric, like her mother; all I had to do was a little unsavory business.

Having a daughter changes a man, apparently.

I brought my hands down on the tabletop and curled my fingers on the edge. Holding them in my gaze, I said, "I'm in."

Cedric and Caspar let out a soft cheer. Cedric filled our wine glasses, to toast to our new venture and the lucre they hoped to reap. Caspar was on the verge of saying something obsequious, but before he could get in a word, I decided to stake the term of my acceptance so that there could be no discussion, no equivocation. The jovial mood disappeared almost as quickly as it came.

"I have one term," I said. "We will split the profits evenly. I take a third."

"Wait—what?" Cedric sputtered.

"Now, Simeon—"

I rounded on Caspar, whose expression, in the span of a moment, turned from surprise, to indignant affront, to fear. For now my voice rumbled like a wolf, one that was snarling to keep a competitor away from its kill.

"There will be no negotiating. I'll have an accounting after each match." I pointed to them each in turn. "I'll rig your crooked bets and earn you fortunes the king could only dream of. But I will have my share of it. And I'll count every pence. The gods won't save you if you ever try to short the Godless his third."

"A fine crowd today," Caspar observed. "A record number, I'm told. Best season opener ever. They're piling them on top of each other in the upper rows." He rested his fingers on his enormous belly contentedly.

I grunted an acknowledgement, busy as I was whipping my arms around in circles to loosen the muscles. The scars from Colm's blade still stung when I moved like this, but the more I stretched, the less they bit inside my body. It had taken the better part of a year, but I'd remade myself into a near approximation of my former prowess. I was good again, very good. The most honest assessment came from one of my door guards, though, and he had the right of it: the Risen Godless was about nine tenths of the former one.

Through the stone walls that surrounded us I could hear the vibration of hoof beats on the earth. There was a gasp, a silence, then an eruption of cheers. Caspar smiled, pleased that the packed crowd in the stadium had been pleased.

We were in my preparation room, a private alcove near the end of my private corridor into the arena. A small, comfortable, relatively quiet place where I could stretch my limbs and eat a bowl of noodles in the hour before my grand entrance. Other than a slit of window with a pane of lead glass, the walls were solid and very thick, which kept the noise outside muffled. The room held a plush rug for my stretches, a table for food, and a couple of chairs. I liked the austerity. Caspar, however, had grown too fine in his tastes to abide asceticism.

"Always the same fare," he said, crinkling his bulbous nose at the empty bowl on the table. "Noodles are peasant's food, Simeon. Let me splurge a little for you. I'll have my chef—"

"A bowl of noodles," I said firmly, "an hour before each match. That's the routine." My arms became a whirl. "Never change the routine."

Caspar held up his hands in mock surrender. "I yield to the routine. Plebeian though it is."

I finished the fifty-count of circles and squatted on the carpet. Another shout arose from the crowd, this one indistinct. More hoofbeats.

"That would be the cavalry," Caspar remarked with approval. "For the opening match of the season they've brought in two teams of skirmishers on horseback, armed them all with javelins. A first for Bajebluff. Beautiful weather for it."

My elbows pressed down into my knees, spreading my legs wide as a butterfly's wings to stretch my groin. Caspar regarded me thoughtfully. His voice dropped low.

"Are you still committed?"

"I am."

"And you're certain you can manage this without risk to yourself?"

I kept stretching but gave him a terse nod.

"Good," he said. His girth shifted in his chair. With a groan, he hoisted himself to his feet and shuffled closer to me. His silken slippers tread heavily over the rug, the jangle of his necklaces rang like tambourines. "Your approach," he said, almost in a whisper, "should be exactly the same. Change nothing, *nothing* that you would otherwise do, except what we discussed."

The muscles of my inner thighs pulled tight as I stretched them to their farthest length. A tinge of pain, then the suppleness. I held the position, pushing my knees down just a bit further, another inch, another wave of pain. My ligaments were as strained as a longbow pulled to the point of breaking.

My teeth clenched. This contortion had always hurt; all the more so since my wounds last season. It was, in a sense, unnatural. But I remember Frederick's incantation: "an unstretched gladiator will soon be an unmoving gladiator." The bends and pulls were also part of the routine. A law unto themselves.

Another roar from the arena.

Another set of muscles to prepare. Scarred but still pliant. Soon it would be time for the gladiator to move.

Caspar was right. It was a gorgeous day.

Standing in the center of the arena, I let my head tilt back, opened my mouth, and drank deeply from the afternoon's sunlight. A chill clung to the air, the last stubborn shred of winter, but the sky above was clear, and bright, and blue. And all around me, a blanket of undulating faces gazed down, a myriad of shapes and hues. With them, the din of a carnival—peals of laughter, hawkers shouting for attention, ushers barking at the scamps who were trying to steal better seats, tens of thousands of voices joined in mindless chatter.

My opponent stood some twenty paces away, facing me.

Benito Zedson was his name. Two years into his sentence on the Rolls, rated a warrior from a school I had never heard of up north in Thuadeigh Duchy, he looked just as I had envisaged him when I had read Cedric's report. Eighteen stone of lumbering anger, as tall and taut as a warhorse, a face marred and purpled with scars from a pox. His head was shaved bald and beaded with sweat already, though the air was brisk. The kind of man who was driven by his cock and his stomach. Zedson's eyes were somewhat crossed, stuck in a kind of permanent leer.

He had fought and won a dozen matches, though. Always in the same manner. According to his records, at the sound of the match's gong, he would launch himself like a catapult, heedless of blows, overawing and overpowering his opponents. His violence always focused on the shortest, straightest line to his enemy. Though I had never attended any of Zedson's matches, from the records Cedric gave me, I had seen them all, just as if I had sat through them in a box on the front row.

An ugly fighting style. Little better than an animal's. The antithesis of Colm Black. I had killed a number of men of this ilk before. Their mode is crude, and easily countered. Just as Frederick showed me that time I was made to fight Posey, if your giant has no skill, you only needed to keep moving aside and strike at his legs.

But I suppose it would make an engaging spectacle, which is why I was paired with this ogre for the season's opening and my first returning match. The handbills proclaimed the contest with breathless letters.

He defeated the great Colm Black,
But can our RISEN GODLESS Gladiator defeat a GIANT?!
Does he have the skill to beat a foe TWICE HIS SIZE?!!

The answer, of course, was yes. Anyone who bothered to skim the records of my prior fights would have known that.

So here I stood across from a "giant," my bare arms goose-pimpled from the cold, waiting for the ceremony to be underway. A pair of attendants had just finished dragging off the corpse of the strangled grappler who lost the last match. I noticed Zedson was trying to tell me something over the noise in the stands. His lips curled as he grunted in a gravelly voice. I could only make out a few of the words:

"Have my way with ... little ... pull you apart ..."

Sometimes they did this, the men I faced. Not the ones who had been properly trained. They knew that I was as impervious to their wasted breath as the arena's walls. Only the lunatics, the villains, the cowards ever taunted before a match. Zedson may have been all three.

I stared at him, unconcerned, unfeeling. My only thoughts were on numbers.

Fourteen and one.

An oddsmaker had put out a privately offered wager of fourteen to one odds that I would make the first charge at this opponent. It was a ludicrous bet. And anyone who had read the records of my former matches would have said so. Godless had always, always, *always* let a larger foe come to him, and then he would fan out toward his opponent's flanks, set the right distance, and do what he always did. It was as constant as the sunset. The very idea that I would charge headfirst into Benito Zedson was ... absurd.

An expectant cheer went up from northeast corner of the arena as two rows of trumpeters announced that the gods' emissary had come into the arena. Today it was a monk from the Ilhuddic Temple. As the horn blowers trilled, a young, nervous-looking man wearing a hair shirt tunic, his locks piled up in a coarse, woven net, crept towards us. He carried a clay vessel resembling a boat. From its stony prow a trail of incense floated in his wake.

Zedson approached him first, and put on quite a display of piety, making no less than half a dozen genuflections of various cults, none of which I recognized. At last, he knelt before the trembling monk, held out his arms, and received in return a couple of bobs from the monk's censer, followed by a blessing that sounded as if it had been given by a man with a knife to his throat. Poor fellow. I'd never seen a holy who enjoyed this duty in the arena. Hopefully, he'd never have to come here again, and could spend the rest of his days pondering the ineffable mysteries of Ilhud.

When it was my turn, I walked casually by the monk and pretended to spit at his feet (the whole routine being strictly for show now). Without a word, I turned my back and returned to my place. There was the usual reaction in the stands: applause, whistles, and encouraging shouts, interspersed with a scattering of boos from those who still disapproved my theatric of heresy. Whatever hard feelings were left over from how I'd managed to kill Colm and still lose were apparently forgiven, now that fresh betting opportunities were open again.

The monk scuttled off, and a troop of sheriff's deputies marched in and outfitted us with our weapons for the day: leathern tunics, platter-sized shields, medium-weight swords, a mercy dagger that I waved off (I tried a mercy blow one time with a dagger and was appalled at how long it took for the fallen man to finally expire).

Then Zedson and I went to our marks. The crowd became still. I noticed a flutter of motion nearby, a sparrow flittering about looking for worms. It really was a beautiful day. The announcer's voice boomed through a speaking trumpet:

"Gladiators, salute your foe!"

Zedson, his weapon before him and rolling his eyes as if this were all a jest, mouthed the words of the salute, "We have one death to die …"

I went into my fighting stance. Zedson looked more like a runner about to start a race. If the runner were the size of a small oak tree. A splotched face with a leering gaze met mine. He was laughing to himself.

The deep, dull clang of the gong, a wild whoop from the crowd, and the wind was roaring in my ears. I sprinted straight for my foe, as swift as my feet had ever run. Before Zedson had lurched into his second step I was upon him. The leer turned into a frown.

I had debated whether to make a stutter-step when I reached him, but as he was mostly on his heels, still in shock at my charge, I decided to make it a clean pass.

Not missing a stride, I whisked past his shield arm. He held the platter wrong—of course he did—had it angled up from his hip so it offered less coverage. But I was too far past to take advantage of his stupidity. Instead I swung my blade back behind me as I went by. It bit harmlessly into his shield's edge, leaving a nick, a loud, unmistakable clash, and perhaps a shudder in Zedson's arm.

The whole maneuver had been utterly pointless.

As I halted my sprint and rounded on my opponent, Zedson came about to face me. He was stunned, I could tell, unsure what to do. I settled back into my fighting position. Feet shoulder-length apart, shield up, sword poised, weight three quarters in the rear, the rest on the toes of my lead foot. Trying to mimic me, Zedson managed to get his shield into something that resembled a defensive hold, and took a stance that might have offered some measure of balance, but his sword arm … gods, how had this man survived twelve matches without ever taking a blade in his armpit? Distantly, I could register some surprised noises, but mostly I heard cheers—loud and lusty— that Bajebluff's own had showed such daring.

The match didn't last long after that first pass. My feet moved swiftly in long curving arcs around his position. Even nine parts of Godless was too quick for Zedson. He kept turning to keep his shield before him and gave a few half-hearted chops from his sword that came nowhere near hitting me, until I got to a distance that was within his reach. The first time he raised that sword arm and showed me that wide stretch of hairy space between his armpit and his kidneys, I accepted his invitation to stick the length of my blade in it.

In and out, then three steps back. That was the way with these blows. About half my weight was all that was needed, so that was all I gave. I felt my sword's blade sliding over bone, a rib most likely. Before Zedson could react, I jerked it free and drew back quickly, well out of his flailing reach.

"B-bastard!"

He let out a groan, a cry, an angry howl, his language already forgotten. Nothing but an animal in the end, I thought.

Zedson narrowed his eye and lurched towards me. It was a clumsy, stumbling charge. He tried to hoist his sword for a chopping blow, but as he lifted his arm he let out a yelp and the blade came back down to his side. His face was dark with pain. His side was soaked in blood.

I circled to his right, his wounded side, made a few feints as if I needed to bother joining with him again. But I didn't. One of Zedson's arteries was rhythmically pumping out his life into the sands. The rose in his mottled cheeks had paled to the color of bone. Time now belonged to me, my weapon to wield.

As I watched, Zedson tried to adjust himself, to stay on his feet, to keep up his defense and at the same time staunch the flow of his wound by pressing his right elbow into his side while still holding his sword before him. It looked ridiculous. Almost like a chicken wing. When the laughter and the boos began to hurtle down on him, Zedson let out a roar, and in his rage threw his shield at me. It clattered well short of my feet. I did nothing, but stayed in my stance and watched my opponent hasten his loss of blood.

He made a final lunge. I only had to pull back a step, and he fell to his knees. His blade dropped behind him. He tried to lift himself, but his legs, his arms, his hands were all shaking uncontrollably. He looked up at me, his eyeballs rolling.

"You—" he rasped. "You think … you're better … than me. B-bastard."

Seldom did I speak to opponents in the ring. From Colm it was well-meant, but I always found talking to my foes unseemly for some reason. The only exception was when a defeated warrior was taking a while to die. If I thought he was the kind of man who cared about his honor, I would ask if he wanted the mercy blow. Benito Zedson was not such a man. But as he convulsed on all fours, barely holding himself upright, unable to lift his head to hurl curses with his remaining breath, it felt as if I was watching a feral dog. One that had broken its back and was left writhing in agony.

I should put the poor thing down.

"Benito," I called to him.

His neck bobbed from the effort of looking up at me.

"Come at me," I said.

His eyes narrowed. He took it just as I thought he would, as a taunt. Zedson took a deep breath, marshaled what little strength he had left, and somehow managed three halting steps with his hands outstretched before him, his fingers clenched as if he would strangle me.

I lunged straight into him, extended my body, my arm, my legs to their widest length, all my weight behind a stab to his belly. The blade went in all the way to the hilt. I pulled it back out, and Zedson fell over in a heap. He let out one final gasp and died.

It was a good ending. The crowd seemed to appreciate the giant's last charge, for they gave the lout a standing ovation. Perhaps he heard the applause; perhaps it brought him pleasure in the end.

But that was no matter. I gave Benito Zedson no more thought.

I spent the rest of the afternoon in my preparation room resting, oiling myself down, and stretching out my muscles once more, listening to the fickle moods of the arena's audience as the last skirmish matches played out to their finishes. After a time, a pair of boys carrying baskets of pence and mark coins came into my chamber. It was the gladiator's gratitude gathered after my match in the ring. Yes, all had been forgiven from last season. I gave each boy a generous tip, bid a good evening to the wardens, and trudged the length of my private corridor back to my villa.

The shadows had grown long inside, the light of the setting sun through the bars on the windows casting dark geometric patterns over my furnishings. The noise of the stadium was slowly dissipating like a rainstorm rolling past. Servants had built up fires in all the hearths. A plate of food awaited me at the table.

I was hungry, but I walked by and went to my bedroom. Underneath my pillow I found the first profit I had ever earned for myself. A spectacular sum worthy of the crime I had committed.

Nestled in the folds of a feathered blanket were eight golden coins, a stack of smaller silver ones, and a copy of a wager slip. Caspar's writing on the margin of the slip showed a sum divided into thirds.

I counted my share. It was over three thousand marks.

The season went on, and Sarabella kept up with her writing lessons. Every ten days or so, she would appear at my villa's gate, and the guard would show her in, and we would spend an hour on her hand, which, in my estimation, had already surpassed mine. To be fair, she was practicing the flowing script much more frequently than I was. And although she could not quite match my speed, her handwriting retained a certain rectitude, a formality in form that mine had sacrificed for the sake of expedience. She had come to admire her own work.

"It's more mine than yours now," she once declared.

I studied the sample she was working on, some verses from the middle of Amadán, and examined her lettering from a variety of angles.

"Do you think?" I asked. "It still looks awfully familiar. Like you've draped your cloak over my frame."

She arched her little eyebrow at me imperiously, and I so wanted to draw her into my arms at that moment. Sarabella held her stylus up, almost like a scepter.

"One of Mother's colleagues," she said, "Divine Agnus Eldarwillow, is a foremost expert on fair and fine hand. She's seen my work. Said it was 'wholly unique.' Her own words, Simeon. It was high praise."

"Indeed."

Sarabella's gaze fell back to her writing book, and I caught a longing expression passing over her face.

"I'm sure they'll be impressed at the Seminary ... that is, if I ... if Mother can find a way."

I patted her on the shoulder, gently, so that she didn't flinch.

"You just keep up with your work and your prayers. The gods will find a way for you."

That night, as the moon's glow pooled through my bedroom window, I brought out my treasure, holding the gold coins up, one at a time, to make them sparkle in the ivory light, and I felt as pleased as I ever had. I stared at my ill-gotten wealth for I don't know how long until I fell into giggling like the Rogues Run scamp I was, as if I had managed to wrangle a half-pence winning out of a crooked carnival game.

After Zedson, the next rigged wager only needed me to buffet with my shield before striking with my sword, which was an uncommon, but not unheard of maneuver. The opponent (who really should have been rated a skirmisher) fell from the blow, so it looked perfectly natural. The match after that had a more challenging wager for me to meet: strike the fatal blow into the back of my opponent's neck (which also came about naturally when the gladiator, who had fought a competent match, foolishly tried to whirl about like a cyclone with his blade). The fourth match, though, proved difficult.

The five-year warrior I was paired against was well-trained and very quick. Gods, he moved like a lynx! Almost as fast as Colm. I nearly gave up on the wager until, after an exhausting stretch of countering his feints and probing attacks, he suddenly ducked. I blinked, and he was underneath my shield arm, prying for a low strike. Now the proper counter would have been for me to crouch even lower, and bring the bottom of my shield aground to make a wall, and from there force him to carry on his attack in the face of my metal, or beat a dangerous retreat. But instead, I kneed him in his side. I couldn't get much force behind it, but it was just enough to push him off his mark. As we returned to our fighting positions he cocked his head quizzically, for what I had done was inexplicable under any fighting method. But, then, he didn't know that a wager had been set at fifteen to four odds that I would strike him with my leg at some point in the match. That little stunt proved most profitable.

It also marked me.

One morning I was in my courtyard, shirtless and training with a pair of heavy rucksacks. They were balanced on my shoulders, each stuffed with four stones' weight of flour. From one length of the garden to the other, I lunged forward on one leg, knelt, brought myself upright, tilted my toes, then lunged again. A hard exercise, but highly efficient. After six lengths with the flour sacks, I was soaked in sweat, and winded, and every bone in my legs felt like kindling being set ablaze.

Lunge, up, tip-toe, lunge.

As I grunted towards the little babbling fountain in the center of the courtyard, I heard a man's voice hailing me from behind.

"That is *most* impressive!"

I kept right in stride with the exercise, not bothering to look over at him. Whoever it was had been checked by both the outer and inner watchmen and permitted to pass without an announcement. One of Caspar's associates. They came around every now and then and were always a bother.

Lunge, up, tip-toe, lunge.

"I hate to interrupt," the man continued, "but may I have a word?"

This was cheek that could not be tolerated. My morning exercises were supposed to be protected. Only Sarabella was permitted to interrupt them.

I pulled myself out of the kneeling position, sloughed off the sacks, and brushed the sweat from my forehead as I turned on him.

"What do you want?"

The man held a pleasant expression, unfazed that he had annoyed one of the deadliest gladiators in the Four Duchies. His skin was darker than mine, his face a collection of hard angles and weathered creases with a terrible scar on his chin, which a cropped gray beard only partially covered. His hairline receded to the top of his scalp. His hands were veined and strong. A man in his fifties, but he could still hold his own, I could tell. Though it was warm outside, the man wore a cloak. It was clasped with a bronze crescent.

I found myself staring at him.

"You look ... familiar ..."

He rolled his head back and laughed as if we were old friends. The crescent on his shoulder gleamed in the sunlight.

"I'll count that as a compliment," he said, "since it's been many years since you last saw me." His eyes darted over me with a playful light. "You look a great deal different. But then not many Rogues Run boys fill out to your size. Gods, your chest is as big as an ox!"

The recollection came to me in a flash. A street in the arena square, not far from here, dimly lit by a street lamp.

"Corporal Downs?"

He laughed again. "You remember me! It's actually Sergeant now, but I don't stand on formalities, Simeon. You can call me John if you like."

"Alright."

Now that I recalled who he was, I took his measure. Downs seemed smaller than I remembered, no doubt because I hadn't come anywhere close to my full height when I knew him last. He was grayer, a little more lined. Overall, though, he had taken care of himself over the years. Most men of his age and station let their bellies get the better of them, but not Downs. He looked like he could still run down a cutpurse if someone raised the holler, so long as it was a straight run, and not too far.

I led him over to a cushioned bench sheltered under an orange tree where we could sit down out of the sun. While I toweled off my sweat, Downs stretched his legs before him, and let out a long sigh. He sounded as if he'd like to slip off his boots.

"Still walking the arena beat?" I asked.

"Always," he replied with a tired expression. "Oh, this feels nice on the old backside. Goose feathers?"

I nodded.

"Very nice."

We sat in silence for a minute, the breeze passing gently over us. The cicadas had come back into season; their chatter rose and fell in hypnotic waves, a blanket of sound that covered the courtyard. I suspected Downs was waiting for me to ask why he had come here. Maybe it was petulance, or maybe it was the knot of worry that had begun to twist in a corner of my stomach, but I would not indulge him. Instead, I sat quietly, slowing my breathing though my heart beat as hard as if I was still doing lunges.

"I remember you were a clever boy," he finally spoke, though he didn't look at me. "A good one, too. You don't do this job as long as I have without learning how to tell apart the good oranges from the rotten ones. Speaking of which, may I?" He gestured at the branch overhanging where we sat. Though it was still early in the season, some of the fruits had ripened from green to orange. A few were already as round and bright as the sun. Half rising from his seat, Downs plucked the nearest one, drew a dagger from his cloak, and used the edge to pry off the peel in a single strand.

"Delicious," he said, sucking the juice of a slice. He tossed the piece aside. "You know what else I remember about you?"

"No idea." I shook my head.

"Good as you were, you were a terrible judge of friends." He let that settle for a moment before continuing. "Paul Little, for example. That one was rotten from the day he was birthed. You know what happened to him?"

I hadn't thought about Paul in years. I suddenly felt a longing for the memories of my childhood, dwindling though they were, and with all the rough edges smoothed by forgetfulness. Paul had been my friend once, an inconstant one. We used to poke fun at one another, made each other laugh, got into trouble together. He was shorter than me. That was all I could remember of him now. Downs kept his attention on the orange he held in his palms.

"I know he was put to death," I replied flatly.

Downs nodded as he cut out another slice of the fruit. A line of juice dripped to the soil in a soft patter. "So he was," he said. "And it was a pity, but not surprising. That's how the rotten ones always end up."

An edge crept into my voice, which, to my pleasure, made the sergeant jolt and shift to the edge of the bench.

"Why did you come here?"

He turned his head, his dark eyes met mine, and he smiled sadly.

"Same reason as last time, I'm afraid. You're mixing with some bad fruits again."

"Eh?"

Downs got up and stretched and let the sunlight wash over him. He seemed intent on appraising the garden and the surrounding villa.

"For a man who ended up on the Rolls," he said, "you've done quite well for yourself. Quite well."

"I'm good at what I do."

He tilted an eyebrow, acknowledging the implicit threat.

"So I hear." He began pacing, rubbing his chin every so often, as if he were trying to think through a problem that had just occurred to him. "It's a fascinating business, your line of work. Not that I pretend to know much about it. I don't think I've ever been to a gladiator fight."

"And the sheriff assigned you to the arena square? That makes sense."

He chuckled and held out his hands helplessly. "I just go where I'm told. Fortunately, I know some people who *do* know about the arena. There's some clever folks in this town when it comes to the matches. The oddsmakers, in particular. All those facts and records and statistics they keep track of ..." He let out a low whistle. "It's amazing. It really is. The way they can predict who's going to win, who's going to die, how it's going to happen. They know it all before it happens. Almost like they're prophets. It's just amazing."

The knot in my stomach clenched tighter. But I held my face in an impassive stare and made myself sound unconcerned.

"I've never paid much attention to the wagers," I said. "I've got enough to worry about not getting killed."

"That's what I thought you'd say. And that would make sense." He came to a halt before me and pivoted slowly until he was looking down on me. He crouched and faced me on the level. "But what the oddsmakers are saying to me, Simeon, well, they're convinced you are watching their wagers. The side bets, in particular. They think you and your agent are placing longshot bets on how your match will unfold—who strikes who first and how, that kind of thing—and then rigging the fight to make sure you win those wagers. They're saying some of your moves have to be scripted. They've looked at their numbers and compared them to some of the things you've done lately … I have to say, they make a pretty convincing case."

It felt as if Downs was reading me, like a scribe unrolling a scroll and tamping down the corners, forcing the paper to reveal its content. I shot up from my seat and threw my hands in the air.

"That's the stupidest thing I've ever heard! You really don't know a damned thing about what a gladiator does."

But he did know what I was doing. Downs knew exactly what Caspar, Cedric, and I had been up to. The sergeant recited a string of facts from memory, and each one landed in my breast like a stone.

"I know that you charged Zedson when no trained gladiator would have. There happened to be a wager given on that which paid out over ten thousand marks. I know that you've done some lunatic things with your shield lately that you never did before, and that's cost the oddsmakers another twenty. I know that your last match had a twenty-to-one side wager that had to be paid out. And I know that Cedric Fallowfield was the one who collected on all four of those wagers. Your agent took a cut, too. Oh, yes. I know all about Caspar and Cedric. They're old acquaintances. Listen, Simeon, you can get ahead of this if you—"

"No, sheriff's man, you listen." My face grew hot as a furnace and my voice rose. It was a bit of a performance, summoning this anger just now, but the rage was genuine. Downs was an envoy of all the armed thugs who had taken away my freedom, made me live under lock and key, and forced me to fight and kill for their masters' entertainment. I wanted to grind that crescent badge beneath my heel and rub the shards into his face.

"When I step into that ring," I snapped, "I meet a man who wants—who *needs*—to kill me. His life is staked on the outcome of the fight. Just like mine. We're not fighting for wagers, we're fighting for our lives. Two strangers …" A tear began to brim and I wiped at it furiously. "Forced to fight to the death. There's no *script* to it, Downs. No performance. No way to rig what happens. We're made into beasts. That's all the arena is. All my life is."

"You really think—" Downs started, but then he seemed to catch himself. A sadness had stolen into his gaze, a genuine one. "I'm sorry," was all he could say.

"You tell your oddsmaker friends," I continued, "you tell those fat whoresons that if they don't like the way I win my matches, come down and try fighting one themselves."

I threw on a shirt and started to leave, but Downs' hand grasped my elbow. He leaned up to my ear, close enough that I could smell his musk as he whispered one last thing before he showed himself out.

"I'm sorry I can't look the other way."

CHAPTER EIGHTEEN

"**M**uch too bold," Caspar said, licking his fingers clean. He pushed a fingerbowl to the edge of a tray, as if it had affronted him. His napkin lay unused in his lap.

We were in the kitchen of his mansion, a capacious room, as big as a barracks, with high, arched ceilings. Yet the space felt cramped from all the ovens, and cutting tables, and warming hearths, and racks of jars, bottles, phials, and carafes filled with condiments of every kind and color. A phalanx of harried cooks huddled over stations, some working sauce pans, others mixing bowls and chopping cloves, while children raced underfoot to fetch whatever needed fetching. The air was filled with delightful aromas.

At the very center of the clamor sat Caspar, like a massive jetty in a tumultuous bay. He had been picking through a tray of sauces in fingerbowls. He dipped his left finger, the only one that was still clean, into a mixture of hummus, tapped it against the tip of his tongue, and addressed one of the cooks hovering at his shoulder.

"This will suffice. The rest is swill." Turning to me, he explained, "We're entertaining the sheriff this evening. The Earl of Lostboat as well. His Grace is notoriously picky when it comes to sauces, and he's not above gossiping if he thinks he's been served fare beneath his station."

"I can come back later," I offered. That Caspar had sent a messenger bidding me to see him as soon as I had refreshed myself from my exercises was not something I needed to remind him of.

"No, no, no. This is important. I won't have my prized warrior bothered." He waved the cook away, settled back in his chair, and dropped his voice so that I had to strain to hear him over the din of the kitchen. "I heard you had a visitor yesterday."

"I did. It was … troubling."

Caspar nodded emphatically. "I'm sure it was." He let out an angry puff of air and launched into a mode of speech I had come to recognize over the years: Caspar, the dutiful agent whose only concern was my safety and comfort. His cheeks glowed pink as he worked himself up with righteous indignation. "As soon as I heard about the intrusion, I was livid. *Livid*, I tell you. Oh, you should have heard the way I bellowed! 'The Godless had his training interrupted by a foot sergeant? I'll have that man's badge melted into his fool head!' In all my years, I don't believe I've ever been so incensed."

Caspar's hand reached out for mine, and though it was a touching (if not contrived) gesture, all I could think of was how much I wished he would have used his napkin first. His fingertips were still slick with his saliva.

"That's why I asked you to come. So that I can allay your worries. You should never have been bothered by this Downs fellow. Cedric has made a bungle of this matter, but now I shall intervene. In fact, I intend to speak to Sheriff Beardley himself this very evening. Don't give Downs another thought. Put him out of your mind entirely."

"Alright," I replied. "Thanks."

"No thanks are necessary, Simeon. I am your agent. It is my duty to take care of trifles such as these. A gladiator should only ever have to focus on his craft." He set the tray of fingerbowls aside. "Speaking of which, I have something to tell you about your next match."

"Oh?"

"It's time you had a sabbatical. A reprieve for the next two months. No matches. No features. The gods know you've earned it. We're going to get you all healed up, rested and readied … for a *special* match I'm arranging."

There was an unpleasant twinkle in his eyes. Nearby, a baker shouted curses at one of the children. He began beating her with a ladle; apparently, she had brought him the wrong tin of butter. Caspar paid them no mind.

"There are still a few final details," Caspar continued, "but we've almost got a contract. If all goes well, it will be the grandest match I've ever

260 *Sword of the Godless*

promoted. Bigger than Colm. The greatest in this city's history! I've got goosepimples just thinking of it. As spectacular as it will be tragic—I speak of your opponent, of course. No, no. None of your questioning gazes. I'm not going to tempt the fates by naming him yet. Once he signs, you shall be the first to know."

Although the prospect of not having any matches for a while was a welcome one, I couldn't fully enjoy it. And I wasn't really thinking about whomever it was Caspar was trying to lure to Bajebluff. I was still bothered about Downs. The image of his hardened face and the sharp pricks of his questions kept tugging at me.

I shook my head. Caspar had said he would take care of it. And certainly he was skilled in these kinds of affairs. I tried to smile.

"Not even a hint?"

Caspar chuckled mischievously and helped himself to a fresh tray of shellfish, still steaming. With a wink and a mouth half-filled with crab, he replied,

"All I'll say is you've met him before. When he comes—and he will, trust me—we'll triple the price for admission and still have a waiting list."

I crept into the temple's narthex, the ambient murmurs of the restive city growing still as I shut the door behind me. Night had just fallen. Inside, a dozen candles burned in sconces, their warm, inviting light revealing a humble place of worship. Though the weather was mild, I wore a thick, hooded cloak, long enough for me to keep the whole of my face hidden, which was very much a necessity now that I had become a figure as well known as the Sheriff of Bajebluff. Reflexively, I made a sign of the gods while the two guards who had accompanied me dipped their heads in a more sincere display of reverence.

A lattice topped wall with an open archway separated the entrance from the sanctuary. I could see the altar at the far end. Centered atop a small dais, it bore a winged goddess wreathed with garlands; Danu was her name, and I could tell, even from a distance, she had been cast from a plaster mold. The altar was flanked by crude wooden beams trussed up with red and blue ribbons and bunting. A small figure stood at the bottom of the dais. She rested her hands on an elderly woman's shoulders and chanted a blessing in a firm, if slightly off-tune voice:

"Light of life, light of the world. We beseech thee to hear us, Oh Danu ..."

I hadn't heard that cadence in many years. The chant drifted through the air in a sad, melancholic key. A somber refrain begging the Mother of the Fifth Pantheon to heal her poor mortals' maladies and misfortunes. A short line of supplicants waited their turn.

As the guards sat in a back pew, I found a place in a queue of Lower Bajebluff's working caste. They were hunched over artisans, and bow-legged goodwives, and a man without an arm, and a bald woman covered with weeping, pink boils, and they all sniffed from head colds and slouched from their arthritis. A few cast sour glances over their shoulders, for my cloak couldn't hide the fact that I was young and hale and towered over them all. But I ignored them, ensorcelled as I was by the chanting. My mouth silently formed the words along with the priestess.

A flotsam of memories began to stir. The rhythmic music of the Seminary, the pattern of days it once held for me, the scent of incense, the sound of hymns. Those had been good days ...

It hardly seemed like a moment had passed when it was my turn to come before the priestess. She paused to drink from a cup of water as I approached the bottom of the dais. When she turned to look at me, I pulled back just enough of my hood to bring my face within the candles' glow.

"Simeon!"

She clasped her amulet and let out a gasp. I confess it was a guilty thrill to surprise her so. Her eyes darted fearfully, as if the icons painted on the walls might take offense at my presence. Through her clenched teeth she hissed.

"What're you doing here?"

I couldn't help smirking. "Why, I came for your blessing, Divinity." I knelt before her so that she could place her hands on my shoulders, and made a plaintive, hopeful expression.

"Stop this sacrilege," she said, pulling at my shoulder to lift me back to my feet. The parishioners in line behind me began to grumble, and one of them even griped, "Who's this young buck think he is?" as she led me a couple of steps away. Her brow furrowed with vexation.

"Why did you come here? If it's to see Sara, I'll bring her by tomorrow. She's asleep in the rectory."

"I told you, I came for a blessing. I really could use one."

Kara made a sign of the gods and pushed my shoulder, hard enough to nudge me back a step.

"There. You're blessed."

I pretended to study my hands and patted down my cloak as if I was feeling for something. The plaster face of Danu stared down disapprovingly.

"I don't feel blessed," I finally said. "You must have done something wrong."

That brought a trace of a smile, though Kara quickly turned her head to hide it. When she looked at me again, it was less as a cleric and more as an exasperated woman.

"I have a paidir to finish." She glanced behind me as the mutter of complaints grew in volume. "I promise, we'll both come to your villa tomorrow afternoon—"

"I have to skirmish, apparently. My opponent's just arrived and we're going to run through a few practice bouts in the arena before our match."

Kara's bottom lip pouted a fraction of an inch. Seeing her standing in her vestments, her hair pulled back and tied with a band, her angular face stretched from what had surely been a long day's work, the glow of candle-light playing in her eyes, I felt a sudden and compelling urge to kiss her. From the way she drew back, I suppose she sensed as much. But before she could leave, I took hold of one of her hands.

"What?"

I fished out a pouch from one of my pockets and slipped it into her palm. "Here."

She looked at it with puzzlement.

"What's this?"

"An offering. For Sarabella. For her prayers. It should be enough, I think."

Before Kara could say any more, I released her hand, drew my hood back over my head, and turned on my heel. As I hurried down the aisle of the temple's nave past the tutting congregants, and flickering candelabras, and fading frescoes of gods I once prayed to, I felt lighter. Kara's voice echoed over my shoulder, blessing the next in line. But it was my blessing that had been bestowed, more powerful than any she could have sung.

The two armed guards picked themselves up from the pew, and we made our way through the throngs of the city back to my compound ringed with caged walls and barred windows. As I returned to continue my sentence, I felt like a free man. A man in full because I had provided for my child.

He had aged.

We sparred in the northern end of a nearly empty Bajebluff Arena, in a part of the ring still shadowed from the stands because, though the sun had not reached its zenith, the air was already as hot as a kiln. There was not so much as a whiff of a breeze, and the padded chest coverings and leather helms we wore smothered us worse than woolen blankets. We had been going at it since early morning. I was huffing, my heart beating at a solid thrum; my opponent was winded, though he did his best to hide it..

Is this what I would look like at forty-nine years, trying to keep pace with a man in his prime?

Frederick let his shield droop and wiped his forehead.

"Is it always this dry?" he asked.

"Usually. Except when it rains. You get used to it after a while."

"Indeed."

He twitched his moustache thoughtfully, the little mane of wiry hair now flecked with gray. Frederick squinted up at the sky, nodded, and took another pass at me. Three quick lunges, a feint to the left, followed by a side-step right, a prodding jab with his training sword, an oaken "prick" he had brought with him. I fended each blow, countered his position with an abrupt wheel, and pretended I was about to strike when I saw he had exposed his collarbone. The show of his neck was a ruse, and a fairly obvious one. His practice sword chopped down hard through the empty air. Had I gone for the blow, and had it been a real blade, it would have cost me a hand.

Frederick shook his head.

"You'll have to venture a strike, Simeon. No warrior can win a match on defense."

He struck again; again I parried, maneuvered around him, and kept my prick close to my side. He was right, of course, but I was not about to offer him a prologue of what my strike would be. Frederick would see it, soon enough, when it mattered.

We had been going at it since dawn. A handful of sentries and a couple of arena children peered over the bottom-most rows as we put on one of the best displays of technique the Bajebluff Arena had ever hosted. He was still proficient, Frederick, but he had slowed. His stamina had diminished. Both would likely prove fatal. But it wouldn't come to that. In a piece of irony only a handful of men could ever appreciate, I had come to realize this technique of his, which really was masterful, would also be his undoing—and it would happen within the opening moments of our match.

After all the years Frederick had spent teaching his pupils where to put their feet, how to keep themselves balanced, how to apportion their weight, he had become like an actor on a stage. His footwork had become exaggerated, almost preposterous, jutting far, or with wide sweeping motions when a little nudge or a slight tilt would have worked just as well. I stopped keeping track of how many times I could have simply dipped my sword's point straight down—and skewered the top of his sandaled feet. Frederick had no idea that the footwork he modeled for others would give me a target that I would exploit. But again, I was not about to tell him so.

At last, he paused. The trainer was bent over at his waist, lathered in sweat, heaving in gulps of air. I waved for one of the sentries to fetch him a waterskin.

He set his sword and shield down, took a deep draught from a dripping goatskin pouch, and shared it with me. Already half emptied; the man must have been parched. I took a couple of sips, though I wasn't really thirsty, and handed the skin back to Frederick.

He took another swig. As he drank, I caught him flexing his knuckles, as if he was working out some kind of stiffness. His eyes caught mine studying him. He quickly dropped the wet spout from his lips.

"Using a water break to spy out an opponent's weaknesses? I taught you well."

"That you did," I replied with a nod.

He took a final drink, this time letting the liquid trickle down the sides of his moustache, down his neck, over his chest and torso. There the water pooled in the crevasse of a paunch that spilled over his belt. Frederick's belly had gone soft. He brushed the liquid off absently.

"You think I've gotten older." He said it as a declaration, not an inquiry.

Blunt as ever, but that had always been Frederick's style of conversation. As it happened, he was right. All morning, I had been contemplating how the passage of a few years could weigh so heavily on a man, but I tried to dodge Frederick with a pleasantry.

"Happens to the best of us," I said. "If you're not dead, you're getting older."

"You know what I mean."

Frederick tilted his head back and narrowed his eyes again, as if the relentless sunlight were a nuisance that should be dealt with. Still catching his breath, he looked back at me with much the same expression. "Check your confidence, young man. I may be a half-step behind you. I might not have the heft in my blows that you do. But I have maneuvers I never taught you."

I held his gaze.

"Whatever you know, I've learned—and surpassed."

His oddly colored eyes flickered for a moment, but his face stayed impassive. To my surprise, he simply shrugged.

"That may be true."

It was alarmingly candid of Frederick. And odd. Frederick had shown an opening. For a moment, he almost seemed like a man, a tired, sad one. I stepped closer to him.

"Then why did you ask for this fight? You served your twenty years on the Rolls. You had a good position at the Escola. Why run such a stupid risk?"

Frederick studied me for an uncomfortably long while. In the distance a gull cackled overhead. All of a sudden, he threw back his head and laughed.

"Why else? For the fortune."

"The—*what*?"

"Don't sound so surprised." Frederick strolled towards the nearest stretch of wall, and I followed him. The shade in the ring was fast retreating. He leaned his shoulder against the stone and seemed to age another decade before my eyes. Lines tore into his brow, stretching from the corners of his eyes. His head seemed to have become too heavy to hold up. He glanced around to make sure none of the spectators might have been eavesdropping.

"I am one of thirty-nine men who ever completed a full term on the Rolls," he said quietly. "I won two hundred eleven matches, and every one of them was glorious. I was … great."

He drew a deep breath of the hot air and held it. Was it wistfulness, reminiscence, or resignation I read in his face? Or was it just a void I was trying to fill? Who could say with Frederick?

"Do you have any idea the fortunes that were made from my suffering, Simeon? Millions. Millions of marks." A pair of heavy lids closed in contemplation over colorless irises. "My agent stole every pence," he declaimed. "Twenty years of fame and fortune, my sentence served, and I was finally free—to be a pauper."

In all my time with this man, in all our interactions, I had never considered his station. When I had been his student, he had always seemed like a demigod, something apart from the world, a force to be appeased. I suppose even demigods yearned for domestic comforts.

"What about the Escola?" I asked.

Frederick pursed his lips. "The Escola gives me room and board, and twenty marks a month. Meanwhile I see my students," he gestured at me, "living like barons … I should like to live as a baron, too. The purse I was offered for besting you is a hundred thousand marks."

That was a staggering sum. I couldn't pretend otherwise.

"Yes," Frederick nodded at my surprised expression. "It's the greatest sum ever offered for a single match. I'll finally have the fortune that was stolen from me. The fortune I deserve. Still think I've made a stupid risk?"

I paused and traced a circle in the sand with one of my toes. "Actually, I think you shortchanged yourself."

He laughed again, and this time a hint of merriment came through. "Oh?"

"I'm in my prime."

"And wounded."

"True. But I still have more weight than you, farther reach, greater strength, faster speed. And now I have all your skill. Besides which, I spent years sparring bouts against you."

"Which you still haven't won," he chuckled. "Since you refuse to show me your attacks."

"I'll be fighting on home ground," I continued. "I have every advantage. The oddsmakers favor me five to one. You should have held out for a hundred million to fight such a senseless match, Frederick."

Frederick tisked. "You shouldn't look at your odds before you fight."

"Why not? They've never been wrong."

"Colm Black would say otherwise, if he were still alive."

Now it was my turn to laugh.

"It will be a challenging fight, Simeon. I'll allow that. But I have one advantage over you. I have my will. In fact, I am nothing but my will. It's a mirror I've kept as clear and hard as a diamond. I have no qualms about killing you. So long as it's done. While you, my student, are still diluted, even after all these years. Sure, you've done a bit of cleaning, but there's still specks clouding that mirror of yours, and I can see them all. Your hope for something greater than yourself. Your trust in others. Love. They're all stuck right there." He pointed at my chest. "Clouding your will. Just as they did the night you first arrived in the Escola. Just as they did when I plucked your virginity and made you murder that poor skirmisher. What was his name again?"

"Aric," I replied. The sting from that night hurt anew, the memory I'd buried brought to light.

Frederick grinned cattishly.

"Still torn over that? How sad. It must be a hard thing to live without keeping your will clear. I wish you had learned that lesson." He heaved himself up from his rest with a tired grunt. "But that will be your undoing."

The day had come, the day that the Risen Godless would face his former trainer, Frederick Noman. Sarabella had made a hasty visit to my villa just before morning broke, ostensibly to wish me well. She had never done so before, and when I asked her why she did so today, she drew herself up, squared her little shoulders, and extended her hand.

"I wanted to thank you … for your generosity. It's—appreciated."

No hug. No tears. No effusions of emotion or love. More like a professional courtesy.

It was the most endearing thing she could have done.

I took her hand in mine, and said, "Think nothing of it. You belong in the Seminary. We need more good priests, like your mother."

Sarabella nodded solemnly. "Yes, we do." And then she said, "Good luck today," and took her leave. I watched her hurry across the courtyard, watched her shoulder past the guard who let her out, watched her barrel out onto the street, chin up, chest out, a little cask of haughtiness. And if anyone had been nearby, they would have had to shield their eyes, for my face beamed with so much pride.

A fine image, very fine, one I would no doubt relish for years to come. But now it was time to gather my straying thoughts together and ready myself for battle.

Time to make myself supple. I hoisted a foot and pressed it against the wall of my preparation chamber and started my first stretch, but paused when I heard a hesitant knock at the door.

"What is it?" I asked.

A doorman peeked inside.

"Your noodles, sir."

He was new, this chamber guard, a gangly, acne-faced youth garbed in a set of cuir bouilli armor that clearly belonged on a stouter man. A tray with a steaming bowl was balanced precariously alongside his spear. I switched legs and continued stretching.

"Just set it on the table. How far along are we?"

"In the matches? Uh, I think they're just about to start the second heat of grapplers."

"That's it?"

At that pace, Frederick and I wouldn't take the ring until mid-afternoon. The hottest part of the day. Frederick would feel scorched before the gong even sounded. I doubt he'd last a quarter of an hour at a full tilt underneath that sun. I felt a tiny twinge of remorse for my former trainer.

"Yeah, they threw a parade for the Sheriff," the doorman explained, "and he ended up giving a speech, and … well, everything's running behind now. Anyway, here's your usual."

He left the steaming bowl, stuck a fork in it, and locked the door behind him. I returned to my stretching. The sound of a cheer drifted into my chamber. One of the grapplers had won his bout. They would have to clean and rake the grounds, wait a while for wagers to be settled, make announcements, and then the next round's blessings could commence. Four more to go before they came for me.

I looked over at the table. The silver mist that had billowed from the bowl had settled. Ordinarily, I waited until there were only two matches left before mine and then I would have my pre-match noodles. It was still a bit early. But the prospect of cold noodles was hardly appetizing. I finished the stretch I was working on and sat down at the table.

Oil, herbs, and a small heap of thick, twining pasta. Simple fare and excellent quality; it came straight from Caspar's kitchen. As bland and filling as ever. I scraped the bottom of the bowl clean.

By the time I returned to the wall to resume my stretches, something felt off.

A low gurgle churned in my stomach. My ears began to ring. Despite the heat, I felt a chill steal over me. I had to sit down.

Somehow I made it to the chair without falling. There were three bowls dancing in my sight where only one had been before. I dropped my forehead into my hand and cursed.

"How do you feel, Simeon?"

Though it felt as heavy as one of my training casks, I managed to lift my head enough to see Caspar. My agent, my trusted confidant, stood in the doorway. Through a foggy blur, I could sense he was trying to look concerned.

"B-bastard," I muttered.

"You're upset. That's understandable."

I shook my head. The motion stirred up a vertigo; I had to bring my other hand beneath my chin.

"All I can say is," he continued, "it was Frederick's idea. Cedric agreed, reluctantly. I was outvoted."

Lies. Or partial truths. Whatever had been slipped into my noodles, whatever poison was now coursing through my veins, had already worked its charm. I'd be a dead man the moment the gong sounded. This kind of thing happens from time to time—drugging skirmishers, lacing poison on a blade, guards putting a fighter through a beating before his match—but not at this level, not with an Escola warrior. We were too valuable.

Only now did I come to realize, I might be more valuable if I were dead. I struggled to form my words.

"Frederick ... gets his purse. And you ... you'll be rid ... of a witness."

"Sergeant Downs' investigation, you mean?" Caspar shifted his weight, causing his necklaces to jingle. He heaved a sigh. "Yes, that was also a consideration. Unfortunately, Downs was immune from the usual inducements. Completely implacable."

"I could've told you that."

"Apparently, he's also some kind of a cousin to Earl Lostboat. So he's as protected as he is incorrigible. A ne'er-do-wrong. I've never met a more upright man." Caspar made a disgusted grimace.

I pulled myself up in my chair and nearly lost my stomach. The whirling was merciless. Round and round the world hurtled and carried me behind in its wake. I tried to tilt my head, to find an angle where the spinning would diminish, but it did no good. All I could manage was to stay in my chair and slouch over the table.

"Try to rest," Caspar said consolingly. "I'm told the effects will dissipate slightly over the next few hours. You'll at least be able to walk on your own. When the time comes …"

Anger gripped me, seized all of my senses. If I were a religious man, I might have called it a demon. A voice that sounded nothing like mine hurled curses at Caspar. I cast a tirade of venomous, horrible, impotent words. All the while, Caspar nodded along, never once lifting his eyes to meet mine, as if he were enduring some kind of penance for betraying me. Which only made me angrier.

"I … I'll tell the guards," I slurred at last. "Wha-what you've done. Tell them … you poisoned me."

He finally looked at me, a bemused expression rippling across his jowly face, but only for a moment, and his mask of sympathy returned.

"You mean the guards in my employment? Whose livelihoods depend on my word? They'll say what I've already told them to say. That Godless drank too much last night, he was too cocky about his match, and it cost him his life." He drummed his fingers on the doorway and stared at them contemplatively. "A sad epilogue. But there will be a moral in it. Which means the people will swallow it whole."

He was right. Of course he was. And all I could say was,

"Bastard."

Caspar's lips pouted. Behind him a great groan arose from the arena. Not far away, a man had fallen, or made a misstep, or, gods forbid, cowered before a foe, and the crowd liked it not. A throng of fools clamoring to watch men spill each other's guts for their amusement, for their wagers. They'd see what mine looked like soon enough.

"I truly am sorry, Simeon," said the agent.

I heard the door shut, the bar and lock fell into place softly, and the familiar, muffled noises of an arena match settled over me.

I cried.

To my shame, to my disgrace, I wept. My stomach finally emptied, a foul burn wracking my throat as the noodles came up. The vomit spread across the table and all over my chest, mixed with my drool, my snot. A man in mourning is not a pretty thing to see. It didn't matter. Now that I was alone, my tears came gushing like an arterial cut, flowing until there was nothing left. No one knocked or looked in on me.

I lost track of the time.

The time.

With a painful heave, I pulled myself up from my torpor. The light pooling through the window had taken an orange hue. I wiped my mouth. My mother's voice mingled with mine:

"Gather your thoughts, Simeon …"

The first one that came to me was an old lesson. Frederick's, actually.

Everything is a weapon.

My eyes scanned the length of the chamber. I took stock and made an account.

I still had many weapons.

There were walls, plain and unadorned, as open as a blank piece of parchment. Mine to use. I had a fork. Two weapons. I had … whatever was left within me. I had time. A little time. But it was mine to spend. The most powerful weapon.

When I had finished cataloguing my resources, a plan had fully formed.

It took a few tries in my addled state, but I was able to bend back two of the fork's tongs leaving only one standing, so that it resembled a makeshift stylus. The prick it made in my wrist was dull, and distant. The blood came dripping out, quick, but not too quick.

I slouched from the chair and crawled, bleeding, to the nearest wall. And then I dipped the fork into my blood. Like a baptism. I brought the fork up to the wall. And I began to write.

I am Simeon Severals.
This is my last testament.

To Sergeant Downs,
You were right …

My severaling was as swift as ever. Such a talent, being able to write fast. As I splayed my life's blood upon my cell wall, I smiled to myself. The old trick I had taught myself all those years ago, what I had passed on to my daughter, it came so easily, so naturally.

I wrote what happened, what had led to my demise. I spared no one. I held nothing back. My testament was true.

After a while, the pricking of the fork began to burn, but it helped keep my focus while I worked. The distractions of the world faded away. All that remained was the stone page before me, the pen I had fashioned, and the words. I was able to write many words. And every one of them was a weapon.

By the time I finished my account, my sight had almost gone. My body shook with cold. A freeze, deeper than any winter.

So weary. A bed. All I wanted was a bed. It was falling dark. Why was I not in bed?

I had a little more blood, a little more to say. The end of the race was near. I could see the finish now, my triumph, my freedom. I kept bleeding words. Mostly they were mine. But I spared a few for Amadán.

The One God is the God of One.

At last, I understood.

As I shed the last vestiges of mortality, my one god came forth, a god of one. An old acquaintance, my only friend.

The One God of Simeon.

EPILOGUE

"**A**nd you must be Sister Sara."

The man who greeted her was gray, and pudgy, and speckled with liver spots. He adjusted his faded red and blue robes and blinked nervously.

"Sister Sarabella," she corrected him.

"Ah, of course. And what do you think of our Vault?"

She made a pretense of scanning the hall. It was a cavernous room, with tall windows that glimmered with daylight. Every inch of wall and every foot of floor was stuffed with overflowing bookshelves or honeycombed scroll cases. Men and women huddled over desks, dressed in the same ragged wear as her greeter, whatever his name was. Here and there a scribe bustled along bearing an armful of papers. It looked just as she imagined it, the way Simeon had once described it for her.

The old man cleared his throat meaningfully. He stretched his lips into a smile.

"I am Marcus. You may call me Master Scribe."

Sarabella raised her brow, as if to say she would no sooner call a scribe by any title than she would have called him "Dad." Though she had only been at the Seminary for a week, Sarabella already knew the castes within these walls. He may have been titled a "master," but he was beneath her. His honorific had been tossed to him like a table scrap to a trusty servant. The man didn't merit her notice.

"Where are the Archlé records?" she asked.

"Ehm," he started and pulled at his sleeves, "may I, uh, ask what your interest is with that Duchy's records?"

Though he was striving to sound appeasing, there was insolence in his tone, she could sense it.

"I wish to see them," she replied. With a cold, smile, she added, "But if you can't help me, I'm sure I could ask Her High Divinity to—"

"No, no." He held up a pair of ink-stained hands in surrender. "I only mean—that is, we scribes do not idly peruse records, unless it's to fill an order."

Sarabella kept him in her glare.

"But I am not a scribe, Marcus."

"Indeed, you're not, Sister."

The old man's shoulders sagged. He seemed to deflate before her. Sarabella softened her tone, now that his proper place had been established.

"I only wish to find one record. A recent one. Then I'll leave you to your work."

He scratched the inside of a hairy ear and bobbed his head.

"Follow me, if you please."

Sarabella glided alongside the scribe. They made their way through a warren of dusty aisles that wended between endless successions of towering bookcases, set out without any pattern or purpose in their arrangement. Whichever way she turned, the shelves loomed over and before her. Whenever they approached a work table, a scribe would look up and start to greet Marcus, but then Sarabella would lift her chin and they would fall still, which gave her a small measure of satisfaction. At last, the two of them reached an area where the wooden bookcases had a lighter tone. The shadows were longer here, for the Vault's windows were partly obscured with clutter. A faint, moldy smell clung to the air. Sarabella crinkled her nose at it.

"These are Archlé's documents," Marcus announced. He waved at one of the higher shelves. "Up there is everything that's been filed since Frostlick Month of the year before last. Oldest is on the left; the newer filings will be on the right. It hasn't been properly audited, so some pages might be out of order."

"I'm sure I can make do."

Despite her clear signal that he should absent himself, Marcus remained. Indeed, he drew a step closer and, much to her annoyance, seemed to be studying her. Sarabella rolled her eyes and snapped.

"I said I can make do on my own. Good day."

"I was only just now thinking," he said quietly, "how much you resemble your mother. Whom I remember quite well."

Sarabella stiffened. The scribe dropped his voice to a gravelly whisper, and the saucy old dog had the nerve to wink at her. "I remember your father even better," he said.

It was not the first time she had had to endure a jibe about her parentage since arriving at the Seminary. But not from a scribe. That was an outrage she refused to bear. But before Sarabella could come up with a suitable retort, Marcus had turned his back on her and scuttled off.

No doubt back to his pence-a-page pathetic life. Inwardly, Sarabella chided herself for not thinking of that quicker.

It didn't matter. She had come to find a document, and once she found it, she would leave that low-bred scribe in this dusty tomb and never return. As a seminarian, there was no need for her to ever set foot in the Vault again. She hoisted the hem of her robe up to her knees and set about climbing up the shelfing so she could search her home city's records.

It proved challenging, pulling herself up the two shelves to reach the top. Her legs, though squat, were unused to any exertion beyond walking. Keeping her balance was precarious. But thankfully she spotted what she was searching for in the second ream of papers she searched. A bound set of documents, perhaps a dozen in all. She clambered back down, sat on the floor against the wall, and leafed through the contents.

It was a court proceeding, a criminal case.

The Most August and Wizened High Court of Bajebluff, having convened this 11th Day of Mending Month, in the Sixth Year of His Majesty Niall the XX's Reign has found the Defendants, Caspar Cartier, Cedric Fallowfield, and Frederick Noman, GUILTY of all counts as charged in the Sheriff's Indictment.

The Defendants Cartier and Fallowfield were taken forthwith on this same day to a Public Square and there they were each put to death by quartering. The Defendant Noman was killed before his sentence could be fulfilled and is hereby posthumously indicted and found guilty of one count of Attempted Escape and six counts of Manslaughter of a Sheriff's Deputy. A coroner has attested to each Defendant's demise …

Sarabella turned a few pages further and located one of the exhibits from the trial. Her eyes went wide. It was what she had hoped to find.

I, Martha Signal, Notary of Bajebluff, have prepared this document as part of the afore-mentioned proceedings. I hereby attest in the presence of the gods and upon my soul, that the following rendition is a true and correct copy of the writing found upon the eastern wall of the deceased Simeon Severals' preparation chamber within the Bajebluff Arena.

I am Simeon Severals.
This is my last testament.

To Sergeant Downs,

Sarabella skimmed the next three paragraphs. She already had an idea what they said. An account, written in Simeon's blood by his own hand, of how he had rigged his matches so his agent and a tavern owner could win wagers from the oddsmakers. Within hours of discovering his body (and once the garrison had restored order to the arena), the details of what the Godless had written on his wall were being repeated all over Bajebluff. One of the local pamphleteers had even printed what purported to be a copy of "The Godless' Testament." The people of Lower Bajebluff hailed his defiance as something almost mythic in stature. Despite her mother's efforts to keep her from learning what had befallen Simeon, Sarabella had gotten hold of one of the pamphlets, had read and re-read it until she almost had it by memory. The pamphlet, she now realized, had been embellished.

That was not all Sarabella wanted to learn, though. As spectacular as his last act in the arena had been, Sarabella had a nagging conviction that the Simeon she had come to know would have said something more. That having opened his wrist to write his final words in his blood, he would have spent the last of his life on something greater than revenging himself on his erstwhile partners.

And so he had.

Sarabella smiled.

"I knew it."

After his confession to Sergeant Downs, Simeon *had* written more. A few final lines. Ramblings. They were hard to decipher, almost like a private journal entry, written to himself. These were his last words:

> *To my agent,*
> *I'm as sorry for you as you were for me.*
>
> *To the people in the arena,*
> *Your praise meant nothing to me,*
> *because I had nothing but contempt for you.*
>
> *To my trainer, Frederick,*
> *I learned every one of your lessons.*
> *Now learn one from me:*
> *The One God is the God of One,*
> *whose will is done,*
> *whose death will be remembered.*

THE END

AUTHOR BIOGRAPHY

Matthew C. ("Matt") Lucas lives in Tampa with his wife, two sons, a dog, and an axolotl. He's the author of the historical fantasy series, *Yonder & Far*, the epic fantasy novel, *The Mountain*, and numerous novellas and short stories that have appeared in various venues. A Florida native with eclectic interests, when he's not writing, Matt enjoys the outdoors, nineties music, Florida State football, and playing the bagpipes. You can find out more about Matt's work at www.matthewclucas.com.